EMPIR

He was breathing heavily now and his legs were on fire. He felt himself slowing down against his will. Try as he might, he couldn't keep going. With a cry of desperation, he stopped, turned and brought his hands up like a boxer.

And still the thing came on. Laz couldn't make out its features in the darkness, but the eyes still glowed an unearthly yellow.

When it came near, Laz swung and hit it in the side of the head. But the blow did nothing to the creature. It was like hitting rotting fish. He swung and hit again, with the same result. He tried to dance out of the creature's way, but tripped on the sand and fell sprawling.

The creature took advantage, pushing through Lazlo's defenses until it was within his embrace. Rotting lips kissed his cheek, then pain exploded as the thing's broken teeth came away with flesh. It swallowed and fell upon Laz again. The speed and ferocity of the attack increased until its head and hands were a blur. It began to wheeze and hiss, the sounds coming from deep within its chest.

Lazlo tried to scream, but the pain kept him from taking a breath.

He was being eaten.

Eaten!

An Abaddon Books™ Publication
www.abaddonbooks.com
abaddon@rebellion.co.uk

First published in 2010 by Abaddon Books™, Rebellion Intellectual
Property Limited, Riverside House, Osney Mead, Oxford, OX2 0ES, UK.

10 9 8 7 6 5 4 3 2 1

Editor-in Chief: Jonathan Oliver
Desk Editor: David Moore
Junior Editor: Jenni Hill
Cover: Mark Harrison
Design: Simon Parr & Luke Preece
Marketing and PR: Keith Richardson
Creative Director and CEO: Jason Kingsley
Chief Technical Officer: Chris Kingsley

ISBN: 978-1-906735-32-6

Printed in Denmark by Norhaven A/S

TOMES OF THE DEAD

EMPIRE OF SALT

W E S T O N   O C H S E

For
Yvonne

ACKNOWLEDGEMENTS

As a reader and a writer I always read the acknowledgements. It takes so much to write a novel, more than any one person can do alone. My first and last thanks go to my wife, Yvonne Navarro. Not only is she an inspiration, but her experience and insight helped me put our heroes in increasingly bloodcurdling predicaments. Thanks to my mom and dad for not buying me that Atari system I so desperately wanted, and for forcing me read everything, and often. Thanks to my children for being the inspiration for two of the main characters. I spent many weary hours trying to keep you alive. And thanks so much to Jonathan Oliver for being there to answer questions, for trusting in me, and for allowing this lone voice in the desert to be heard so far afield. Lastly, thanks to the real people of Bombay Beach and the Salton Sea. This novel is entirely fictional except for those locations. I can't imagine that there is a real zombie factory. I've exaggerated the destitution and devastation of the communities surrounding the Salton Sea. The people who live there are of hardy stock and not easily dislodged from the places they love. This book is meant as homage to them, sometimes tongue-in-cheek, celebrating their ability to survive, even in the face of such desperate odds.

CHAPTER ONE

"Sorry, Frank. No more fish."

Frank stared over his empty beer glass at Lazlo Oliver, the bartender and owner of the Space Station Restaurant. Frank's used car salesman expression melted. His eyes narrowed. His grin receded, exposing a mouthful of broken and grimy teeth. "What do you mean, no more fish?"

"No more. Sorry, Frank." Lazlo squared his shoulders. At six foot three, he was a big man and, for all of his seventy years, still in pretty good shape. He hoped there'd be no trouble, but with Frank you never knew. Sometimes the drunk would teeter off into the night, and sometimes he'd go off like a roadside bomb. One just never knew.

"But it's fresh fish. It's real fresh, Laz." Frank reached down and jerked a string of tilapia from a battered Styrofoam cooler and held them over the bar. The years slipped away as he grinned like a teenaged boy, proud of a day's catch. A full head of unruly brown hair atop a creased and creviced deeply-tanned face – somewhere between a hard-drinking thirty and sixty – told this man's tale as someone who'd spent his life in the sun.

Lazlo examined the milk white eyes of the three tilapia, mouths gaping around the waxed yellow stringer. The scales were still a mosaic of bright greens. Sometimes Frank would get red tide fish he found rotting on the beach and try and pass them off as freshly caught. Not this time. These had been caught this afternoon, probably between Frank waking after passing out last night and this evening's dinner and beer. Such was Frank's drunken cycle: drink, sleep, fish, drink, sleep, fish.

"Listen, Frank. I'd love to take your fish, I really would, but I have three freezers full of the damned things and, if I were to bet, half of them would be from you. Honestly, Frank, I have fish coming out my eyeballs."

Frank looked back and forth from his fish to the bartender at this unfathomable turn of events. For a moment he seemed as if he was going to cry. His mouth formed a little circle.

Lazlo stepped away and wiped down the bar. Gertie was in the kitchen. By the looks of it, she had almost finished closing down for the night. Business had been brisk until dark, then had fallen off like usual, leaving only locals and the occasional tourist too stunned by the reality of the Salton Sea to know that they never should have stopped here.

He poured a fresh beer for Andy, their local daft. The man claimed to be a rocket scientist but looked more like a mad scientist. The only thing more guaranteed than Frank trying to trade fish for beer was Andy sitting in his usual spot, mumbling to himself, doodling in his little notebook as he sat with his ever-present tortoiseshell glasses and clothes – a wrinkled conspiracy of a white laboratory coat over an Hawaiian shirt, shorts and flip flops.

José sat by the door. Laz didn't know if the man was illegal or not, but he was the all-around handyman no one could do without. He didn't talk much and had a haunted look in his eyes. Whatever the reason for the expression, the rail-thin Mexican took his own counsel.

The Cain and Abels – real surname Beachy – were sitting at their own table. They'd come in for fish and now sat and talked low amongst themselves. The Space Station was the area bar, restaurant, and general store, which is why the Amish family of five more often than not found themselves in for a night's dinner.

Then there was the tourist from Maine, who'd stopped on his way to Los Angeles and ended up sitting down next to Frank. Laz never caught his name, but it didn't matter. In the morning he'd never see the man again. He could tell by the look in his eyes and the eyes of the other seven tourists who sat at tables interspersed around the restaurant, that none of them would ever return.

Laz had seen it a thousand times. A tourist family, tired of the long trip through Texas, New Mexico and Arizona, riding along Interstate 10 or 8 towards the Pacific Coast, too blitzed to drive any farther, sees the old signs pointing to the Salton Sea promising resorts and fun in the sun. They didn't realize that it wasn't really a sea, nothing more than a large inland lake choked with salt and no outlet. Instead of driving another four or five hours to their destination, they'd convince themselves that staying the night in an "Ultra-Cheap" Seaside Resort would be a reward for long hours in the car. Their intent would be to wake the next morning and, maybe after a morning swim at the resort, drive the rest of the way at a leisurely pace. But when they finally witnessed the dark, beer-colored Salton Sea and rolled down the windows to inhale the ever-present bouquet of rotting fish, they probably hadn't known what hit them. Most of the time they pulled out as fast as they could, continuing on their way, eager to be free of the awful stench and horrific sight, but there were always a few who decided to tough it out.

How bad could it be? they thought.

The smell will go away, they told themselves.

But it never did. The smell of dead and rotting fish worked its way into everything – their clothes, the fabric of the seats, the carpet, their hair, their skin, even into the depths of their luggage.

"Get away from me!"

Lazlo grabbed his bat from beneath the bar and rushed over to where Frank was manhandling the man from Maine.

"Come on, one beer," Frank begged. "Three fish for one beer. My God, man. Can't you people do math in Maine?"

"Let him go, Frank!" Laz commanded in his characteristic deep voice.

Frank had one hand on the man's collar, his other holding the fish up for the tourist to see, brushing them against his nose and leaving a wet mark on his T-shirt.

"But Laz, he wants to trade."

"Frank, if I have to tell you again, I'm going to knock that head of yours right out the door." Laz brandished the bat. "Do the math, Frank. One bat! One head!"

Frank glared at Laz like a cornered rat that knew there was cheese to be had and wouldn't be deterred until it had its fill.

"Go sleep it off, Frank."

Frank hesitated another moment, then let the tourist go and backed away. Tears rose in his eyes and, with a sob, he grabbed his Styrofoam cooler, cradled it like a child, and ran out the door. Everyone was silent for a few moments, then resumed their conversations.

Laz hated when Frank got this way. The drunk never remembered when he got carried away and wouldn't remember what he'd done the next day. More often than not, Laz would forgive the man, his sorrowful puppy eyes working on the soft side of him that wanted everyone to be happy. But he'd be damned if he was going to let Frank come back in as if nothing happened. Not this time. No way.

He replaced the bat and hollered at Maude.

"Watch the register, sugar. I'll be back in a few."

His fifty-five year old ex-girlfriend who still worked as a waitress and *de facto* front-of-house manager for the Space Station glared at him. He grinned in return. His relationship with her, as with Gertie – his other ex-girlfriend who was the cook and *de facto* back-of-house manager – was founded on stoked anger.

Laz walked past the walk-in reefer and continued out the back into the warm night air. The smell of the sea struck him like a wet washcloth and clung to him. He grabbed the trash Gertie had bagged by the door and hauled it around the side of the building to the collection of cans. He'd have to pay someone who owned a truck from Brawly to come and take them to the dump. It was a long time since the city of Bombay Beach had enough money for trash pick-up, and he'd be damned if he was going to be like some of his neighbors, and turn his property or the land around it into a privately owned garbage dump. He tossed the bags into the cans, returned to the back door, reached inside and grabbed his cigarettes and a notebook.

Laz walked around to the front of the restaurant, crossed the street and sat on a retaining wall. He lit a cigarette and inhaled the welcome smoke; one thing that could be said about the smell of cigarettes was that it hid the stench of rotting fish. From his vantage point on the wall, it was ten meters to the edge of the water. In the moonlight, he could make out a dozen small shadows along the foaming edge of the water. Most likely fish. More *dead* fish. Would it never end?

In the light of the bar's neon sign, he opened his notebook and turned to the first unused page. He pulled a pen from his pocket and wrote today's date, and after checking his watch, added the time beneath. Next he wrote a few sentences in what to anyone else would be a nonsensical code, then sat back and began to watch the sea.

He'd been keeping track since he first noticed the lights. It hadn't taken long for him to find a pattern to them, so on nights when he knew they were going to occur, he made sure to bear witness and record the events as he saw them. He wasn't a scientist, nor was he very smart in a bookish sort of way, but he knew that if he watched and listened long enough, he might understand what was going on.

He didn't have long to wait.

First it came as a gentle lightening of the water. From black to gray, the water brightening as if powered by an invisible source. He inhaled the last of the smoke, held his breath and tossed the cigarette into the sand. The pressure began to build in his chest for him to exhale, but he kept the smoke trapped. He knew it wouldn't be long. As the pressure built and built, he *hoped* it wouldn't be long.

Then it happened.

The water flashed a brilliant green, then returned to gray.

He exhaled slowly, relishing the acrid bite of the menthol cigarette. He grinned as the water flashed again. Lasting less than a second, it happened so fast that if he'd blinked at the wrong time, he'd miss it.

Then a third time, it flashed.

Then darkness.

Then nothing.

Whatever it was, it was over.

Laz looked at the time and began to scribble down his observations and thoughts. It took longer than plain writing, because of the code he used. But then one never knew who might read your book.

A faraway scream made him look down the beach into the darkness. He waited to see if the sound would come again, but he didn't hear anything except the gentle lapping of the almost dead sea. It had sounded like Frank. Laz shook his head. There but by the grace of God... Laz knew that it could have just as easily been him trying to weasel fish for beer had he not been able to conquer his own demons. He amended his thought – had he not found Gertie and Maude to help him conquer his own demons. He could have never done it without them.

Laz heard the sound of feet on sand and pavement coming from the street behind him, probably Maude or Gertie seeing where he'd gone, wanting to rehash some old slight or beer-soaked memory. He'd let them have at him once he finished. The sound of feet shuffling was accompanied by the horrible stench of rot.

Not one of the girls.

"Frank, is that you? I told you to go sleep it off."

The sound and smell came closer.

"Frank, you really need to get –"

Something jerked him from his perch.

"What the *fuck*?"

He was hurled to the ground so hard his ribs cracked. He gasped, winded. Framed by the neon image of a space station that served as the restaurant's logo stood something man-sized, green skin a match to the sign.

"Who – ?"

Instead of answering, the strange man fell upon him. Lazlo fought to keep him away, but the other's strength was unbelievable. Laz gagged at the miasma of decay. His attacker's staring eyes glowed yellow; dimly, he wondered how they could do that.

But Laz wasn't going to let whatever it was get him. He kneed the thing in the side, sending it onto the sand, then struggled to his feet and began to run. The thing blocked the way to the restaurant, and was even now rising to its feet. Laz turned and headed off down the beach as fast as his old legs would carry him.

After a dozen meters, he turned to look, hoping the thing had been a figment of his imagination, or perhaps the opening salvo of dementia. But he wasn't to be so lucky. It was after him. And it was fast.

Laz kept running, but his strength was already waning. He was seventy years old and could take care of himself with the likes of Frank, but against... against... what was he against? A black and white image came to his mind of dark water and a creature rising to the surface to carry away a vivacious blonde. *The Creature from the Black Lagoon?*

He was breathing heavily now and his legs were on fire. He felt himself slowing down against his will. Try as he might, he couldn't keep going. With a cry of desperation, he stopped, turned and brought his hands up like a boxer.

And still the thing came on. Laz couldn't make out its features in the darkness, but the eyes still glowed an unearthly yellow.

When it came near, Laz swung and hit it in the side of the head. But the blow did nothing to the creature. It was like hitting rotting fish. He swung and hit again, with the same result. He tried to dance out of the creature's way, but tripped on the sand and fell sprawling.

The creature landed on top of him. Like before, Laz held it at arm's reach. Now he could hear teeth gnashing, but curiously no breathing. In fact, he couldn't feel the chest move at all. It radiated a deep sea cold.

Jesus-Mary-Christ in a basket! It's not alive!

Laz felt his arms weaken.

The creature took advantage, pushing through Lazlo's defenses until it was within his embrace. Rotting lips kissed his cheek, then pain exploded as the thing's broken teeth came away with flesh. It swallowed and fell upon Laz again. The speed and ferocity of the attack increased until its head and hands were a blur. It began to wheeze and hiss, the sounds coming from deep within its chest.

Lazlo tried to scream, but the pain kept him from taking a breath.

He was being eaten.

Eaten!

And then death claimed him.

CHAPTER TWO

The Rolling Avocado roared past a pile of road kill on the side of Highway 10, just north of Buckeye, Arizona. The heat waves made it seem as if the world was one immense stove in which the road was a griddle, cooking dead animal, well done. Natasha didn't know if it had been a zebra or a pig or a herd of wild geese. She didn't know anything about wildlife, other than what she saw on the television when her parents felt it was time for her to watch something educational. She didn't know what it was, but as they passed it, she opened her mouth and wrinkled her nose in the universal sign of teenage disgust.

Her brother Derrick happened to look up from the game of Death Fantasy III he was playing on his personal player deck just in time to see it. He sneered and asked, "What was it?"

"Another zoo animal," Natasha said, flipping her hand back toward where the creature lay dead and mutilated.

"Cool," Derrick said, his mind once more diving into the realm of hand-held video game land. "Tell me when you see another one. I want to see it too."

"When I puke on you, you'll know," she said.

Derrick grinned wickedly, then slew a roomful of tiny elf creatures with his Broadsword of Magnificent Doom.

As much as the idea of more road kill sickened her, Natasha returned her gaze to the window, where the desert rolled by. She and Derrick sat in the reverse facing seats in the back of the Rolling Avocado, their endearment for the 1970s Oldsmobile Vista Cruiser with unearthly green paint that was their sole family vehicle.

The middle and top of the car were packed with all of their worldly possessions. A bad economy, the shutdown of a Chevrolet parts plant near Philadelphia, and a year of hospital bills that the insurance company wouldn't pay had conspired to send them into bankruptcy and a three room apartment more than a year ago. That her grandfather had passed away and left them his home and restaurant had been what Auntie Lin had called a godsend.

Then again, Natasha didn't believe in God.

God wouldn't have let the economy turn to shit. God wouldn't have let her grandfather die. More importantly, God wouldn't have let her mother die of breast cancer last year.

No. Natasha didn't believe in God and she'd continue to deny His existence until He gave her mother back and admitted that it had all been one big, tremendously cruel joke.

Until then, she had to leave all of her friends and travel, hat in hand, to a place she'd never heard of and meet people she'd never met so that she and her family could actually afford to eat and have a home. It was hard for her not to feel as if her life had been ripped off.

"Stop feeling sorry for yourself," Aunt Lin said from the middle seat. She sat wedged against the passenger side door, rope and bungee cords controlling an impending avalanche of suitcases and a giant bag of cheese balls that Derrick had begged her dad to buy at a truck stop in the middle of New Mexico. "It makes you look ugly and your mother never wanted you to be ugly."

At the mention of her mother, Natasha closed her eyes.

Aunt Lin wasn't really their aunt. She'd been her mother's Chinese nanny when she was little, had stayed after she got married, and become nanny to both Derrick and Natasha.

Derrick mimicked Auntie Lin's accent in a bad parody of a Charlie Chan movie. "Yes Auntie. Natasha *no rike ugry.*"

Natasha flipped him off, then quickly hid her finger in her other hand. Thankfully her father hadn't seen, couldn't see, what she'd done. He hated "the bird" and would punish her if he'd seen her do it. She sighed, and let the weight of her woes bring her down.

Her father said that they were going to live in a resort, or what used to be a resort. Natasha supposed that something had happened for the place to lose its status. Whatever the case, Bombay Beach *was* in California. And it *was* a beach. And there *was* water. This was her mantra whenever thoughts about Willow Grove and her previously-perfect-then-turned-to-shit life intruded upon the reality of the Rolling Avocado and a life with no mother.

California.

Beach.

Water.

The sun was setting as she stared out the window at the scenery rolling away behind them. Where Eastern Pennsylvania was filled with lush trees, grasses and bushes, the desert of Western Arizona was empty except for the occasional cactus. Some were multi-armed giants, some small and white-furred. She didn't know what any of them were called, but they all looked alien and deadly.

One of the things she liked to do in the woods by herself was track down sassafras trees. Usually only tiny saplings, no bigger around than her thumb, they stood only a few feet high. Their three-pronged leaves let off a citrus smell, reminiscent of lime when squeezed. Sometimes she'd pull them out of the ground so she could get to their roots, which had been used for tea or as a sweetener by the Native Americans long ago. Once she'd been brave enough to wash the root free of dirt, and then sucked on it for several hours. The taste had been pleasant, like gum but without the necessity of chewing. Even so, she'd probably looked ridiculous, like some wild frontier woman.

But like everything else in her life, those days were gone.

The old Natasha would have found the cacti intriguing. She would have wanted to know everything about them. She would have wanted to touch them, maybe even smell their bark. Now all she thought about was how ugly and disconcerting they were. The best she could do was squint her eyes and imagine them as people standing beside the road and waving at them. As if they were herding the Rolling Avocado and the people within it along to a certain destiny.

She wondered what her father was thinking about this whole change of life. She'd never really met her grandfather. He'd left her dad when he was very young, and never returned. There had always been a vacuum in her life when talking about grandparents. Everyone else seemed to have two sets of them, but Natasha only had one set – her mother's parents – who they'd left in Eastern Pennsylvania.

Grandpa Lazlo had represented an entire side of her family she knew nothing about. And now *he* was dead. They'd already had the funeral, the will had been processed through probate, and notification had gone out to Natasha's dad. According to the letter, her grandfather had been found washed up on the beach, missing a head and an arm. She shuddered. The letter her father had read said wildlife had probably been responsible for the missing body parts, even though he'd only been in the water for twenty-four hours. It didn't matter how many times Natasha thought about it, the idea of a missing head creeped her out.

Suddenly the car hit a pothole and bottomed out at seventy miles an hour. Her father swerved violently to the right, then managed to correct to the left.

Natasha held her breath and grabbed hold of the armrest on her seat as she watched the fish-tailing view through the rear window.

Then an immense *pop* filled the inside of the car.

The tire?

The air was suddenly filled with a fine orange blizzard. The top of Derrick's black hair was almost entirely covered, as was her own, in a dusting of orange. Her father coughed and opened all the windows in the car.

"Cheeseballs!" Auntie Lin hacked and shuddered. "Ack!"

Natasha couldn't help herself. She released the breath she'd been holding and burst out laughing. Maybe everything was going to work out fine after all.

CHAPTER THREE

They arrived at a rest area north of Bombay Beach just after midnight. The four of them were far too tired to unpack or even get out of the car. They'd collapsed in place, postponing their new resort life on the edge of a sea until the next morning, when they could see it and appreciate it more in the light of day.

As the next day dawned, they awoke to the screams of a thousand birds.

Patrick Oliver jerked awake. The cacophony was amazing; he couldn't hear anything else, including Auntie Lin's snores. He peered through the windshield, but saw nothing but a Vaseline-smeared sunrise, which is what he normally saw without his glasses. He sat up and groaned. His back felt as if he'd strapped a board to it and rode down a mountain. Worse. He'd driven across country in a car with a 30 year old suspension. Frankly, he thanked his lucky stars he was alive.

He pawed around on the dashboard for his glasses and found

them about the same time that Auntie Lin woke in the seat behind him.

"What? Are the children okay?" she asked, with her hands blocking the light of the dawn from her eyes as she licked her dry lips.

Patrick slid his glasses into place and dug around on the floor beneath his seat for his flask. His mouth felt like eight miles of desert. He'd rationed himself as they'd crossed the breadth of America. He was proud of himself for managing the craving for so long. From the heft of the flask, there was still a quarter left.

"What's that noise?" Aintie Lin asked.

"Birds, I think." He grabbed a water bottle from the empty passenger seat, took a long swig, then handed it to her. "Here. You might need this."

"What? I can't hear you over the birds. Jesus. Where did they come from?"

Patrick turned to gaze through the windshield and for the first time saw the conflagration. He couldn't identify a single bird. Their wings, beaks and talons created a single, frenetic, ravenous beast, undulating along the edge of the sea, as it at once dove and rose, fighting against itself in a violent collage of motion.

"What the hell?"

He went to open his door, but Auntie Lin grabbed the back of the seat.

"Are you sure it's safe?"

Patrick grinned. "Come on. They're just birds."

Despite her protests, he opened the door and climbed out, allowing his back to stretch for the first time since 7 PM yesterday when they'd stopped to clean the residue of giant cheese balls from everyone's hair. He brought the flask to his mouth and took a deep refreshing drink.

And then the stench hit him.

"Oh my God!"

The alcohol burned acrid as he covered his nose and mouth with both hands. His eyes watered.

"Oh my God," Auntie Lin echoed from inside the car. "Mr. Oliver, for God's sake, please close the door. You're killing us."

He slammed the door, but remained outside, his desire to drink overruling his desire to get out of the stench. He leaned against the car, wondering how he was going to survive the reek, and swallowed the vodka he'd been holding in his mouth. If he took shallow breaths, he could breathe.

He took another drink, keeping his eyes on the birds, lest they turn and think he was Tipi Hedron. There had to be thousands of seagulls fighting to get to the shoreline of what appeared to be a beer-colored inland sea. The noise was as deafening as the smell was rotten.

Then, by some miracle, the wind shifted to an offshore breeze and the air was clean once more. Patrick stood straight and watched the sun rising over the far edge of the sea, its golden rays illuminating the water and the edges of the birds' wings in a glistening nimbus of light. Everything had gone from hellish to heavenly in a moment.

Suddenly a man appeared, stick held high, screaming in barbaric rage as he ran, all elbows and knees, towards the birds. They ignored him until the last second, then rose heavily out of his way. He swung madly, screaming over the shrieks of the birds with an edge of madness in his voice. His fifth swing sent him twisting in the air, his legs entangling as they failed to keep up. He fell face first into what the birds had been feeding on and lay there for a moment.

The back door of the station wagon opened and Natasha and Derrick rolled out.

"I gotta pee," Derrick murmured, looking around, then running to where a trashcan stood overflowing beneath a "Do Not Litter" sign.

"Is this it?" Natasha's hair was tangled into a brown-tentacled nightmarish mess that sought to go in every direction at once. Her narrow face still held the imprint of the seat. "This can't be it."

"Do you see what I see?" Patrick asked.

The man by the water pushed himself to his knees, retched mightily into the surf, then stood. Twin rivulets of yellow drool fell to the ground. The man ambled off the way he came, his gait uncertain.

"A drunk puking in the surf?" Natasha asked.

"Hey, we have those at home," Derrick said, having finished his business and rejoined his family.

"No. What's on the shore. What the birds were after." Even as he said the words, the first of many birds began to return. Within moments, the sky darkened and those that had fled returned to their interrupted meal of rotting fish.

"How many are there?" Derrick asked.

"What? Fish or birds?" Patrick asked in return.

"Dunno. Both?"

"Hundreds. Thousands."

"Is this really the Salton Sea?" Natasha asked.

Before anyone could answer, the wind shifted once more, drawing the stench back over them like a heavy oil cloth. Everyone groaned as they covered their noses and mouths. They rushed to the car, jumped inside and slammed the doors behind them. Then they sat in stunned silence watching the rotting fish, the birds and the barbaric drunk who had once again found a stick and was ready to resume his Don Quixote stand.

CHAPTER FOUR

Gerald Duphrene sat behind the wheel of his golf cart, glaring in morose fascination at the remains of the coyote lying in the middle of Highway 111. The crushed body was perfectly perpendicular to the double yellow line, crossing it like a "T". It wasn't just the positioning of the body that had transfixed him, but also the juxtaposition of the absolutely flattened body with the perfectly undisturbed head. The long snout, the lolling tongue, and the wide bright eyes seemed alive on the dead creature. They stared back at Gerald in surprise, as if to ask, *how did I get here?*

The sight reminded him of Private Abner Johnson back in '53. Old Ab had perished in a similar way on the hills north of Seoul when the Chinese were pushing them back and back to Pusan, though Abner never did see Pusan. They were lying on the side of a hill, trying to sleep amidst the cold rain and the constant shelling when it happened. No one could have foreseen it. Nothing could have stopped it. An American Sherman tank had crested the top of the hill, maneuvering backwards as it fired 76.2 mm shells at the ocean of Chinese soldiers. The tracks slid on the mud, sending the 32 ton machine skating down the backside of the hill. It crushed Ab's entire body flat, blood and guts shooting from the sides like a jelly sandwich that had just been hand slammed. One minute Ab had been talking about life on his daddy's tobacco farm in North Carolina, the next he was Korean War road kill... all except for his head. His head, like the coyote's, was perfectly undisturbed and seemed to be caught in mid-sentence.

Gerald remembered staring at old Ab for what seemed like a whole minute before he got up and ran. And it was a good thing he did, too, because the rest of the tank battalion followed the first, backing blindly down the hill as they scrambled to escape the tidal wave of slant-eyed yellow murder. Maybe Old Ab's death had saved him. Gerald nodded to himself. Good thing he was paying attention.

A cargo truck carrying cucumbers towards Tucson roared by, finishing the job on the dead animal. As the truck disappeared down the road to Niland, Gerald turned the golf car around, and drove back into Bombay Beach, reflecting – not for the first time – how cut off from the world they were. As he passed the *Welcome to Bombay Beach* sign he noticed that weeds were hugging the wooden supports. He made a mental note to return with clippers. They might not have many tourists, but that wasn't a reason for them not to look their best.

That sentiment went to the heart of his problems. What had once been a proud little community on the shore of a thriving inland sea had turned into a scene of all-out Armageddon. He'd seen Korean villages in better shape after UN Forces and the Chinese had steamrolled over them.

Now parked at the corner of Avenue A and Fifth Street, he glared at his community. He remembered in 1958, when he'd first moved here, how pristine and beautiful everything had looked. The trailers were rectangular pastel homes arrayed in perfect rows. The developer had sprung for fake grass for everyone, which provided impossibly green plots in front of every porch that only needed to be occasionally swept and cleaned with a hose. A service provided fresh flowers in pots set at the base of everyone's mailbox. The roads were new, nary a piece of litter in sight. The water of the Salton Sea was a Sultan's paradise of crystal blue water. And bikini-clad water skiers crazed the horizon.

He adjusted the brim of his baseball cap with his right hook, put the cart in gear with his left, and headed off down First Street at a slow roll. Things never stayed the same. Change was the nature of the universe. He'd had a drill sergeant in basic training who'd told him once that the measure of a man was not how he dealt with success, but rather how he responded to adversity... and life had sure given Gerald Duphrene his share of that.

The stainless steel hooks that were his hands and the Salton Sea were both examples of what could have been. They were *if onlys* and if he spent his days dwelling on *if onlys* he'd never get anything done. *If only* frost bite hadn't murdered his fingers. *If only* the land hadn't conspired to murder the dream of the Salton Sea. Nothing more than *if onlys*.

As he drove down the street, he managed to see past the ruin and degradation of the trailers, ticking off, instead, those which were still occupied. Now nearly half of them were empty with more and more emptying every day.

Some left by land, moving their worldly goods – or sometimes leaving them – and heading off on Highway 111 to better times.

And some left by other means.

A chill ran from his shoulders to his elbows where the prosthetics started. These were what bothered him most. He'd seen the monsters coming out of the water. He'd watched them creep into a house and ravage the occupant, sitting on the sofa watching television. He'd seen far worse in Korea, so one person eating another hadn't been what scared him.

He had scared himself.

Not because he was willing to do anything to stop the creatures.

Not because he wanted to protect the people of his town.

Not because he knew the price of war.

No. He scared himself because sometime between being a twenty-something badass in Korea and being a seventy-something cyborg in California, he'd turned into a wimp. Every time he saw the damned things he'd start shaking. He'd find himself frozen in place. He couldn't even speak.

And he hated himself for it.

After each occasion he vowed that the next time would be different. He promised himself that he'd do something, save someone, be that hero he'd once been.

But every time he failed himself.

Gerald turned down Avenue C, eyeing the dark and broken windows of the abandoned trailers. But this time would be different. He'd face his fear if it killed him.

He pulled to a stop in front of the old yellow and white trailer where George and Paula Silva had lived. That Porta-Wop and his wife had been good friends while Gerald's wife had been alive. But soon after his dear Jane died of lung cancer, the Portuguese-Italian ex-Army sergeant and his wife moved back to Kentucky where her family was from. The trailer had remained abandoned ever since and year by year it fell into more and more disrepair. Now, it was little more than a ruin.

Staring at the doorway, he felt the old fear return. He had to fight it. He had to conquer the feeling. Nothing bad would happen. Nothing could happen.

He'd captured one of the creatures using a bear trap and it was still inside. What better way to conquer his fear than with a real live – or in this case, real dead – test dummy?

All that bravado evaporated, however, as he stared into the dark maw of the doorway. He regarded the blackness inside. A niggling thought made him wonder which one of them was the real dummy.

Gerald set his jaw.

He'd find out soon enough.

But not this time.

He backed the golf cart out of the yard and into the street, and resumed his patrol. For now, there were other things that needed his attention.

An hour later, after washing at a nearby campground, the Olivers managed to find Grandpa Lazlo's restaurant, beneath a sign bearing a gigantic neon space station that looked capable of docking miniature intergalactic starships. One story and made of sun-faded yellow and blue painted cinderblocks, the restaurant had only one window by the front door to let light in. On the left was an alley between the restaurant and an abandoned gas station set back from the road, the pumps standing as skeletal monuments to a time of more plentiful tourists. The restaurant's wall bore a faded mural of space ships doing battle in a galaxy far, far away. Trash cans were gathered near the back corner. A laundromat was attached on the right, its huge windows painfully reflecting the sun.

On the fly-speckled window was a sign that said "Open." Natasha wondered why it would be open so soon after her grandfather's death two weeks ago. Although she hadn't really known him, she decided to take a dislike to Gertie, who greeted them at the door. The older woman was tall and thin with long white hair. She had high cheekbones above a ready smile, and wore flip-flops, orange dungarees and a bikini top.

"Frank told me there was a family parked by the beach. I figured it had to be you. Hi, I'm Gertie. I was Lazlo's girlfriend." She gave Natasha's father a hug before he could put his arms out. She grasped his shoulders when she was done and held him at arm's length. "You look so much like him, you know. Especially in the cheeks and the jaws. Soft eyes, though. Hmmph. Must be from your mother."

She turned and went back inside without saying another word.

Patrick looked at his family, who looked back at him and shrugged. Derrick helped Auntie Lin out of the car and they entered the restaurant together.

Whatever Natasha expected, it hadn't been to see a place so clean. The walls, counters and tables gleamed. She'd never liked cleaning, and really hadn't paid attention to how clean things were, but after the shock of the Salton Sea, she'd grown a sudden appreciation for sanitary surfaces.

Gertie stood imperiously in the middle of the room with her hands on her hips. "Laz always liked the place clean. He used to say that it might be a natural disaster on the outside, but on the inside it has to be a place people want to come to."

"I'd come in as long as there were no dead fish," Derrick muttered. Then he saw the crazy man they'd seen on the beach, sitting at the bar and drinking beer through a straw.

Another woman came out of a swinging door from what must have been the kitchen. She was the same age and body type as Gertie but her skin was the color of dark chocolate. Her grey hair was closely cropped to her head, and she wore an apron over a bikini top, dungaree shorts and flip-flops.

"So are you going to sell the place and put us out on the street?" she asked, without even a "hello." She crossed her arms and stared at Natasha first, then turned her attention to Patrick.

Patrick stuttered. "I don't – we don't –"

Auntie Lin saved him by asking, "Who are you and what business is it of yours?"

"I'm Maude," the woman said, stepping closer. "I was Lazlo's girlfriend."

Natasha turned to Gertie and pointed. "I thought she was –"

Maude and Gertie exchanged looks as the Oliver family watched.

"We were both his girlfriends," Gertie finally said.

"Although lately he could barely stand us," Maude added.

"I think he was getting old."

"I don't know about that," Maude said mischievously, her gaze somewhere else. "Laz could perk up every now and then. Boy could he perk up."

"Maude!"

Patrick grinned and so did Auntie Lin.

Natasha closed her eyes and shook her head at the thought. "It's okay," Natasha's father said. "He had that effect on people, I was told."

Gertie nodded. "You were told right."

"There wasn't a soul who met your dad who didn't like him," Maude added.

A lump formed in Natasha's throat and her face tightened.

Then her father took a tentative step toward the women. He looked back at Natasha and Derrick, and took another step and held out his hands. Gertie and Maude took them and they stood there for several minutes, united in their loss.

Natasha began to feel uncomfortable. She felt the weight of the moment, but this seemed absolutely the wrong place for it. She looked around the restaurant and saw that although there was room for about thirty people, there was only one customer, the man she'd seen acting crazy on the beach. He'd cleaned up since then and looked almost respectable, if you discounted the wild eyes, wind-blown hair and broken teeth.

Gertie was the first to break the silence. "So what is it going to be? Are you kicking us out or what?"

Her dad didn't know what to say.

Auntie Lin saved him from having to. "How about some breakfast and then maybe we can talk about it? The kids need some food. We drove all the way from Pennsylvania in three days and could use a break."

"That's a terrific idea." Maude grinned. "Breakfast coming right up. How do you like your eggs, young man?" she asked Derrick.

"Hatched," he said.

"Derrick doesn't like eggs," Natasha said.

"Doesn't like eggs? Then he takes after his grandfather. I have just the thing for you, young man."

Auntie Lin pushed her way behind the counter despite Maude's protests and began to help in the kitchen.

Breakfast arrived within twenty minutes. Maude served them while Gertie wrangled coffees, waters, milk and orange juice. Auntie Lin brought toast, butter and an assortment of jellies for everyone. They even fed the man at the bar. He turned out to be Frank Gillespie, a local from back when the Salton Sea had actually been a resort.

Derrick was served French toast dusted with confectioners' sugar. Three strips of bacon and two links of sausage rode the top, all covered in syrup. By the way he inhaled it, Natasha was convinced it was the best thing her brother had ever eaten. When he finished, he looked around for something else to eat. Lucky for him Maude saw his glum face and brought him another helping of what she called Lazlo's Toast. From then on, as she moved about the restaurant, the boy's eyes never left her.

Auntie Lin found a spot at the bar and had wheat toast and coffee, her sparkling gaze taking in the new people and the new place.

As the family ate, customers began to trickle in, including a group of four elderly tourists in shorts, black socks and T-shirts. They were as old as Gertie and Maude, but acted much older. The difference was plain in the way the two old women goofed around with each other, compared to the two at the table, clucking and fussing over each little bit of life that was thrust before them, the cleanliness of the forks they were shining with their napkins and the way their husbands were sitting on their chairs. The final straw was when one of the women, her hair the color of an electrified smurf, tried to send her eggs back for the third time, claiming they weren't scrambled hard enough.

Gertie threw both hands in the air and headed back to the kitchen, muttering something about knowing where a bucket of spackle was. And that was that. The tourists saw neither hide nor hair of Gertie, and Maude patently ignored them, whenever she strode by. They finally stood, tossed a twenty dollar bill on the table, and left.

It was just about then that Patrick said to Natasha. "Why don't you and Derrick go and explore? Me and Auntie Lin need to talk with these ladies for awhile."

Natasha sat for a moment staring at her father, stunned that he'd just treated her like a child. She was eighteen, she'd graduated high school, and was as much as an adult as anyone else in the restaurant, with the exception of Derrick, of course. She glared, counted to ten, then jumped up from the table and stomped out of the restaurant. Derrick followed close behind. She'd moved across the country because she'd known that her brother would need her. If it wasn't for him, she'd have never come.

She fumed until she hit the outside air. As soon as the door closed behind her, she wished she'd never left the restaurant. The temperature had risen to at least a hundred without a breeze or cloud on the horizon. "Oven" was the word that came to her mind. She turned to Derrick, whose face had slackened from the sheer weight of his breakfast.

"You gonna make it?"

"Ugh," he said.

Natasha looked longingly at the door. She wanted badly to go back inside but knew that if she did her father and Auntie Lin would once again probably send her away. As hot as it was, unless she was going to burst into flames, she wasn't going back inside.

She gazed at her surroundings, musing that the town of Bombay Beach more closely resembled some war-torn East European town seen on a television news snippet. She'd been to Sandy Hook on the New Jersey coast. It was a seven mile stretch of perfect beach with the nearby town of Highlands seemingly transported from the suburbs. Food franchises and stores were the same there as the malls around Philadelphia. Even the people were the same, just more tanned and windblown, the cool sea air scouring their skin clean of big city grime.

Yeah, she'd been to beach resorts before and this place was no beach resort. Everything here was the opposite. Of the people she'd seen, the extraordinary old women Gertie and Maude included, none of them wore clothes she associated with success. The beach was a putrid stretch of rot. The water was the color of old soda. The buildings had either collapsed beneath the weight of their own decay or were on the way. And everything seemed to be encrusted with salt.

The Space Station Restaurant was probably the best-constructed building in sight. Rows of trailers, some clearly abandoned and others in questionable states of occupation, ran off to her left, each surrounded by rusted chain link fences. The occupants of a blue trailer down the line had woven a banner which said "God Lovs U" between the links of their fence.

To her right were several regular buildings. All but one, a

corner market with a window filled with paper signs advertising specials on fruit and vegetables, had been abandoned. Three women sat on a bench in front, chatting amongst themselves in the shadow of the awning. Each of them wore shorts and bikini tops, although Natasha felt seriously that none of them should have been allowed to wear the latter. As nice as they might be, their days of showing cleavage had passed when Bill Clinton had been president and parents still let Michael Jackson play with their kids. Now their bodies were more a study of geography than anatomy.

She peered between the trailers as movement caught her eye. At first glance it appeared to be a dog chained to a doghouse in a chain link-fenced yard. But interspersed weeds and the heat of the air made it hard to make out. She stepped closer, moving a foot or two into the alley beside the restaurant. Then the dog snuffled at the ground.

She sucked in her breath. For a brief moment the creature wasn't a dog but a person. The face was covered by what looked like a baseball catcher's mask, metal bars sheathed in leather and fastened at the back of the head.

Then the creature wrenched its face to the sky, made a strange barking noise and ran into the doghouse.

Natasha turned to Derrick, who was admiring the mural on the alley wall.

"Did you see that?" she asked.

"Mmm?" he turned towards her, and by the look on his face, it was clear that his attention had been riveted on the fading space battle.

"Over there, in that yard." Natasha pointed. "It looked like..." She didn't know how to finish the sentence.

"Like what?"

Natasha shook her head. Had she really seen it or had it been a mirage?

"I thought I saw someone chained to a doghouse."

"'Someone'?" Derrick laughed. "As in a person?"

"I know. I know." She shrugged. "It sounds stupid. Forget about it."

She looked once more at the empty yard and the chain trailing into the dog house, then strode back to the front of the restaurant. She began walking down the street, gravel and sand crunching beneath her feet.

A portable arrow sign down the road announced a sale on salt. The arrow pointed to an immense tent with a banner above the entrance which read "Duvall Brothers Imperial Salt Exports."

"My uncle said if the Duvalls can sell salt in the Salton Sea then they could sell water to a drowning man."

Natasha turned at the new voice and saw a girl in her mid-teens, with long brown hair twisted into tight braids. Freckles danced across a wide nose on a light brown face, and her smile was one her mother would have called "petulant." Even though the girl was younger than Natasha, she wore eyeliner, mascara and blazing red lipstick.

"Those your uncles?" Natasha asked.

The girl shook her head. "Nuh-uh. My uncle collects salt for them. He goes out and brings it back so that they can press it into bricks. He says they have a good market with the Chinese."

She spoke quickly with just a hint of Spanish to her pronunciation.

"Why would the Chinese buy salt from here?" Derrick asked.

"Who knows?" The girl shrugged. "Why do they sell dried bear penis? Or goat spleen? Sometimes you shouldn't ask."

Derrick's jaw dropped as he looked at Natasha. "Did she say bear penis?" he mock-whispered.

Natasha grinned. "I think she did." She held out her hand. "Natasha Oliver. This is my brother Derrick. We're new here."

"No shit," the girl said, taking Natasha's hand then letting go. "I could tell by the way you're looking at everything that you weren't from around here."

"Is it that obvious?"

"You all do it when you come. Someone probably told you about the resort and about the sand and the sea. You might have even heard about some of the problems with the place, but you said to yourself, *How bad can it be?*"

Natasha found herself nodding as the other girl spoke.

The girl held out her arms as if to encompass Bombay Beach, the Salton Sea and the universe. "How bad can it be? It can be this bad." She shook her head and laughed. "Name's Veronica Lopez. I used to be like you when I first got here, then I got used to it."

"I don't know if I can get used to this."

"You'd be surprised how easy it is to get used to something. Hell, girl, give it a few weeks and you'll be telling someone else the same thing I'm telling you right now."

"Where are you from?" Derrick asked.

"Los Angeles."

Derrick's eyes rounded. "Really?" His expression was a mix of incredulity and puppy love. He tried not to grin, but had no control over his mouth.

"Oh, Lordy." Veronica shook her head. "This one's going to be trouble."

Although the girl can't have been more than two years older than Derrick, there was an epoch of experience between them that was clearly noticeable. Veronica was sixteen going on thirty.

"Did you ever meet anyone famous?" Derrick asked.

"My cousin."

"Which movie was he in?"

"He wasn't in no movie. Raul was arrested by the cops in South Central. He was a gangbanger. Everyone knew Raul. It's why I'm out here living with my auntie and uncle. Mom didn't want me getting hooked up with the same crowd."

"Gangbanger?" Derrick said. "You mean like drive-bys?" He made a firing motion with his fingers.

"For some of us drive-bys aren't something on the evening news. I bet where you're from you can walk down the street just as plain as day and not worry about who's gonna shoot you for wearing the wrong color shirt." She shook her head and her eyes softened. "Never mind. Listen, let me give you a tour. There's some funny shit in this place."

Veronica walked with a strut, like she had something to prove. She guided them down a side street and began to point at different homes and cars, telling stories about each one. The streets were arranged in a simple grid system. Numbered streets ran east and west and lettered avenues ran north and south. There were no lawns or plots of vegetables. Everything was covered in sand, even the road, which at times couldn't be seen for the sand blown across it. The only plant-life –aside from weeds – was palm trees that grew stubby, browning leaves and gray beards as if they were old men of the sea. Giant satellite dishes were prominent in many yards, as were aluminum antennas growing on the roofs of homes like the strange technological horns of prehistoric animals. When asked about these, Veronica responded that Bombay Beach didn't have cable, so if someone wanted more than the three static-laced channels broadcast from El Centro, they needed these antique satellite dishes. None of the regular subscription satellite companies made Bombay Beach part of their territory, so it was a retired rocket scientist who, for a few bucks a month, came by and serviced everyone's dishes.

They came to what looked like three trailers welded together and Veronica told them that it belonged to an Amish family who'd come out to the Salton Sea for the "simplicity of life," whatever that meant. Natasha and Derrick were quite familiar with Amish people. They saw them all the time coming from Pennsylvania in their horse-drawn buggies, old-timey clothes and existences free of creature comforts. In fact, Lancaster County, where they were from, had a large Amish population, so their presence here provided a strange comfort. Still, Natasha had never expected to see Amish people in the middle of the desert, much less on the shores of a rotting sea. Although the trailers were a modern contrivance, there were no antennas, satellite dishes or electric lines running from the poles alongside the road to the home, like in the other trailers. The shades were drawn and the sun glinted off the siding in places where the paint had worn. Nothing stirred in the yard.

"Creepy," Derrick said.

Veronica laughed. "I know what you mean. I've had better feelings about crack houses than this joint."

"How many kids did you say they had?" Natasha asked.

"Three. Two boys about Derrick's age and a girl nearer my age.

They don't talk very much and their father doesn't let them out."

"What do they do?"

Veronica gazed solemnly at Derrick as she considered the question, then her eyes turned to slits as she smiled wickedly. "They worship the dark gods and will hearken in an age of savagery the likes of which the world has never seen."

The air was still for a moment. Derrick stared at the trailer with wide eyes, his mouth forming a small circle of surprise. Even Natasha stared at the U-shaped compound, wondering if there was an altar inside covered with the carcasses of small furry animals, or maybe something larger and with tentacles, or even a block of salt carved into the figure of a Dark God.

"Gotcha!" Veronica laughed.

Derrick and Natasha both jumped, caught in their own imaginations. They smiled self-consciously, feeling like rubes.

"You guys are too easy." Veronica snorted.

Natasha laughed, but was irritated at the girl. She kept a smile on her face, though. Instead, she turned it back on her. "Did you just say 'hearken'? Gandalf called, he wants his word back."

Veronica glared for a moment, clearly not used to the challenge, then let herself laugh again easily. "If you know Gandalf then you're a closet gamer, aren't you?" She said it as fact, rather than as a question.

"My dad made me read the books before he'd let us see the movies," Natasha said. "I thought some of them were too long. Derrick here is the gamer. I don't really care for them."

"What do you play?" Veronica asked Derrick.

"Death Fantasy."

"Which one?"

"All of them. I'm on III right now."

"Have you reached the Demon Lich yet?"

He shook his head.

"Wait until you do. It's awesome. If you get stuck, I know some ways to help."

Derrick smiled, then stepped back and pointed at one of the windows.

"Did you see that?"

Natasha looked but didn't see anything.

"The curtain moved. I swear it did."

Veronica laughed again. "It's not like it's haunted. People live there. They're just weird people."

"Who hearken the coming of savagery," Natasha added.

"An age of savagery."

Natasha rolled her eyes, but relaxed. At least the younger girl would make the summer livable, if not enjoyable.

They continued down the street, passing three empty houses for every occupied one. Some were burned-out hulks. Natasha wasn't certain if it was because of fire run amok or because burning down empty trailers had been someone's strategy to alleviate the boredom. No pets roamed, although she could hear an occasional dog bark. No children played. They only glimpsed people now and then, through windows or in their back yards, never long outside, intent on getting back inside. They'd passed a community center with a basketball court, but the rims were bent, falling and rusted to uselessness. A jungle gym made of tires was home to an Africanized beehive which Veronica said they should leave alone if they knew what was good for them. Still, Natasha had never seen killer bees and knew only what she saw on television.

The tiny town on the edge of the inland sea was a postage stamp, built in a square grid and surrounded on three sides by a twenty foot high seawall of sand and dirt, reinforced with a mesh of iron bars. Veronica explained that the seawall was to keep the sea from flooding the town. When the rainy season hit the Empire Valley, the irrigation ran off the fields and into the Salton Sea. The sea level could rise quickly, sometimes with dire consequences, so most trailers had been set on concrete pylons. It also accounted for the wooden-framed roof decks that had been built atop nearly every trailer, allowing the residents to sit high and dry in their lawn chairs and watch the sea over the seawall that surrounded the town.

Strange machines chugged in the ground at the four corners of Bombay Beach. At each one, a pipe ran from a huge propane tank down into a manmade well covered with wire mesh. Gurgling emanated from the depths, echoing in the concrete tube like a monster's growl. Derrick dropped to his knees in front of one and gripped the mesh as he tried to plumb the shadowy depths with his gaze. The smell coming through the grate was a putrid distillation of everything horrible about the sea, but it couldn't quash the boy's curiosity.

"That's a sump," Veronica said. "This is actually Sump Pump Number Two, if you want to be specific."

Suddenly the machine growled.

Derrick jerked back at the sound, then laughed self-consciously. "Sounds like a dragon down there."

"Whatever it is, the Army Corps of Engineers put it here to suck out the ground water. They say that without it, we'd be nothing more than a salty swamp." She stomped on the cracked clay underfoot. "Instead we have the luxury of this."

Derrick growled into the sump, matching his tone with that of the mechanism. His voice filled the concrete void above the machinery.

"Follow me," Veronica said, snapping her fingers. "I want you to see this."

Across the road from the sump was a set of stairs, broken and sun bleached like the bones of a whale. When they reached the top, the sea in all its inglorious decay spread out before them. But that wasn't why Veronica had summoned them up there. She pointed to what looked like a power plant less than a quarter mile across the quay.

"What's that?" Derrick asked.

"If you believe the Mad Scientist, it's a top secret government facility where they build things and hide them from prying eyes."

Derrick's eyes glowed at the idea of a secret government compound.

Natasha rolled her eyes.

The low gray building had three immense smokestacks. White fists of smoke punched out from two of them, first expanding, then withering under the heat of the all-powerful sun. A row of heavily-tinted square windows ran along the front of the building. Two white Suburban SUVs were parked in the side lot.

An access road ran around behind the building. A twelve-foot-high chain link fence protected the entire setup from intrusion from the outside. An access gate could open to the quay, but was now closed and locked with a chain.

"What do they build there?" Derrick asked.

"Don't be a sucker, Derrick. She's pulling your leg."

Veronica put on a *Who, me?* expression.

"Puh-lease," was Natasha's response.

"Seriously. I did not make that up about what the Mad Scientist said and I'm not pulling your leg." Veronica added as she noticed the doubt in the other two faces, "It's really not me. It's the Mad Scientist who's pulling your leg."

"Is there really a Mad Scientist?" Derrick asked.

"Derrick." Natasha shook her head and sighed. "I have got to get you out more."

Veronica laughed. "He's just another one of the crazy people left in Bombay Beach. He used to be some sort of real scientist for the government. His name is Andy Gudgel. I'll show you where he lives. It's kind of cool." She gave Natasha a twinkling look. "Think hobbits."

Natasha mouthed the word then shook her head and gave voice to the question that had been boiling inside of her. "Why are there so many crazy people here?"

Veronica scoffed at Natasha's question. "Look around you. We're kids so we have no choice, but if you were grown up, would you stay? I mean, come on, would you want to live here?"

"Not for a second."

"There you go. Those who could leave, left. They didn't even sell their homes. They just left. Those who couldn't leave, for whatever reason, stayed. And so you're left with the desperate or insane."

"Which one are you?" Natasha asked.

"I think I'm desperate, but I might be insane. They say you never know when you're insane." Veronica poked Natasha in the arm. "And which one are you?"

"Oh, we're not staying here, at least I'm not."

Veronica nodded and grinned. "Sure you're not."

Natasha ignored her and descended the stairs back into the town. She kept a forearm over her nose to help keep out the stink. She wondered if her clothes smelled of the place already. And what about her hair? She glanced back at the others, wishing they'd come down so she could find someplace with air conditioning.

"What is it, really?" Derrick asked, standing at the top of the seawall, gazing intently at the mysterious facility.

"Do you really want to know?" Veronica joined him in staring at the long, gray building perched on the edge of the sea, smoke billowing from two of its three smokestacks.

Derrick nodded.

"It's a desalination plant. Uses osmosis to remove the salt from the water so we can drink it."

"Osmosis," whispered Derrick. "Sounds like the name of a wizard."

Natasha shook her head as she watched the others descend the stairs and join her. Who's to say they all weren't crazy?

They continued trudging through town, eventually arriving at an immaculately-painted, robin's-egg-blue trailer bordered by a chain link fence. The ground was covered in empty beer cans several feet high. A man with poufy black hair and thick black sideburns sat in a bench swing attached to an awning that ran the length of the trailer. He had a beer in a camouflage foam sleeve, and sipped from it like a man of leisure.

As they approached, a car with bumper stickers from Magic Mountain and Disneyland eased past. The man in the swing leaped from his spot, sending cans into a crashing cacophony. He wore a white tank top and hot pink bellbottom pants with rhinestone studs down the sides. He spun, dropped his pants, mooned the passing motorists, and shook his ass in the hot desert air for all it was worth. He shouted something that sounded like *Love me tender*, then hitched up his pants, and with a thunderous clatter of cans beneath his feet, sat back down in his swing. It didn't appear as if he had spilled even a drop of beer.

"That's Kristov," Veronica indicated. "My uncle says he's an ex-Romanian freedom fighter from the days of the Soviet Union."

"What's with the Elvis getup?" Natasha asked.

"He's a little touched in the head. He just sits there, drinks beer all day, mooning the tourists, pretending to be Elvis."

"Is he dangerous?"

"No."

"What happened to him?" Derrick asked.

"He told some of the other kids he'd been in a gulag and had been experimented on."

Derrick asked, "What's a gulag?"

"A prison, I think," Natasha said.

"So he was a criminal?" Derrick asked.

"Who knows?" Veronica pointed to the moat of empty beer cans surrounding the house. "See those cans? The reason he has them all around his trailer is to warn him if someone comes near."

"Veronica, come and drink beer with me. I will teach everything I know to you." His accent was a little slurred, but held a note of playfulness.

"No thanks, Kristov. Gotta show the new folks around."

"These are new peoples? I love new peoples. Come to Kristov and drink beer."

"There's more to life than beer, Kristov," Veronica said.

"Says you." He turned to Natasha. "Hurry and leave while you still can," he shouted. "Look!" He leaped up, spun around and treated them with the view of his ass usually only reserved for tourists.

Natasha and Derrick both recoiled at the hairy protrusion.

"Oh my god," Natasha said.

The ex-Romanian freedom fighter in the Elvis clothes sat back on his swing and began rocking himself back and forth. "You should go now, before it's too late and the monsters get you."

They left him there and continued on their tour of the town. Natasha tried not to think about the warning, especially coming from someone as clearly crazy as Kristov was, but she couldn't get it out of her head.

CHAPTER FIVE

CHAPTER FIVE

With the breakfast rush finally over, Patrick, Auntie Lin, Maude and Gertie sat at the table ruminating over cooling cups of coffee. The only other customers in the restaurant were Frank at the bar and an old retired school teacher named Abigail Ogletree, who always came in late with her little toy poodle and read her latest bodice ripper while eating oatmeal and drinking coffee. The dog sat on the seat beside her, its attention focused on her plate of food.

The four of them absorbed the silence for ten minutes, knowing the importance of what was about to be said.

Patrick had bounced the possibility of running the restaurant with Auntie Lin half a dozen times. One moment he was certain he could do it, the next he was convinced he'd be a sheer and utter failure. What he knew about running a restaurant he could write on the head of a pin. Eventually, somewhere in the middle of Nebraska, they'd agreed that he'd come in, look things over, sell the restaurant, and start a new life with the proceeds, maybe find a good school for Derrick, and somewhere for Natasha to embark on adulthood. But now, after looking at the town of Bombay Beach and talking with his father's two ex-girlfriends, the prospects for a sale seemed astronomically doubtful. Who would want to buy anything out here? Wasn't that the problem?

Patrick was beginning to come to terms with why his father had never returned. Maybe it was because he couldn't sell the business. Maybe he'd wanted to come home but couldn't. But the moment Patrick thought those things, he knew he was reaching, trying like always to find a reason why his father had left and never come back. Anything other than what he thought in the darkest hours of the night, when the trees scratched at the window and the house was quiet except for the creaking, that made the emptiness grow in his stomach until he felt like he could swallow the universe... the idea that it was him that made his father leave.

Patrick desperately wanted a drink. He'd snuck several in the bathroom but his flask was empty. He couldn't help but glance to the door. He remembered the store around the corner. He bet that they sold liquor. He itched to go out and get some.

Auntie Lin never said anything, but she didn't have to. Every time she looked, it was through his dead wife's eyes that she saw him – like judgment from the grave.

"So what's it gonna be?" Gertie asked.

"You selling or staying?" Maude asked.

Patrick snapped back to the situation at hand. He'd already had a confab with Auntie Lin, whose opinion he found himself counting on more and more. There was really nothing else to do. His job on the assembly line had dried up. There were no prospects other than to fight teenagers for cashier positions in supermarkets or as fry cooks at fast food franchises. With two kids as a single parent, no prospects and an opportunity to work and live in a new town standing before him, he'd be foolish to pass it up. In fact, as soon as they executed the will, the restaurant was theirs. Bottom line was that they had no place to live or work, and the restaurant and Bombay Beach offered both.

He stared into the eyes of the two older woman, knowing now just what to say.

"We're staying," he said.

Gertie broke into a huge smile.

"And us?" Maude asked. "You gonna ask us to stay on, too?"

This was something that they hadn't agreed on. Patrick wanted them gone, more because his father had chosen them over him than any other reason. Auntie Lin had argued that they shouldn't be punished for his father's choices and she was right, as usual.

Although they had a brightness about them, his father's ex-girlfriends were on the downhill side of everything good in their lives. Although they smiled hopefully at him, he couldn't help but notice their leathery-tanned skin, wrinkles yanking hard at the corners of their eyes, and gray hair eating away at the color. They were alone now. All each had was herself. In a strange way Patrick was also alone. He'd always had his father's ghost to haunt him before. Now that his father was dead, his ghost had passed on as well. The only way he had to learn about his father was from these two women sitting across the table, and he could either kick them to the curb or invite them to stay.

"Why are you looking at me funny?" Gertie asked. "You getting sick or something?"

"No. Not sick. Just tired is all." He sighed, wishing once again for a drink. "I guess I'd like you to stay on, if you can. We don't know anything about running a restaurant and would appreciate if you taught us what you know."

"A reprieve." Maude leaned back and whistled. "I owe you twenty, Gert."

Maude took a rolled twenty out of her cleavage and handed it to Gertie, who immediately placed it in her own cleavage. Patrick allowed himself a smile. Amidst all the melancholy, he actually felt good.

"We'll definitely stay. So what's next?" Gertie asked.

"I need to find a judge to execute the will. Make everything legal, you know."

"We don't have one of those." Gertie shook her head. "They shut down the courthouse."

"What is this, the Wild West?" Patrick asked. "What town doesn't have a judge anymore?"

"This one, apparently," Auntie Lin noted.

"Where's the nearest one?" he asked.

"Down in El Centro," came Frank's voice from the counter.

Patrick turned in his chair to look at the disheveled head and rheumy eyes of the town drunk. Frank had already been served a beer, which he was drinking through a crazy straw. He looked almost childlike as he sucked the alcohol through several loops. As strange as it looked, Patrick would give a pinky and a thumb to join the man if given the opportunity.

"Where's that?" Patrick asked, licking his dry lips.

"About forty miles as the crow flies."

"What about by road?"

"About three hours."

"Why so long?"

"Construction and farming equipment. Lots of farms around the Salton Sea."

"You serious?"

Maude snapped her fingers. "What about Will Todrunner?" she asked Gertie.

"What about him?"

"Isn't he a Justice of the Peace too?"

"He sure is." Gertie said. "Listen, let me give him a call and I'll get him over here. He's going to want to meet you anyway, seeing as how you're going to be living here now. That reminds me. Are you going to be wanting to move in to your father's place?"

"I think so. We really don't have a place to stay and can't afford a hotel. We've driven an awfully long way." He glanced quickly at his hands, then shoved them into his pants to stop them from shaking. "But if it's going to be a problem we can make some –"

Gertie shook her head. "It's no problem. We don't really live there anymore. But Me and Maude had some stuff we might want to get out first. The will gave you everything and we don't want to do anything that Laz didn't want."

Patrick felt like he needed to say something but he didn't know what it was. He'd wondered why his father had made him the sole heir, especially when he had had these two women who clearly adored him. There'd been no mention in the will about Maude or Gertie. He'd have thought there would have been some direction if his father had shared the sentiment. After all, he'd spent more years with them than he'd spent with Patrick. He'd been thirteen when his father left, and other than a card with a twenty dollar bill every now and then, he hadn't heard from the man in more than thirty years.

"He talked about you all the time," Maude said, as if she was reading his mind.

Patrick shook his head. "He didn't know me."

"Oh, yes he did. He used to travel to Philadelphia twice a year. He watched you play in your school band. He went to your high school graduation. He even went to your daughter's Christmas pageant last year."

As she spoke, Patrick's eyes widened, and his jaw dropped. Suddenly, his mouth felt dry. Why had his father been there and never said anything? He was about to ask that question when a man in a wide-brimmed hat, white shirt and black dungarees burst into the restaurant. All eyes went to him as the door slammed open, then closed.

"My boy is missing. I think something happened to my boy," he said. He was out of breath. His eyes were wild.

"Abel, take it easy." Gertie stood and rushed to his side. She tried to grab his elbow but he jerked away. "We'll find him. Which one has gone missing?"

"Obediah. He was getting driftwood and now no one's seen him."

"It's the green," Frank said. "The green got him."

"You hush your mouth, Frank," Gertie hissed. Back to Abel she said, "Do you know where he was collecting the wood?"

Abel shook his head.

Patrick stepped forward. "What about foot prints?"

They all looked at him.

"You're Amish, right?"

Abel nodded.

"If he's wearing boots like yours, which I bet he is, then all we need to do is look in the sand for the hobnailed prints."

Abel's eyes brightened. "That's a great idea, Mister..."

"Oliver," Maude said. "He's Lazlo's son, come to take over the place."

Abel removed his straw hat and held it to his chest. "Sorry for your loss, Mister Oliver. Your father was a good man." His words came out in a rush. "He took care of our family and treated us well... always set a nice table." His gaze darted towards the door.

Patrick felt an odd sensation of pride for the man who he'd never really known, but he didn't allow the thought to linger. He wanted nothing more than a couple of shots of something hard and wicked, but he found himself offering to help. "Listen, let me go with you and see if I can help."

"Good idea," Maude said. "You go too, Gertie, and I'll call Will. With any luck, by the time he gets here Obediah will be at home drinking milk and eating some of his mother's bread. He's probably just goofing off."

Abel shoved his hat back on his head. "Thank you," he said. Then he turned and bolted out the door.

Gertie and Patrick followed. As they got to the door, Frank spoke one more time. "Green means no," he said. "If you see it. Don't go."

The sea began right across from the restaurant between a break in the seawall. The break hadn't always been there. According to Gertie, Laz had bulldozed the seawall out of the way as soon as the Army Corps of Engineers had left. He wanted an ocean view from his restaurant even if the ocean was rotting.

Will Toddrunner, who happened to be the Deputy Sheriff and the Justice of the Peace for the towns of Niland and Bombay Beach, arrived an hour into the search. After brief introductions between Patrick, Auntie Lin and Will, they set off down the beach, looking for tell-tale Amish boot prints.

The sheriff ran down some of the vital statistics as they

walked. The town had 345 people according to the last census, but he doubted that half of them were still living here. The unemployment rate was 25%. On a scale of one to ten with the average U.S. city at a three, the crime in Bombay Beach was at five. This was mostly the result of the unemployment rate and the air of hopelessness. Besides the unfortunate disaster of the Salton Sea, Bombay Beach – which was located squarely along the San Andreas Fault – was also blessed with earthquake swarms. Just last week three 4.7 earthquakes had struck the area. The only damage that had been done was to knock down the skeletal remains of a few of the teetering deserted homes. The only death had been Lazlo Oliver, which couldn't be and hadn't been connected to the geological events. Truth be told, earthquakes were a part of life around the Salton Sea. The residents enjoyed the frivolous violence of the quakes. Each one broke the monotony of another otherwise dreary day. Another interesting fact was that the nearest gas station was twenty miles away in Niland so the average Bombay Beach citizen got around on golf carts, or using the "often-preferred California flip-flop-powered locomotion."

The deputy was pure Californian. As it turned out, Will's father had been a deep sea fishing master out of San Diego and his mother had been an artichoke picker from Brawley. When it came to a choice on what to do with his life, Will had done four years in the Marine Corps then joined the Imperial County Sheriff's Department. Now going on ten years, he'd kept his father's *laissez-faire* outlook on life, while maintaining his mother's concentration and attention to detail. Although both traits seemed to be necessary to be a successful warden of the people, often times the latter helped more, for it was Will who spotted the first boot print.

"Here!"

Will ran forward three steps and knelt. Using his baton, he circled the boot print to separate it from the wavy lines in the sand nearby. He also used the baton to remove a piece of seaweed that had come ashore sometime after the print had been left. The green leafy length sprawled across the impression of the heel in the print, as if to lay claim to whoever had made it.

Patrick turned and hollered down the beach to where Abel and Gertie had gone the other way. They ran to him.

Patrick squatted next to Will and pointed. "See how those nails are square? Those are definitely Amish nails. Everyone else uses round nails, if they use nails at all."

The print's angle of travel suggested that Obediah had been heading along the sea's edge. Patrick glanced back to try and see the other prints, but they'd either been eaten by the waves or were buried under the detritus of the sea. He thought he saw an edge here, and a heel there, especially now after having seen a full print, but he couldn't be certain.

Suddenly the stench of rot and putrefaction washed over him. He nearly gagged. A mat of seaweed floated in the beer-colored water. The vines had trapped several fish and an egret, its white upturned eye staring into a sky within which it would never again fly. The bird's chest had been torn wide open. Maggots wriggled in the noonday sun.

Near the bird a pacifier lay enshrined in the weed. With a light green handle, the teat upturned like the egret's eye, it brought Patrick a sense of foreboding. He had to find out if his worst fears were only imagined. Without thinking, he waded into the tide. He immediately felt the sting of the warm water, the alkalinity like an acid to his skin. He plowed past the dead fish and the bird and grabbed for the pacifier. He missed it and instead pushed it under. With a shout, Patrick leaped for it, shoving his arm and head under water, until he felt the familiar shape. When he came up, he turned around. He held the pacifier to his face and was gratified beyond belief not to have found a baby's finger hooked through the ring on the other end.

"My god, man! What have you done?"

"Get out of there!" Gertie shouted. "That water ain't safe."

The skin of his face and scalp had begun to burn. The smell he'd all but forgotten assaulted him anew, this time from him. He climbed out of the waist-deep water and dripped along the shore toward the others.

Auntie Lin held her nose with one hand and used her other to point back towards the town. "You better go back to the restaurant and find some way to clean up."

Gertie shook her head as she backed away from him. "Tell Maude to show you the utility room. You don't want to get anywhere near your new home before you burn those clothes and get the stink out of your hair."

Patrick nodded and headed back the way he'd come. He was happy to have the pacifier, in a way that he couldn't put his finger on, almost as if amidst the horrible decay of the resort there glowed one pure thing.

A few minutes later, after scolding him for swimming in the lake, Maude showed him the utility room in the back of the restaurant and took his clothes to burn after he removed them. It took Patrick an hour of using everything from hand soap to powdered bathroom cleanser to get the stink of the sea off, but he finally managed.

Maude brought his suitcase in from the car, from which he pulled a pair of shorts and a *Fresh Prince of Bel Air* T-shirt. He tossed these on and went into the restaurant. For a moment he considered going back out and helping with the search, but the proximity of cold beer changed his mind. He told himself that he'd have just one, maybe two, before heading back outside, and sat down at the counter beside Frank. Maude poured him a cold one, which he heartily drank down to the suds.

He pulled out the pacifier and held it in his hand, turning it this way and that as he considered it and waited for a refill. Now that he was in the cool confines of the restaurant, alcohol soothing his blood, it seemed strange that the pacifier had attracted him so. He'd never responded to something like that before.

When Maude came back around to refill their beers, she saw the pacifier and stopped cold.

"Where'd you find that?"

Patrick held it up as if to ask her if it was what she was referring to. She nodded as he placed it on the counter.

"In the sea."

"Where in the sea?"

"I don't know. Where we were looking for the Amish boy, I suppose. Why?"

Maude paused for a long moment. She licked her lips, never once taking her eyes from the pacifier. Finally she nodded, as if she'd made a decision. "You might as well know. That belonged to your father. Well, to you, I suppose."

Patrick stared at the plastic thing on the counter and drank the cold beer while Maude explained how it had belonged to Patrick as a baby. One day about fifteen years ago, Lazlo had found it in one of his boxes when they were unpacking. He'd decided to wear it, so he'd put a shoe string through it and placed it around his neck, where it stayed for most of the next twenty years. Lazlo took it off infrequently, mainly to change the string; otherwise it had been on him like a charm, and had served to remind him of his son each day – morning, noon and night – right up until he died. In fact, he'd been wearing it *when* he'd died.

When she moved off after refilling his beer, Patrick sat stunned, trying to digest the information and match it with the idea that his father had deserted him. If his father had intended to leave forever, why had he kept coming back? Why had he kept the pacifier?

Frank dug around in a pouch at his waist and found a length of string. Although it smelled vaguely of fish, the drunk inexpertly made a necklace of the pacifier. When it was done, he handed it to Patrick, who placed it around his neck. Doing so made him feel a connection with his father that he'd never known before.

Patrick fell deep into thought as he tried to imagine his father and what things would have been like had they known each other and been friends. He was still sitting there and thinking two hours later, when the search party returned empty handed.

CHAPTER SIX

The dog was diabolical. Abigail Ogletree had finally managed to pull in her favorite soap opera from a Mexican television station – it was an American soap opera, rebroadcast with Spanish voice-overs and English subtitles – and the dog wanted to steal her attention. God forbid she sit for a few quiet hours and watch the grainy lives of happier people with more interesting lives played out on her all-but-useless television. Trudie, her sassy miniature poodle, just wasn't having it.

Abigail muted the television and jerked her head towards the kitchen. "Shush!"

The dog stopped barking and Abigail returned her attention to the television. And for the ten thousandth time she cursed her husband, Roger, for dying and leaving her in this backwater cesspool. Her television was ten years past its prime and the cable companies had long ago moved on. She was relegated to using an old antenna that kept shifting in the wind – always, it seemed, at the most inopportune times.

She could just make out a man and a woman through the ever-present snow on the television. The man was Charles Hargrove and had just recovered from a traffic accident. He had amnesia; Abigail counted that it was the third time he'd lost his memory in eleven years. The girl was Genevieve. She was his best friend's daughter, but was pretending to have been a long time mistress, acting on a crush she'd had on Charles since she was a child.

Abigail couldn't wait to see what would happen when Charles finally remembered who he was. Would he burn so many bridges he'd never be able to return to a normal life? Would he consummate his relationship with Genevieve, thus destroying his lifelong friendship with his best friend? Would she succeed in trying to convince him that he'd asked her to marry him, and elope to Cabo San Lucas?

Abigail had long ago given up trying to guess what would happen on the show. The story writers were too good and always kept her guessing. She shivered in anticipation, leaning forward to make out what was happening.

Charles and Genevieve were close enough to be kissing, but the distortion of the television made it questionable. She had to pay careful attention to try and discern what they were actually doing. Plus, in addition to the fact that the actors and actresses were always in a blizzard of electric snow, the soap opera had Spanish voice-overs, with English closed captioning amidst the snow which always seemed thickest at the bottom of the screen.

Trudie started to growl, deep throated and low.

Suddenly, on the television, a door opened and a man entered the picture.

Abigail covered her mouth and inhaled deeply. It was Genevieve's father.

Charles held the girl tighter, not recognizing the man.

Trudie's growl turned into a bark.

Abigail turned her head towards the sound for a moment, but the snowy soap stars drew her attention back to the television. But whatever had happened, she'd missed it. She didn't speak

Spanish, and the text was already past. Now all she saw was a jumble of three figures wrestling in a winter storm.

Damn that dog!

She threw her remote control down on the couch hard enough that it bounced. She pushed herself to a standing position using the arm rest and slid her feet into her slippers.

"What is it, Trudie?" She shook her head and headed towards the barking dog. "Why is it that whenever I sit down to enjoy myself and leave you alone, you find it necessary to –"

The white and gray poodle barked louder now that she was in the kitchen. A man's hand gripped her hind leg. He'd tried to crawl through the doggy door, but become wedged. At first fear leaped into her chest, but then she remembered the Klosterman Kid, who'd stayed the same four year old he was thirty years ago. More than a little slow, his grandparents kept him out back with a catcher's mask on his face so he wouldn't chew anything and boxing gloves on his hands so he couldn't grab anything. It wouldn't be the first time he got loose. But it would be the first time he tried to break into her house... or for that matter, try and get her dog.

Abigail grabbed the broom from where it leaned against the wall between the doorjamb and the refrigerator.

"Let her go you –" She refused to use the word "retard," and instead shouted "– bastard!" She swung the broom, hitting the man in the back of his head.

The dog barked and snarled at the hand that was around her leg. She reached out to bite, but couldn't bring herself to actually do it.

Abigail switched her grip and began to poke the Klosterman Kid on the side of the neck.

"Get out! Get out! Get out!" she screamed over and over, each time shoving the rounded wooden end into tender flesh.

Trudie broke loose and dodged behind Abigail, and took up barking even louder.

The man's hands moved to follow, and as it did, Abigail caught a glimpse of the face. It was not the Klosterman Kid. This man, whoever he was, had a much older face, skin wrinkled and gray and green.

A hand grabbed at her foot. She stepped back, but lost her slipper in the process. He pulled it to his mouth and began to chew savagely at the furry purple and orange fabric.

Abigail broke the broom over the man's head.

He began to hyperventilate, wheezing coming from somewhere deep in his chest.

She reached atop the refrigerator and grabbed a heavy lead crystal bowl that she'd once used for fresh fruit, when there'd been fresh fruit to be had. She brought it down on the man's head as hard as her brittle old fingers could propel it.

The head made a hollow squishing sound, and blood oozed out of the left ear as the bowl rolled to a stop in front of the stove, none the worse for wear. The dog suddenly stopped barking.

Abigail took a step back.

And was glad she did, for the man lunged forward, hands encircling the spot where her legs had just been. She let out a little scream, terror blossoming inside her.

The creature on the floor, for it was no longer human to her, gazed at her through unholy yellow eyes. Saliva that reminded her of the frothy green pollution lining the edge of the sea fell from its lips and down its chin.

She lifted the broken broom handle. Its sharp, broken end could easily pierce those eyes. Then it began wheezing louder, the sound coming faster and faster, until the sound filled the trailer. It lunged forward, pulling itself farther into the house.

Abigail lost all sense of courage. She turned and ran to the back of the trailer. Thank god Trudie was close behind because if she hadn't come, Abigail was doubtful she'd have gone back for her precious poodle.

She hit the door to her bedroom, running as fast as her legs could carry her. It slammed open, then shut. It was on a spring hinge and more substantial than the rest of the trailer. Her Roger – before he'd died, God rest his soul – had spent a small fortune disaster-proofing the bedroom. Not in case of hurricane, tornado, earthquake, or anything like that; Roger's greatest fear had been illegal aliens surging across the Mexican

Border. So he'd built a room lined with metal, a door made of steel, and put enough weapons inside of it to obliterate Kansas.

Just as Abigail snapped the lock into place she heard a wrenching sound followed by an explosion of wood. Then the wheezing came toward the bedroom like a muffled freight train, accompanied by the pounding of the creature's feet.

It hit the door with a clang and began to beat upon it.

Abigail found a 45 caliber pistol and crawled onto the bed. She clawed for her husband's pillow which she'd kept in the bed ever since he'd passed and hugged it to her chest. Trudie followed and curled up in her lap. She eyed the door, her tail hugging her belly, too afraid to bark. Abigail was afraid to move.

And she'd stay that way a very long time.

Another hour of skulking through the heat found Natasha and Derrick at the opposite corner of the town from the restaurant. Veronica had had to run home, remembering that she'd promised to help her Auntie with cleaning. As much as she hated cleaning, she loved her Auntie more, so she'd bid the Olivers farewell and run home.

After Veronica had left, Natasha realized that she didn't know where the girl lived. How could she find her later if she had no idea where to start looking?

But that was the least of her worries. The heat was beating down, and she stood in the middle of the street, staring blankly in all directions. The prospect of looking for home seemed overwhelming. The heat sapped her energy to the point where putting one foot in front of the other was the best she could do.

"So what do you think?" she asked Derrick.

"I think we need to find an ice cream truck and take it home." Derrick grinned. "What'd I give for a Bombpop."

"No kidding. Or a Creamsicle. Even a shaved ice would be great right about now."

Derrick looked up and down the street. "What are the odds that there'd be an ice cream truck around here?"

"Same odds there'd be a pizza delivery truck or a Chinese restaurant."

"Or a Burger King," Derrick chimed in.

"God, can you imagine if we had a joint that sold chicken wings? And with some serious hot sauce like Plasma Heat or Volcano Hot like back in Willow Grove at Tonelli's?"

Derrick sighed. "One can only dream."

"Hey, I haven't seen him before."

Natasha pointed to man in a golf cart zipping up the road. As he passed, he nodded, but didn't offer a wave, a word, or even a smile. He looked old, a Veterans of Foreign Wars hat perched on his head. The golf cart was painted in camouflage and had a large basket on the back to carry things, which was currently empty. They watched as he headed towards the entrance to the town.

"Did you see his hands?" Derrick asked.

Natasha shook her head. "What about them?"

"I swear he didn't have any."

Natasha made a face, dubious.

Derrick nodded vigorously. "I swear, sis. He didn't have hands at all. He had little hooks." Derrick made his fingers into the shape of hooks, mimicking driving.

"Derrick," Natasha hissed. "Don't make fun of him."

"I'm not. I thought it was cool is all."

Natasha started down the street, pushing one foot in front of the other, back the way they'd come.

"Wait up. Where you going?" Derrick asked.

"Back to the restuarant. It's too hot out here. The heat's frying your brain."

"My brain?"

"Or what's left of it."

Derrick mock-laughed then ran to catch up to his sister.

Natasha suddenly stopped, and Derrick almost knocked her down. "What is it?"

"Over there." She pointed through a gap between two trailers.

"Looks like a statue."

"I swear to god it moved."

"Now whose brain is frying?"

"No, really." She began walking towards the statue, but Derrick grabbed her from behind. "Let me go!"

"What if it's one of those monsters?" he said, his voice like a spooky movie star.

Natasha laughed hoarsely. "Yeah. Like there are any monsters. That old drunk Kristov doesn't know what he's talking about." She tried to shrug off his grip.

"Oh shit!" Derrick whispered.

She turned back to the statue. The head seemed to be moving, as if it were looking for something. The statue took off, moving towards something behind the trailers. It ran spastically, lurching from side-to-side. Then it was gone, hidden by distance and trailers.

As hot as it was, goosebumps danced along Natasha's arms. That she had no idea what it was made it worse. It could be anything.

She laughed once, still staring at the place where the statue had stood.

CHAPTER SEVEN

Gertie let Maude know that although the rest of them had decided to leave the hundred degree heat and wait to see if the boy would turn up, Abel Beachy had refused to quit, even in the face of Sheriff Will's argument.

"If he was out here we would have found him by now," he'd said. "Chances are the print was a red herring and your boy is doing what all boys do, going through all these empty homes we got here in Bombay Beach, looking for something cool."

Patrick had overheard Gertie tell Maude that the leader of the Amish clan had shaken his head and taken off down the beach, searching for any sign of his son.

Sheriff Will had left, responding to an accident between a station wagon and a combine on Highway 111. He'd said he'd be back and and that he felt certain that the boy would turn up before dinner time.

Patrick continued drinking throughout the afternoon, even

when Auntie Lin made a comment about it. He told her about the pacifier and what it stood for, which kept her from saying anything else. So while he sat beside Frank getting the sit-down-drunk's-tour of the town, Auntie Lin, Natasha and Derrick were shown the ins and outs of the restaurant business.

Patrick learned about the town locals as each one came in for something to eat or read. The Amish family stayed out, but Andy the Scientist and Jose the Laborer spent considerable time that afternoon sitting at a table by the front window, drinking iced teas through straws. Patrick learned about the Duvall Brothers – Jose Mara and Rico – who'd come from Miami to harvest salt to sell to the Chinese. They were the town's largest employer, sometimes hiring a staggering five or six people. He met Kim Johnson, a laid-back woman with tattoos covering her body, who had moved here from the mountains of Montana to save souls and return them to Christ's embrace. He met Carrie Loughnane, a voluptuous woman with flaming red hair. She'd once been a cheerleader from Costa Mesa but an upwardly mobile crack salesman had turned her onto his product, gotten her hooked, and now she had seven children all by different fathers, health problems, and ran the town's only Laundromat. Her favorite comment when asked why she'd reopened the old Laundromat was that "Even in Hell people deserve to have clean clothes."

His kids came in wanting to lay down and rest awhile. He'd tossed them the keys, with orders to unpack the car and get things situated in their new home.

About three in the afternoon, Kristov Constantinescu, the Romanian Frank had told him about, came in dressed in clothes like a neon lounge singer. He had puffed-up black hair and sideburns like Elvis. He'd brought an empty hand truck with him, and when he left it was stacked with eight cases of National Bohemian Beer. Patrick thought that strange, especially since he knew it was one of the local beers his cousin in southern Maryland loved to drink. How Kristov got it all the way out here was a mystery. Patrick tried to catch Kristov's attention as he was headed out the door so he could ask him, but all he got was a hasty "*Thankyouverymuch.*"

At about three thirty in the afternoon Patrick realized he was sauced. He managed to get Maude's attention, but when he opened his mouth it wouldn't work properly. She worked out what he wanted and began making him a plate of fried fish and fries.

Patrick saw Auntie Lin shaking her head at him out of the corner of his eye. He knew he was going to hear about it when he sobered. He turned his attention back to his glass. Who cared what they thought anyway?

When the food arrived it was sizzling hot. He heaped malt vinegar and ketchup over the top and stuffed it down as fast as he could. Then he chased it with a glass of water, hoping to dilute the beer already in his system. But it had no effect other than to make him even thirstier.

Auntie Lin reminded him that he'd wanted to tour his father's trailer. Patrick wanted to go, but he knew he wasn't ready for it. He needed some time to get used to the idea that he'd be living there before he actually moved in. He was pretty sure that the first time he went in, he wanted to do it alone. So he said as much to Auntie Lin, and, of course, she didn't understand, figuring that he wanted to drink cheap beer instead of viewing the place his father had called home. She couldn't be more wrong.

When she finally left him alone he ordered another beer, then thought better of it and ordered one for Frank, Jose and Andy as well. If he was going to be miserable, he might as well have company.

Auntie Lin came back about two hours later to tell Patrick that she and the kids had unpacked the car. The kids filed in after her to get something to eat.

He tried to thank her, but Patrick's mouth had stopped working long ago.

"I drink you handled that well," Frank said.

Patrick circled his head.

"What's gonna be the encore?"

Patrick opened his mouth to speak, but all that came out was "futh," a lowly cousin to the curse word that he'd tried to say.

He turned to look at Frank and they both cracked up.

Suddenly the night was split by the sound of a shotgun going off –

Blam! Blam! Blam!

Patrick tried to jump to his feet but fell off his chair instead. He pulled himself to a sitting position and, from his spot on the floor, watched Natasha and Derrick and a host of locals run outside to see what was going on. He should have joined them.

Another blast hammered the night.

Patrick examined his useless legs. He suddenly wished that he'd never started drinking. He gazed towards the open door, silently slipped the pacifier into his mouth and began to suck on it.

Natasha sprinted out the door even before she knew what was going on. It never occurred to her to be afraid until she heard the fourth shot, which made her jump and scream. She found she'd grabbed Derrick, who was also holding her. They separated, briefly embarrassed.

"I think it came from over there," Jose shouted, pointing down the street.

The air had cooled somewhat, a relief from the staggering heat of the day. A million stars lit a cloudless sky, reminding Natasha that she wasn't in Philadelphia anymore. Only a few of the streetlights still worked, casting intermittent halos of sickly yellow light.

A dark figure rushed across the street two blocks down.

"There!" Derrick pointed.

"Did you see who it was?" Carrie asked.

Gertie shook her head. "Can't be Abel. That was too small."

Derrick turned to Natasha. "Maybe it was Obediah?"

"Could be, but why would he run?" Gertie shouted back towards the restaurant. "Maude, you make sure you call Will and tell him we have shots fired."

Shots fired. Natasha had never heard those words said outside of television.

Suddenly another figure, this one much larger, ran into the

middle of the street, raised a shotgun, and fired in the direction the other person had gone.

"Abel, is that you?" Gertie called.

"Ms. Gertrude." Abel's voice was an octave higher than it usually was from the excitement and exertion. "I saw one of them things. I think it got my boy."

"Things? We have things?" Frank asked.

"Just leave it be, Abel Beachy. You're going to kill someone with that shotgun." Gertie shouted.

Even from two blocks away, Natasha could see the whites of the man's teeth as he grinned and said: "That's the point, is it not?" He patted the gun, then took off.

"What the hell?" Andy came out and peered down the street. "What's all the shooting?"

"Abel had one of them things in his sights." Gertie glanced at Natasha and Derrick.

"He did?" Andy's eyes widened and he took a step back. Then he turned and ran, staggering a little as he went, back towards his house.

"What do you mean by things?" Natasha asked, remembering the *thing* she saw running between trailers earlier in the day.

"*Bad* things," Frank replied, then giggled.

Gertie stared at him for a moment, then shook her head in disgust. "Go back inside and keep these kids' father company. He can't even walk and we surely don't need him outside with Abel Beachy acting like it's an invasion of the Body Snatchers. We don't need no –" She glanced quickly at Natasha and Derrick "– new comer getting lost or hurt in these houses."

Natasha smiled grimly, but beneath it she knew what Gertie meant to say was that they didn't need *no drunk*. As if to prove it, Gertie patted Natasha on the shoulder and told her everything was going to be okay. Then Gertie ordered her and Derrick to come with her and split the others who'd come outside to watch into three parties of three. Before they separated, Maude brought out flashlights for each group.

Soon Natasha and Derrick were following Gertie, who strode into the darkness like a gunslinger. Her fearlessness was what kept the kids going, because as soon as they left the neon-lit front of the restaurant, all the bogeymen of their nightmares began to play across the possibilities of who they might meet, and what the *thing* was that had gotten the Beachy kid.

Natasha wanted to press the issue. What were the things everyone was talking about? But she didn't want to do it in the dark.

They entered a burned out hulk of a trailer through the space where the sliding glass door used to be. Most of the furniture had burned to unrecognizable black shapes. A single blue marble stood stark against the soot-stained floor.

"Jessica Sullivan used to live here," Gertie said. "She collected those tiny stuffed animals. This must have been one of their eyes."

"What happened to her?" Derrick asked.

"Her son packed her up and sent her to an old fogies' home."

"But he left her stuffed animals." Natasha pointed to where the blue eye rested.

"Didn't matter to him. He just wanted her out of his hair." Gertie picked it up and put it in her pocket.

"So what happened to the trailer?"

"Vandals burned it like they burned most of the others."

The three of them moved from one trailer to the other. Occasionally they'd come to one that was occupied. Sometimes Gertie would peer in the window, and sometimes she'd knock and have a few soft words with the occupants, but they never went inside.

Down the street they saw the Romanian's trailer. As they drew near, Gertie held up her hand for them to stop. Holding the light as steady as she could, she continued towards the fence. Even from where Natasha stood, she could see a body lying atop the sea of beer cans. She ignored Gertie's command to wait and followed, Derrick pressing right against her, his hands on her back as they edged closer to the body.

She heard a droning sound, something like a remote control airplane.

"What is that noise?" Derrick asked. Gertie walked to the fence and shone the light on the body. It was the Romanian for sure. His pants had fallen down revealing white buttocks the color of dead fish bellies, as if he'd passed out in mid-moon. The sound was coming from him, not an airplane – snoring.

"Kristov's passed out." Gertie scoffed. "Lot of good those will do him," she said, pointing at the beer cans. She leaned over the fence and shouted, "Can't hear them if you're passed out!" He never stirred.

They were on their seventh or eighth house when they heard a rustling behind one of the trailers, followed by a groan. A figure separated from the shadows and lurched in their direction.

Gertie brought her bat around as she shone her light into the shadows.

"There you are." Auntie Lin stepped into the beam of the trembling flashlight. "What got into you, going out when there's a madman with a gun blasting at everything that moves?"

"That madman is Abel Beachy," Gertie said.

"It doesn't make it any safer if you know his name. Anyone firing like that with houses all around is still a madman." Auntie Lin grabbed Natasha's and Derrick's arms and pulled them toward the street. "Come on. We're going back to the restaurant. You haven't eaten yet."

"But –" Derrick began.

"Don't 'But' me. I'm sure we'll see what happens before it's all over. Now let's go." She turned to Gertie. "And you should never have brought kids outside when it was so dangerous. What were you thinking?"

Although Natasha allowed herself to be tugged away, she shot a resigned look at Gertie. Gertie receded into the darkness as she went. Part of Natasha was happy to be going back inside. But another part of her, one she really hadn't known existed, suddenly wanted to know the unknowable. She wanted to be a part of the adventure and the events that were transpiring in the darkness, where Abel Beachy ran with a shotgun firing at God knew what.

Strange how a little change of scenery could alter your attitude, she considered.

Gertie silently bid young Natasha goodbye. That one had an inquisitive streak in her that reminded Gertie of herself. Still, in some places knowing too much could hurt you and she was glad that the girl and her brother had been taken under the protective wing of their Auntie Lin.

What the old Chinese woman had said had hurt, but the she was right. What *had* Gertie been thinking? Lazlo's family seemed a nice sort and Gertie was happy that she hadn't told them the totality of what she knew about Bombay Beach. Not that she had any hard evidence or facts, but running the restaurant she'd heard so much that even if a tenth of them were true they cast a deadly shadow across the community... especially the things that came from the water.

Gertie trembled slightly in the darkness. Now alone with the rumors, she could finally see if they were true. If she'd seen what she'd thought she'd seen Abel Beachy chasing, then she had no business continuing. Then again, she wasn't about to be chased out of the darkness like some weak-kneed Catholic. Her father had been a bouncer and her mother had been a truck driver, and she had the best and worst traits of both of them; primarily the same bull-headedness that had caused them to separate and get back together a dozen times. So she continued on. She held her bat in one hand and her flashlight in the other. If she saw anything, she'd use both as weapons.

Her search took her to the sea shore. Seaweed lay lank and rotting on the water's edge. Dead fish, beer cans, red plastic cups and all manner of trash floated in the tide.

Gertie played her light back and forth, acutely aware of the sounds around her.

Fear crept along her spine as she imagined things in the darkness, silent deadly things, watching her as she walked the tide line.

It sounded like a fish surfacing, or something slapping the water with the palm of its hand.

But her light found nothing but dead sea.

She heard someone calling in the distance. Although she couldn't make out the words, she thought it sounded like *Obediah*, which meant they still hadn't found the boy. Gertie heard a great slurping sound and almost jumped out of her skin, even though she recognized it as Sump Pump #2.

She chuckled and pushed her hair back, then stuck the baseball bat under her arm as she rearranged her pony tail. She decided that she'd give it a few more yards, then return to the restaurant. She'd already done more than was necessary, and out here alone, she didn't know what might happen.

The beam of Gertie's flashlight swept past something white and filmy. She stopped and adjusted the light, circling until she saw what looked like the blind, cataracted eye of an immense dead fish.

As she stepped closer flies erupted from the seaweed to buzz madly about the beam of the torch, making it almost impossible to see. She waived a hand to clear away the pests and stepped closer to examine her find. What she saw, however, wasn't the eye of a fish but a human.

She inhaled sharply.

Oh my God, she thought. Was this Obediah? Had the poor boy drowned?

She turned and glanced behind her, wondering if she should call out. She returned her gaze to the head and tried to make out the features, plus see where the rest of the body lay. But everything was too obscured by the seaweed, the trash and the way the light played off the surface of the water.

Then, for a moment, Gertie could have sworn that the eye blinked. Suddenly she wondered if Obediah might still be alive.

The eye blinked again. This time she saw it.

Or was it the waves pushing it open and closed?

She stepped into the surf and was now close enough to see yellow ichors seeping from the thing's neck.

What kind of person has yellow blood?

Then she saw it in all its gory reality. The thing beneath the water couldn't possibly be Obediah. It was too old. It had the face of a middle-aged man. The neck was all but severed from the body. The head hung by only by a few pieces of skin. The spinal cord had been shattered and swayed like a broken rope in the water. The skin was a mottle of greens. The blood wasn't simply yellow but seemed to glow in the water.

This must have been what she'd seen run across the street.

Then it hit her. All the rumors were *true*, even those far-fetched things that Andy had been spouting to the other drunks in the restaurant when he thought she and Maude weren't paying attention. Gertie tried to step back but found she couldn't move her foot. Looking down, she saw why and screamed. A hand had wrapped around her ankle, green and gray tinged skin, yellowing nails that, even as she watched, pierced the flesh of her foot and slid against her ankle bone.

She screamed again before she was jerked off her feet. She landed hard against the sand, the back of her head slamming the ground. Air left her in a *whoosh*. The flashlight and bat went flying.

Another hand gripped her leg. First one tug, then another and another and Gertie was all the way in the water. She felt teeth slide against her skin and screamed hysterically and breathlessly. Teeth bit into her thigh and ripped away a huge chunk of flesh. They tore in again and again, each time ripping and shredding. When it hit her femoral artery, she screamed a final time, then was pulled beneath the tide. The red of her blood mingled with the yellow of the creature, resulting in a wide, orange slick that held together for a moment, before being washed under by the tide.

CHAPTER EIGHT

Abigail wasn't sure how much time had passed. It was dark outside. The only light came through the window from a streetlight over on Avenue C. For a moment she didn't know where she was. Then she saw the gun lying next to her on the bed, glistening in the moonlight like a nightmare made of oil.

She sat bolt upright. Her eyes went to the door as she remembered the creature who'd scrambled through her doggy door and chased her into the bedroom. She'd thought it was the Klosterman Kid at first, but it couldn't have been. Yellow soulless eyes shone through the layers of her memory that were like nothing she'd ever seen. There was a savagery about the creature that absolutely terrified her. Like the Rottweiler that had chased down her beloved Trudie that one time. It had paused in its mauling once after she'd kicked it a dozen times, and the look it gave her was nothing short of monstrous. That was the look the creature gave her.

Abigail realized she had no idea where Trudie was. She opened her mouth to call the dog, but then paused. What if the creature was waiting outside the door? What if it was outside her window?

She craned her neck and listened for a sound, any sound. It took a moment, but she was able to discern breathing. It took a moment longer for her to detect where it was coming from—under the bed.

She leaped off the bed and fell to her knees, lifted the bed skirt, and peered under the bed. Trudie lay with her head on her paws, staring fearfully at the door. Abigail reached until her fingers brushed the dog's curly coat. Then Trudie turned, recognized her, and ran towards her face, licking her, as elated to see Abigail as she was to see the dog.

Abigail rose to a sitting position. As she reached for the pistol on the bed, the dog jumped into her lap and curled up. She held the pistol to her chest with her right hand as she petted the dog with her left.

"Do you think it's still out there, Trudie?" she whispered.

The dog glanced up at her, then resumed its vigil on the door.

"Can you smell it? Can you sense it, little one?"

The dog growled low in its throat.

Just then something scraped against the outside of the bedroom door. Was it the creature? Or was it her imagination?

The scratching came again, ever so lightly, as if it *was* in her imagination and not even there, a trick of the mind that told her it was probably okay to open the door.

Probably.

Patrick pushed the fly down to the bottom of the bowl and held it there with his spoon. Eight sodden Cheerios floated in the milk, looking gray in the morning light.

Or was it his eyes?

Storms snapped across the front part of his brain. The rest of it seemed shrunken to rattle against the inside of his skull. He tried not to move. Even blinking hurt. But under Auntie Lin's watchful eye, he had no choice but to pretend he hadn't been hammered last night, which meant he couldn't possibly be hungover.

Oh, if only that were true.

The fly somehow fought free of the spoon and shot to the surface of the milk. It came through one of the Cheerios and held onto the miniature life preserver. He imagined it staring at him through faceted eyes, condemning him for the attempted drowning and begging him with its tiny fly voice not to do it again.

Patrick prepared to finish the job when Auntie Lin spoke.

"More coffee?"

He hadn't touched what she'd poured earlier, yet she stood poised to refill it. He tried to smile but lacked the coordination to pull it off, and instead made a pathetic lopsided frown.

"No thanks."

"You're not fooling anyone, you know."

He looked up from his flyacide. He was about to say something but was saved by raised voices coming from across the restaurant.

"I don't care about that. We need to get people here to help."

Abel Beachy had brought his family in for Saturday breakfast, as he did every weekend. Noticeable was the empty seat where Obediah normally sat. Jedadiah, Marlene, and Abel's wife Rachel sat stone-faced and bleary-eyed, staring at their untouched plates of eggs and sausage, while the leader of the clan shook his fist at the deputy sheriff.

"Honestly, there's nothing more we can do. Did you check his room? Maybe there's a phone number or some –"

"We don't have phones! We're Amish, you idiot!" Abel boomed.

Will held his hands out. "Did Obediah meet a girl recently? What about school? Was there someone special?"

Abel shook his head fiercely and was about to reply when his daughter caught Will's eye.

"What is it, Marlene?"

She glanced at her father, then returned to staring at her plate.

"Abel, please tell your daughter that it's okay to speak. If she has anything that can help us, then I need to hear it."

Abel fumed for a moment longer before softening. He reached out and put a meaty hand on his daughter's thin shoulder.

"Marlene, do you have something to tell Deputy Sheriff Toddrunner?"

"No, papa."

"Marlene?" Will asked. "This is serious. If you were asked to keep a secret by someone, you need to reconsider. This is starting to become a big deal."

She looked up again, a deer caught in the headlights. She bit her lip and began to cry. "He has a girl he likes in Brawly."

Abel seemed ready to launch himself out of his chair, but Will quelled him with a look. To Marlene, he asked, "What's her name?"

"Mary Jo something. He met her at the farmers' market three weeks ago."

"Did you get a last name?"

She murmured something that sounded like *no*, then shook her head.

"At least we have somewhere to start," Will said, writing in his notebook.

Abel glanced around the room and noticed that all eyes were on him. He seemed about to say something, but then set to his breakfast instead, bringing the food woodenly to his mouth without enjoyment.

Jose and Kristov sat far at the other end of the counter. The Duvall Brothers sat at a table, as did Andy Gudgel, Kim Johnson and several other locals.

Auntie Lin carried around the coffee pot offering refills. Derrick bussed dirty dishes. Natasha carried plates of food two at a time to waiting customers. She'd been offered a tray to use, but was afraid she'd upend whatever she carried right onto the customers. Maude had been in the kitchen most of the morning and only now came out, wiping her hands on her apron. The dark skin of her face was flushed. Heavy bags hugged her eyes.

Will got ready to leave, but stopped when Maude put a hand on his arm.

"What is it?" He looked around. "Where's Gertie?"

"I was going to ask you the same thing," she said, her voice drawn and tired. "She didn't come home last night."

Will nodded. "It's not like her to miss breakfast."

"No, it's not." Maude shook her head. "I don't know where she is, but I don't want you to have to go looking if she's just sleeping in or something."

The deputy sheriff thought about it for a moment, then placed his hand atop hers. "Don't worry about it. She's always turned up before. You know how she used to get with Laz." He glanced at the Beachys, "I'll track down this Mary Jo in Brawly and see if Obediah headed that way. I've seen hormones tear even the best of families apart." He took his hat from the table and put it on his head. He nodded to the room before leaving, held the door for a moment to allow someone else to step inside, then was gone.

The door clanged shut behind the newcomer as he took in the interior of the restaurant. He was in his mid-thirties and bald. He smiled, waved once at the room, and took an empty seat at the counter beside Patrick. "Cup of coffee?" he asked.

The words broke the tension in the room. Auntie Lin rushed to fill a mug and everyone else returned to their meals and private conversations.

The new guy introduced himself as Hopkins. He told Patrick he'd come from the Salton Sea Ecological Authority to investigate the effects of the recent earthquakes on the fish die-offs. Many of the locals barely even acknowledged his presence.

Half an hour later, Hopkins finished his meal and excused himself to begin taking readings of water and soil samples.

Finally alone, Patrick took the moment to remove the fly from his cereal. He placed it gently into a napkin and folded the material into a delicate square. The creature deserved a proper burial. If Patrick was feeling better later, maybe he'd even honor it with a wake.

Natasha was glad to be free from the restaurant and back in her grandfather's trailer. The walls were dark paneled and the floor was carpeted in thick blue shag. Her grandfather's things were everywhere. Standing in the sunlight filtering through old, yellowed curtains, Natasha could feel him everywhere. His things had a smell about them that reminded her of barbershops, liquor stores and cut grass, and she could only imagine that that was what her grandfather had smelled like.

The living room was at one end of the doublewide and held two long leather couches, perpendicular to an easy chair on one end and a giant screen television on the other. She and Derrick had slept on the couches last night, an old VHS tape of *Weekend at Bernie's* playing on the television as their nightlight.

They'd unloaded the car, and several suitcases and boxes of their most important things were stacked against a wall. But there was no room for their stuff while her grandfather's things were still there. Removing them should be left up to her dad.

Her dad... he'd already fallen into a depression and, as Auntie Lin put it, was trying "to solve the word's problems with alcohol." Natasha could certainly understand how it might feel to be deserted by a parent and the thought sent a dagger of emptiness slicing through her gut. But then again she'd always thought that she was made of tougher stuff than her father. One thing was for sure: if he wanted any quality of life at all, he needed to get over it.

Suddenly the place felt confining.

"Come on," she said to Derrick. "Let's go outside."

Derrick was more than ready and, for the first time in an hour, cracked a wan smile. "About time."

His thoughts were probably running along the same lines as hers. She reminded herself that her brother might also be feeling deserted by their father and need some attention.

She grabbed a pair of sunglasses she'd found on her grandfather's dresser – the kind worn by fighter pilots – and put them on. She like the way they felt; they made her feel cool.

It was ninety-two degrees in the shade of the palm trees in the front yard. Derrick ran back inside and snagged a Pirates baseball cap. His love for the Pennsylvania baseball team was a continuing bone of contention between him and his father. Natasha didn't think her brother even liked baseball. He just enjoyed their father's frustration with a traitorous son who liked the Pirates over the Phillies.

When he returned, she and Derrick stood beneath the palms and stared out at the sandy streets. The water was hidden by a giant seawall. Only the birds were visible, rising into the air and diving back down, presumably eating the fish that swam lethargically to the surface to die.

"Don't you two look as out of place as a Mormon in Compton," Veronica said, leaning against the chain link fence.

"What?" Derrick drew the word out as he silently repeated her mysterious statement.

Natasha adjusted her glasses. "I thought we looked good."

"Right. Sure you do. So did the Clampetts."

Veronica wore boy's shorts that came down to her knees and a yellow and purple basketball shirt with Kobe Bryant's name and number, and basketball shoes without socks. A smile lit her clean face. Her hair was pulled back in a pony tail and red mirrored punk sunglasses protected her eyes.

"Where'd you go last night?" Natasha asked. "You missed all the fun."

Veronica's smile dropped. "You can have that kind of fun. My uncle doesn't want me out at night. We hear all sorts of things when it gets dark."

"What? Like monsters?" Derrick teased.

Veronica shrugged and pushed herself away from the fence. "There's something that makes the noise at night and, whatever it is, I'm going to stay away from it."

"I might have seen some of those things," Natasha said carefully. She didn't want to be treated as if she were stupid, but she wanted some answers, if there were answers to be had.

Veronica shook her head. "Watch what you're looking at is all I have to say. Sometimes you shouldn't be looking too closely at things, you might see what's really there."

"That doesn't make any sense," Derrick said.

"Sure it does. It means mind your own business. Keep to yourself. You gotta live that way if you're going to survive where I came from. You got to live that way if you're going to survive here too."

Her words hung heavy in the air, and Natasha couldn't tell if the other girl was being serious or not. She had a rough side to her that came out every now and again, as if it were a defense mechanism. Natasha thought about her life in the malls of suburban Philidelphia and realized how different her world was from Veronica's.

Veronica glanced at Derrick who was staring at her. "What are you looking at?"

"Is there really a chance we won't survive?" he asked in a low voice.

Veronica canted her head, then laughed. "Listen. Half the stuff out of my mouth doesn't mean anything. I'm just talking smack. Nothing more than smack. So you ready to go, or what?"

But Derrick persisted. "Which half?"

"Which half what?" Veronica asked.

"Which half is smack?"

"Oh." She grinned evilly. "That you'll have to figure out for yourself." Seeing his doubt, she added, "It's what makes living so much fun." She bounced on her feet. "Anyway, you all want to do something?"

Natasha had wondered the same thing Derrick had. People had a habit in this town of making mysterious remarks, Veronica included. She had to wonder if there was anything to them, but now wasn't the time to press it.

"I don't know," she said. "What do you want to do?"

"There's lots of ways to get into trouble around here." Veronica said.

"Are we going to steal a car? Rob a liquor store?" Derrick turned his cap sideways and made a gun out of his finger as he took aim and shot at the trailer across the street.

Natasha pulled his hat over his eyes and shook her head. "Calm down, Tupac." To Veronica she said, "So what shall we do?"

"Like *anything*... Hey! Let me show you the Mad Scientist at work. Come on."

Veronica took off walking. Both Natasha and Derrick had to hurry to catch up with her. They went down two streets, then began to pick their way through an alley filled with cast-off appliances. The refrigerators had had their doors removed.

Natasha had heard how it was to stop children getting locked in them. The stoves seemed older than any of the ones she'd ever seen. Here and there a microwave lay broken and rusty, like a forgotten shrine to bad cooking.

Veronica guided them to a non-descript but well maintained trailer. Behind it was another trailer of the same size, only this was buried in the sand almost all the way to the roofline. Stairs had been excavated down to the front door. At the top of the stairs was a swinging gate with a sign that read "KEEP OUT." Music came from inside – Gilbert and Getz's *The Girl from Ipanema*.

"This is it."

"Where are we?" Natasha asked.

"The La-bor-a-tory," Derrick said, in a mock Eastern European accent.

Veronica giggled. "Your brother's funny."

Natasha shook her head. "Please don't encourage him."

"But he's right. The Mad Scientist is down there even as we speak, working on God knows what." She pointed to the door with the small, lit red bulb above it. "See that? It means he's in there working and doesn't want anyone coming in. He says sometimes he's developing pictures and daylight could destroy what he's working on."

"It's so buried you can't even see the windows," Derrick said. "Weird."

"What is he really doing?" Natasha asked.

"Making monsters is my guess." Veronica grinned. "Hell, I don't know. But can you think of anything better to do than find out?"

"How are we gonna see in if there aren't any windows?" Derrick asked.

"Easy. Follow me." Veronica turned and looked at them sharply. "But watch your step. You slip and you might just die." She held their gaze for a moment, then turned and chuckled.

Natasha shook her head. More smack. There were odd moments when Veronica appeared to be some sort of cross between a deadly gangbanger and an insane Pippi Longstocking.

Veronica went to the right of the stairs and walked carefully toward the end of the trailer. She stepped lightly onto the roof and began to take tiny steps along its length.

"What are you doing?" Natasha stage whispered.

Veronica beckoned her to follow. "Trust me," she mouthed. "It's okay."

Derrick moved to go first, but Natasha grabbed him by the back of the collar and hauled him back. Instead she went, creeping across the sand and stepping atop the rusted metal roof of the submerged trailer as if it were made of egg shells. Her brother followed.

They clumped together near the middle of the roof. The black roof tiles were too hot from the sun for them to sit. Even touching it for more than a few seconds became painful. So instead, they squatted. Veronica peeled back a piece of roof tile and rotated it on the nail that held it in place, revealing a hole underneath, the size of a quarter. The music became louder, and might have been loud enough to cover any accidental sound they might make, but Natasha wouldn't put money on it.

Veronica put her eye to the hole and stared into the trailer for a moment. Then she turned to Natasha, "Here, take a look."

Natasha scooted next to Veronica and peered into the hole. At first she thought her vision might be blocked, but then she realized that it was the top of a man's head, bouncing to the beat of the song. Then she began to make out more of the man. His arms were raised as if working on something, but try as she might, she couldn't see what it was. Tools were scattered along the surface of a stainless steel bench.

She felt Derrick tap her shoulder and shrugged him away.

"Come on. It's my turn," he hissed.

She ignored him, instead trying to will the Mad Scientist to move his head so that she could see what he was working on. Here and there she'd get a glimpse of something green, but nothing more. It reminded her of the frogs they'd been forced to dissect in eighth grade science. Most of the girls had cringed and feigned illness when it was their turn, but it hadn't bothered Natasha. She'd always thought frogs were gross and slimy and had no compunctions about cutting them open. As a matter of fact, she'd enjoyed touching their nerves and watching their legs twitch. A part of her worried at how much she'd liked it.

"My turn."

Natasha shushed her brother, then realized too late that the sound had carried into the trailer.

The Mad Scientist's arms stopped working. His head lifted as if he were listening. After a moment, he shook his head and resumed his work, his head bobbing once again to the beat. He reached for what looked like a voltage meter, and when he did so, what he'd been working on was revealed.

She gasped and jerked her head back.

"Finally," Derrick whispered in exasperation.

He knelt and placed both hands on either side of the hole, as he peered inside the trailer.

Natasha stared at roof of the trailer open-mouthed.

"What did you see?" Veronica asked.

Natasha turned to the girl. She couldn't get her mind around the idea, much less her mouth around the words.

Derrick cursed and stood up so quickly he almost lost his balance.

Veronica reached out to help him. "What is it?"

Derrick's eyes were bugged. "He saw me."

Just then they heard the music cut off and the locks rattling inside the door.

Veronica grabbed Natasha's hand. "Come on!"

Derrick hopped off the roof and took off. Veronica pulled Natasha after her. They ran for five minutes until they came to rest within the warm shadows of sump pump #2. All three of them were bent over double, grabbing their knees or waists and gasping.

"What did you see?" Veronica asked.

Natasha thought about the frogs she'd studied at school and how she could make the legs jump and kick. Then she thought about the hand she'd seen on the Mad Scientist's workbench, the drab green fingers jumping and kicking like the legs of the frog. Unless the Mad Scientist had found the dismembered hand of an

alien, she had no idea where it'd come from. All she knew was
that seeing a body part on that workbench, a *human* body part,
sent shivers down her spine.

CHAPTER NINE

Gerald Duphrene and George Silva had played cards every night after the sun had gone down. Whether it was Tonk, Cribbage, Nerts, Gin or Stud Poker, they never failed to play some sort of game. Rarely did they ever exchange a word. They didn't have to.

George had left a deck of cards on the kitchen table after he'd gone back to Kentucky with his wife. There wasn't a note, or any direction, but Gerald had known what to do. So every night after dusk he sat at his table and played solitaire. The game kept George close: when Gerald won, he beat George, and when Gerald lost, George beat him.

The day found Gerald once again at George's old yellow and white trailer. It seemed perfectly reasonable that this was the place he'd decided to trap the monster, and deep down he believed that George would have liked it that way. After all, the old card shark was always telling Gerald that he "wasn't too old to still take it to the enemy."

Gerald turned the battery off on the golf cart and set the emergency brake. It was time.

It had been many years since the Korean War. Then, Gerald had been brave out of necessity. Someone else had forced bravery upon him. It was simple: either be brave or be dead. But now it was his choice. He could leave Bombay Beach and never turn back. But this was his home. This was really all he knew, and he wasn't about to be driven out by the monsters. So if he was going to stand and fight, he had to get used to the monsters.

"Enough thinking," Gerald said out loud. "Now get to the doing."

He stepped up the wooden steps and entered the trailer. The living room was open to the sky, the ceiling looking as if it had been ripped open by a giant hand. He stared at it for a long moment to put off doing what he needed to do, but reluctantly turned his attention to the hall. It extended before him, seeming longer than it should have been.

There was a time he would have taken a hill without a thought. He did it for his country. He did it for his friends. He did it for the spirits of his family. Gerald tried to grasp that feeling again as he put one foot in front of the other and began the long trek down the hall.

The sound of his teeth gritting could be heard over the beating of his heart. He began to notice a smell, like bloated fish and pollution. The closer he got to the room, the stronger the smell became, until it was all he could breathe.

The door had been smashed in and hung on its hinges, the upper half sagging and unsupported by the middle hinge. He focused on the cheap brass door knob, and then pushed the door open a few inches.

He didn't look at it, but he saw it in the reflection of the knob as a big black blur. He could make it out in his peripheral vision. Arms, legs, a head. But still all a blur. If only he could keep it blurry he might not be so scared, for as God was his witness, his mind reeled with fear, as if it was his first day in the Land of the Morning Calm and the Chinese were massing beneath his hill.

Fear had a taste and it tasted like steel. The taste of a bayonet in the rain, or of a rifle shell clenched between the teeth to keep from screaming.

Gerald turned his head and beheld the monster.

Its skin was a universal green, like necrotic skin around an untended wound. A military uniform clung to the monster, torn at the sleeves, across the chest and at the knees. Its feet were bare and had rotted partially away. The monster's arms hung at its side, long, muscular, mottled green, its hands opening and closing. The face was half gone. Cheeks gave away above the jaw, the tip of the nose was gone, an ear was missing. Hair hung in clumps, leaving spots of baldness. The eyes were the only things still intact, but they were changed, replaced by a yellow so incandescent, it was like urine on freshly packed snow.

It lunged at Gerald, and he screamed.

But the monster drew up short as the chain attaching the iron-jawed trap on its leg to the trailer's axle snapped taught. It wheezed loudly in the small room as it pulled against the chain, less than a foot from Gerald's face.

But Gerald kept his eyes shut. He felt his insides shrivel. Something clamped around his heart and constricted it. Urine soaked his pants. He realized that his hooks were trembling on the end of his arms.

He remembered what his old sergeant had told him when he was in Korea. There was a phrase he was told to repeat over and over and it had worked for a time, keeping the fear at bay.

He opened his mouth to speak, but the sandpaper that his lips had become refused to work. He ran a thick tongue over them several times until he was able to speak.

"Fucking gook bastards," he whispered.

He willed his eyes to open just a crack.

The monster leered at him with yellow eyes.

"Fucking gook bastards," he managed to say with a little more conviction.

The monster lunged at the end of the chain but couldn't get any closer.

"Fucking gook bastards!"

Gerald felt the power of the words come back to him. He remembered their entire platoon screaming the phrase over and over as they were attacked on his third night in the country. The mantra had rang out over the valley, even louder than the rifle fire. They hadn't lost a man that night. The power of the words had held them together.

So now, as then, Gerald crowed the words to the ceiling, as if his friends in heaven could hear him. He began to laugh, a strange laugh that he hadn't heard come from his mouth since the war.

And he screamed the mantra. Over and over, the words that had kept him alive so long ago bounced off the snarling face of the green-skinned monster that stared back at him with mad glowing eyes.

"Fucking gook bastards!"

He screamed it again and felt better for it.

Her nose was inches away as she tried to see under the door. But the hallway on the other side was all darkness and shadows. No matter how hard she tried, she couldn't pierce the gloom.

Was it gone? Was it still out there?

She'd caught herself several times with her hand on the door knob, prepared to open it. Only at the last second did she recognize the danger, remembering her husband's words after he'd finished the construction.

"Don't open the door no matter what happens," her husband had said. "When the end comes, and it will, you want to be the last one standing, so let the rest of the world fight it out while you wait here inside."

Only one thing kept her from following his instructions – her hunger. It was devastating. It ate at her inside, clawed at her throat and needled into her psyche.

Feed me. Feed me. Feed me.

She hadn't had a thing since yesterday morning.

"Are you there?" she whispered.

No answer.

She turned back towards Trudie, whose gaze remained fixed on the door. The dog had been her danger barometer and still believed that the thing was outside. But could it be wrong? Could the dog merely be as scared as she was?

"Please. Are you there?"

And then she heard it, the slight wheezing sound of the creature.

She tried to peer into the darkness and see where it was, when an eye suddenly appeared before her on the other side of the door. Yellow and unholy, it stared back at her.

Trudie barked, breaking the spell.

Abigail scrambled to her feet and ran back to the bed. She grabbed the pistol with one hand and her dog with the other.

Sooner or later that creature had to go.

Abigail glanced down at her dog as she stroked its downy fur. Hopefully sooner, because she was getting hungry.

"What about a mermaid?" Derrick asked drowsily, still smirking at her story. He lay on the couch, his head pressed into a pillow.

Natasha stared at the snow on the television and tried to ignore the thousandth question Derrick had posed on learning about the hand she'd seen. He'd run the guess gamut from the Hulk to green M&Ms. It was clear that he didn't really believe her, but she knew what she'd seen and the vision still haunted her – the Mad Scientist applying surgical clamps to the tendons of an amputated hand. It occurred to her that Derrick would have more readily believed her if she hadn't said the hand was green. As strange as it was, the idea of a regular dismembered hand was normal compared to the reality of the green one.

"What about the Creature from the Black Lagoon?"

She sighed, took a sip from a coke that had long ago turned warm and flat, then returned the can to the end table. "The hand wasn't webbed," she said flatly.

"Aha!" Derrick pumped his fist. "Now we're getting somewhere."

Natasha shook her head. They'd turned in for the night, lying once again on the leather couches. Her dad had come in late in the afternoon, talked to her and Derrick for a moment, and gone into her grandfather's bedroom. She'd heard him crying. She'd heard it a lot, but it still disturbed her and wasn't something she wanted to hear again.

Later, Maude had come over and made shrimp tacos on the grill. Auntie Lin made fried rice. They'd all sat on the roof patio with a view of the sun's dying rays across the red-hued Salton Sea. Her dad and Maude drank a few beers. Natasha was happy to see that he only had a couple.

They talked a little about the missing Beachy boy, then spent the rest of the conversation talking about Gertie. It seemed that she was prone to going off by herself. Something that had driven Natasha's grandfather crazy when he'd lived with her, but as Maude pointed out, he was also often the reason Gertie left. As of yet, there was still no sign of her, but then again, for increasingly obvious reasons, no one had really looked.

Maude explained to the Olivers how she and Gertie had both dated Lazlo. Maude had met him first and been with him for ten years. When they separated, he'd spent the next ten years with Gertie. During the last five years, both of them had dated him on and off, but at their age, it was nothing like when they were younger.

Maude also emphasized that neither she nor Gertie were the reason Patrick's father had left his mother. That had been a woman truck driver named Emily Ferger, with whom he'd decided to start a new life in El Centro. Within months he'd regretted leaving, but knew that he could never go back; he'd broken a trust that could never be mended. To return would have been "a Band-Aid on cancer": he hadn't wanted to do more harm than he already had done.

Maude explained that she'd always been more independent than Gertie. Maude came from a family of eight children and Gertie had been an only child. She'd needed Lazlo as both a friend and a lover and was taking his death harder than Maude.

Natasha replayed the conversation in her mind several times. She'd had friends, but she'd never felt as if she couldn't live without them. She'd wondered if there was something wrong with her, because everyone else she knew, Derrick included, seemed to need their friends as if they were extensions of themselves.

But not Natasha. She had an independent streak a mile long. She'd been picked second to last once on the kick ball team and, instead of playing, had walked away. She hadn't needed to play to have a good time. She'd just wanted to be around people, to see them laugh and play and to live vicariously through them. Although she hadn't been able to think about it in those terms back then, she was coming to understand it now.

"What about a man from the moon?" Derrick asked, his voice on the verge of sleep.

"He'd be made of cheese," Natasha said.

"Could be green cheese," he murmured.

"Stinky cheese. You would have smelled it."

Derrick nodded sagely. "We would have. Good point, Watson."

Natasha stared at the television screen for awhile, letting her mind drift. So much had happened. Looking around Bombay Beach, other than Veronica, she didn't think there were any other kids – and the Amish kids didn't count.

"Natasha?"

"Yes, Derrick."

"Why do you think they call static on the television snow?"

"What does it look like to you?"

Derrick considered for a moment, then answered. "An electronic Etch-a-Sketch."

"Do you see shapes?" She felt sleep only moments away.

"Sure. Like clouds."

She was beginning to drift along the current of her dreams when she felt a tug at her arm.

"Natasha, wake up."

She didn't want to leave. Everything tasted like peppermint, even the air. There was a rumble as if a volcano was erupting purple, molten chocolate far away –

"Natasha, come on. Wake up."

She opened her eyes. The rumbling was still there.

"What is it?" She levered herself to a sitting position on the couch.

"Something's going on outside." Derrick headed for the door. "Come on."

Natasha followed, careful to close the door quietly so she wouldn't wake Aunt Lin or her father, and hurried up the steps to the rooftop patio. On one side, the moon shone down on the Salton Sea, creating quicksilver waves in the darkness. On the other was the highway, where three bull-nosed buses were pulling off and heading into town. They had no markings, and the windows were heavily tinted.

"What do you make of that?" Derrick whispered.

Natasha shook her head. It was a little late for a tour group, plus, those buses didn't seem to be the type to be carrying octogenarians out for a discount week of sun, fun and adventure.

Natasha and Derrick watched from the roof as the vehicles drove into town, turned at sump pump #1 and ran the length of Fifth Street to sump pump #2. Instead of turning then, the buses went straight; the metal barrier that usually blocked access to the desalination plant had been removed. The buses followed a sandy road across the quay which was lit up like a Christmas tree.

Her grandfather's telescope rested on a homemade wooden tripod near the far edge of the patio. She tugged on the telescope and, with Derrick's help, was able to get it free. She carried it over to the opposite rail, knelt and tried to see through it to where the buses idled at the gate to the plant.

She saw a man dressed in a black jacket and blue jeans checking items off on a clipboard as the buses entered the gates. He waited until the last bus had come to a stop, then, after glancing back along the quay toward Bombay Beach, he closed the gate.

It was in that moment that she recognized him. It was Sam Hopkins, the ecologist who'd come into the restaurant earlier that day.

Gerald woke from a nightmare, sitting up with a start. In his dreams the Chinese had stormed over the hill and had infiltrated camp. This had happened only once in his memory– never to his platoon, but to a sister platoon farther along the line, nearer Inchon.

He reached over and grabbed his left prosthetic. He always kept one on. Without his wife around, he had no one to help him into them, so each night he rotated, removing one or the other, but never both.

He dressed as quickly as he could, then went to the living room.

He heard the cries from his dreams again, this time from down the street.

He grabbed his old carbine from where it sat beside the door and exited onto the porch. It was hot and muggy, little more than a breeze stirring the night. He slid into the seat of his golf cart, backed out, and headed down the road at a walking pace.

He kept his headlights off, knowing that they'd attract attention if lit. The screams came again. He turned down Avenue F, heading for the water. Figures ran into the street and back out of it.

He rested the carbine across his lap so he could use it if necessary. The big wooden and steel rifle was the only thing he could shoot with any accuracy. Pistols were out of the question. As were shotguns, their recoil ruining his tenuous grip.

But the carbine had gotten him through the Korean War and had proven itself many times.

As he crossed Third Street, he was able to make out a commotion coming from the Beachy place. He rolled a few more feet, then halted.

A monster stumbled into the street, dragging someone.

Gerald leaned forward. It was Mrs. Beachy. Her face had been all but bitten off and her stomach ripped open. The monster looked around, then headed towards the seawall.

"Fucking gook bastards," Gerald murmured.

Gerald heard the sound of a vehicle. At three in the morning, it was a wonder anyone was up. He backed into the shadow of a trailer that used to belong to Jessica Sullivan. He'd always thought she was pretty, even when she started barking like a dog and they took her away.

Soon two vehicles turned into Avenue F. He recognized them as SUVs from the plant.

Gerald watched silently as heavily armored men engaged the monsters, wrapped them in netting, and packed them in the back of one of the SUVs, while the other was filled with the bodies of the Beachys.

Gerald remained in place until it was almost dawn, then he slowly drove by the scene. It looked like hell had come upon the Amish family. The home had been broken into, and belongings were scattered all across the yard.

He continued past and waited outside the restaurant until it opened. Maude served him a cup of coffee in a Styrofoam cup which he took with him. Other than being polite to Maude, he never said anything to anyone, neither about what he saw, nor what he knew.

They'd find out soon enough what happened to the Beachys.

They didn't need him to tell them.

CHAPTER TEN

Natasha woke with the feeling that she was being watched. The sun shone through the slats of the window blinds, golden motes of dust spinning in the dry trailer air. Derrick lay curled into a ball on the other couch, the blanket gripped in his hands like something he'd killed in his sleep. The fan rotated slowly, moving just enough to keep the air circulating in the low-ceilinged living room but not really enough to cool her.

Natasha glanced at the television, which someone had shut off while she'd slept. She grabbed her cell phone from the coffee table out of habit. But she didn't have service in Bombay Beach so it was nothing more than an expensive clock with a few games and a calculator. She'd planned on networking with her friends. Several of them were Twitterholics, and she counted on these to keep her abreast of the latest happenings. But the cell phone was next to useless. Not only didn't it work, it wasn't even good enough to play music. It was just a clock to her. And the clock read 9:30 AM.

She found it strange that she'd been allowed to sleep in. Auntie Lin had woken her at 5 AM. the previous morning so they could get the restaurant ready for the breakfast rush. Maybe her mom and dad had decided to keep the restaurant closed for another day.

As Natasha rose from the couch, she noticed Auntie Lin staring at her from the doorway, a bandana covering her hair. In her hands she held a mop and a bucket.

"Were you watching me, Auntie Lin?"

"No, I was holding up the doorway."

Natasha grinned. She thought about trying to get out of cleaning, but she didn't have any reason not to help. Plus, she could try and understand everything that had happened recently while she cleaned. Her father had already left. She woke Derrick and soon the three of them were scouring the inside of the trailer. Derrick found empty boxes in the shed behind the trailer, and they filled them with their grandfather's personal effects, marking them so their father could go through them if he wanted. Meanwhile, Auntie Lin and Natasha scrubbed everything in the house bar the ceiling.

While they worked, Natasha told Auntie Lin everything they'd encountered thus far, including seeing the hand and the mysterious buses pulling into the desalination plant. Auntie Lin didn't have much to say, but that was normal. Natasha was used to the old woman being a sounding board. Sometimes just talking to Auntie Lin was enough to get her thoughts in order.

As Natasha sorted through her grandfather's effects, she found two letters, from Gertie and Maude. She couldn't help but read them. Natasha thought she'd get a peek into her grandfather's personality, but instead the letters left her depressed.

They finished cleaning around noon. Natasha didn't really understand her grandfather any more than she had before, but her thoughts were better organized. Plus, she and Derrick now had clean rooms to sleep in. They had once belonged to Gertie and Maude and both, much to their delight, had waterbeds. As she lay on hers Natasha thought about the gentle swells of the ocean, not the rotten sea they now lived beside.

They headed towards the restaurant. There Derrick and Natasha found their father, Maude and a few of the other locals sitting around the big round table in the center of the room, drinking iced tea and engaged in a heated conversation.

Natasha went right to Maude and handed her a packet of letters, bound by a rubber band. Maude looked at her, and she apologized.

"I'm sorry. I read these. I know I shouldn't have, but they were so..." She couldn't find the words.

"Romantic?"

"Yeah. That's what they were." Natasha knelt beside Maude and embraced her. After a moment's hesitation, Maude returned the embrace.

The others were talking about the sea and the reason it was like it was. Some of the older residents – like Frank, Kim Johnson, and Kristov – thought it was because of the government, some disaster manufactured to hide their secret shenanigans. But the newer residents, such as Maude and Andy – who Derrick and Natasha were careful not to stare too closely at – felt that it was nothing more than the result of a natural disaster.

Some of the town-folk relented and agreed that it might have been a natural disaster, but it was the government who'd exacerbated the problem, and so the argument went.

Maude eventually went into the kitchen and made everyone turkey sandwiches, macaroni salad and iced tea, before returning to the debate, chipping in here and there.

Natasha recognized the conversation for what it was: nothing different than from what she'd done with Auntie Lin, an exercise in frustration avoidance, allowing everyone to give voice to their ideas. So she sat and ate and watched and listened and, although the opportunity arose, never mentioned that she'd seen Andy Gudgel, the Mad Scientist, experimenting on a green monster hand in his lab.

Just as the debate was simmering down, the front door opened and Deputy Will entered, with Sam Hopkins close behind. He strode to the counter and asked Maude for an iced tea, then took off his baseball cap and wiped his brow with a napkin.

"What gives, deputy?" Andy asked.

"When's the last time any of you saw Abel Beachy or a member of his family?" He eyed everyone carefully as he asked.

"Why?" Patrick asked. "What happened?"

"We got a situation."

Maude brought out two iced teas and passed them to the men. When they were finished drinking, they handed the glasses back with a nod of thanks, then Deputy Will explained: "The Beachys are gone."

"What do you mean, gone?" Andy Gudgel shouted. "Where'd they go?"

"That we don't know. They could have left town, but by the looks of things, I don't think they did. I didn't have time to go over the scene. After I determined that no one was there, I was more interested to find out if any of you knew anything."

"If they didn't leave, then where are they, Deputy?" Patrick asked.

"We don't know." Will shook his head and put his cap back on. "There's evidence that something happened though."

"Something? What something?" Kristov asked. Today, he was wearing a peach-colored tuxedo with a ruffled, open-collared shirt. On his feet he wore cloud-white loafers. No socks.

"You'll have to see for yourself." The Deputy headed for the door. "Come on. I want you all present when I go over the scene. Consider yourselves deputized."

That last bit made everyone exchange glances, as if they couldn't believe their ears. Natasha looked at Derrick, who seemed ready to explode with a mix of pride and excitement. She rolled her eyes. "Easy, Wyatt Earp."

As if they were some Wild-West posse, the party marched out of the restaurant and down the street, fists clenched, curious as to what they might see. But when the group rounded a corner and saw what had become of the U-shaped trailers that comprised the Beachy compound they drew up as one and stared.

Two of the windows were broken and the front door hung from one hinge. Clothes were scattered in the yard, as if someone had dragged them from the house to the chain link fence. A hole gaped beneath a window, looking as if a shotgun blast had blown through it. Blood stained the bottom step of the front porch.

"Don't you think we better wait before we go in there?" Andy asked the deputy.

"Wait for what?"

"Evidence. We might destroy what we find."

"Look where we are." The deputy swept the area with his arm. "Does it look like we have a forensics unit on hand? You're lucky you got me!"

Everyone was taken aback by Will's tone. He was clearly pissed off and Frank called him on it.

"Why you so mad, Will?"

The deputy whirled on the lanky drunk and grabbed him by the wrist. "Because I think someone died here. I also think someone in this town did it. I don't know who it was, but I'm going to find out. This might be Bum Fuck Egypt, but I'm still the deputy sheriff and there's law here whether you-," he let go of Frank's wrist and looked around, the fire dimming in his eyes as he got himself under control, "-like it or not."

Patrick was the first to break the uneasy silence that followed. "Hold it, Deputy. We're not the ones who were involved in this."

Deputy Will Toddrunner raised his eyebrows. "We'll see about that when I'm done talking to everyone. In the meantime, let's see what we can see."

"What are we looking for?" Natasha asked.

"Anything. Everything. Whatever can shed light on what happened to the Beachys."

"But if we're guilty, who's to stop us from messing with the evidence?" Derrick asked.

Deputy Will answered without turning. "Because I lied earlier. I've already been over the scene and I know what's in there. If something suddenly goes missing, then I definitely *will* have a suspect."

Everyone looked at each other.

Natasha couldn't help herself. Deputized or not, she gulped.

Abigail had spent a night and a day in her room. She'd eaten one and a half tubes of toothpaste last night, sharing a bit of it with Trudie and washing it down with water. The dog was so starved it had almost bit her as it licked the paste from her hands. Then later it had crapped in the corner something awful. Abigail had wiped it up with tissue and flushed it down the toilet, but the smell still lingered in the room.

She'd stopped trying to be quiet, too. No longer did she tiptoe around. She walked normally. She spoke to Trudie in a normal voice. She even spoke to the creature in a normal voice, on occasion even knocking on the door to elicit a response.

Almost always the damned thing would reply by scrabbling on the outside of the door; sometimes almost imperceptibly, sometimes grating and loud, always the sounds sent chills up her spine.

What was it to keep her in the room like this?

What kind of creature was it that terrorized old women?

She'd thought about this for a long time and wondered if it wasn't a more widespread phenomenon. How many other residents of Bombay Beach had this or some creature like it attacked and killed? Was she the last surviving person in Bombay Beach, or were others holed up like her?

If she'd have to bet, it would be that Gerald, Kristov and Frank would survive. Both Gerald and Kristov had fought in wars, each returning with their own scars, although Kristov's were a bit harder to see. Clearly he'd done and seen things he never wanted to think about, and Elvis was his protector.

Then of course there was Frank. Good old loveable, drunken Frank. He'd tried more than once to reintroduce romance to Abigail's life, occasionally bringing her stolen flowers and offering to share what booze he had left. Abigail always declined these invitations, but couldn't help but be a little flattered that there was someone out there who wanted her in that way.

Even if it was Frank.

No, Frank would survive because of the old adage that *God watches out for drunks and fools*. Frank so perfectly fulfilled both categories, he was sure to be the last man standing on the planet.

Abigail wished she had either the fortitude of Gerald and Kristov, or even the pure dumb luck of Frank. Anything. Anything other than starving to death or being ripped apart by the creature, but those seemed to be her current options.

Then she remembered something.

Roger had died the day before Valentine's Day four years ago. While going through his things, she'd found a box of chocolates with a card, her name scrawled across the envelope in his handwriting. She glanced around the room. She hadn't thought about that in more than a year. She'd meant to keep it as a souvenir and had never been able to bring herself to actually eat the candies.

But now... now things were completely different. Now the chocolates might just save her if she could only remember where she'd put them.

She went to the dresser and fell on her knees, flinging open the drawers. She searched through her clothes, discovering old purses she hadn't seen in ages, and silken scarves she'd never wear again. But no chocolates.

Then she rememebered the closet. She'd put a box of Roger's things on the shelf, things she'd never wanted to get rid of. His favorite fedora, his pipes still smelling of vanilla tobacco, and other personal things, each with their own special memory.

She scrambled to her feet, jerked open the closet door and pushed aside a pile of blankets and several pillows to get to the box. It wasn't heavy, but she lost her balance as she pulled it off the shelf and fell into an end table, her hip screaming in pain as she fell to her knees.

She got back to her feet and threw open the top of the box. And there it was. Right beneath the fedora, with the words *Fannie Mae Candies* scrawled across the top. She tore the lid off, and removed the top layer of foil, revealing twelve pieces of chocolate, only slightly graying with age. She immediately shoved two candies into her mouth – hazelnut and dark chocolate – and they tasted like heaven.

Her dog leaped atop the bed beside her and sat wagging its tail. She was about to give it a piece when she remembered that dogs were allergic to chocolate. So instead she turned away from Trudie, holding the food close to her breast lest the dog see her.

She ate another piece, this one filled with coconut.

Trudie changed positions and moved into Abigail's lap.

Abigail pushed the dog away and walked to the corner of the room by the closet. She stood, eating the chocolate, watching the dog out of the corner of her eye.

Trudie growled low in her throat.

She wanted some chocolate.

She growled again.

CHAPTER ELEVEN

Everyone met at the restaurant when they finished examining the Beachy place. All were present with the exception of Kristov, Jose and some of the other locals. The restaurant was open for dessert and drinks only; Maude had taken off, mentioning something about Gertie, and was nowhere to be found. So Auntie Lin took orders for cake, pies and ice cream and, with Natasha's help, ensured that everyone was taken care of.

Will and Sam Hopkins had stayed behind at the Beachy place, calling the crime into central dispatch and submitting requests for the state to get involved.

Now inside the Space Station Restaurant, Patrick listened as the residents of Bombay Beach propounded a host of unlikely explanations, including alien abductions, government conspiracies and doomsday cultists run amok.

Kim Johnson talked about Fred and Rosemary West, a British couple who'd killed a dozen people – including their own daughter – and postulated that there might be a similar group in the Imperial Valley area who targeted Amish people.

Carrie Loughnane reminded everyone about the Manson Family.

Frank murmured about little green men from outer space, then slid into a diatribe about *Mork and Mindy* re-runs and how the show had really been a dissertation on the failure of capitalism. He was soon ignored, though, as everyone began to talk amongst themselves.

Patrick called Natasha and Derrick to him. They agreed something was going on that they didn't understand. So far Gertie and an entire family had gone missing. The rumors of aliens and monsters notwithstanding, they agreed that it was possible that someone in this dying town might have snapped. Wasn't it a fact that serial killers always seemed to be normal, law-abiding neighbors?

So they came to a decision.

Patrick stood and gestured for quiet. It took a moment, but with the help of Kim Johnson whistling through her teeth, soon everyone had stopped talking.

The attention made him uncomfortable.

"I don't know what's going on. I have the safety of my kids to think about. Probably nothing's going on, but I have to be sure. Bottom line is that I'm going to stay home with the kids for a few days. I don't expect Maude to run the restaurant alone, so..." He held his hands higher as protests began. "Anyway, we'll reopen as soon as all of this... subsides. We're going to stay home. Until then, we think it might be a good idea if you all do the same."

As he sat back down a chorus of complaints and pleas arose, but Patrick ignored them.

Rico Duvall stood and proclaimed that he and his brother weren't going anywhere. As one of the only employers in town, he stressed that they were still looking for three to four people a day and that they would pay in cash during this emergency if people so desired.

Columbus Williams – a retired Navy officer – unfolded himself to his full height and told the folks that they were all crazy, because anything could have happened. Even now the Beachys could be at the hospital because of an accidental gunshot or from getting cut on flying glass. He stressed that not all answers have to be far-fetched and that most things could be explained using rational, intelligent deduction.

Everyone gave him a moment's serious consideration then returned to their musings. The clamor of their conversations only halted when the missing Kristov and Jose, followed by several others, entered the restaurant with hunting rifles in hand and bandoliers crisscrossing their chests like banditos.

As the room fell silent, Kristov belted out a few verses of an old Soviet marching song. No one knew the words, but soon all eyes were on him. The song did its trick.

Clearly having changed from his previous garish outfit into another for the occasion, the cut-price Elvis now wore a robin's-egg-blue leisure suit with an open-collared French-cuffed white shirt. On his feet were black platform shoes. Silver reflective glasses covered his eyes. His hair had been raised into an impressive black Elvis pompadour. The belts that crossed his chest held more than a dozen shotgun shells. In his hands was a 12 gauge shotgun.

Patrick and Natasha exchanged glances. Patrick was once again reminded what a collection of misfits they had living in Bombay Beach. The notion that an Romanian freedom fighter turned Elvis Impersonator could be the voice of the people was something no one could have predicted.

When Kristov stopped singing he marched to the counter and climbed up on it, ignoring Auntie Lin's glare. Kristov then sought Patrick in the crowd and pointed at him.

"I am here to speak with Olivers. I want to say what needs to be said and it is what I am here to say. I want everyone to know that Kristov Constantinescu and his friends are heavily armed and know how to use their weapons. There is no need to close down the Space Station. We have you protected."

Patrick glanced around and saw his confusion reflected on the face of those gathered before him.

"The monsters," Kristov said. "We will shoot the monsters with our big fucking guns." When he heard a few chitters of laughter from the crowd, he turned and aimed the barrel of the gun across the tops of everyone's heads. "We are not being jokesters. We are being serious. We will protect you. We will kill the monsters; so eat, drink, and be merry. We will protect you because we are the Bombay Beach Brigade."

Patrick peered at Natasha, who had a bemused look on her face. She mouthed the word "monsters" and raised her eyebrows.

Someone in the crowd began to laugh. It turned into a titter as several others joined in. Finally Patrick couldn't help himself as he imagined the Elvis Impersonator at the head of the newly-formed Bombay Beach Brigade, protecting the town's residents from monsters that didn't really exist.

Natasha and Derrick escaped the restaurant at about five in the afternoon. Patrick had decided to keep the place open for one more night. He hadn't taken much convincing, once he'd started drinking with the others. Maude had returned from another exhaustive yet uneventful search for Gertie and had begun getting the dinner service ready, working listlessly and automatically. It was clear that Gertie's absence was affecting her, but Natasha didn't know what else to do other than go from trailer to trailer knocking on doors.

Derrick followed her as she went in search of Veronica's trailer. Although the trailers looked nothing alike, they were of a kind, all just this side of a *Mad Max* movie.

She stood in the street for a good minute. The heat of the day had dissipated and a cool but foul breeze brushed past them. Once again there wasn't a cloud or bird in the sky. Natasha realized that the stillness had been bothering her since she'd arrived. In every neighborhood she'd ever been in, there had always been movement, the sounds of life during the daytime. But here in Bombay Beach no kids played outside, no pets scampered about, no people walked along the roads. Except for the flies, there were no insects: no lightning bugs, ants, beetles, roaches, nothing. Everywhere she looked there was nothing moving, as if the entire town had been abandoned but no one knew it yet.

Suddenly the ground began to shake.

Derrick stumbled and fell to one knee. Natasha held out her arms and spread her legs for balance as everything shook and trembled. It took a moment to register that she was in an actual earthquake. The palm trees quivered, dead leaves rattling like *papier-mâché* skeletons. The trailers screeched on their foundations, trash containers and beer cans fell from porches, chain link fences rattled.

And then it stopped.

As suddenly as it had begun it stopped. Once again the world returned to its former stillness, with only a few beer cans rolling back and forth on the ground to prove that anything had actually happened.

A screen door swung open as Natasha helped Derrick to his feet. Veronica shot out of a trailer, jumped from the porch and ran to the chain link fence that surrounded her home.

"Did you feel that?" She took a look at Derrick. "Never been in one of those before, have you?"

Derrick smiled weakly and shook his head.

"Do they always last so long?" Natasha asked.

"Long?" Veronica giggled. "Wasn't more than five seconds."

Natasha doubted that could be true. It had felt much longer.

"Come on in," Veronica beckoned. "We have the swamp cooler going and it's almost habitable inside."

Natasha glanced at the ground and the palms and wondered how bad it could get. How much could the ground shake before it opened up and swallowed them whole? She shuddered at the idea and hastened to follow Veronica.

Soon they were all safe inside Veronica's trailer, with a cool draft blowing over them. Old blinds cut the light into slits, throwing lines of shadow across everything. The room was clean and furnished with green vinyl chairs and a long sofa.

An older Hispanic woman wearing shorts and an LA Dodgers T-shirt, with her graying black hair pulled back, was busy picking up things that had fallen over in the earthquake. As they entered she was tutting over a broken dish depicting the Statue of Liberty. In the kitchen, an older Hispanic man fiddled with the back of a radio with a screwdriver.

"Auntie, these are the people I told you about," Veronica said. "This is my Auntie Hermana and that's my uncle in there."

The old woman greeted them and immediately put them to work helping her repair the minor damage the earthquake had caused. All told, there wasn't much. She'd used earthquake wax to hold things against the walls and tables, so most of her ornaments were unbroken.

Afterwards, Natasha and Derrick followed Veronica to her room. Veronica immediately flopped onto the bed, lying on her stomach, feet in the air.

Natasha and Derrick stood in the middle of the room, mesmerized by the conglomeration of images on the wall. There were thousands of magazine photos of musicians, sports heroes, politicians, Bible characters, animals, insects and all manner of things. There wasn't a single space on the wall or ceiling that hadn't been covered, sometimes repeatedly, by black and white and color images.

Veronica saw them staring. "After my brother was shot, my parents kept me inside the house for almost a year. I didn't go to school. I didn't even go into the front room for fear that someone would spray the front of the house with bullets. Because my room was in the back of the house, it was the safest, so I stayed there. To keep from getting lonely, I cut pictures out of magazines, books, cereal boxes, anything I could get my hands on. I would have gone crazy without them. It got to the point where these became as much my family as anything."

"But why here? Why do it now that you're living with your Aunt?" Natasha asked.

"Because I got used to them." Veronica smiled self-consciously. "I realized that I missed them, so I raided abandoned trailers, took the magazines and removed the pictures. It's funny. Although I can leave anytime I want, sometimes my Auntie has to kick me outside. I like *mi familia*," she said, pointing at the walls. "I know them better than I know anyone."

"Do you know who everyone is?" Derrick asked.

"Some. The famous ones."

"And the others?"

"I invented names for them. Like that one," she said, pointing at a straight-haired man, sitting in a barber chair about to get a haircut. "I call him Charles and he's a butler for a Duke and Duchess living in San Diego. He hates dogs and cats but loves birds. His favorite color is violet and he sleeps with a teddy bear."

Natasha grinned, but couldn't help asking, "Are you serious?"

"Of course."

"What about that one?" Derrick pointed.

"That's Roger Daltry, the lead singer of The Who."

"And this one?" It was a rail-thin young woman with her blonde hair seemingly glued to her head.

"That's a woman who has just been fired from her first job. I call her Susanna. She lives in London and hates driving on the left side of the road. She wishes she were American, and is a fan of Country and Western music. She has a tattoo of Bigfoot on her ass."

Natasha leaned in close and put her finger on the picture in question. "Are you talking about this one?" When Veronica nodded, she added, "Her real name is Twiggy. She was a model in the 1960s, I think. My mother had a picture of her in her scrapbook. She wanted to grow up and look just like her."

"So says you," Veronica said without blinking. "To me she's Susanna."

Natasha was about to argue, but then decided against it.

She plopped down on the bed next to Veronica. "Was that a big earthquake?"

"Not really. I'm told there are a lot larger ones, but that's about what we get here. It scared the shit out of you, didn't it?"

"Well, yeah. Who wouldn't be scared, you know?"

"What about this one?" Derrick asked, ignoring the girls' conversation, too entranced by the images to care.

"Sissy Spacek in *Carrie*."

"She looks pissed," he said. He moved along the wall, his fingers flowing across the images like they were Braille and he was a blind man.

"Do the earthquakes cause any damage?" Natasha asked.

"Not really. I mean, some of the old trailers in Bombay Beach are real dumps to begin with. Each one of the tremblers takes them a step closer to collapse. That's why Will and that asshole Hopkins tell everyone to stay out of them. They say it's dangerous."

"And you don't believe them?"

Veronica made a face like she'd smelt something bad. "Oh, I believe them, but what do they really know about danger? I just have a problem with *them* telling *me* to be careful. It's like telling a woman who has cancer to look both ways when she crosses the street."

Natasha wasn't sure the metaphor was accurate but she could tell that she'd struck a nerve. "What about Hopkins? Why doesn't anyone like him?"

"I don't know. He just comes across as a know-it-all, and I hate know-it-alls."

"What about this one?" Derrick asked.

"That's Kevin Bacon. He's an actor."

Derrick moved on.

"You know, I saw him," Natasha said.

"Kevin Bacon?" Veronica sat straighter.

"Nuh-uh. Hopkins. That government guy. We saw him last night over at the desalination plant."

"Out there? Why would he be over there so late?"

"There were buses that came in and he was keeping track of them or something. He had a clipboard."

"Who was on the buses?"

Natasha shrugged.

"And this one?" Derrick poked his finger at the ceiling.

"John Wayne."

"The Duke. I thought that was him, but I've never seen him with the eye patch."

Natasha looked at Veronica and rolled her eyes. Then they began to laugh. Soon, Natasha had joined in the game and she was dancing around the room, pointing to picture after picture, taking turns with Derrick, and letting Veronica either tell them who it really was or making up a story to fill out their two-dimensional lives. All was hilarity until Veronica mistook the made-for-TV band the Monkees for the Beatles, which almost made Natasha hyperventilate at the insanity of the error. Soon she was telling Veronica the truth of the Monkees, and the state of American television in the early days: *Happy Days, Laverne and Shirley, The Love Boat,* and the best show in the entire universe, *Lancelot Link, Secret Chimp.*

The dog was ill, there was no denying it. Abigail had broken down and fed it two pieces of chocolate. It had vomited several times and kept crapping in the corner, noxious streams of yellow-brown liquid. When it wasn't in the corner, it was pacing back and forth, unwilling to lie down.

Abigail had left a third of the chocolate in the box and had placed it back on the shelf so that the dog would leave her alone. She knew she shouldn't have given it chocolate, but what was she to do with the dog begging, starving, whining in front of her and not understanding why Abigail was eating and she couldn't.

When she could, Abigail fed it water. They had a never-ending supply of the stuff, and if they could wait out the creature and stave off her hunger, they could survive this episode.

Abigail lay back on the bed, her husband's fedora clenched in her arms, and stared morosely at the door. God, she'd love to live somewhere else, but all of their money had been sunk into the land and this trailer and no one, but *no one*, was buying land around the Salton Sea.

She was trapped in Bombay Beach as surely as she was trapped in her home. Any way she looked, she was trapped. It was all just so hopeless. She was just marking time until it was her turn to die.

Scratching came from the bathroom.

"Stop that, Trudie."

The scratching continued unabated.

"Trudie, I said stop that."

Trudie leaped on the bed beside her, panting rapidly.

And the scratching continued.

Abigail sat up in bed. If Trudie was right here, then what was it making that noise?

She got to her feet and crept to the bathroom door. She peered in and cocked her head. When the scratching came once more, she pinpointed the sound. It was coming from beneath the toilet.

What could be making that –

Was it the creature from the hall? Had it decided to try another way in or was it another creature come to get her?

She took a few steps towards the toilet. And why was it scratching there? Roger had steel-plated the walls and floor and ceiling. There was no getting in.

Except...

She remembered when she'd had Jose come over and repair a busted pipe. He'd said something then about the steel flooring. The price he'd quoted was unreasonably high, she'd thought, and she remembered telling him so. He'd brought the price down to a reasonable amount she was willing to pay, but had told her that he'd *have to cut corners*.

Was one of the corners the steel plating?

The scratching answered her.

CHAPTER TWELVE

Patrick's head should have exploded sometime between when it hit the pillow at 3 AM and when he was woken with a shove at 9 AM. If it had, he wouldn't be experiencing the pain he was feeling now. The dull throbbing he could take, but the hundreds of screwdrivers lancing his brain was another thing altogether. If he had the keys to the world he'd put a stop to it, but for now all he could do was gulp aspirins and glower at all things noisy – which apparently was everyone except himself – and hope to survive the next few seconds.

The restaurant was in full swing, although how long that was going to last he didn't know. Maude had handed in her notice. She'd said that with Gertie having run off and Lazlo dead, there was nothing left for her but bad memories. Patrick realized that her leaving would be a crippling blow to the restaurant, but in his condition he couldn't bring himself to care.

Auntie Lin slammed a plate of pancakes in front of him. He stared at them. Normally he'd dive in, especially with boysenberry syrup and butter, teasing his eyes and nose with the luscious look and taste, representing everything he loved about breakfast. But his stomach gurgled at the very idea.

Sam Hopkins slapped him on the back and plopped down on the stool beside him.

"That was some hell of a time, wasn't it?"

Patrick nodded as parts of it came back to him. Kristov had promised to guard them and escort each of them home last night. Patrick had an image of the mad Elvis impersonator holding a shotgun in the crux of his shoulder, leading a group of them to the safety of their trailers, a velvet-clad pied piper of drunken fools, singing *Suspicious Minds* like it was a military cadence.

"Yeah. Hell of a time," Patrick mumbled. He sipped a glass of water. It seemed to be the only thing he could keep down.

Auntie Lin approached with a menu, but stopped when Hopkins said, "I'll have what he's having."

Patrick shoved it over. "Here. Take it. Not hungry."

Hopkins gave him a surprised look, then eagerly dug in. "Thanks, man."

Whatever, thought Patrick.

He knew he was a miserable sight. Patrick pushed out of the restaurant and was assaulted by the bright light of the desert day. He took eight steps, staggered against the wall and puked beneath the mural of spaceships doing battle with aliens.

Boy, was his Auntie Lin pissed.

Derrick couldn't wait to get away. Not only was working in a restaurant the *lamest* thing he'd ever done, it seemed as if his dad had gone off the deep end. The irony that his dad was acting like the man they'd all laughed at the first day here wasn't lost on him.

Somehow Natasha had managed to slip out earlier. She'd left when he was in the back, elbow deep in scalding dish water.

He shoved open the back door and headed towards the beach.

He knew he should probably go home and check on his father, but that was the last thing he wanted to do. He'd seen his father drunk too many times to count; in fact, he'd hoped that the trip might give them all a new start. Everyone at Derrick's school knew about his father and he was tired of seeing the sympathetic looks in their eyes. Now it seemed as if he'd have to face the same looks when he started high school in the fall.

The heat beat down from a hard orange sun. It was definitely hotter than it had been earlier. Flies were the only thing that moved.

He started picking up rocks and throwing them at the birds. When he tired of this, he found a long metal rod and poked at the detritus in the polluted tide. After about half a mile, he turned around, this time concentrating on the beach, poking at odd mounds of sand. He wasn't looking for anything in particular, just something to take his mind off his present situation.

When he'd almost drawn even with the restaurant he found a mound that offered resistance when prodded. He bent and uncovered a vinyl-bound diary.

On the inside front cover was his grandfather's name, but that was the beginning and end to what he could read. There was writing in it, but it was complete gibberish, for more than a hundred pages. It looked as if it was written in code, but who would write anything in code unless they were a secret agent or something?

If only there were other boys around. He could show it to a friend and together they would have figured it out. Like back in Philadelphia when he and his friends had unraveled the mystery surrounding the homeless man named Jimmy Ten Hats who always wore ten hats on his head at the same time. No one knew why he did such a thing, until the boys figured out that those had been the occupations the man had had during his former life. The first hat was that of a porter on a train, and the last one was a hard hat from the same plant his father had worked at.

Derrick shoved the book in his back pocket and continued searching along the shoreline. He found a few interesting pieces of metal, and a patch of scaly skin from some kind of dead fish, but his mind kept being drawn back to the book. What kind of code was it? And who would be smart enough to decipher it?

It was mid-afternoon and Patrick sat on the floor of what used to be his father's closet. The kids had boxed everything up and now he was going through them. He had the pacifier in his mouth as he leafed through a shoebox full of greeting cards.

Bobby Gentry's *Ode to Billy Joe* played on the stereo. It had been one of his favorites when he was a kid and he remembered that he and his father had sung it over and over on the way to the Monongahela River to fish for trout; he remembered the words like it was yesterday. He and his father had been the only fishermen on the river that day, and had caught a dozen fish in the rain. It had been the last time that he and his father had ever gone anywhere together. A week later the man had taken off.

The shoebox was filled to bursting and as he looked, he realized that all of the cards in the box had been meant for him... but they'd never been sent. It didn't even look like his father had intended to send them, so their presence was curious. Why would someone buy cards for someone and never send them? Patrick found himself sucking on the pacifier and wondering what his father had wanted all these years. Had he felt trapped here? Had he been too embarrassed to come home?

There must have been a hundred cards in the box. Birthday cards, Christmas cards, Easter cards, Hallowe'en cards with pictures of ghosts and goblins. They were in chronological order and, as he looked at each one – each bearing a scrawled, simple *Dad* – Patrick thought about what he'd been doing each day.

For some of the days, like his sixteenth birthday, Patrick knew exactly what he had been doing. His mother had bought him an old Dodge Duster. It was all rust and fiberglass molding, but he hadn't cared. A boy's first car is one of the most special things in the universe, right up there with his first taste of pizza, his first time with a woman, and the feeling a man has when he realizes he is a father.

Patrick let the pacifier drop from his mouth as he grabbed the bottle of Old Crow from the floor and took a deep swig. He laughed at his own sentimentality. If having a kid was so damned important, why had his father left?

He started to jam the cards back in the box. Twice he dropped them, scattering them across his father's old shoes. The cards had been a tight fit in the box when he'd found them, and now that he had them splayed across the floor, he couldn't figure out how to get them all back inside.

Finally Patrick gave up and shoved the cards that wouldn't fit down his shirt, and lurched to his feet, the box pressed to his chest with one hand and the bottle in the other. He steadied himself, then left the trailer as the record reset and started playing *Ode to Billy Joe* all over again.

Gerald parked his golf cart in the shade of sump pump #2, raised his binoculars to his eyes and peered through them, watching the front of the desalination plant at the other end of the quay. Things had been sideways there for a long time. He tried to remember when it was that he first knew something was wrong. He figured it was sometime during the 1970s. They'd had a busload of hippies descend on them then, staying an entire summer until their spirits were smashed by the oppressive heat and the constant rot.

That was also when he first noticed the nature of the vehicles and people going in and out of the compound. He'd returned from the war an insomniac, lying awake in bed, unconsciously listening for the sounds of Chinese soldiers crawling up on his position.

So it was that he noticed the military vehicles coming and going from the plant in the wee hours of the morning, soldiers driving the trucks and manning the gates. Why did a desalination plant require soldiers to function properly?

The answer was that it didn't, which meant that something else was going on.

Over the years Gerald had been gathering more and more

information. He was surreptitious in his spying, careful that he didn't put himself in a position to be seen or captured.

In recent years that had been more difficult. Five years ago he'd spied the first camera. Since then he'd counted over a dozen. At first he'd believed them put in place by the man known as Colonel Hopkins – sometimes Sam Hopkins the Ecologist – but Gerald soon rejected that idea. Someone else had put the cameras in place. Far too many were pointed towards the plant, as if someone else was keeping track of the events as they transpired. If the government was concerned about the town's people and their proximity to the operation, Gerald believed that the cameras would be pointed at them. How better to keep track of the locals than to monitor them 24/7? But that wasn't the case. He still hadn't discovered who put up the cameras, but he had it narrowed down to a few individuals.

Still, it had been a long time since Gerald had cared what other people thought... a very long time. Once upon a time he'd thought of himself as a good Samaritan, someone whose job it was to help the community; that was until his hooks, and the looks they received from those he'd once thought to call friends.

Sure there were those like George and Paula, but friends like them were few and far between. Most of the people in Bombay Beach had taken one look at his hooks and viewed him with disgust and horror – never mind that he lost them in defense of a patriotic ideal that they only thought about during holidays, when fireworks and BBQs were their only expressions of solidarity.

Yet despite this treatment, he still cared for Bombay Beach. But it was the place, not the people, that had found a way into his heart. He still dreamed of a day it would be like it had been when he'd first arrived. He remembered how beautiful the water was and how pristine the trailers looked in perfect rows, with perfect lawns and perfect paint.

So he'd continue to do what he could to protect the town. And if the citizens benefited from his benevolence then bully for them. As his wife had once told him, *they're lucky that they have someone like you looking out for them, even if they don't know it.*

Gerald slid the binoculars back in the case, snapped it shut and made sure it wouldn't slide around on the seat. He put the cart in gear and headed back up Isle of Palms Avenue, looking for a chicken salad sandwich.

"So what do I do with it?" Derrick asked. He was out of breath and excited as he sat on the floor of Veronica's room. The girls had been talking on the bed when he'd burst into the room but, after a moment of outrage at his intrusion, now seemed nearly as excited as he was.

The book was open on the bed between the girls as they delicately turned the pages. Here and there were letters that randomly made a word in the middle of a sentence, but other than that, the pages were indecipherable.

"Can you decode it?" Derrick prodded.

Veronica glanced towards him and grinned.

"What does that mean?" he asked. "Is that a yes?"

"No, it's just a smile to tell you how cool you are for finding this." She beamed her lipstick-smile at him for a moment more, then returned her gaze to the book.

Derrick's face burned with embarrassment. He tried not to notice Veronica's knee-high white socks, red and black checkered mini-skirt, and tight white halter-top. To hide his awkwardness he sought out images on the wall. Something ugly and normal. A picture of Richard Nixon calmed him enough to regain his dignity.

"Look at this. See how the margins are even on the right and uneven on the left?" Natasha said.

Derrick tore himself away from the wall and scooted over to where he could see. He was all too aware of how close he was to Veronica. Her knees were pulled up just on the other side of the book, and when she leaned over, he could smell her shampoo. He looked down at the book and saw that his sister was right. The words had been written as if the writer had started on the right hand side of the page.

"I hadn't noticed." Veronica turned several pages, then flipped from back to front. "They're all like that."

Derrick liked the way her freckles danced when she scrunched her nose. "All of them?"

She nodded and glanced his way, warming his heart, then resumed examining the book.

"You know," Natasha began, "I think that Grandpa Laz wrote it backwards."

This brought Derrick out of his trance. His grandfather had written the book backwards? If there was anything more cool, he didn't know what it was.

"The code must have meant that he didn't want anyone to read it."

"I can see that," Natasha agreed. "And he wrote it backwards as a double code."

A double code. *That* was more cool. Derrick grinned.

"But what does it say?" Veronica shifted her feet under her to get a better vantage point.

"I've done codes before," Derrick said. "Simple things in school, like substitution codes. You know, like the Caesar cipher, where an 'A' is really an 'M,' and a 'B' is really an 'N' and so forth."

"Could it be that?"

"I tried that on the way over here." Derrick said. "Didn't work. I've also seen codes where lists of numbers refer to letters of the alphabet, only not always in their natural order."

"I don't see any numbers," Veronica said.

"Me neither. I was just thinking out loud. Maybe I should sit down with a pencil and a piece of paper and see if I can figure it out. The trick is to look for the most commonly occurring words, such as 'the' and 'a' It's also important to find double letters, like two 'L's or two 'P's. Once you can find those, then you can figure out the alphabet." His eyes got wide as he peered at the page.

"What is it?" Natasha asked.

"It could be an Atbash cipher."

Natasha and Veronica looked at each other, then back at Derrick.

"What's an Atbash cipher?" Natasha asked.

"It's another substitution cipher, but the last letter of the alphabet is really the first letter and things run in reverse. So 'Z' is 'A' and 'Y' is 'B' and so on."

"Was Atbash a person?"

Derrick glanced at Veronica. "I don't know, maybe."

"How do you know all of this stuff?" Veronica seemed to look at him for the first time. Really *look* at him.

Derrick felt himself starting to blush and looked again at Nixon. "I read it in a book somewhere. I don't remember."

"You read all of that in books?"

Now it was Derrick's turn to look at Veronica. He realized that she was an ex-gangbanger from Los Angeles and probably hadn't grown up in a home where Sundays could be whiled away reading a book. He almost said something sarcastic, but instead he just nodded. "Sure. No telling what I've read that may be useful." He examined the first page closely and eventually shook his head. "Nah. Not an Atbash. Too bad, really. It would have been the easiest thing."

"Yeah, too bad," Veronica echoed.

"Hey," Natasha said, getting everyone's attention. "Do you think Grandpa Laz knew what was going on in Bombay Beach and wrote about it in this book?"

The three of them gazed at the book with new respect. If it did have the secrets to what was going on here, then they could finally see if the locals were right about it being a government conspiracy. That there was a book lent credence to that idea. After all, why would their grandpa go to so much effort just to write about ordinary stuff? Codes such as these weren't meant for normal diaries. They were meant to keep secrets.

Than a thought occurred to Derrick. Was it possible that his grandfather was killed *because* of this book?

He glanced wide-eyed at Natasha, who shared his expression. She'd evidently thought the same thing.

The scratching had gone on for hours. Abigail stood in the doorway to the bathroom, her hand shaking as she held the pistol. It was impossibly heavy, but she was terrified to lay it down. It was the only thing that could save her if the creature burst through, so she had to hold it. She couldn't afford to put it down for even a moment.

Trudie lay beneath the window. She hadn't moved for hours. She was barely breathing, yellow bile staining the fur around her mouth. The chocolate had hurt her more than Abigail had anticipated. All she'd wanted to do was feed her poor Trudie, take away the edge of hunger for a bit.

Abigail had known that dogs were allergic to the candy, but she'd had no idea the allergy was this severe. That she blamed herself was an understatement. She looked in the mirror and saw a dog killer.

So as she stood holding the pistol to protect herself, other uses for the weapon came to mind, ideas creeping in under her determination to survive. If she made it through this crazy episode, would she be able to live with the knowledge that she'd killed her own dog? Would she be able to live with that truth?

That there was nothing she could do made her want to scream. What was this creature to hold her trapped in her own home? If it wasn't for this thing clawing through her floor this never would have happened.

She thought again of Trudie begging her over and over, whining, starving, entreating her for just one small morsel to eat. Abigail had given the dog one piece, then another – only two pieces really. Maybe three.

Abigail was so caught up in her miserable reverie that she almost missed the fact that the scratching had stopped. She glanced over her shoulder at Trudie who still lay beneath the window. The door to the room was still locked, the deadbolt secure. She could see a bulge beneath the mauve carpet where the creature had been working at the floor beside the toilet.

Then a hand burst through. Mottled-green skin tipped with hard gray nails tore at the carpet, ripping pieces away as the hole opened larger. Soon an entire arm wedged through, the hole widening quickly as a shoulder pushed through behind it.

Abigail brought the pistol up and held it with two hands. She aimed down the barrel like her husband had told her to and pulled the trigger.

The gun jumped. The explosion seemed impossibly loud in the small space. The back of the toilet exploded, sending shards of white porcelain and water raining across the room.

The creature continued undeterred.

She fired again, this time taking out the toilet bowl. Water sprayed from the pipes, drenching the opposite wall.

Still the creature came. It pushed its head through, hands tearing at the carpet and wood to enlarge the hole.

She fired again.

Part of the creature's lower jaw disappeared in a mist blood and bone.

But it wasn't even slowed.

She had to run.

She ran first to Trudie and scooped the dog into her arms. As she headed for the door, she saw the creature pushing its torso up through the floor, yellow eyes fixated on her. Was it the only one? As she unlocked the deadbolt and slammed open the door, she knew it was too late to ask that question.

She ran into the hall, dog in one hand, pistol in the other. She slid around the corner of the kitchen on the linoleum floor, hitting the refrigerator with her shoulder, caught her balance and began to fumble with the locks on the door to the back yard. She couldn't get her hands to work properly.

She dropped to all fours, shoved Trudie through the doggie door, and began to crawl through herself. She heard the sound of crashing come from her bedroom. She knew she had only had a few seconds. Moving as fast as she could, she pushed herself through the tiny square door, but dropped her pistol.

She reached back inside and searched blindly for it. The sound of pounding feet got closer. Her fingers brushed against the dustbin.

She could hear the creature's wheezing breaths from the other side of the door. She knew she should flee, but she needed the gun. Suddenly she felt the skin of the creature, screamed and yanked her hand back. It held it for a moment, but then her fingers slipped free and she fell backwards. As she found her balance, she saw the top of the creature's head as it began to follow her out the door.

Abigail scrambled to her feet, grabbed Trudie and hurtled down the stairs. It was night. Late. The only sounds she heard were from the occasional generator. She glanced back, running, and saw the creature glaring at her as it climbed out of the flap and got to its feet, half its jaw missing.

Oh, if only she hadn't dropped the gun.

The fence separating her home from the Klostermans' stopped her momentarily, it was so high that her old legs refused to clear it. So she leaned over the fence and flopped into the yard, winding herself and almost losing her grasp on Trudie.

Somehow she managed to get to her knees. She wasn't used to this sort of activity. She crawled as quickly as she could. The Klosterman Kid's doghouse rose up before her.

She found the bolt that kept it closed at night, lifted it, pried open the door and slid inside. She fell several feet; the floor was much lower than ground level. She was again surprised as she landed softly atop padded carpet.

Curling into a ball, she held Trudie to her chest and began to rock back and forth. She'd run as far as she could. All she waited for now was for the creature to break down the door. But it never happened. The creature never came. Her sobs gradually subsided until she heard the sound of heavy breathing. In the darkness all she could think of was a bear in a deep, dark cave. But she wasn't in a cave, and nor was it a bear she was hearing. She was in the doghouse and the sound could only be coming from the Klosterman Kid.

She wondered fearfully what he'd do to her.

She wondered if she was any better off than before.

CHAPTER THIRTEEN

Patrick woke drenched in moonlight and flies. He was slow to come around, his mind foggy with nightmares of birthday parties, bloody cakes, and *Ode to Billy Joe* playing unceasingly in the background while everything spun as if he was on a crazy carousel.

He'd gotten a mouthful of sand while sleeping and the grit was caught between his teeth and his gums. He tried to spit, but his mouth was too dry. He managed to open his eyes. He was on the shore. In his hand, he held a single card, from an Easter when he was fifteen; he searched his memory and wondered why he'd kept that one, but couldn't figure it out.

He rolled to his knees and vomited onto the sand. Drool and saliva dripped from his mouth. There was more in his stomach that wanted out, but it wouldn't come. Until the stench of what had already come up hit his nostrils.

It took a few minutes for him to collect himself. As he got to his feet, still a little unsteady, the moon slid behind a mountain of clouds, leaving him in gray darkness. On the ground in front of him were the remnants of a fire – pieces of cards, some singed, most blackened beyond legibility, in a pile that had been soaked by the tide sometime after he'd passed out.

Patrick glanced at the card in his hand, and let it fall to the ground. Then he thought better of it, picked it up and shoved it in his back pocket. He looked around and spied the Old Crow bottle wedged in the sand like it had brought a message from a deserted island. There was an inch of booze left in it. He glared at the offending bottle for a moment, then tossed back the rest of the warm brown liquid.

A sound came from down the beach.

He switched his grip on the bottle, holding it by the neck, and peered into the darkness, but couldn't see a thing through the grit and tears in his eyes.

The noise came again. Several people dragging something huge, a muffled curse, a harsh command.

He blinked the tears away and saw several black shapes dragging a boat ashore. They were wearing masks and black clothes. One turned toward Patrick as he hit the sand and lay flat, but they appeared not to see him. After a few moments, they left the boat and headed inland.

Patrick found himself following them. Part of him said it was a bad idea, but he wanted to see what was going on.

He stumbled twice as the wet sand gripped his shoes, but was too far away for them to hear. He crept as close as he could along the seawall, then, when he thought the coast was clear, climbed over and slid down the other side. He tried to land on his feet, but when he hit the ground, he fell on his hip, crying out in pain.

The men stopped and squatted at the sound. One turned in his direction.

Patrick kept very still. He lay against the seawall and hoped that his form would blend into the darkness.

Then came another sound, this time from the opposite direction. The men turned toward what sounded like a bottle skittering down the asphalt street. One brought up a rifle. The sight of it sucked the air from Patrick's lungs. The man sighted down the length of the weapon.

A drunken voice spoiled the quiet with a refrain of *Now or Never*. The next verse was replaced with the sound of retching, then the sound of a gate opening and the clatter of cans as the Romanian waded through his alarm system. The trailer door closed and Patrick breathed easier.

The man with the rifle lowered his weapon and the three were once again on their way.

Patrick followed them for another half a block before they came to a burned-out hulk that had once been a double-wide. The top deck was nothing more than twisted wood. The chairs had melted to the roof.

The leader used a radio; the static-laced conversation was too soft to understand.

Patrick heard someone running behind him. He dove into the nearest yard, wedging himself beneath a propane tank painted like a jack-o'-lantern.

Three more men raced past, dressed in black like the others, carrying a net between them. They ran to the other three and, after a moment's conversation, began to move towards the open glass door of the trailer.

Patrick shifted to make himself more comfortable. His hangover had all but disappeared. He knew he shouldn't be seeing what he was seeing. If they were to catch him, there was no telling what would happen. The feeling both thrilled and terrified him.

The three men continued toward the opening. They held the net between them, as if preparing to capture a wild animal. The halogen lights on their helmets came on, revealing something large retreating into the darkness of the trailer.

The two riflemen took positions on either side of the men with the net. After a moment of hesitation, the net was thrown at the creature hiding in the trailer, but it missed. As the men were retrieving the net, a creature burst forward and knocked one of them down, before fleeing back into the shadows.

The fallen man stood slowly, clearly shaken. His fellows, ready once more, feinted once, then threw the net deep into the shadows, and the one in the middle hauled on a rope and jerked it tight.

Something was struggling in the trailer, furiously straining and rolling until the strangers closed in on the net.

The lights were turned off and they headed back the way they'd come, directly towards Patrick's hiding place. He tried to squeeze further underneath the tank.

They came towards him in single file. The rifles came first, stocks firmly against their shoulders as the weapons swept back and forth along the street. Next came the two dragging the net. The thing inside writhed and struggled furiously. A third man held a rope extending from the net, keeping it taut. Last came the leader.

As the net was dragged past him, Patrick risked a glance. What he saw was nothing like what he'd expected. It was a man, or what had been a man. His mottled green skin was peeling away, revealing putrid gray flesh beneath. He looked dead, except for his eyes, which glowed an unearthly yellow. The thing groaned once as it passed Patrick, but thankfully the men in black weren't paying attention.

Patrick closed his eyes, desperate not to be discovered, and the footsteps faded in the distance. Patrick relaxed. All but the last man slipped over the seawall, presumably going for a boat. Once they were gone, the leader removed a rubber hood. He looked vaguely familiar, but from this distance, Patrick couldn't be sure. He took off his jacket as well, revealing a T-shirt beneath.

He began walking back towards Patrick, striding purposefully and whistling a sea shanty.

As he approached, Patrick recognized Hopkins. The man turned his head and looked right at Patrick as he passed, but didn't seem to see him. Patrick remained stock still, and Hopkins turned his head and continued on. Soon he was far down the street, the shanty echoing softly in the night.

Patrick pushed himself away from the tank and struggled to his feet, his legs leaden and crampy. As he shifted to get the blood back into them, he clicked the bottle against the tank. The sound rang through the night like the tolling of a bell. Patrick froze.

How he'd maintained his grip on the bottle, he didn't know. He dropped it like it was poison and, without waiting to see if the noise drew anyone, rounded the burned-out trailer and ran, not stopping until he was home. The door was locked; he knocked once, then instantly regretted it. He stood at the door praying that he hadn't woken anyone.

Tomorrow morning he'd talk to his kids and tell them what he'd seen. He'd spent more than enough time feeling sorry for himself. Now he needed to act like a man, like a father. He needed to stop feeding his depression. Bottom line, he needed to stop drinking.

He stood and stared at the trailer for a long time, working through it all. After a while, he stumbled over to the restaurant and poked around the back, eventually finding a window that had been left open. He slept in a booth with his legs curled beneath him, dreaming of Hopkins and the green man in the net...

A Chevy Suburban rumbles down the street and stops at the front of the restaurant. Two men exit the SUV and kick open the front door, wood splintering and flying into the room. The men shine flashlights into the darkness until they find what they are looking for. They rush to Patrick, hit him, grab him, throw him into the backseat of the SUV and roar away.

When they hit him the second time the dream dissolves. Only he's no longer in the restaurant curled up comfortably on the booth. He's in the SUV with two masked men. Hopkins is behind the wheel, his eyes laughing at Patrick in the rearview mirror.

There was *no way* Natasha was going to get any sleep. She'd heard her father banging on the door and wasn't about to let him in. She was pissed at how he'd fallen so hard off the wagon. They needed him to be a dad right now, not a drunk.

He hadn't set the most perfect example growing up. The

idea that he could go missing for a few days and then return as the perfect dad had always confused her. But as she grew older, she understood that her father had a problem; something was missing in his life and he continually tried to fill the emptiness with alcohol.

After she watched her father leave, she decided that she needed some fresh air, and went up on the roof to lay on one of the lounge chairs and stare at the stars. She tried to find sleep once more, but the quiet night was ruined by the roar of an SUV passing by the house doing at least eighty miles an hour. It raced towards sump pump #2, then down the access road to the desalination plant.

She shook her head. The first sign of life in this dead little town and it was someone late to work.

Natasha pulled a chair to the telescope, deciding to take in the town, just to see what she could see. Not that she was intent on spying on her neighbors, but it would be nice to observe someone having a normal life for a change, even in this second cousin to a normal town.

But not everything was normal.

She could make out the inside of the Romanian's home, his front room lit like a stage. He was passed out on the couch, fully clothed, a blow-up doll in his arms.

She could distinguish Veronica sitting on her couch and watching a late night movie in black and white.

On the other side of town, Kim Johnson stood on her rooftop porch completely naked. Cloaked only in moonlight and the warm salty air, her arms were open to the sky as if she were praying. Even from this distance Natasha could make out the tattoos covering the other woman's body. What had they said about her? She was a priest, or a reverend, or whatever they called the leader of the local church. She didn't say much, but she always seemed to be in the thick of things.

Lu Shu worked by a small lamp in his garage, repairing his nets. Natasha appraised the old man and wondered if he might be the right type for her Auntie Lin. She wasn't beyond matchmaking, especially for the old woman who'd been everything but a real mother to her. How interesting would it be to have an Auntie Lin and an Uncle Lu?

Natasha thought about this for a time as she looked in on every trailer within her vision. Here and there she saw signs of life but, for the most part, the town was asleep.

So she turned the telescope on the sea. First she scanned the shoreline to see if there was anything out of the ordinary. Try as she might, it was too far for her to really make out anything. The lights on the far shore were dim in the hot night haze. She knew that more people lived on the other bank than on this one. There'd actually been planned communities, laid out in parcels, bought and paid for, then left empty when the sea had begun to rot. How many hopes and dreams had been shattered because no one back in the 1950s had been able to foresee what would happen to a lake with no outlet?

She was about to pull away when the sea flashed a brilliant green for a split second. It happened so fast she wasn't even sure it had been real. She rubbed her eyes and looked again. The sea flashed once more. This time she kept her eye against the eyepiece and saw a third and final flash. She remained fixed to the telescope for about a minute before she sat back and regarded the placid sea.

What had that been?

She leaned back in her chair. Everything had been so *odd* since she'd arrived.

Natasha slept for a time, but was woken by the sound of buses passing in the night. She peered through the telescope, her eyes bleary.

The moon illuminated two buses chugging slowly along the edge of town, down Isle of Palms Avenue and towards the access road to the plant, exactly like the ones she'd seen before. They crossed the quay and entered the plant through a gate. She recognized Hopkins standing there with a clipboard. He seemed impatient, speaking into a radio as he stared back down the access road.

Natasha followed his gaze. The seawall must be blocking his view of the highway, but she was able to see it just fine. Sure enough, there was one last bus, but it seemed to be having problems. Smoke billowed from the engine as it jerked and jolted forward; it stopped and started, with a great grinding of gears.

Like the others, the bus was an unmarked, uniform dark grey with tinted windows. That three busloads of people had come, in addition to the other two buses the night before, suggested that there was more going on at the desalination plant than anyone knew about.

She corrected that thought: more than anyone except the Mad Scientist knew about. Natasha was convinced that he knew what was going on. She would talk to him tomorrow morning, and bring Veronica and Derrick with her. That would be safest. What could one man do against all three of them?

The bus continued to limp forward in jerks and starts, passing sump pump #2 to the access road, where it coughed, choked, and finally died. Smoke poured from the engine.

The door opened and a man in camouflage fatigues jumped out and sprinted the two hundred yards to the waiting Hopkins. Shortly after the first man came another ten, twenty, then thirty men out of the bus; all dressed in uniforms and fleeing the bus. Each carried a dark green bag half his size, so their progress was much slower than the first one, who Natasha presumed was the driver. He was waving them on, urging them to follow him.

Why were they in such a hurry?

As if in answer to Natasha's question, man-shaped creatures surged from the water on the left side of the quay, scrambling up the embankment to the road to intercept the men. The driver looked like he was going to escape, but Hopkins closed the gate when he saw the creatures, locking it with an immense padlock and chain and flipping a switch on a nearby light pole.

Screams drew her attention back to the men from the bus. She squinted into the telescope to get a better look. The creatures moved fast, and all she could see was an arm here, a leg there, and brilliant yellow, glowing eyes.

She pulled back from the telescope, not believing what she was seeing. *Ohmygod ohmygod ohmygod.* Her heart beating in her throat, she again put her eye to the telescope.

She watched the hand-to-hand fighting. The soldiers seemed capable of defending themselves, kicking and punching accurately, but they had little or no effect. Each of them was overpowered and slammed to the ground, and the creatures followed them down, biting and gnawing...

Eating.

Her stomach turned. Bile leaped into her throat.

A sizzling snap drew her attention to the fence around the desalination plant. The driver had tried to climb it and was now sparking and jerking as electricity ran through him. He finally fell to the ground, his body smoking.

When Natasha looked back at the creatures, they were drawing their victims back into the water. The soldiers were still struggling. Within moments, it was all over.

The only thing left on the access road were the soldiers' bags and pools of blood.

Natasha realized she'd been holding her breath and released it, then gasped again.

One creature still remained. It stood in the bus's headlights, head cocked as if listening for something.

Then she noticed the soldier huddled behind the bus. He looked terrified, his hands covering his face. Even from where she stood, she could tell he was shaking. Her heart went out to him. She desperately wanted him to escape.

The creature approached the bus. Its wrinkled skin was mottled green, and black hair lay lank against a balding skull. The nails of its hand were long and malformed. It was bare-chested, but tattered and ruined pants covered its crotch down to its knees and it wore black boots.

The soldier scooted to the left side of the bus and seemed about to peer around to see if anything was coming.

The creature came around the same side and Natasha knew that if the soldier were to look, the creature would most certainly see him. She began to repeat to herself over and over: "Don't look. Don't Look. Don't look."

As if he had heard her, the soldier backed away, glanced upward and saw a pair of handholds on the engine access panel.

He pulled himself onto the roof of the bus, where he lay perfectly flat and still.

The creature suddenly sprinted the length of the bus and rounded the corner to the back, but it stopped when it found nothing there. It cocked its head.

The sound of an air horn tore through the night, and the creature turned and sprinted for the water. It dove awkwardly, without using its arms, and was soon lost beneath the tide.

The soldier let himself down, grabbed his bag and headed towards the entrance to the quay. Sump pump #2 chose that moment to belch; both Natasha and the soldier jumped at the sound.

The air horn cut through the night again, and the gate opened. A strange military vehicle with no windows and heavy armor exited. Two uniformed men came from the back and set about picking up the bags left behind and preparing the bus to tow it inside the fenced area.

They found a soldier near the water's edge. He moved slightly as the uniformed men approached. But instead of being helped to his feet, one of the men put a pistol to his head and pulled the trigger.

Natasha jerked her head back in surprise.

When she looked again, the body had been removed and the vehicle was returning from whence it came.

Natasha tried to find where the surviving soldier had gone, but she'd lost him when her attention had been drawn to the vehicle. If he was smart, he'd hide inside one of the abandoned trailers.

But which one?

She settled into her chair, drew her legs beneath her and sat staring at the night sky for a long time, staring into the night sky and listening for the creatures. The last thing she thought about before her dreams stole her away was what Veronica and Derrick would say when she told them what she'd seen.

CHAPTER FOURTEEN

All her muscles hurt, burning beneath her skin. She wanted to sit up, to change position, but she didn't think she could even move. It took a moment for her to remember where she was: the creature, her flight, her destination.

And Trudie.

She looked at the unmoving dog in her arms. Her little tongue stuck out from her mouth, her eyes were mere slits, her chest didn't move, and the skin beneath her fur felt cold and hard.

Abigail drew in a rattling breath and sobbed, whispering the dog's name. The worst of it was it was her fault.

Her sobs caught in her throat as she felt a hand press against her head.

Another hand reached for Trudie and pulled the dog free from her grasp.

She had no choice but to let it go. She remained still, straining her ears to hear what was happening, and was shocked to hear the sound of a child making cat sounds to her dead dog.

"Meow. Meow."

As strange as it sounded, the tiny fake cat sounds soothed her for a time. So she listened.

Natasha had been aching to leave all morning, but Auntie Lin had her and Derrick moving furniture and cleaning the inside of the trailer. Natasha had thought it clean, but it wasn't to Auntie Lin's standards, so the greater part of the morning was spent wiping down walls, baseboards and the floors.

Derrick had known that something had happened; Natasha had tried several times to tell him, but it seemed like every time she'd been able to get a moment alone with him, Auntie Lin had popped into the room with yet another cleaning directive. Auntie Lin was probably Natasha's closest confidante, but she couldn't see herself telling the old woman about the creatures she'd witnessed the night before.

She realized that she should be scared; and she was, a little bit. But more than scared, the prospect of the creatures excited her, for the first time since she'd left Pennsylvania. As morbid and terrible as it seemed, Natasha wanted to see these creatures again and find out what they were about.

On a more sobering note, her father hadn't come home last night. Although she doubted something bad had happened, she wasn't about to leave Bombay Beach without him, no matter how troubled he was, no matter how terrible he was at being a father. The fact was that he was their father and the only parent they had. Natasha dreamed of a day when he'd come to terms with his problems, and wanted to be there for it.

Every now and then, during the course of the morning, she'd stop and think about what she'd seen, reliving the terror she'd felt for the soldiers when the creatures had surged from the sea, while simultaneously trying to put it in a context she could understand.

It all just seemed so unreal. Perhaps part of the reason she wasn't as afraid as she should be was because of her distance from the events. She hadn't been down there on the ground with the creatures when they'd attacked. She'd viewed everything through the telescope's lens and, by doing so, had removed herself from the event. It had been little different from watching it on television, except that what she'd seen was real.

Or was it? her fickle mind tickled back.

They worked until ten o'clock, and then Auntie Lin left, with the reminder that they'd need Natasha's and Derrick's help for lunch at the restaurant.

So now, with Derrick close behind her, Natasha made a beeline for Veronica's trailer. Not that the girl would know what to do, but she was Natasha's only real friend in town.

As it turned out, Veronica wasn't home and her aunt didn't know where she was.

Derrick kept pestering Natasha to tell him what had happened, but she just told him to shut up and let her think. Kim Johnson had been on her roof last night as well. Maybe the older woman had seen something.

Natasha grabbed Derrick and they ran the four blocks to a quadruple-wide trailer, so big it was square. The sign read *Lot's Church of Redemption*, and a bunch of smaller signs plastered over the structure's bright yellow siding asked if you wanted to be "Born Again."

Natasha knocked for several minutes before giving up.

So much for *that* idea.

She knew Veronica's uncle worked for the Duvall Brothers, so they tried there next.

Half of the inside of the giant tent they used as an office was filled to the ceiling with blocks of compressed salt. A set of workbenches ran along one wall holding various tools and several dive tanks. Rico Duvall was sitting at a large light table going over a map of the bottom of the Salton Sea. The area nearest Bombay Beach was colored in red hash marks with the words "RESTRICTED AREA" marked prominently across the space.

Rico looked up when he heard them enter and greeted them. He told Natasha that his brother and Veronica's uncle had gone out harvesting salt in the region just south of Bombay Beach and wouldn't be back until mid-afternoon. He didn't know where Veronica was.

Natasha was disappointed. She'd been so excited at the prospect of telling Veronica about last night, but now it all felt kind of flat. She and Derrick walked out of the salt warehouse and into the heat of the day.

And there was Veronica, walking down the street with Carrie and three of her kids, having an animated conversation. She waved at Natasha, said something to the Carrie, and ran over to join them. She wore white shorts that ran past her knees, a long white tank top that could have been her uncle's, and basketball shoes.

"What's up?" Then: "What happened?" She looked at Derrick.

"I don't know. She won't tell me."

"I just wanted to wait until we're all together." Natasha glanced around. "Come on. Let's go somewhere cooler so I can tell you what I've been waiting to tell you."

They went to Veronica's room. This time Derrick was too interested in what secret his sister was keeping to look at the pictures.

So it was, with Veronica and Derrick sitting on the bed with their mouths hanging open, that Natasha relayed what she'd seen. Awed, they grilled her, asking her questions, which she answered as completely as she could. Finally Natasha announced that their next step had to be finding the missing soldier.

"Do you think he's still here somewhere?" Derrick asked.

"Where else could he be? Look around you," Veronica said. "This is the middle of the middle of nowhere. That's exactly why my Mom sent me here in the first place. Trust me, there's nowhere to go from here."

"We have to find him," Natasha insisted. "You know that Hopkins and his men will go from house to house looking for him tonight. Then it will only be a matter of time."

Veronica held up a manicured hand. "Wait. No one has asked the most important question."

Natasha raised her eyebrows. "What's that?"

"Who all is involved with this? You said Hopkins is involved, which doesn't surprise me. People have suspected him of bad things for a long time. But who else? The Mad Scientist? The Deputy Sheriff? The Duvalls? I mean, if there are creatures in the water then this is big. Super big. There have to be a lot of people involved. It can't just be that Hopkins guy."

"We can leave out my dad and Auntie Lin, and probably Maude too," Natasha said. "We weren't even around when this started. The only one here was my grandfather. I bet if we're ever able to decipher that notebook, we'd learn that strange things have been happening for a long time."

"Then leave out my aunt and my uncle too," Veronica said.

"Not so fast," Derrick countered. "Doesn't your uncle spend all of his time on the water? If there are creatures out there, how come he doesn't get attacked? Maybe he knows something."

"Fuck that," Veronica snarled. "No way could my uncle ever be involved in something like that. He's given up a lot for me."

"But we can't rule them out," Derrick persisted.

Veronica surged to her feet, eyes narrowed and fists clenched.

"Whoa! Stop, Veronica!" Natasha held her hand out. "We're not saying they are involved. We're just pointing out that it could be anyone. I mean, don't forget Lu Shu. He fishes every day too. Or Kim Johnson. She runs the local church."

"Or Carrie Loughnane for that matter. Or that Elvis guy with the cans. Or even that guy we saw in the golf cart with the hooks for hands. What's his name?

Veronica stared at them, steaming. Finally she said, "Gerald. His name's Gerald." Veronica breathed through her teeth for a few seconds, as if to relax. "Okay. You guys have made your point." She put her hands on her waist, and began pacing back and forth. "It could be anyone – Will, the Duvalls, Maude, the Mad Scientist, even Kristov the Elvis guy could be involved. We don't know so we can't tell anyone about this."

"You can scratch the Mad Scientist off that list. I know that he isn't involved," Derrick stated, crossing his arms.

"What makes you so certain?" Veronica crossed her arms

too. "I thought we just came to the conclusion that it could be anybody."

"Almost anyone, yeah, but not the Mad Scientist." Looking at the two girls, both waiting expectantly for an answer, he added, "It's obvious because of the hand we saw him working on. It must have belonged to one of the creatures. Why would he work on it in secret in his laboratory if he was part of the whole thing and had access to the plant?"

Both girls stared at him, then Natasha nodded.

"Okay then, the Mad Scientist goes on the good-guy list," she said. "Auntie Lin and my dad are on it already, but we should add Maude too. I don't think she's involved."

"Why do you think that?" Veronica turned her stare on Natasha. "Her boyfriend is dead and her girlfriend is missing. Of course she could be involved."

Natasha groaned. "I can't believe that." She remembered how warm the woman had been to her when she'd made grilled shrimp on the deck of their trailer their second night in Bombay Beach. "I refuse to believe that." Then a thought came to her. "We need to warn people so they can –"

"No!" Veronica hissed. "That's the last thing you want to do. You tell anyone and Hopkins will find out. He probably has snitches all over the place. He probably even has snitches who don't know they're snitches, just passing information along because they think it's the right thing to do. And do you really think your father will keep quiet about this? Do you really think he won't try and call in the state police or the FBI or someone?"

"How's he going to call? There's no cell phone service and no internet here. If someone wanted to, they could cut the telephone lines too, like they do in movies. Hell, we don't even know where he is."

"So let's say your father resurfaces and finds out and then tries to get the word out and fails. That makes the situation better? He'd be a sitting duck."

Natasha saw the grave truth of Veronica's words. "And we don't know to what level this goes. There's no telling who in the government has knowledge of this." Then she paused; she'd been holding the question back, but now seemed the perfect time to ask it. "You mentioned before that you didn't go outside at night because of what's out there," she asked, carefully. "Was it these creatures you were afraid of?"

Veronica smiled for a moment, then let it slowly fall as she noticed that Natasha was deadly serious. "Stories," she finally said. "Rumors. There wasn't anything concrete, just people saying, 'watch out after dark,' or 'beware of the green.' Just stupid stuff that was enough to make you look behind you at night."

"So you didn't know about this already?" Natasha asked.

"No. Just what people talked about. People talk about a lot of things around here."

"That guy Frank told me to beware of the green," Natasha said. "And Kristov told me to watch out for monsters. I thought they were drunk and stupid."

"They probably were, but it makes you wonder, right? How much people really know about what's going on."

"So what are we going to do?" Derrick asked.

Natasha clapped her hands. "First we're going to find that soldier. He's probably scared and hungry. Then we ask him what he's doing here in the first place. My guess is they brought these soldiers in to fight the creatures, so he probably knows something about what's going on."

"Doesn't sound like they did too well last night," Veronica said.

"Last night they didn't have any guns. If the bus hadn't broken down, then they'd have stood more of a chance." Natasha snapped her mouth shut and frowned. "Do you think Hopkins has Gert?" She turned to Derrick. "Do you think he has Dad?"

Derrick suddenly looked young and frightened. "I don't know. Maybe. Unless they're –"

"Don't even say it," Natasha snapped.

Derrick looked down.

The silence settled over them

Veronica put a hand on Natasha's arm. "Come on. There's no sense worrying about things over which you have no control. You're right, we need to find that soldier. He has more answers than we have questions."

Natasha thought about Auntie Lin and how she'd wanted them to help with the lunch service. They were already late and Natasha really didn't want to help out in the restaurant anyway.

"What are we waiting for?" Derrick's face brightened.

"Nothing," Natasha said.

"Nothing." Veronica smiled as she readjusted her pony tail. "Just let me get some things from the fridge for him to eat. He's sure to be hungry."

Veronica grabbed three green chili tamales, a can of Mountain Dew, a vanilla pudding pack and a plastic spoon, and tossed them all into a bag. Natasha told her to add one of the bottles of water. On their way out the door, Veronica's aunt asked why they were taking the food, and Veronica said it was for a picnic. Her auntie made a comment about the nutritional value of their choices, but the kids were gone before she could finish.

It was already two in the afternoon; the sun beat down from a cloudless sky. Even so, they began their search by sump pump #2. Veronica climbed the stairs to sneak a peek at the quay. When she came back down she said that she couldn't see any blood, although there were a lot of flies on the road.

They worked together, deciding to start at the quay and move their way inward towards the center of town. There'd been some talk of separating, but they knew that might be dangerous. Natasha figured that when they found the soldier he was going to be scared. The last thing they needed was to be alone in a dark, abandoned trailer with a man who was scared and had been trained to kill.

So the idea was to announce themselves whenever they went into a trailer. Deciding who would go first was another matter. Natasha and Derrick thought that Veronica should always go in first.

"Oh, sure, send in the Mexican."

Derrick snickered. "You're Mexican?"

"Veronica Lopez sound Chinese to you?" She sniffed.

"I was just kidding," Derrick said.

"Not because you're Mexican," Natasha pointed out. "Because you're from L.A."

"Just to set the record straight, we don't have creatures coming out of the Pacific Ocean attacking soldiers in L.A., so I don't think I have any particular expertise."

"But you've been involved in..." Natasha let it hang. "You know."

"What do I know? I've been involved in what?"

"Gangs."

"Yeah," Derrick repeated, "Gangs."

"Oh, hell. Gimme that!" Veronica grabbed the flashlight from Natasha. She stomped towards the first trailer, mumbling to herself something about how kids from Pennsylvania couldn't find their asses with both hands if it weren't for a certain Mexican chick. She shone the light inside. "Hey soldier? You in there? I'm a bad ass Mexican gangbanger who's going to make enchiladas out of your ass if you don't come out." She turned to Natasha. "Is that better?"

"Uh... I think you scared him," Derrick murmured.

Veronica shook her head and frowned. She mumbled under her breath as she stepped through the broken front door and onto shag carpet that had been new a long time ago, before disco was dead.

Natasha and Derrick followed close behind.

Veronica played the light across the room and into the kitchen. Spider webs dominated the room, and a thick layer of dust coated everything. Tattered cheap paintings hugged paneled walls. The once white popcorn ceiling was gray. As they stepped into the trailer, the vibrations sent a plume of dust trickling down from the ceiling, making them sneeze.

The trailer was in a standard configuration, with three doors coming off a short hallway. The two on the side were a second smaller bedroom and a bathroom, and the door on the end led to the master bedroom. They checked each room and found them empty.

The second and third trailers they searched were burned-out tin hulks, with the residue of those who'd once lived there scattered around the wooden floors, singed and sodden souvenirs of better times. By the time they searched the fourth trailer, the idea of going into one of the dark and dingy interiors no longer sparked fear in Natasha's heart.

Now Derrick wanted to lead the way. They had to pass two occupied trailers first – Lu Shu's and Carrie Loughnane's. On the other side of the ex-cheerleader's home lay a yellow and white trailer half covered by buffalo grass. Golf cart tracks had worn a path through the weeds to the rusted remnants of the doorframe. Although the windows were broken, the screens behind them covered with cobwebs, it was clear that someone had been here recently.

Yet Derrick was undaunted. Holding his flashlight before him, he turned and grinned infectiously as he stepped boldly into the front room.

And stopped.

He stared at something in the darkness, his light fixed somewhere deep inside the trailer.

Natasha called to him twice, but he refused to answer. She saw his knees buckle and called to him again.

Veronica stepped inside, glanced once down the hall, grabbed Derrick and jerked him out of the doorway. They fell together in the weeds. Veronica tried helping Derrick to his feet, but he was staring blankly at the sky.

"What is it?" Natasha asked. "What did you see?"

Veronica shook her head as she glanced worriedly at the doorway. "Not here," she whispered.

Together the girls got Derrick up and stumbled into the middle of the street. The distance was enough to snap Derrick out of his stupor.

"What is it, Derrick?" Natasha pushed his lank hair out of his eyes. "What did you see?"

He gasped, and wiped his eyes. "I felt something. There was something inside."

Natasha looked at Veronica.

"I felt it too," Veronica said. "I thought I saw one of those things in there."

"What things?" Natasha asked.

"Your *creatures*. I could just make it out standing in the shadows of the master bedroom. Watching us. *Waiting* for us." Veronica shook her head. "It was hard to see. Maybe it was nothing."

"It had no face," Derrick whispered.

Natasha made a move to go inside the trailer, but both Veronica and Derrick grabbed at her.

"You can't go." Derrick shook his head. "The soldier isn't in there."

"How can you be so sure?"

"I'm sure. Trust me."

She jerked her arms free. "Fine. Let's just check the next trailer."

The lot next to the yellow and white trailer was empty. It had been cleared long ago and only held the detritus that the wind had blown on it, trash captured by the weeds.

Beside the lot stood an empty trailer painted in shades of blue. A faded logo of a flock of birds flew forever on the edge across the front door, their painted wings flaking away. The trailer's door was closed.

"Do you want to go in first again?" Natasha held the flashlight out to Derrick.

He shook his head.

Natasha turned the light to the door and tried to shine it through the small window set in the middle, with little luck. It looked as if there was a curtain blocking the flashlight's beam. She tried the doorknob, and opened the door an increment, then glanced around and beckoned the others to follow her. "Anyone in here?" she asked loudly. "If there is, don't be afraid. We're not here to hurt you." Taking a deep breath, she pushed the door open the rest of the way and stepped inside.

The living room had once had a mural – a painting of the galaxy – on one wall, now marred by time and dust. In the kitchen, the filthy refrigerator stood half open.

Natasha turned to her left and peered down the hall. It was laid out like all the other trailers.

"Hello? Can you hear me?"

The sound of something shifting down the hall made her jump. She thought she saw something round and black at floor level suddenly disappear from view. Was it a boot? Had the soldier been lying against a wall with his legs extended, or was it one of the creatures?

She waited a few moments until her heartbeat returned to normal. Then she called, "My name is Natasha. I saw what happened last night. I... we... live here and want to stop what's happening. We want to help you."

Natasha frowned. She sounded like an idiot.

Still no response.

She tried another tack.

"We have some food for you. I know you're hungry. Probably thirsty, too. We have a Mountain Dew and some water. Do you want some?"

Natasha heard the almost imperceptible sound of fabric brushing against the rug in the other room. Other than that, there was no response. Veronica and Derrick had entered, sticking close to each other. Derrick glanced fearfully down the hallway.

"I think he's here," Natasha whispered.

"Are you sure?" Veronica's eyes widened.

Natasha shrugged. She couldn't be positive, but she felt like he was the one back there making the noise.

"Listen, I know you're back there. I can hear you, so there's no reason to hide." She waited. Nothing. "We're here to help, but come nightfall, either the people from the plant or the creatures are going to come after you." She paused again, but still nothing. "So you can face me or you can face the creatures. And I'm just a girl. So how about it?"

A groan came from the master bedroom. It was followed by a scraping sound as if someone were using the wall to help them stand, sliding their back up for support. "Who are you?" came a weak raspy voice.

Natasha felt her heart leap.

"Natasha Oliver. We own the Space Station Restaurant here in Bombay Beach. I'm here to help. Can we come in?"

"Who else?"

Natasha turned and was about to reply when she saw Veronica point to herself and shake her head. Natasha started to say something, but stopped when Veronica shook her head more violently. Then she got it.

"Just me and my brother," Natasha said.

"Hi. I'm Derrick," Derrick said.

"Come on then. Slowly."

The voice sounded sick. For the first time, Natasha felt a twinge of fear. What if it was some kind of disease that turned the people into those creatures? It happened in the movies.

Derrick prodded her in the back.

She grabbed the bag of food and water and walked slowly down the hall. She entered the room and found the soldier sagging in a corner. Derrick entered and stood in the doorway behind her, eyes wide.

The soldier stood about a foot taller than Natasha. Closely-cropped dark brown hair topped an angular, but not unpleasant face. His sand-colored camouflage uniform hung loosely on him, as if it was made for someone bigger. The duffel bag was at his feet and still bore the imprint of his head from when he'd been using it as a pillow. Her attention was drawn to his dirty hands, which kept opening and closing.

"Hi," she said.

He was appraising her just as she was him. He kept thrusting out his jaw.

"You have food?" he rasped.

Natasha looked at the bag in her hand, then offered it to him.

He stepped forward and snatched at it, then fell back against the wall. He looked inside and pulled out the water first, downed half of the liquid, and ripped into one of the tinfoil-covered tamales. He crammed two bites into his mouth, then chugged the rest of the water. He chewed furiously for a moment, before swallowing.

Then everything changed. He dropped the bag and fell to his knees. Water and pieces of tamale hit the floor in a sickly spatter. The soldier wretched again, rolled onto his back and clenched his stomach, wiping spittle from his face.

"It's the DTs," Veronica said from the doorway. When Natasha gave her a blank look, Veronica gestured toward the writhing soldier. "Look at him. He's an addict, and he's been one for a long time."

"An addict?"

"Look at his hands and face. Looks like he lost a lot of weight too. He's been using for a long time."

"What drug is he on?" Derrick said.

"Meth, crank, whatever you want to call it. Makes you feel like Superman for a while, then breaks you down until you can't even eat someone's homemade tamales. Some Superman he turned out to be."

"Kryptonite," whispered the soldier. "It's the kryptonite that's killing me."

Veronica rolled her eyes. "And he's a comedian to boot." She took his duffel bag, pawing through it while the soldier struggled to bring himself under control. "Not much here. A couple of changes of clothes, some comic books and a box of medals."

"Let me see those."

She passed the medals to Derrick.

He opened them and whistled. He mouthed a *wow* as he looked from the solider to the objects in his hand.

"Those are mine," the soldier said. He struggled to get to his feet, sliding himself up the wall. He licked his lips and wiped his face with the back of a hand. "I said, those are mine. I thought you were here to help me, but now you're stealing from me?"

"I was just looking, Mister." Derrick handed back the box.

"Are you okay?" Natasha asked.

"Yeah. Just not used to regular food." He glanced at the others. "It tasted good. Did you make this?"

"My auntie did," Veronica said.

"Tell your auntie she did good." When he got no response, he added, "You held back in the hallway to make sure I wasn't going to attack your friends, didn't you?"

Veronica nodded.

"Smart."

"Is what she said true?" Natasha asked.

"About the meth?" The soldier shrugged. "Sure. And I used to be Superman too. Now I'm just..."

Derrick used the opportunity when the man trailed off to ask, "Did you win those medals in the war?"

The soldier laughed hollowly. "You don't *win* a medal. You get one for surviving."

Derrick laughed with him for a moment, but then stopped when he saw the man's eyes.

"So what's your name?" Veronica asked.

"Metzger."

"Is that all your parents gave you? Just *Metzger*?"

"Shane. Shane is my first name." He looked down, realized that his hands were clenching and unclenching and stuck them into his pockets. "But everyone calls me Metzger."

"I'm Veronica. This is Natasha and this is her brother, Derrick. We're the Bombay Beach Welcoming Committee." She looked around to see if anyone would add anything. When they didn't, she opened her arms and declared in a mock-dramatic voice, "Welcome."

"Uh, thanks. I think."

"So what is that place you and your soldier buddies were being driven into last night?"

"Don't know. A bunch of us were in Track 3 Rehab for Meth Addiction. A Colonel came and enrolled us into a special program. He said we'd get clean and earn bonuses besides."

"Some special program," Veronica repeated. "Did he say it involved those creatures?"

Metzger stared at Veronica beneath heavy lids. "Of course not. They just said we'd get clean and never have to worry about it again. The Colonel told us we were going to be like astronauts. Lots of rigorous training, he said. He said we'd be astro-mechanics or some shit like that."

"Astro-mechanics." Derrick said. "What do you suppose one of those does?"

"Fixes astros?" Veronica said, then realized it sounded like a joke. "Seriously, what's an astro?"

"I think it means space or something like that. Like in astronomy." Natasha shook her head. The soldier was a piece of work. He looked like he was standing two inches from death's door. She'd only known one other drug addict before and she'd died in gym class her senior year. The soldier, Metzger, had the same hollowed eyes and cheeks as that girl had had. "I think they lied to you, Metzger. I think they had something else in mind."

They talked for the next few hours.

Natasha told him about her life in Pennsylvania. She told Metzger about her mother and how she'd passed away. She told him about her father, and how she wanted to hug him sometimes because he looked so miserable, but she knew that if she did he'd get mad because his unhappiness was supposed to be some big secret.

But more than telling him about her life, she listened and began to understand why Metzger was the way he was. She didn't press when he talked about the war, but when he mentioned the ocean she probed further.

As it turned out, he'd been raised in Destin, Florida. His father had been in the Air Force. Metzger had wanted to become a Green Beret, so he enlisted in the Army instead of following in his father's footsteps and joining the Air Force. He'd grown up on the type of war movies where red, white and blue heroism didn't carry with it the smell of blood, guts and shit. He'd wanted to be a hero. He'd wanted to be someone they'd make a movie about. So Metzger spent his childhood preparing and pretending at every possible opportunity to be a soldier.

Living on the Florida panhandle, there'd been no end of trips to the white, sandy beaches where he'd sit back and stare at the water. Then when a roadside bomb in Iraq ate a great hole in the side of his Hummer and his friends had evaporated into nothing, he'd spent the next three weeks on a hospital ship in the Persian Gulf, haunted his friends and by the moans of the wounded below decks. He spent as much time as he could on deck, away from the others, staring at the depths of an ocean that connected halfway around the world to the beach he'd once called home.

But now the sea no longer calmed him.

It made him nervous.

The Army brought him back stateside and stationed him at Norfolk, Virginia to recuperate, and the water messed with him.

He didn't even need to see it. He could smell it, hear it, feel it in the air. And then he would be transported back to the Hummer ride along Highway 80 in Iraq – to the explosion – to the MEDEVAC chopper – to the sight of bloody bodies in the bowels of the hospital ship, the gray deck flooring splotched with the blood of wannabe-heroes and other mothers' sons.

At first Metzger had thought he would get used to it, but it got so bad he couldn't even look at the water. His mother called it anxiety, but the government called it Post Traumatic Stress Disorder. And they spent the next three months trying to cure him while he self-medicated meth.

When the sun went down, Derrick left with Veronica to get more food, water and some candles.

Natasha felt perfectly safe on her own with the soldier.

She saw Metzger differently than she had before; he was more than an anonymous addict. Still, his face looked worn, and his eyes seemed old even though he was really only a couple of years older than she was.

They could have been two people together anywhere in the world, talking, resting, looking each other in the eyes. Anywhere else they would have been allowed to continue. Not in Bombay Beach.

Tommy Klosterman wasn't at all what Abigail expected. Seeing him outside all of these years she'd expected him to be much more an animal; after all, the only thing she had to go by was the way his own grandparents had treated him, and they kept him chained outside. And oddly enough, she felt safe with Tommy.

After he'd taken Trudie from her, he'd held the small body for a very long time. Abigail didn't think that he knew the dog was dead. He acted as if it were a stuffed animal, clutching it tightly to his chest, making noises to it, petting it with his sausage-sized fingers. But then he'd gotten hungry and had gone out into the yard to the length of his leash. He'd hollered loud and long for his "Omammie," but he'd never received an answer. It wasn't until midday that he came back inside, grumbling and pounding the floor with his fists.

While he'd been outside she'd taken the opportunity to stretch her muscles. She'd sat up, trying to get as comfortable as possible. Inside, it was nothing like a doghouse. It was like a shed, or a small house, or a child's fort. There was enough room for her to stand; light filtered through the door and the ventilator in the roof illuminating walls with crayon-scribbled characters, a stained futon and an immense box of toys.

She found Trudie lying atop the box of toys. She touched the fur gently, telling herself that what had been her dog no longer occupied the body. Trudie's spirit, that thing that made her such a special dog, had gone elsewhere leaving nothing but dead flesh behind. She told herself this, because she had to, or else she'd go crazy with the knowledge that Tommy was playing with the corpse of her dead dog.

When he'd returned after his grandmother had failed to feed him, she'd gone back to her original position, curled into a ball near the entrance. He'd ignored her when he entered and had thrown himself onto his futon, whining into the mattress and rocking back and forth.

Abigail wondered what had happened to his grandmother and why she hadn't come outside to feed her grandson, as she always did. But as Tommy Klosterman cried on his mattress like a small child, Abigail came to believe that she knew the reason.

An hour later, after Tommy fell asleep, Abigail gathered her courage. In a burst of energy, she rolled out the door. She scrambled to her feet and ran as fast as her old legs would take her until she reached the porch.

Behind her came a growl of frustration as Tommy awoke. The door opened, followed by the crash of chain against wood as Tommy ran towards her, but then was forced to stop as he reached the end of the leash. He hollered after her, "Omammie! Omammie!"

As scary as Tommy was, the plaintive wail tugged at her heartstrings. "I'll see where she is, Tommy," she said. "Don't worry."

A baseball bat leaned against the outside of the trailer beside the door. She held it ready in one hand as she tried the handle. It was unlocked and she went inside.

The interior was awash in cool air. The kitchen area was empty, as was the living room. She noticed the front door was open and went to close it, scanning the front yard as she did. No one was there.

"Agnes?" she called. "Henry? Where are you?"

Down a short hallway, she checked the bathroom and both bedrooms, but the trailer was empty.

As she turned around, she noticed that several of the pictures on the walls were hung askew. She straightened them, discovering several drops of dried blood on the glass.

She returned to the front door and looked at the doorjamb. She ran her fingers across the splintered wood. Something – or someone – had forced its way in here. Abigail looked around at the apparently tranquil home. She knew how quickly it had happened. Had it not been for her Trudie, she might have fallen victim to the same fate, for it was the warning her dog had given her that had given her the chance to survive.

"Omammie!"

Tommy was still calling from outside. He had to be starving.

But first things first.

Her bladder was about to burst. She went to the bathroom, and after taking care of business, washed her hands, face and neck in the sink, relishing the feel of hot water and soap against her skin.

Finally feeling human again, she entered the smaller of the two bedrooms. There was a twin bed, but it appeared to be little used. She found a clean set of clothes and was about to take them into the kitchen, when she heard a noise from the other bedroom.

She set the clothes down on the bed, grabbed the bat with both hands, and crept into the hall.

The noise came again.

She stepped into the room, prepared to swing the bat with every ounce of strength she had. She was a small woman and had never thought of herself as particularly strong, but the events of the past several days had created a rage within her. She focused on the image of her beloved Trudie lying atop Tommy Klosterman's toybox.

"Hello. Is anyone there?"

A rustle answered her, from where the bed met the wall on the other side of the room. She saw a dark gap.

She stepped to the foot of the bed, then back, wary of something beneath the bed reaching out to grab her feet. She scooted to the wall and tried to peer into the shadows next to the bed.

"Agnes? Is that you?"

A groan came from the space beside the bed.

"Agnes, if that's you, say something." Abigail wished she had the pistol. She glanced at the bat. It would have to do.

The bed shuddered.

Abigail stepped back until she was stopped by a bureau.

A hand appeared, grabbing the top of the bed. The skin was mottled green, the same shade and color as the creature that had held her hostage in her home. Then Agnes managed to climb to her feet... or what Agnes had become.

She still wore her nightgown, lavender with butterflies stitched into the gossamer. Her white-gray hair was still in curlers, some now fallen. Her face and skin were the same color as her hands, and her eyes glowed with a yellow ferocity. Saliva dripped from teeth that seemed too long to be human.

"Agnes?"

The thing growled at her. It tried to step towards her, but was partially trapped by the end of the bed.

Abigail glanced at the door. She knew she could leave, probably run and get away, but what would happen to Tommy?

She ran across the room with her bat held high. When she was near enough, she brought it down on top of Agnes' head. The impact sent a vibration into her hands so hard that she almost dropped the bat.

She swung again, this time catching Agnes on the side of the head.

Abigail stepped back. Blood poured from the wound on top of Agnes's head. Her head hung sideways as if her neck was broken.

Abigail swung again. But as she swung, Agnes exploded into action and leaped at her. Abigail held her arms out to try and stop the attack and dropped the bat. The weight carried her crashing into the bureau, then to the ground. A music box, jewelry and a hand mirror avalanched to the ground beside her.

Agnes held her down, teeth snapping.

Abigail grabbed the side of Agnes's head to hold her away from her.

The teeth snapped. A wheezing sound began to emanate from her chest.

She wasn't going to be able to hold Agnes for long. Her strength was already waning. She freed one hand and searched blindly for the bat, while Agnes snapped at her. All her hand found was the hand mirror, which she grabbed and brought up as hard as she could into Agnes's face. The plastic frame shattered, along with the top half of the mirror. Realizing she now had something sharp enough to cut, Abigail shoved it into Agnes's neck and began to saw savagely. Blood gushed over her hand and onto her arm, making the mirror slippery, but she'd done severe damage. Agnes no longer snapped. Her head flopped to one side. Her eyes closed to slits.

With the last of her strength, Abigail pushed the woman off and onto the floor. As she did, her forearm brushed against the woman's face. Agnes bit down and into Abigail's arm.

She screamed and rolled to her feet. She found the bat and hammered at the woman's face until there was nothing left, splitting the head and scattering the brain on the carpet. The eyes were open and empty. Finally, Abigail sagged to the bed, exhausted and breathing hard.

After a few minutes, she returned to the bathroom and cleaned up again. She searched the medicine cabinet and found a bandage which she used to cover the wound on her arm, after coating it with antibiotic cream.

Then she stumbled into the kitchen. She'd forgotten why she'd wanted to go in there in the first place.

"Omammie!" she heard Tommy cry.

It was then, standing with the refrigerator door open, that she realized that she was hungry. But for what, she didn't know, other than the hunger was growing inside her something fierce.

CHAPTER FIFTEEN

Gunshots rang out, followed by shouting.

Natasha checked her watch. It was past nine already. Derrick and Veronica should have been back long ago.

Metzger was already on his feet and peering through the window.

"What do you see?" she asked.

"It looks like Elvis, only shorter."

"What else?"

"I dunno. There must be a couple of dozen people. Some of them have guns. Hey, there's Derrick. It looks like he's been crying."

"What?" Natasha leaped to her feet and rushed to the window. There were at least twenty people outside, most of whom she recognized. Derrick stood behind Kristov, his head hung low. He pointed towards the trailer they were in. She knew exactly what had happened. They'd made him talk.

"They're coming in."

"They have guns," Metzger said. "Should I be worried?"

Natasha saw his feeble attempt at a smile. "Let me see if I can explain. Whatever I say, though, roll with it."

Banging came from the front door.

Natasha ran to open it but the door flew open, catching her in the head and flinging her back against the wall and stunning her.

By the time she came to, the people had Metzger by the arms and were shoving him out the door. Auntie Lin knelt and put a hand to Natasha's forehead. Natasha tried to stand, but the small Chinese woman, who was much stronger than she looked, kept her from getting up. "You had me worried sick."

The truth was that Natasha had been so captivated by Metzger that she'd completely forgotten about the fact that other people might be looking for her. She recognized a little bit of her father in her.

She pushed Auntie Lin's hands away and staggered to her feet, grabbing for the doorjamb to keep her steady. The others were dragging Metzger down the street. What had Derrick and Veronica told them? What was going on? She tried to get near him, but there were too many people in the way.

When Natasha stepped from the darkness of the Salton Sea night into the fluorescent-lighted interior of the Space Station, she looked around for her father. He'd put a stop to this. All she had to do was explain. But she didn't see him there. She did see Metzger, standing to attention before Deputy Sheriff Will Todrunner.

Derrick slid next to her. "They made me tell them where you were."

"Have you seen Dad?" she asked.

Derrick shook his head. "I'm sorry. Auntie Lin was just so –"

"Sshhh." Natasha made a chopping motion with her hand and took another step forward to get within earshot.

"Just passing through, you say," Deputy Will said, his face deadpan, eyes shadowed by the bill of his baseball cap.

"Yes, sir."

"Are you discharged or are you still in the Army, son?"

"Still in, sir. I had some leave built up after my time in Iraq and thought I'd head towards the ocean."

Natasha became aware of Auntie Lin and Maude standing together, whispering to each other with their arms crossed, gazing suspiciously at everyone. The soda fountain had been turned on and plastic cups were stacked on the counter for people to serve themselves.

Small pockets of conversation continued in hushed tones while the Deputy Sheriff quizzed Metzger. Natasha glanced around and was relieved to see that Hopkins wasn't there. There was no telling what he'd do if *he* saw Metzger. She locked gazes with the Mad Scientist; he stared at her for a long moment, his mouth twisted into a knot of worry. She'd all but forgotten about him and his green creature hand. How much did he know? How much would he share with them?

"You got a number I can call to check?" she heard Deputy Will ask.

Metzger rattled off a number and said it was for his unit in Norfolk, Virginia. Then he asked if he could go to the bathroom. The Deputy relented, and Kristov, still carrying his rifle, showed him the way. The deputy turned to Natasha once Metzger was out of earshot.

"What were you thinking? You had your aunt worried."

Natasha felt a spark of indignation at the man's chiding and before she could control it, her mouth opened. "What's the problem? Never seen a soldier before?"

The deputy started to scowl, then allowed a grin to cross his face. "How old are you again?"

"Eighteen."

"Old enough to know better, I'd think," he said.

"You'd think."

"And you think you know all sorts of things about people, don't you?"

"Yes. I think so."

"Can you tell the difference between a good guy and a bad guy?"

An image of the deputy and Hopkins having a conversation came to her. "Sure," she countered. "Can you?"

"Natasha Renee Oliver!" Auntie Lin gasped and shook her head. "Why are you talking to the deputy like that?"

Natasha shrugged off the hand. "Why is he talking to *me* like that?" She pointed toward the bathroom. "Metzger is back from the war with a box full of medals and a head full of bad memories. If anyone should be feeling bad about the way they talked to someone, it should be the deputy. Metzger's not a criminal. He's a soldier who fought for our country."

Natasha stopped, realizing she'd been shouting. All the other conversations had stopped and everyone was staring at her.

Finally it was the deputy who broke the tension with a low rumble of laughter. "I suppose you may be right. You gotta understand that my responsibility lies in protecting this community. In doing so, I sometimes need to check and see who people are. It's my job. No offense."

She tapped her foot as she said, "None taken."

The deputy turned away from her, but Natasha wasn't done. All the frustration and confusion and anger that she'd been keeping inside was coming out.

"Now *you* should get back to protecting us. My dad's missing. Gert's missing. There's a whole Amish family missing. No telling who else is missing. If you don't watch it, the whole town will disappear with you none the wiser."

The deputy seemed as if he was about to say something. Instead, he pushed himself away from the bar he'd been leaning on and headed towards the door. He waved for a couple of the men to follow, then he was out and into the night.

"Natasha!" Auntie Lin hissed.

Natasha put her hand on the older woman's arm. "I know what you're going to say, so don't bother saying it. Everything's going to be fine. We just need to find dad."

Natasha kissed Auntie Lin on the cheek, then noticed Metzger standing by the kitchen, wiping his hands dry with a paper towel. She walked over to him. "Are you okay?" She said.

He nodded. "What happened to the deputy?"

"Your girl here chased him away," Veronica said, sidling up.

Metzger stared at Natasha. "What'd you say?"

"Just that you were too much of a weakling to do anyone any harm so they should let you go," Veronica said.

Metzger's eyebrows rose.

"I did not." Natasha punched her friend in the arm.

The bell above the door rang as Rico Duvall entered the restaurant and halted. He looked worried. "The Weather Band on the radio said a tropical depression has formed south of Cabo San Lucas. They've projected the track of the storm and have it driving right through the Sea of Cortez and through Puerto Peñasco."

Derrick looked from Veronica, to Metzger, to his sister. "What does that mean?"

"It means we have to board the windows," said Columbus Williams, on his way to the bathroom. He tossed his empty beer can into the trash. "Last time we had a tropical storm, it dropped ten inches of rain on us. The sump pumps failed and half the homes went underwater. That was ten years ago and they haven't made the pumps any better since."

Natasha remembered that the tall black man was a retired Navy officer. She didn't like the idea of being flooded within the walled town.

"Will we be safe?" Natasha asked.

"We've survived worse." Maude sipped a cup of coffee and shrugged.

"Gimme snorkels or give me death!" Frank cried from a corner.

Kristov snorted. "No shit. That's the point."

Andy Gudgel spoke for the first time in a long time. "No reason to get excited, everyone. We're more than a hundred miles inland. Even if the storm does come this far, the worst we'll get is wind and rain. No chance of a storm surge here."

Natasha nodded at the Mad Scientist's words but, by the way he glanced worriedly at the door, there was clearly something troubling him.

"What's a storm surge?" Derrick asked.

Natasha was glad he had asked because she didn't know either.

"It's when the wind and the storm get behind the waves and push them onto the land," Columbus said. "I lost a thirty-two footer in Annapolis after Big Bertha." He *tsked* and shook his head. "A storm surge can kick your ass when you're not looking."

"How long do we have?" Lu Shu asked. He'd been nursing a beer in the corner, but now he stood, frowning in concern.

"About a day," Rico said. "We'll know what happens if Puerto Peñasco gets hit. If it does, then we're next. For sure."

After a few moments, everyone started talking again, planning for the worst. They left one by one, each nodding at Maude and Auntie Lin as they went. Even Frank tipped an imaginary hat as he grabbed six beers and wobbled out the door.

Natasha glanced at where Metzger stood talking to Veronica and Derrick. She was about to join them, when she noticed her Auntie Lin and Maude staring at her. Natasha braced herself for what was about to happen.

"I expect you home tonight," Auntie Lin said. "Derrick doesn't need to be staying out so late and he'll follow you anywhere." She stared at her for another moment as if trying to decide to say something more, then said, "Plus, your father still hasn't come home. No telling where he is or what he's doing." Then she turned and began to help Maude clean the empty plastic cups off the counter.

Natasha felt a pang for the old woman who'd done everything for her, from change her diapers to help her get dressed for her graduation dance. Lin hadn't signed up to be mother and father to them; she'd started her life in America as a Nanny and now, at an age where she should be readying herself for retirement, she was cleaning someone else's restaurant.

Where was her dad?

Natasha felt a stab of anger.

She watched Auntie Lin and Maude, feeling her old sadness return. She was just feeling sorry for herself; she really should stay and help. But part of her was torn by Metzger and Veronica waiting for her outside. If only she could be in two places at once.

CHAPTER SIXTEEN

It was a funny thing. One minute Metzger was being grilled by the Deputy, the next folks were asking him about Iraq and what he'd seen. He'd seen it a thousand times since he returned: even the most diehard peace lovers and military haters couldn't help but be cordial. Their curiosity and, he hoped, respect for his survival brought them to him like moths to a flame.

Outside the restaurant, he found himself speaking with a tall older black man and a thirty-something woman, tattoos poking out the collar of her shirt. The man had introduced himself as Columbus Williams, and had spent 25 years in the Navy before retiring. The woman's name was Kim Johnson, or Reverend Kim as she liked to be called. She led a local church.

"We do appreciate your service, son," Columbus said.

"That's true for all of us. I'm not a fan of the president, but I do appreciate that there are people like you out there to protect us if need be."

"What'd you do over there?" Columbus asked. The years were carved into the dark, strong-jawed face.

Metzger glanced at the man. It might take a lifetime to answer his question. Metzger had done so much, and so little. That which he wasn't proud of he was trying hard to forget, only the forgetting was turning out to be an even harder task.

"I spent most of my time guarding convoys. I was a spotter in my vehicle."

"What's a spotter do?" Kim Johnson asked.

"Watch out for the enemy and try and get him before he gets us."

Aside from the three of them, the street was empty. Here and there a streetlight provided a nimbus of light, and starlight could be seen through breaks in the cloudy night sky. He hadn't paid too much attention when they'd driven into town last night. In fact, he hadn't paid too much attention at all until the bus driver had told them to run for it, and then the creatures had attacked.

Columbus put a hand on Metzger's shoulder. "Sorry, son. You've got better things to do than stand around and tell me war stories. Maybe I'll catch up with you later."

"Naw, it's okay." Metzger glanced back at the restaurant. Derrick and Veronica stood in the door, trying to get Natasha's attention. She wouldn't be long now.

"Ever spend time aboard a ship?" Columbus asked.

"I was on the *Mercy*." Metzger stood with his hands in his pockets. "It was a hospital ship," he added.

"What happened?" Reverend Kim asked. "Were you injured?"

Metzger shrugged. "A little. Our Hummer was hit by a roadside bomb."

"Jesus." Columbus shook his head. "We never had those in Vietnam."

Derrick and Veronica bounded towards him.

"I think I gotta go," he said.

A moment later, Natasha came out the door. Her hair was pulled back in a ponytail. She was damned cute.

She grabbed his arm and pulled him. "Sorry, we have to go."

Metzger gave Reverend Kim and Columbus an apologetic look

as he was pulled down the street, almost losing his balance. He took his hands out of his pockets, and removed her grip on his arm.

"Easy," he said. "Where are we going in such a hurry?"

"Anywhere but here."

She was smiling, but looked as though she'd been crying.

"Okay then. Let's go."

They all jogged to Veronica's house. The lights were on inside. Through the window they could see Veronica's aunt and uncle sitting on the couch watching television.

Her trailer had a porch as well as a roof deck. They sat on metal chairs on the porch.

Derrick was the first to talk.

"I'm sorry, Metzger. I didn't mean to tell them."

"Don't sweat it. You had to answer them. It's not like I'm Billy the Kid or something. I'm no outlaw."

"To Hopkins you are," Veronica said.

"You're not talking about Colonel Hopkins, are you?"

"Colonel?" both Veronica and Natasha asked together.

"We didn't know he was a colonel," Natasha said, "We were told he works for some sort of ecological agency for the government."

"What does Colonel Hopkins look like?" Metzger asked.

After the three described him, Metzger nodded. "Sounds like the same fellow. He came to our clinic in Virginia on a recruiting trip."

"But what about the ecology thing?" Derrick asked.

"Probably a cover. If he went around as an Army colonel you all might be suspicious."

"People around here found him pretty suspicious anyway." Veronica frowned. "So the question is, how is he connected to those things?"

"Yeah," Natasha said. "We figured you were going there to fight the creatures."

Metzger didn't see the logic in that at all. If there was truly a threat from the creatures he'd seen, the government would have sent in Special Forces or some elite infantry unit, not a bunch of PTSDers.

"Then what's the connection between the creatures and the buses of soldiers?" Derrick asked.

Metzger shrugged. "I don't have enough information yet. We need to see one of those things up close, then maybe we can discover what they were before they became..." He gestured uncertainly.

"So all we need is a creature who will stand there while we look at it." Veronica made a face. "Simple, right?"

"Maybe it is." Natasha stood. "I think I know where one is. I saw someone, or something chained behind a house the first day we were here."

"Like someone was keeping them as a pet? Hey!" Derrick snapped his fingers. "That's what you were talking about. Why didn't you tell me what you saw?"

"It was hot and smelly. It could have been my imagination."

"It's not your imagination," Veronica said. "And who you're talking about isn't any creature, it's the Klosterman Kid."

"The who?" Metzger asked.

"Klosterman Kid. Although he's not a kid, really. He's about thirty-five. His grandparents keep him outside. He lives in a doghouse."

"What?" Metzger stood, his face expressing his incredulity.

"Serious. He has some sort of brain damage from a car crash when he was a kid. His parents were both killed and he was in a hospital for a long time until it closed down. Now the grandparents take care of him as best they can."

Metzger still couldn't believe it. "By keeping him outside?"

"They say he's violent."

"I thought he was wearing a mask and some gloves," Natasha added.

"They make him wear a baseball catcher's mask so he won't bite anyone. He wears boxing gloves so he can't pick up anything."

Metzger couldn't believe what he was hearing. It was the craziest shit he'd ever heard.

"Okay. We have *gotta* go see that."

Derrick grinned. "Yeah. Let's go."

Veronica shook her head. "We better not."

"Wait a minute. Since when are you scared of something?" Natasha asked.

"I'm not scared. It's just..." she fought to find the words. "It's just that he shouldn't be living the way he's living and everyone knows it, but no one has ever done anything about it."

"Does the Deputy know?" Metzger asked.

"Yeah."

"Then don't sweat it. I think if there was something illegal, he would have put a stop to it. Know what I mean?"

Veronica nodded. But then she added, "But it sometimes feels immoral."

Ten minutes later they were all staring at the Klosterman Kid and Metzger knew what she meant. He lived like a dog.

The backyard of the trailer was lit by a spotlight. The Klosterman Kid sat in the middle of the yard playing with a ball. His legs were splayed like a toddler's as he repeatedly bounced it against the wall of his doghouse. Sometimes it would come right back to him, others he'd have to scramble for the ball before it got farther than his leash could take him.

Metzger followed the leash from the thick leather collar to the dog house. The structure was sound and, from where he was standing, seemed to be more than a mere dog house. A vent spinning on the pitched roof kept the air circulating inside. The entire structure was about five feet high, with light emanating from somewhere inside.

He was relieved that it was less a doghouse than it was some boy's fort. Now he saw a little of the reasoning the locals used to justify the man remaining outside.

"Wow," was all he could say.

"Feels like the Twilight Zone, doesn't it?" Veronica asked.

Metzger nodded. "Everywhere I turn in this place, it seems that things are just a little bit off."

"Sometimes a lot," Derrick said.

"Sometimes a lot," Metzger agreed. He turned to Natasha. "But we're back to square one. We don't have one of the creatures to examine."

"Actually, we might," Veronica said, glancing at Derrick. "We think we might have found an abandoned trailer with one inside."

"You think? You didn't check?"

"We're not soldiers. Are you kidding me?" Veronica shook her head.

"What did you see, Derrick?" Metzger asked.

"I didn't really see anything. I just felt it. I kind of, I don't know, knew it was there." Derrick glanced at the soldier hopefully. "Do you know what I mean?"

Metzger knew exactly what the boy meant. His own sixth sense had saved him on countless occasions during building clearing in Baghdad.

"It's getting late," Natasha said. "Let's go back to that trailer tomorrow and check it out in the light."

Veronica and Derrick nodded, clearly liking the idea.

Metzger would have rather gone tonight. He had to keep reminding himself that the others weren't soldiers.

They headed back towards Natasha's trailer. Truth be told, he was exhausted. He'd love to get a good night's sleep. He hadn't had one in more than two years.

CHAPTER SEVENTEEN

Derrick and Natasha brought Metzger home around eleven o'clock. Auntie Lin had taken a liking to the young man, but wasn't sure if it was a good idea to let him into the house while everyone was sleeping. Luckily, even with the storm blowing up the Sea of Cortez and having not yet reached Puerto Peñasco, they had twelve hours of good weather left before it hit. So Auntie Lin's solution was to have a camp out of sorts.

Everyone took advantage of the cool air and slept on the roof in lounge chairs. Auntie Lin watched over them, sleeping in a lounge chair at the top of the stairs to the roof deck, a Sudoku book perched in her sleeping, gnarled hands.

The next morning, Natasha was the first to wake. She, Derrick, Veronica, and Metzger had talked long into the night about what they were going to do. First they were going to talk to the Mad Scientist and get him to explain about the green hand he had stashed in his laboratory. They decided to do this instead of investigating the place where Derrick had found a monster, hoping that they could use what they learned from the Mad Scientist to their benefit.

An hour later everyone had eaten breakfast and taken a shower. Veronica went home to change and promised to meet them at the Mad Scientist's.

The day dawned hot, like Hell's oven had been turned up and the door left open. The superheated air nearly took their breath away. Derrick, Natasha and Metzger headed to the restaurant first, moving slowly. Where before they'd cut through yards, today they were happy to trudge down the street, heads down, hands in their pockets, their attention on the road before them.

The restaurant was closed. The front window had been covered with plywood. The door was locked and no lights were on inside.

"Better hurry and get inside." Carrie Loughnane smoked a cigarette as she leaned against the wall beneath the awning next door at the Laundromat. Her windows had yet to be covered, and by the looks of things, she didn't plan on doing it herself. She wore red Capri pants and tank top, making her look like a red pear. "I said hurry, before you melt." Carrie held open the door.

All three hurried in and were suddenly soothed by cool air as the twin swamp coolers on the roof fired like turbo jet engines straight into the entryway. It would have been a peaceful paradise had Carrie's seven kids not been running around playing Cowboys and Indians.

Her children ranged from four to eleven years old. Carrie had been continually pregnant for seven years. Once a vivacious cheerleader from a Costa Mesa high school, she'd traded community college for crack cocaine and had spent the next seven years drifting through a fog of sex, crack, and rock and roll.

"Is this the soldier I heard about last night?" Carrie asked, looking Metzger up and down. She'd killed her cigarette in the ashtray outside, but the acrid smell of smoke still lingered on her clothes, mingling with her heavy, clove perfume.

"Metzger, ma'am." He held out his hand.

"What a gentleman," she said, winking at Natasha as she gripped his hand.

Natasha didn't find it funny at all. She felt a bite of jealousy as they shook hands. Carrie was in her early thirties, and had lost little of her former beauty.

There was a shrill scream of agony. One of the kids had stuffed another halfway into a washing machine.

"Die, space toad!"

Carrie shoved her hands onto her hips. "Five, let seven go. What the hell are you thinking?"

The kids scurried off to do something out of sight.

Carrie turned and shook her head. "Kids."

Metzger looked at Natasha and mouthed the words, "Seven? Five?"

Carrie saw it and laughed. "I know. It's stupid. Sometimes I forget things, like their names." She thumped the side of her head. "But I remember numbers really well, so I give them numbers. One is the oldest and seven is the youngest. Sometimes I sort of feel like Charlie Chan."

Metzger nodded slowly, but by look on his face he thought it was one of the strangest things he'd ever heard.

"Did you hear about the storm?" Derrick asked.

Carrie turned her attention to him and shook her head.

"They said it might be the worst in twenty years if it clears Puerto Peñasco. We're supposed to batten down the hatches."

"Do you even know what that means?" Natasha asked. "How do you batten down something?"

Derrick glanced at Metzger, clearly embarrassed to be called out like that by his sister.

Metzger came to his rescue. "Easy now, Natasha. It's a pirate thing. We should all know how to batten things down. Ain't that right, Dread Pirate Derrick?"

Derrick grinned. "Yarr!"

"Are you going to need help with the windows?" Natasha asked.

"Windows?" Carrie said.

"Yeah. For the storm that's coming," Metzger added.

"Storm? What storm?"

Derrick was about to open his mouth, but Natasha elbowed him in the ribs, then pointed out on the street. Veronica was trudging through the heat heading towards the locked restaurant.

Natasha grabbed Metzger by the elbow and began pushing him towards the door. "Listen, we gotta go, but if you need some help, come and ask us, okay?"

Carrie stared at Natasha for a moment, then her eyes seemed to clear. "Okay. I will." Then she turned and hollered for children one, three and four.

A moment later, Natasha and the others were out the door and calling for Veronica, who was already past the Laundromat. "Hey girl!"

Veronica turned sluggishly. "Ugh," she said. "I feel like a zombie. It's so damned hot."

A sluggish breeze had come up while they were inside, bringing the smell of hot, putrefied fish with each gust of air.

They turned back the way Veronica had come and headed up Avenue A.

"Is she okay?" Derrick asked. "She acted kind of... I don't know."

"You mean Carrie?" Veronica nodded. "She's a winner for sure. God knows where she goes when she goes, but she goes somewhere."

"Lost brain cells. They say that when you lose them, they never grow back," Metzger said.

"Damn. Then she has a lot of empty space to traverse inside that head of hers." Natasha frowned. "It must be hard."

Veronica nodded. "It is. She knows she's messed up, but not really how bad. We're a close community. You know she doesn't charge anyone to use the Laundromat, right?"

All three looked at her.

"I had no idea," Natasha said.

"Yeah. She said she found the place, so she doesn't feel comfortable charging people. That would be like stealing, she says."

"So how does she eat and feed the kids?" Metzger asked.

"She trades. She cleans houses too, sort of."

All four of them laughed at the idea of Carrie and kids one

through seven descending upon a dirty trailer. Then they let the laughter die as they realized how hopeless the woman's life would be if it weren't for the people of Bombay Beach. It made Natasha realize even more how unusual the town was. She'd hated it horribly at first: the town was literally rotting away on a sea that no one could swim in. But she was coming to understand that Bombay Beach had far more of a sense of community than any where else she'd lived.

"It's like the Army, sort of. We take care of our own. It's like a big family," Metzger said.

Natasha watched him as they walked. He'd held breakfast down. That was a good sign.

They made the turn down Third Street, and found themselves in front of the Mad Scientist's set of trailers. The main trailer on the left was light blue and white, and cleaner than most. The weeds in front had been clipped to within an inch of the sandy soil. A lime green garden gnome had a Star Trek uniform painted expertly over its body. To the right and set back was the other trailer, mostly submerged: the laboratory.

"Which one?" Derrick asked.

Veronica pointed to the red light beside the door on the sunken trailer. "That one."

"Do we just walk right in?" Metzger asked.

Veronica shrugged. "We should probably knock first." To Derrick she asked, "Do you have the book?"

He nodded as he pulled it out. He held it carefully as though it were fragile.

"Then let's go," Metzger said. He walked towards the trailer, but before he could descend the stairs to the door, the door opened.

"Go away," came the thin voice of the Mad Scientist.

"It's Natasha, Dr. Gudgel. I brought some friends with me. We need to talk." She glanced at Veronica and Metzger for support. They both nodded grimly.

"I don't have time. Sorry."

He pulled the door shut, but Metzger pounded on it hard.

"Leave me alone."

"We can't," Natasha said. "We need your help."

"I can't help you."

"You can't or you won't?" Metzger countered.

Gudgel flung open the door. "Listen, just leave this place. You shouldn't be here now. It's just too..." He let his voice trail off, his eyes full of worry.

"Dangerous? Is that what you were gonna say, Mister?"

The Mad Scientist tried to close the door again, but Metzger jammed his foot into the gap. They struggled for a moment before it became obvious that the soldier was the stronger of the two. The Mad Scientist just turned and shuffled back into the laboratory, leaving the door open behind him.

They followed him in. Derrick was last. He closed and locked the door behind them.

The inside of the trailer was nothing like any of the others. The entire place had been gutted, leaving one long rectangular space. The trailer's walls were covered with schematics and charts, most of which were indecipherable. Natasha recognized a map of California and the Salton Sea, but not much else. Tables lined both walls. All sorts of instruments covered every available surface, including several telescopes and enough beakers and test tubes to populate a high school chemistry lab. A smell lingered in the air, a combination of unwashed clothes and a sharp, eye-watering chemical.

"Let's get this over with," the Mad Scientist said. He turned and sat on a stool. His hands shook slightly where they rested in his lap. He wore a white, unbuttoned lab coat over shorts and a *Mork and Mindy* T-shirt. He didn't look scared, just defeated.

"Get what over with?" Veronica asked.

"Him. I know why he's here." He shook his head. "Just know that I was never a part of what the project has become."

All four of the newcomers exchanged glances.

"Project? What project?" Derrick asked.

"Him. His project." Gudgel pointed at Metzger.

"I'm not sure I get what you're saying," the soldier said. "The astromechs?"

The Mad Scientist frowned. "Is that what they're calling it these days? Where did they tell you that they were taking you?"

"To a project that would get us straight and teach us how to work in space."

"I suppose none of that was a lie. Of course, it begs a lot of questions... especially why a space program would be hidden on the coast of this horrid inland sea. Did any of you ask yourself that question?"

Metzger shook his head.

"Clearly you don't know as much as I thought you did." The Mad Scientist sighed. "Tell me why you've come."

"We thought you would show us the hand," Natasha said.

The Mad Scientist blinked for a moment, then shook his head. "I don't know what you're talking about."

"We saw you," Derrick said.

"Ahh. So it was you on my roof the other day." Gudgel shook his head and laughed. "I convinced myself that it was a bird."

"So what about it?" Metzger asked. "Can we see it?"

When Andy hesitated, Natasha added, "It's not like we don't know about the creatures. We saw them. Hell, they almost killed Metzger."

The Mad Scientist visibly deflated, all fight gone from him. Without a word, he went to a refrigerator towards the rear of the trailer, removed a covered stainless steel tray, and brought it back to where everyone stood. He set it on the table and removed the metal lid, revealing a shriveled green hand that twitched and moved of its own accord.

"Oh my God!" Metzger stepped back into Veronica. "I thought you were kidding."

"Easy, big boy. It's only a hand," Veronica said.

"Man, oh man, oh man." Derrick looked around, excitement and fear racing across his face.

Using stainless steel prongs, the Mad Scientist grasped the hand and held it to the light. The fingers tried to grip the steel holding it, but couldn't get enough purchase. The sight of the hand so close to Natasha's face sent a shiver up her spine.

"Is... is... it alive?" Derrick stuttered.

"It's as dead as the sea outside."

"Then how is it... why is it *moving*?" Natasha said.

"It's not the why of it, but rather the how. I've been trying to reverse engineer what we started twenty years ago."

He offered the prongs holding the hand to Metzger. "Here, hold this."

Metzger grabbed it. Once it was in his hand, he remained still as a post, staring fearfully at the thing writhing in the grasp of the tongs.

Meanwhile, as the other three waited, the Mad Scientist went to the refrigerator and returned with a stoppered test tube half-filled with a glowing yellow substance. He placed it in a wooden stand and regarded it with reverence.

"This is what it's all about. I've been able to extract this over the years, but I'm still trying to find out how they did it. When I was part of the program, we were still banging our heads against the scientific wall, but so much has been discovered or invented since then. Not least the modern computer; calculations that used to take days or weeks now take seconds." Gudgel sighed and shook his head.

"Hey, can you take this?" Metzger asked, his eyebrows raised as he held out the green hand.

The Mad Scientist took the hand and put it back in the tray. He bade his guests sit and told them what he knew about the green hand, where it came from, why it existed, and why he remained behind to discover what was going on.

"It started during the Kennedy Administration. Two initiatives were created, the Apollo Program and the Hadrian Outpost Project. One would take man to the moon, and the other would keep him there. But because of the sensitivity and the fear of the Soviet Union, the second project remained hidden in plain sight, on the edge of a once famous resort now abandoned for the glitz of Palm Springs. Despite the secrecy, the program was well funded and made great progress from the start.

"The idea was to make it possible for humans to work in space. It was one thing to plant a flag, but another thing altogether to take possession and build upon that first step. Hadrian's Outpost was named after the Second Century Roman Emperor who conquered and held far-flung reaches of land on the very edge of Roman civilization. For the project to work it would require that humans develop the ability to function in low-gravity, zero-oxygen environments; something that wasn't possible without the use of vacuum suits.

"Terminally-ill prisoners in federal custody became willing test subjects when their families were promised significant sums of money. With nothing to lose, those in their last days signed up... and died, one after another. For the first four years, there was little advancement except for an understanding of virus delivery mechanisms and the affects of ionizing radiation on cells.

"Through the Nixon Administration the project continued, and it didn't hit a glitch until Ford came into office. President Ford learned about the project and insisted on a visit. He was appalled at what he saw and tried to pull funding. But Ford had little power and only succeeded in redirecting the budget from NASA to the Department of Defense.

"Sadly, that was what did the project in. After the unsuccessful Carter Administration, President Ronald Reagan entered office and cleared the books of all old projects. With no representative or senator to stand up for the program it was disbanded.

"At least it was *supposed* to have been. Most of the staff left, but a select group continued to work, funded by donations to environmental research which were funneled by friends in congress to a tiny annual budget called the Salton Sea Desalination Environmental Project. Barely enough money to keep the project going with a skeleton staff, it was still enough to maintain operations, until a more friendly and open-minded administration was able to resurrect the foundering project."

Natasha and the others learned that the Mad Scientist – aka Andy Gudgel – had been one of the head scientists from 1972 to 1981. He'd been a civilian scientist until Ford took office, then was released as part of the downsizing efforts. He could have gone anywhere, but his heart was with the project, so he'd stayed, hoping that someday he'd be rehired and return to the project he'd helped create. Until then, he lived in Bombay Beach on the money he'd banked all the years he'd been working, trying from his trailer to keep up with the scientific advances that were being made behind the scenes.

But he had to be careful. The project had placed two security personnel within the population of Bombay Beach. In all of his years, the Mad Scientist had only found out the identity of one of them – Maude McKinney. And she was always watching him, making sure that he kept his activities quiet and private. As long as he didn't broadcast the truth of the project to the world, she and the others let him live in peace.

When the revelation surfaced that Maude knew about everything, Natasha groaned inwardly. She stole a glance a Veronica. "What do you mean, she knew? She knows about *all* of it? Even the creatures?"

"I'm not sure what she knows about the progress."

"Progress? I saw more than three dozen creatures rise out of the water and kill soldiers. And trust me, the soldiers never even had a chance. Is that what you mean by progress?" Natasha's face was purple with fury.

The Mad Scientist shrugged and smiled weakly. "Actually, yes. What you saw were creatures who should not exist, functioning with cells that can do little more than maintain a power charge. They don't need to breathe, eat or drink. I'd call that an achievement."

"That's just sick," Natasha said.

"They're zombies, aren't they?" Derrick asked.

The Mad Scientist regarded the boy for a moment, then nodded as if the idea hadn't occurred to him before. "Not zombies in the Haitian sense. But semi-mindless, unliving creations that attack everything that moves, yes."

Natasha was only half listening. She was furious that Maude had known what was going on and had never told anyone. All those dead soldiers could have been saved if the woman had spoken out. "So if they were created to work in space, why do they want to attack people? I don't get it." Natasha said, rejoining the conversation.

Metzger nodded. "Yeah. Good question, Natasha."

The Mad Scientist shook his head. "I don't know. I wasn't

privy to the trials. If I succeed in reverse engineering the isotope, then maybe I can tell you. Until then, it's all just guesswork, hardly real science. Frankly, I don't care. They were meant to be disposable workers in space. Side effects are bound to occur."

"Can we ask him about the book now?" Derrick held it out in front of him. "Mad Scient – er... Mr. Gudgel. Can you take a look at this for us? I think my grandpa wrote it, but it was in code and we can't figure out what it says."

Gudgel took the book and glanced at the kids. "So they still call me the Mad Scientist, huh?" He shook his head. "I suppose there are worse things. Let me see this." He paged through it, stopping now and then to look closely at a page, or to inspect the margins. "It is indeed a code. What was your grandfather doing, I wonder?"

"We thought he might have been writing about what he saw in the water. Maybe he knew about the project."

He looked up sharply. "Do you think so? Hmm. No wonder Maude was so into him."

Natasha decided at that moment that she was going to have a word with the woman.

"Can you decipher it?" Derrick asked.

"Possibly, as long as the crib is included."

"The what?" Metzger asked.

"The crib. This is clearly a substitution text. It doesn't appear to be Caesar's, although I can't rule that out without checking. Look here, at the end of every odd numbered page, are these same twelve letters. Different books traditionally use different cribs, so this was a way for the owner to keep track."

He held the book out for everyone to see:

GDOQSGHOHWCB

"The fact it appears so often tells me that it has to be the crib, or the key to decoding the text. You decipher these 12 letters and you have the key to the rest of the text. If you can't, then the text is useless. It's probably a simple shift. This was drawn in freehand, so unless he was a genius, then he probably shifted the alphabet so that he could write this easily."

"And when you say shift you mean...?" Metzger trailed off.

"Say you assign 'G' for 'A,' then that means that 'H' would replace 'B,' 'I' would replace 'C' and so on. A simple shift."

"Simple shift," Derrick mouthed, as he took the book back. He opened it and stared at the characters at the bottom of each odd page with wide careful eyes.

"So what's next?" Metzger asked no one in particular.

Nobody answered.

CHAPTER EIGHTEEN

They returned to her grandfather's trailer, overwhelmed by information. The whole way back no one said a word. Auntie Lin saw their pensive faces when they arrived and fixed them heaping bowls of fried rice. Veronica handled her Chinese hot sauce well, but Metzger had sweat pouring from his scalp as he wolfed down the food with an equal amount of water. He never complained, but eating the fried rice was clearly an unanticipated ordeal.

After lunch, they gathered in the living room, sprawling stickily along the leather couches. The single air conditioner in the front window whined tiredly; with the curtains closed and the ceiling fan on full, the room was barely tolerable. Still, it was better than the rooftop patio.

Natasha passed out pieces of paper and pencils. Their first order of business was to find out what the crib was. They had 12 characters. What made it more difficult was that there were no spaces between any of the letters in the book at all.

But at least they had the crib.

With the crib written at the tops of their pages, each of them sat for an hour, writing guesses, then seeing if the letter sequences and frequencies were the same as in the crib. Sadly, and frustratingly, none of them had any luck.

They heard the sound of two vehicles squealing to a stop outside, then the crunch of many boots on gravel, running toward the house.

Metzger took off for the back of the trailer only a moment before someone began hammering on the door.

"Open up! We know you're in there."

Natasha frowned as she stood. She exchanged looks with Veronica and Derrick.

"I said open up. We have the house surrounded."

She went to the door. "What's going on? This is Natasha Oliver. I live here."

She heard whispers from the other side of the door, then came a voice she recognized. "Natasha, this is Mr. Hopkins. Can you open the door, honey?"

She turned to Veronica and scrunched her nose. She hated being called *honey*.

Veronica made the universal sign for shooting oneself in the head. Derrick, meanwhile, gathered the papers into a pile, then shoved a comic book over the top of them.

"What's going on, Mr. Hopkins?" Natasha asked, pouring on as much innocence as she could. And it wasn't easy. In her mind's eye, he was standing out by the buses watching all the soldiers being killed.

"Nothing, dear. I have some men with me who are looking for an escaped prisoner. They need to come inside and conduct a search."

She hated being called *dear* worse than she hated being called *honey*. "Do they have a warrant, Mr. Hopkins?"

Hopkins didn't answer right away. Instead, there was more muffled conversation from the other side of the door.

"Natasha, dear, they don't need a warrant. In the interests of National Security and the PATRIOT Act, they have a right to enter your home whether you want them to or not. I'd open up if I were you."

Veronica shook her head vigorously, while Derrick stared at her with eyes the size of clocks.

Where was her dad when she needed him? Frustration and fear shot through Natasha. Everyone back in Willow Grove knew that the reason Auntie Lin had stayed around was because the kids needed someone that they could count on to raise them. But there were some things her nanny couldn't do and standing up to armed men was one of them.

Natasha could just imagine something horrible happening, the armed men breaking down the door and doing something to her and Derrick and Veronica. The best thing to do would be to let them in and hope for the best. After all, it appeared as if Mr. Hopkins was trying to make this look legal, so if she played along, maybe she'd have a chance. Besides, if they did find Metzger, they couldn't rightly take him straight to the zombie factory. Not with all of them as witnesses.

"Natasha, are you there?"

"Yes. I'm opening the door now. Hold on a moment." She glanced back to find that Metzger had disappeared. She didn't know where he'd gone, but she had to trust that he'd find a place where he couldn't be found.

She took a deep breath to steady herself and opened the door.

Two soldiers dressed in black, combat helmets atop their heads, stood to either side of the door, rifles pointing right at her. Mr. Hopkins stood between them, dressed in a red polo shirt and jeans, wearing a self-satisfied smile.

"Mind if we come in?"

She stood aside. Never having had a weapon pointed at her before, Natasha was stunned. The very idea that she was one trigger pull away from death made her chest tighten. She felt hot tears prick her eyes and fought them back as all three men entered the house.

"So where is he?" Hopkins asked Derrick. "Have you seen him, son?"

"Leave him alone." Veronica started to stand, but one of the soldiers pushed her down. "Don't tell them anything, Derrick."

"Don't pay attention to Ms. Veronica, Derrick. Her rap sheet is bigger than her common sense. Did she tell you that she has a criminal record? Did you know that she liked to burglarize people's homes when they were away at work?"

Derrick looked from Veronica to his sister.

"Stop bullying Derrick," Natasha said, recovering from her initial shock.

"Then tell us where he is."

"He's not here."

"Then why are there four glasses and only three of you?" Hopkins pointed at the coffee table.

Hopkins glanced down at the comic book resting atop the pile of papers with their decoding efforts. If Hopkins picked it up, he'd most assuredly see what they'd been working on.

Then, of course, Hopkins did exactly what she was afraid of, picking up the comic book and holding it up to the light. "I thought I heard that Batman was dead. Did he come back to life or something?" He waved the comic book at Derrick to get the boy's attention.

"He is dead," Derrick said. "That's Robin. He took his place."

"The kid? I thought he was short."

"I suppose he grew up."

Hopkins grinned at the comic and shook his head. "Kid stuff." He dropped the comic back on the stack of papers. "So about those four glasses?" he asked, pinning Natasha with a glare.

"The fourth one belongs to my Auntie Lin," Natasha said. She couldn't even breathe. The words came out barely above a whisper. She added hurriedly, "You met her at the Space Station."

"Your Auntie Lin, huh?" Hopkins sucked air through his teeth. "If only we could all have an Auntie Lin." He snapped his fingers. "Phillips, search the trailer and let me know when you find him."

"Yes, Sir," said one of the soldiers, turning and heading down the hall, weapon leading the way.

Natasha moved to follow, but Hopkins held out his hand. She stopped and stared fearfully down the hall. All she could do was watch as the soldier searched the kitchen, opening the cabinets.

He even checked the refrigerator and the oven, as if Metzger could somehow shrink himself.

When Phillips was done with the kitchen, he moved down the hall to the first bedroom and eased into it as if something deadly lay within.

She had to wonder herself where Metzger had gone. Had he escaped out a window? Was he hiding under one of the beds? The way the soldier was searching it seemed inevitable that Metzger would be caught. What would they do with him once they found him? Would they still turn him into a zombie or would they execute him on the spot?

The soldier cleared one bedroom and headed for the next, which Natasha had claimed as her own, then came to a locked door: Auntie Lin's room.

Phillips called out to the other soldier, who joined him at the door. While the new soldier guarded the door, Phillips concluded his search by going through the master bedroom. An immense crash could have been the dresser going over. Natasha pictured her father's things scattered on the floor and crushed under booted heels. She frowned at Hopkins, who stared placidly into the distance.

When the soldiers met again at Auntie Lin's door, Hopkins pulled a radio from his back pocket and spoke into it, asking if there'd been any sign of Metzger. The reply was negative. He told them to keep watching, then shoved the radio back in his pocket, turned to Natasha and said, "Let's stop dicking around."

He marched down the hall and turned back to Natasha. "I'll give you one chance. You call to him and get him out here and it will be the safest thing for him. If Phillips and Roscoe go in after him, there's no telling what will happen."

Natasha just stared back at Hopkins. She knew the truth of what he said, but what was she to do? If she was even to acknowledge that Metzger was there, it would be his death sentence. The only thing she could do was wait it out and hope for the best.

Hopkins shook his head, then knocked on the door. "Hello in there?"

There was no answer.

He knocked a little harder. "Open up, please."

A female voice came through the wood, speaking in Chinese. *"Bié jìnlai! Bié jìnlai! Wo shi chiluóluó."*

Hopkins glanced at each of the soldiers, who shrugged in response, then shook his head and frowned. "Open the door or we're going to break it down."

The voice repeated, *"Bié jìnlai! Bié jìnlai! Wo shi chiluóluó."*

Hopkins stepped back and pointed to the door. One of the soldiers kicked hard at the door knob. The door shattered at the lock and flung open.

The soldier spoke for the first time. "Oh – my – God!"

"Please! Get out of here!" came Auntie Lin's hysterical shriek.

Natasha ran over to see what was going on, imagining monsters. This time no one stopped her. When she looked in, she was as startled as the soldier beside her.

Hopkins averted his gaze, a look of disgust on his face. "Get in there and check for Metzger," he said.

The soldiers didn't move, but he yelled at them until they entered.

Auntie Lin backed away and sat on a cedar chest, almost knocking over a picture sitting on it. She crossed her legs demurely and stared daggers at the soldiers checking under her bed and inside her closet. When they didn't find anyone, they turned to Hopkins.

He was far from pleased. "Wherever he is," he snarled, "know that we'll be watching for him. Specialist Metzger is a dangerous man. Listen to him at your own risk."

He glanced once more at Auntie Lin, then turned his head and left in disgust. The soldiers followed him to the front of the trailer. When they left, Veronica slammed the door behind them, then locked it.

Natasha turned to Auntie Lin with a *What the hell were you thinking?* look.

Auntie Lin cackled happily as she stood, crossed the room, and donned a robe.

"What's so funny?" Natasha asked.

"This old body still has its uses."

Natasha couldn't help but smirk. And the smirk turned into a full-fledged smile when the cedar chest opened and Metzger climbed out.

It had become a daily regimen to face off against his captured monster. Gerald Duphrene had finished a lunch of tuna salad and sliced apples, washed his dishes, dusted the inside of the trailer, and now found himself parked in front of the Silvas' trailer once again.

He couldn't be certain, but he believed that the monster scared him a little less now than it did yesterday. *Knowledge will set you free*, he told himself. For that matter, *whatever kind of monster this is it can't be as bad as the thousands of Chinese soldiers who charged your position every day for three years.*

"Fucking gook bastards."

He grinned as he said it. Funny how things he'd thought left behind in the war could come back and help him in the present day. He trundled up the steps into the house. The bedroom door was still cracked. He heard the monster before he saw it. It made that peculiar wheezing sound, as if it were trying to breathe but had forgotten how.

Gerald thought of an asthmatic he'd known in basic training. The poor sap had wanted to join the army so badly. His brother had served in the Pacific against the Japs and all he wanted to do was share in the family fame. But try as he might, even a round of push-ups would leave him gasping helplessly for air. Gerald couldn't remember the boy's name, but the sound he made was like the sound the monster made. The comparison helped him. After all, who could be afraid of an asthmatic monster?

Taking a deep breath, he stepped into the room. For a second he wanted to turn and run, but he beat that feeling into submission with his mantra.

The monster hadn't changed much. Its uniform still hung in tatters over green skin. Its hair grew in clumps, like grass in the seams of the sidewalk. The eyes still shone with yellow determination. More importantly, the jaws of the trap still held the leg.

"How ya doing, you fucking gook bastard?" Gerald kept his voice under control.

It didn't answer. Of course, Gerald had never thought it would.

"Your pals have been chewing their way through town. They got the Beachys last night. Not very neighborly of you."

The monster's wheezing increased. Its face drew into a half-smile, lips pulled back from teeth that chattered against each other.

Gerald took a step closer. "I bet you'd like to eat me, wouldn't you, you fucking gook bastard? You'd like nothing more than to have a Gerald Duphrene sandwich, isn't that true?"

The monster suddenly exploded into action, lunging for Gerald with arms outstretched.

Gerald backed away until his back hit the door. He clamped his mouth shut to keep from screaming.

The monster lunged again and again at him, as if it could break the chain around its foot. It extended its arms and clawed the air with its hands.

"Fucking gook bastard," Gerald mumbled. His heart was in his throat.

Then he noticed the jaws of the trap. During the commotion they'd slipped down the leg, scoring the monster's calf to the bone. The jaws now rested on the ankle, too low, it seemed, to be as effective as they had been. Had this been a man, he'd be screaming with pain, but the monster didn't seem to feel it at all.

Gerald wondered how much longer the trap would hold his pet monster.

The answer came right away.

The monster lunged again, this time peeling away the skin from the ankle to the tip of its toes as it freed itself from the jaws of the trap. Without the chain to hold it up, it fell, and in doing so, knocked Gerald to the ground.

Gerald kicked out with his feet.

The monster grabbed one, and used it to pull itself towards him.

Gerald kicked harder, catching the monster in the face several times until it let go. Then he turned to run, scrambling to his feet. A piercing pain in his leg made him scream. Had the thing bitten him?

Gerald leaped into the hall and ran into the bathroom. He slammed the door, pressed his back to it and howled his mantra, his eyes closed, prayers shooting like machine gun rounds into the heavens.

The monster beat on the door for a moment, then continued down the hall and out the door. Gerald counted to ten, then jerked the door open and ran after the monster.

What if it came into contact with someone else?

Gerald knew that he could not let that happen.

Veronica stood at the window, peering through the curtains. "I can't see anyone, but that doesn't mean that they aren't there."

Metzger sat on the couch, running his hand though his hair. "There are probably some men around back that we can't see. If I was setting up surveillance, I'd sure as hell have someone back there. Damn." He shook his head. "Sorry to have brought all this trouble here."

Natasha sat beside him. She wanted to put her arms around him, but was afraid of what he might do. In fact, she was more afraid that he'd let her, than that he'd reject her.

"I got it!" Derrick suddenly yelled. He held up his paper. "This is it. I know it."

Veronica turned. "You figured it out?" She grinned. "Look at the little genius."

"Who're you calling little?" Derrick strutted to the end of the coffee table and stood in front of the TV. He held up the sheaf of papers. "Look at this. We knew what the crib was before we even knew the crib existed. Grandpa had wanted us to find it out all along. Heck, it was in front of us all the time."

"So what is it?" Metzger asked.

"It's really too perfect." Derrick grinned. "Where were the zombies meant to work?"

"What?" Veronica didn't understand the question.

"You mean the project?" Natasha concentrated.

Derrick nodded quickly.

"Orbit?" Metzger guessed.

"Space," Veronica said. "The zombies were meant to work in space."

"Right. And what do we have in this town related to space?"

Natasha snapped her fingers. "The Space Station Restaurant."

"Booya! Kewpie doll for my sister. Space Station is twelve letters. That's the crib."

"How can you be so sure?" Metzger asked.

"Because I've already begun translating and it fits right in. Now to figure out the other letters and we'll have this completely translated."

"How hard will that be?"

"Not so hard. It's like a jigsaw puzzle. Think of the crib as the outside edges. Once you have that, it's only a matter of time before you fill in the middle."

They spent the next several hours poring through the book. Now that they'd found the key to decoding the text, there was an avalanche of information regarding tides, the appearance of strange lights, earthquakes, missing people, and all sorts of events, all laid out with links to one another. Grandpa Lazlo had even tracked the comings and goings of trucks and the "mysterious dark buses" entering and leaving the "desalination plant," or what Natasha now thought of as the *zombie factory*.

The sheer amount of information was overwhelming. Taken separately it would appear to be the rantings of a crackpot. But as a whole, this information was undeniable. One couldn't ignore that the flashing green lights were always preceded by an earthquake, which always resulted in someone missing, a fire in one of the trailers, or increased activity at the zombie factory. The question was what to do with the book. Should they turn it over to the police? Everyone had an idea as to who was responsible, from Simon Cowell to Oprah Winfrey to CNN to the local police. But at this point they couldn't trust anyone. Who knew who else worked with Hopkins? Maude had already proven to be a traitor. Maybe even Gert. Perhaps she was even – as Natasha thought – in the zombie factory working in some office, doing whatever it is they do in zombie factory offices.

No one could really decide what to do. Derrick and Veronica fell asleep on the couch, Metzger in one of the easy chairs.

But Natasha was too riled up. She had something she needed to get off her chest.

She headed to the trailer next door and, without hesitation, knocked on the door.

CHAPTER NINETEEN

Maude's pearl-blue eyes fluttered, then blinked. She stared at Natasha with an expression that seemed to be a mix of embarrassment and relief.

"You knew," Natasha said. "You knew all this time and never told anyone."

Maude fell heavily onto the couch in her living room, looking as though the words had beaten her down.

Natasha closed the door behind her. "How could you have known and not said something? For all we know, they killed my grandfather and Gertie. I thought they were your friends. I thought you *loved* them."

When Maude said nothing, Natasha closed her eyes and sighed. "Did grandpa know who you were, or did you keep it secret all this time?"

"So you talked to Andy."

"We talked to Andy."

Maude nodded. It took a while for her to say anything. She licked her lips several times and glanced around, looking as if she wanted to be anywhere but where she was.

"I do love them. I love them more than you'll know. Laz and Gertie were my life. I would have stopped if I could have, but in the end I had no choice."

"You had no choice?" Natasha's eyes flashed. She was insulted by the remark. "Of course you had a choice. We've all been wracking our brains trying to figure out what's going on, and here you knew all along. I can't fucking believe it. How can you not feel like an accomplice?"

Natasha's question echoed in the silence that followed. When Maude finally answered, her voice was barely audible. "I *am* an accomplice. It's my fault people are dead. Had I told them in the beginning, they would still be alive. You're right on all counts. I am a terrible, terrible human being."

Natasha's rage, which had known no bounds, suddenly broke against Maude's guilt. She wasn't yet ready to quit, but her expression softened as she stared into the devastated face; for truly, if there was a woman who looked as if she'd lost everything, it was Maude.

"So why did you do it?" Natasha finally asked.

"Why did I do it?" Maude breathed more than said the words. She picked at the cuticles on her fingers, her gaze locked on the motion. "I never thought it would come to this. I mean, when I came here to work, everything was over, or at least it was supposed to be. Reagan came into office and cut the budget. We were all out of a job. Andy hung on because he couldn't bring himself to ever do anything else. He was always hoping the project would open back up. I hung on because they said they'd pay me to tell them if anyone came poking around and asking about the program. And I was thinking about Russians." She smiled weakly, then looked down once more. "But no one ever came around... no one at all. The more the years passed, the further I left it all behind me. I essentially forgot about it... That is, until..."

"Until people started to go missing," Natasha offered.

Maude nodded and repeated, "Until people started to go missing. Then I began to wonder, *What if?*"

"When did you know it was for real?" Natasha asked.

"When Hopkins came to town." Maude made a face like something had died in her mouth. "He only comes around to check on me the first Tuesday of every month. When I saw him the other day I knew there was going to be trouble."

"The zombies, you mean."

Maude flicked a smile, but it was gone almost before Natasha saw it. "Is that what you guys are calling them?"

"Sure. What else would we call them?"

"I don't know. It never really occurred to us to call them something back then."

Natasha nodded.

"It was really a terrific idea. Imagine creating a worker who didn't need to breathe or eat. A worker who could survive the radiation of space. Imagine what we could have accomplished had this worked."

"But it didn't."

"That was Reagan's fault, not ours. Kennedy approved the idea, Johnson funded the initial research, and it took a third rate actor to crush any hope of space travel for the next hundred years." Maude gripped the spoon in her hand until her fist shook. "Oh, I used to be wedded to this program so completely. I loved the job so damned much, and then one day, *poof.*"

"You know that we only took terminally-ill prisoners when I was with the program? I never would have been a part of a program that took healthy people. I never would have allowed it."

But Natasha wouldn't let it be. "I suppose the thing to do is forgive you. It's pretty easy. It sure would make me feel better." She took a picture out of her back pocket and stared at it. It was a picture of her grandfather when he was a boy, all elbows and knees as he held aloft a fish for everyone to see, his ebullience projecting through the gap-toothed smile of a kid who never imagined he'd be a zombie's dinner. "But the dead can't forgive. They can't return to hear your excuses, no matter how good they are. So if my grandpa can't forgive you, I'll be damned if I'll do it for him."

Tears ran from Maude's eyes. She asked, "What are you going to do now?"

"Find my dad. It's about time I sobered him up and we got the hell out of here."

Natasha turned and stormed outside.

She marched to the restaurant and found it closed. Likewise, the Laundromat was empty. One could only hope Carrie had taken her children home.

The wind had picked up and was tossing her hair. The sky had gone from blue to gunmetal gray as the storm drew towards Bombay Beach.

Natasha turned around, glaring at the seawall, the trailers, the storefronts and the never-ending sand. She balled her fists to her sides and screamed in frustration.

"Daddy, where are you?!"

She shook with rage.

Then something moved far down the street towards the trailer which they'd been afraid to go into. A figure ran into the street. She couldn't make it out this far away, but whoever it was, it was moving fast and coming straight at her.

Fear supplanted her rage. What if it was one of those zombies? She looked around her as if the locked buildings would suddenly be unlocked and open. But to no avail.

When she looked back down the street the figure was halfway towards her, lurching more than running. Her heart leaped into her mouth.

Then a golf cart erupted from a side street, crashing into the side of the zombie, the collision rocking the cart and hurling the zombie into the seawall.

The driver swerved towards her. Behind her the zombie clambered unsteadily to its feet.

The cart was driven by the hook-handed man, Gerald. Barely slowing, he yelled for her to get in. Without any more urging, she ran beside it for a second and jumped aboard. She turned around and saw that the zombie was still coming.

"Hold on and lean left," he yelled.

Natasha grabbed the handle on the side of the seat and did as he said. They took the ninety-degree turn as fast as they dared; the cart ran on two wheels for a moment before slamming back to earth.

Then they sped away. When she finally looked back, the zombie had disappeared. They made two more turns before pulling into the driveway of an impeccably-manicured trailer on First Street.

When they pulled to a stop, Gerald took a moment to set the break and plug the battery into a cord that ran from a pole beside the trailer. Meanwhile, Natasha sat stock still in the seat.

"Why don't you come inside for some iced tea?" he offered, finally.

Gerald limped up his porch steps without looking back and entered his home.

Natasha waited a moment, undecided on what to do, then hurried inside and locked the door behind her.

"Don't know if that's necessary," Gerald said. "I haven't found one smart enough to turn a knob yet."

She flashed him a look and he nodded.

"You're right. It's probably bound to happen sooner or later. Better to lock it." He handed her a glass of ice tea. "Here, drink this and then tell me why you were out there hollering at the sky."

He went into the bathroom and was gone for several minutes. When he returned, he still limped slightly. He smiled through gritted teeth.

She drank deeply. The tea was sweetened and went down clean and cold.

"Thank you for saving me."

"Wasn't nothing. Damn thing got away from me anyway. Been trying to catch it all day."

"Why was it trying to get me?"

Gerald shrugged. "Not so sure it was trying to get you as much as it was trying to get away from me."

"Where was it when you found it?" she asked.

Gerald stared at her for a moment, as if deciding how he was going to answer her. Finally, he said, "I'd captured it. I thought maybe if I had one to look at, I might not be so damned afraid of it."

"Easy to be afraid of something that isn't supposed to exist."

Gerald took a sip of his iced tea. "I suppose."

"Where'd you keep it? It was in the blue and yellow trailer, wasn't it?"

Gerald blinked several times, then nodded.

"We could tell it was there," Natasha said. "We were too afraid to go inside. Where do you suppose it went?"

"I'm guessing it went back in the water."

"Not the plant?"

Gerald appraised her as he refilled her glass and handed it back to her, gesturing for her to take a seat at the small breakfast table beside the kitchen.

When they were both seated, he spoke. "So you know about the plant, huh?"

She nodded, looking at the old man. For the first time since he'd picked her up, she really noticed the hooks on his hands. Made of stainless steel, they had a utilitarian look to them. She'd always thought of hooks at the end of arms as something scary, a main ingredient for urban mythology about lonely places along the road and serial killers. But the hooks weren't scary at all. What had Veronica said – that he'd lost them in the Korean War? His face was friendly, carved by decades of living. He wasn't a large man, but the combination of his hooks, his piercing blue eyes and his firm jaw made him seem almost larger than life. She felt tears burn her eyes as she wondered about her own grandfather and then, of course, her father.

"Are they really zombies?" she asked.

Gerald stared into his drink. "Not sure what they are. Not sure that calling them something makes them any better or worse. Maybe it would be best if you and your family leave."

"I can't." She barely got the words free. "My father is missing."

He looked at her and shook his head. "Sometimes people go missing around here through no fault of their own."

Natasha opened her mouth to speak, but couldn't. Her worst

fear had been voiced by someone who knew more than she did.

"But that doesn't mean it happened to your father," Gerald hastened to add. He leaned down and adjusted his pant leg. It rode up and had caught on a wide white bandage soaked with red.

"You're bleeding," Natasha said.

Gerald shook his head. "It's nothing. I deserve it," he glanced at Natasha. "Anyway, when's the last time you saw your father?"

Natasha told him, then explained about his alcoholism.

To that he smiled. "Believe it or not, that gives us hope. I've seen my share of drunks holed up in these trailers and know which ones are best for that sort of thing."

"So you'll help me?"

"Course I will. Not like I have other things to occupy my time."

CHAPTER TWENTY

Mexican television told the tale of Tropical Storm Hiawatha. It had slammed into Puerto Peñasco, uprooting anchors and sending fishing boats sailing down main streets normally trod by tourists. By the time it left, the death toll was twelve and climbing. Meteorologists predicted that the storm would lose power as it raced inland. Yuma, Arizona should expect winds in excess of seventy miles an hour and five inches of rain. The Salton Sea, half that.

Veronica finished translating the news and switched back on the video tape of old *Three Stooges* episodes. Metzger stood staring out the window. Natasha and Veronica sagged on the couches, and Derrick sat at the kitchen table, hunched over his papers, transcribing his grandfather's code.

No one laughed at the antics on the television; the show was just on to keep them from dwelling too deeply on the zombies living less than a mile from them.

Natasha had returned less than an hour ago and kept her conversations with Maude and Gerald to herself. She wanted to do something, to get out of Bombay Beach. That Gerald had offered to search for her father was of immense help. The old man knew the town better than anyone, and knew places where people tended to hide. With any luck, they'd be on the road heading away real soon.

Veronica sighed, went to the kitchen, poured herself a glass of water and drank it down. When she was finished, she returned to the living room, shaking her head. "This is all just so damned far-fetched, you know?"

"Straight out of a movie," Natasha said.

"Or a comic book," Derrick added.

"So what would a comic book hero do?" Veronica asked.

"He would –"

"Or she," Natasha interrupted.

"He, or she, would go to the source. They'd find out where the zombies are, blow up the lab – the lunar outpost, the stronghold, wherever the zombies were – he or she would go there, kill all the bad guys and save the world."

"And what would happen to the hero?"

"He'd live on to the next issue."

Veronica sighed. "Remind me to come back as a comic book hero in my next life."

"Better watch what you're wishing for. You might come back as Howard the Duck," Metzger said.

Derrick laughed. "That's funny."

Veronica didn't understand the reference, and stared at Derrick, but he was steadfastly ignoring her, instead working diligently on his decoding and transcription.

Natasha snapped to a sitting position. It took a moment for her to speak, but when she did, her words were low and clipped. "You're all being childish. People have been killed, for God's sake." She glared at everyone. "Tell me, what are we going to do when night comes? We going to read comic books? We going to watch television? We're sitting ducks in here."

Everyone exchanged glances.

Metzger was the first to break the silence. "You're right, Natasha's right. But we can't go anywhere without your father."

"But that doesn't mean we have to sit around like a bunch of idiots," she said.

Metzger turned to Veronica, "Do you think your Auntie and Uncle would come if you told them the truth?"

She shook her head. "They wouldn't believe me if I swore on a bible. It's just too –" she struggled for a word.

"Crazy?" Derrick offered.

"Yeah. Crazy."

So if we can't leave, then what shall we do?" Metzger asked the room.

Everyone watched Moe beat the shit out of Shemp and Larry with an axe handle. No one laughed.

"What if we had one to show them – your aunt and uncle, the town, everyone?" Derrick suddenly asked. "What if we blew this whole thing out of the water by getting a zombie and showing it to the world?"

"And how are we going to do that, little man?" Metzger asked, turning from the window.

Derrick made a face at the comment, but continued. "Remember the zombie in the trailer? The one I was afraid to go into?"

Metzger snapped his fingers, his face brightening. "That's right. We almost forgot about that."

Natasha shook her head. "I think that one's gone."

All eyes went to her.

"What do you mean?" Veronica asked.

Natasha sighed, then told them what had happened, and about Gerald.

"You mean you almost got eaten by a zombie and you didn't think it was important enough to tell us about?" Derrick asked, his mouth agape.

"It was a far cry from being eaten. It didn't even get near me, really," Natasha said.

"What do you think this guy Gerald was doing with the zombie?" Metzger asked.

Natasha shrugged. "I don't know. Whatever it was, he wasn't happy about it."

Veronica shook her head. "Then that's that. Scratch one more idea."

"Wait," Derrick said. "My idea isn't dead. My grandpa had all the information here. He just didn't have enough time to put it all together. According to this, right before there was any significant event, there were strange green flashes in the water. They were quick, but if you were looking right at them, you could see them plain as can be."

"I wonder what the flashes are?" Natasha murmured.

"It says that the flashes were always preceded by earthquake swarms," Derrick added.

"We had those earthquakes a few days ago," Natasha said.

He nodded. "And then the big zombie attack along the road. Do you know what I think? I think the flashes are some sort of power release, like a bleed-off. When the power builds too much, then they have to release it in the form of light energy."

Veronica's eyes widened. "How the hell can you know that? What school did you go to?"

"The Robert Heinlein and Iain M. Banks school of science fiction."

"The what?"

"Also don't forget Marvel and DC comics. Tolkien. *Star Trek. Star Wars. Watchmen.*"

Veronica clapped her hands and laughed. "Oh my God. You're a nerd."

"If that's what you call people in L.A. who actually read something besides the sides of milk cartons and wanted posters in the post offices, then yes, I'm a nerd."

"Bill Gates was a nerd and now he's one of the richest men in the world," Metzger put in.

Derrick shot Metzger a thank you look.

"But all this is from comics, books and movies," Veronica pointed out. "It can't really work, can it?"

"Why not? The best science fiction uses some science to make it look real, otherwise it's too far-fetched to believe. I've learned

more about science from those things than I have in school,"
Derrick said. "Anyway, it's just a theory."

"But it's as good a theory as anyone's," Metzger said, again
returning to the window. "Hey, the weather is picking up outside.
This storm looks like it's going to dump on us soon."

"How soon?" Natasha asked.

Metzger shook his head. "Don't ask me. I'm not the weatherman.
I run from zombies for a living."

"We have an hour or two before the worst of it arrives,"
Veronica said.

"We need to find out," Natasha said, coming to a decision. She
swung her legs onto the floor. "We need proof." She thought
about Gerald and the zombie that he'd been chasing. If only he'd
been able to capture the creature, she wouldn't have to suggest
what she was about to suggest.

"And how do you figure we're going to get that? Just walk
up to the zombie factory, bang on the door, and ask to see the
zombies?" Veronica asked, sarcasm twisting her lips.

"Not necessarily." Natasha turned to Veronica. "I saw some
dive tanks at the Duvall's. Do you know if they use them?"

Veronica nodded.

Light twinkled in Natasha's eyes. "You do know how to dive,
don't you, living all those years in Florida?"

Metzger stared at her with the beginnings of terror as he
figured out her idea. He nodded reluctantly. "Yeah."

"Good. Then you can go down there and see what the lights
are about."

"Go down where?"

"In the water." She told them about the map she'd seen Rico
going over with the off-limits area right beside the quay. They all
agreed that if there was to be some sort of underwater entrance,
or exit, it would be there.

"You're volunteering me to dive into the water and look for
zombies?"

She nodded.

"Might as well ask me to put my head in a lion's mouth."

"They have two sets of tanks," Veronica said.

Natasha shook her head at Veronica, but the other girl didn't listen. Instead, she repeated herself.

"So they have two pairs," Metzger said with macabre glee. "Then you can join me, can't you Natasha?"

"I don't know how to use them."

"Oh, it'll be easy."

"But maybe we should –"

"No buts, Natasha. You're right. We do need to check." To Derrick, he said, "We'll need the two of you onshore to make sure nothing comes in after us. Think you can handle it?"

An hour later found Derrick sitting on an overturned barrel at the edge of the Salton Sea, near the quay that ran to the desalination plant. Behind him the sump pump growled angrily as it fought to keep the water out of the streets. The sky was a mat of grey steel, and the wind blew offshore, raising white caps on the waves.

Veronica sat beside him. She held a speargun across her lap. The combination of the L.A. Lakers basketball jersey and basketball shoes, her wild hair, her mocha skin and the weapon made her look like a gangbanger from the *Jonny Quest* cartoon.

Derrick had the urge to kiss her, but he'd never kissed a girl before. Her lips were only a foot away from his. All he had to do was lean over and do it.

What's the worst that could happen? he asked himself. Eyeing the glint of sunlight off the wickedly-barbed tip of the spear, he had his answer.

But looking out at his sister and Metzger with their SCUBA gear on, wading through the dead fish and seaweed, he had a feeling that this was going to be his only chance. This could be the end of things, and if it really was going to be the end, he didn't want to go out without having kissed a girl. After all, didn't all the heroes in his comics, books and movies kiss the girl? Then why shouldn't he?

So he leaned over and kissed her square on the lips.

And to his great surprise, Veronica kissed him back.

When they finished, Derrick stared out at his sister as she fully submerged, with the biggest shit-eating grin that ever graced a teenaged boy's face. He never once looked at Veronica, but could feel the heat of her gaze.

"You're gonna be something else someday," was all she said.

The water felt nasty, like olive oil mixed with fish guts. Natasha knew she was going to stink when she got out of it. And she didn't like the way the mask enclosed her in its claustrophobic embrace, stealing her peripheral vision. In fact, she hated the whole enterprise and couldn't believe she'd been talked into joining Metzger.

He swam a little forward and to her right. The idea was to hug the shoreline along the quay until they found some indication of something man-made. The water wasn't very deep; her gauge read twelve feet. Off to her left the sea was deeper, but the slope was gradual. In fact, it was shallow enough that light from the sky above filtered through the water and provided enough illumination to guide them.

They'd found the SCUBA gear at the Duvall's place right where Natasha had last seen it. The tanks had been recently filled, the date scribbled on a sticker on the side of each one. Metzger said everything was in good working order, so with a quick lesson on how to use the equipment, he guided her into the water.

Now she swam next to him, her flippers doing most of the work, her hands out in front of her. She felt clunky. Her legs didn't move as smoothly as they could, and certainly not as smoothly as Metzger's. His long, bare legs swished slowly back and forth. He'd removed all of his clothes except his underwear. She'd kept her underwear on too, and a T-shirt.

A layer of bird and fish bones, probably from the multiple die-offs over the years, made the sand-covered bottom look like a battlefield where the dead numbered in the thousands. Visibility in the dark green water was reduced to about ten feet. She could just make out Metzger's head as he swam beside her, but there was nothing else except darker water beyond, where the shadows lay.

They swam for a minute or two before they encountered something. The sand gave way to a squared corner of concrete. They stopped and reached down to touch it. One edge of the concrete ran parallel with the quay. The other ran straight into the sea.

They followed the edge along the quay for a while, but it kept going far out of sight. They backtracked and began to follow the other edge out to sea. Natasha noticed that the depth of the water was still relatively shallow, no more than twenty feet. She also noted that the expanse of concrete, larger than multiple football fields as far as she could tell, was devoid of bone or other detritus. It was as if someone, or something, kept the surface clean.

Metzger tapped her on the arm. He pointed towards the middle of the concrete expanse. Natasha nodded and gestured for him to lead.

They swam languidly. Here and there she could feel the swells above as the wind from Tropical Storm Hiawatha ripped the surface. She wondered how Veronica and her brother were doing. Leaving them topside with the speargun was the best they could do, but the weapon was for monsters. If Hopkins were to arrive with soldiers, what could they actually do?

Beneath Natasha, the concrete remained clean of debris. If it hadn't existed on the bottom of the murky sea she would have thought of it as a parking lot. A shadow appeared in the distance, and she touched Metzger's leg. He nodded without turning, indicating that he'd seen it too. They swam slowly, minds racing at the possibilities of what the murk might unveil.

But what they eventually saw didn't make a lot of sense. Four thick chains covered in moss and algae were piled on the concrete. Each chain was attached to an immense eyebolt embedded in the cement, and beside this was a metal box with a blinking red light. Beneath the light was a circular hole, but Natasha couldn't figure out what belonged there.

Metzger reached down and hefted the chains. By his ponderous movements, Natasha could tell that their weight was considerable.

They stared at the box and chains for a few more moments, then moved on, trying to maintain their original heading. Soon other shadows appeared, each one a dozen or so feet apart. The next one they swam to was virtually identical to the one they'd just left. The only exception was that the chains didn't have as much algae, and a nozzled hose ran from the mysterious hole inset beneath the curiously blinking red light.

They moved on to the next shadow and stopped dead. The use to which the chains and nozzle had been purposed was no longer a mystery. For in front of them was one of the zombies, bound at the wrists and ankles by the chains, the hose running from the box into a metal pucker on the back of its neck.

Thankfully it faced the other direction, but that did little to still Natasha's hammering heart. Its skin was mottled green. Here and there she could see bone, along the spine, on the left hip and right shoulder blade. The zombie couldn't stand up straight. The chains pulled it down so it was almost on all fours.

She thought back to the empty chains she'd seen. Were those evidence of zombies who'd escaped, or were they evidence of zombies yet to be made?

Metzger grabbed her attention by waving a hand in front of her mask. She jerked back, startled momentarily, then looked at him. He indicated that they should move behind the zombie to another shape down the line. She agreed that that would be the ideal, allowing them to look at the zombies without affording the creatures the same opportunity. There was no telling what the zombies might do if they saw her and Metzger. So they headed off at a right angle, swimming slowly towards the next large shadow in line.

This one was much like the last, except it had no hair at all. Parts of the skull showed through the skin. Darker greens indicated that it might have been in the water longer, or at least dead longer.

They continued, swimming past zombie after zombie. She quickly lost count, but they must have numbered in the hundreds. Natasha suddenly realized the immensity of what she was seeing. The broad, unbroken expanse of concrete had been created to hold zombies in rows so that they could be tested. Water was a far cry from space, but just as unbreathable. That this immense slab existed just beneath the surface of the sea within a stone's throw of the town of Bombay Beach was terrifying.

Finally she and Metzger came upon a connection where a zombie had broken free of one of its manacles. Not broken free, Natasha realized, but the hand on that arm had rotted away, leaving nothing more than a stump. As they swam past, it turned towards them and for the first time she saw the eerie yellow glow in its eyes.

They stopped cold.

As did the zombie. It seemed confused at first, but then its stare turned into a predatory scowl. Teeth gnashed slowly in the water, as if it could taste them from five feet away. Then suddenly it exploded into a fury of movement. Its arms, legs – its entire body thrashed against the chains with such madness that both Metzger and Natasha found themselves backing away. So violent was its attempt to get at them that its left arm broke in two, allowing the second manacle to fall to the concrete floor. Then it tried to rush towards them, but was held back by the chains attached to its legs.

Both Metzger and Natasha turned to flee, but found themselves face to face with another zombie. Natasha screamed, losing her breathing apparatus in a bubble cloud of terror.

Metzger swam towards her, clamping his hand over her mouth to once again create a seal. But instead of cooperating, she fought against it.

Natasha was caught in between lines of zombies, thrashing creatures on either side of them. The metal boxes on these zombies had blinking green lights rather than red ones. Their eyes were an unearthly yellow, radiating madness. And they were all going to break free and get her, they were going to eat her like they ate everyone else. Watching the line of zombies gnashing at the water, struggling violently to break free, she knew her fate resided in those teeth.

Natasha shook her head as Metzger tried to get her mask back on. She reached out and pushed at his face, causing a stream of bubbles to explode from his mouthpiece as it, too, dislodged.

Natasha could no longer breathe. The weight on her chest grew unbearable, and Natasha's vision began to blacken along the edges. She was going to die right here, right now, and become a zombie like the rest of them. Somewhere there was an umbilical cord ready to be shoved into her neck, manacles ready to be clasped around her limbs.

Then she found herself shuttled upwards. When they finally breached the surface, it was into the teeth of the storm. The wind howled. Rain slashed at their faces. Waves slapped their heads with each passing moment.

She inhaled deeply, half water, half air. She began to cough.

Metzger grabbed her hand and began to pull her to shore. The zombie factory was to her left and Bombay Beach was to her right. Two tiny figures broke the uniform dullness of the beach: Veronica and Derrick, or were those zombies awaiting their dinner?

She closed her eyes as she tried to catch her breath. Golden points of evil greeted her as zombies frolicked wickedly in her imagination.

She knew she was whimpering, but she couldn't stop.

She couldn't stop anything.

CHAPTER TWENTY-ONE

Night slid in with the storm like a thief, stealing the light. Wind sang along the edges of the metal trailers, like a chorus of banshees. Rain raged against the outside of Grandpa Lazlo's double-wide, a million tiny beasts pounding to get inside. Natasha lay on the couch, tossing and turning, slipping in and out of consciousness.

When Metzger had brought Natasha to shore, she was coughing water. Derrick had run to her, watching fearfully as Metzger turned her on her side and let her cough out what she'd breathed in.

Now, with Veronica peering through the window as lookout, and Metzger cradling Natasha's head on his lap, Derrick knew what was coming. That he was the youngest of them all meant nothing. His experience came from living vicariously through others who'd survived and died on his behalf.

From Borimir in *The Fellowship of the Ring*, to Jimmy Nightshade in *Something Wicked This Way Comes*, to Cory Mackenson evading the rendering truck in Zephyr, Alabama, to Ghost Rider chased across the land of the living by the legion of the dead, Derrick had vicariously survived good and bad plans, some created whole-cloth from the ether of necessity, some devised by careful consideration of all the facts. Even *Encyclopedia Brown*, as childish as the books now seemed, had taught him the need to analyze things, and understand that most often what seemed to be the obvious thing, no matter how outlandish it seemed, was what was going to happen. Derrick knew that no plan went unscathed, but he also knew that they did indeed need a plan.

They *would* be attacked.

Of that he had no doubt.

There was no way that Natasha's and Metzger's undersea reconnaissance could have gone undetected. Hopkins had their number. They'd gotten away with everything so far because the man was willing to play within the rules. He could have put them all in one of his SUVs earlier and taken them away. Derrick had seen it in the man's eyes, and for a moment there in the trailer with Auntie Lin sitting naked on the trunk hiding Metzger, Derrick had thought that Hopkins was going to do just that. It was only a matter of time before soldiers or zombies were sent after them, and their only hope of surviving was to have some form of plan.

So it was with this knowledge that Derrick leaned over his papers on the table, tongue poking out the corner of his mouth as he drew boxes and lines. Here and there he'd shake his head and erase something, only to draw it again.

Next to some of the boxes, he made notations. He made "Xs" through some of the others. Although he'd been in Bombay Beach less than a week, it felt like an eternity. He'd run through – or fled through – almost every yard in the desiccated town already, and he'd remembered what Veronica had told them about who lived where and which places were empty.

As his pen moved across the page, Derrick realized that he wasn't just drawing a map, he was drawing up battle lines.

"Someone's coming," Veronica said.

All eyes went to the girl holding the speargun, standing by the door.

Metzger and Natasha put down their mugs of hot cocoa and stood up.

Derrick grabbed his papers, took them to the kitchen, found a large Ziploc bag and shoved them inside. He grabbed another Ziploc for his grandfather's book.

"I see flashing lights. Hey! It looks like Deputy Todrunner." Veronica turned and flashed a smile.

"Do you think he's involved?" Natasha asked.

"The Mad Scientist said that there were two others. One was Maude, but he didn't know who the remaining one was," Derrick reminded them.

"Good point. Shit." Veronica eyed the spear gun in her hand with trepidation.

Auntie Lin appeared in the hallway. She too wanted to know what was going on.

Veronica shot a look back to the others in the room. "He parked outside. He's coming to the door. What should I do?"

Metzger looked around. "Get in the bathroom with the speargun. If he does something crazy, it's up to you to save us."

"What? Like leap out and shoot him with this?" She held up the speargun.

"Just go. Hurry!"

Veronica hesitated a moment more, then bolted for the bathroom.

No sooner had she turned the corner than there came knocking at the door.

Metzger went to the door and opened it.

The deputy sheriff pushed in with rain and wind behind him. He pulled the door closed as quickly as he could, but it wasn't fast enough to keep the carpet from getting soaked. "Everyone alright in here?" He removed his baseball cap and slapped it against his leg a few times.

Metzger noted that he had a pistol on his hip, a Ruger .357.

Without waiting for an answer, Todrunner looked at Natasha and said, "I've had some calls. Things have been dead-on strange around here. Any word on your father?"

Natasha shook her head. "I was hoping you had some information."

The Deputy frowned. "Nothing here, I'm afraid."

"So who'd you talk to who told you something strange was going on? Who was it who called?" Natasha asked.

"It was Maude," the Deputy said.

"What'd she say?" Metzger asked.

"Something about monsters and a government conspiracy." The deputy frowned and shook his head. "It didn't make much sense, but she was crying on the phone, so I dropped everything down in Brawly and headed here through the storm and all the chaos to see what was happening."

Derrick grabbed the phone and checked the dial tone. Nothing. "Phone's out, now."

The deputy nodded. "Went out about a half hour ago. Power lines fell across the road about 5 miles south of here. Probably won't be until the storm blows over before it's fixed."

"What do you make of Hopkins?" Derrick asked suddenly.

"You mean Sam?" The deputy shrugged. "What do you mean?"

"You heard me."

"Now wait a minute." The deputy looked at the three people in the room. "What about Sam? What's really going on?"

"Just answer the damned question," Metzger said.

"He's just some guy doing his job."

"No, really," Metzger added. "What do you *really* think of him? Do you really think he works for the Environmental Protection Agency?"

The deputy took a long moment. Finally, he said, "I think that maybe he's a little too secretive for his own good."

"Did Maude tell you that he came into this house with soldiers looking for Metzger?" Natasha asked. "Since when does the Environmental Protection Agency have soldiers working for them?"

"They don't, as far as I know." He stared at Natasha, then to Auntie Lin. "Did he do that? Is that true?"

Both Natasha and Auntie Lin nodded.

"They saw me naked," Auntie Lin added.

"And they saw her naked," Metzger repeated.

The deputy nodded respectfully to Auntie Lin, then took a seat on the couch. "Aw, hell. You better tell me everything that's happened."

"Everything?" Derrick asked dubiously.

"Everything."

Natasha began by telling him where they'd been. She described the concrete, the chains, the umbilicals and, most of all, the zombies. When they got to the part about the buses, Todrunner's eyes widened. Clearly he'd had no idea what was going on. By the time he learned about the hand kept by Dr. Gudgel, Veronica had come out of the bathroom, tired of waiting for something to happen. She'd left the speargun behind, which was probably a good thing.

When they were finished with their stories, the deputy sat stock still for a few moments. Finally he stood, pulled out his radio and tried to contact his headquarters. He got nothing but static in reply.

"Damn it all." He shook his head and cursed. "Okay, get something waterproof to wear. I'm getting you out of here. You need to be in protective custody until we can get some backup, someone in here to help me ask a few people some questions."

Natasha looked from Metzger to Derrick. "Are you serious?" she asked.

"Absolutely," he said.

They were ready to go in moments. Metzger wore an old green windbreaker that had belonged to Natasha's grandfather.

Just as they clambered out the door, the ground heaved beneath them and everything began to shake. The light beside the door cracked and broke. Everyone grabbed each other to keep from falling down; even the Sheriff's SUV seemed to rock in place.

Then it was gone, as quickly as it came.

Everyone glanced at each other, fear alive in their eyes.

Soon all five of them were in the SUV, heading down the street toward the Space Station Restaurant. The rain had let up and reduced to a drizzle, but the wind continued to howl.

Suddenly two white Suburbans roared in from side streets. One rammed into the back of the deputy's SUV, rocking it dangerously, the impact knocking people against the headrests and side windows. The second SUV came to a stop in front, blocking any escape.

Deputy Todrunner was the first to move. He unlatched the shotgun from the central lock with one flick of his hand, then rolled out of his door and came to position behind it. He brought the gun to bear on the window of the Suburban in front of him and fired twice.

Metzger bailed out of the door behind the driver. "Give me your pistol," he shouted.

"Not on your life, kid," the deputy said, as his shotgun roared again, this time taking out a black-clad soldier who had appeared from the rear of the Suburban. The soldier fell in a heap, his rifle sliding free and clattering to the ground.

Natasha screamed. Metzger turned and saw that a soldier was trying to pull her out of the other side of the SUV. Glass from a broken rear window was all over the seat. Veronica had a grip on Natasha's arm and was pulling her in the other direction.

Deputy Todrunner jerked his pistol free and fired three times across the hood towards the soldier. The soldier fell to the ground, spraying crimson as he fell.

Metzger dove for the automatic rifle the dead soldier had dropped, wrapped his hands around it and tried to bring it to bear, but found a boot holding it down and the barrel of a rifle pressing against the side of his head. He froze.

Behind him, he heard the sound of shouting. When he was finally allowed to stand, he saw the deputy with his hands on his head, blood running from his mouth and nose. Derrick, Natasha, Auntie Lin and Veronica were being pulled from the backseat and made to stand beside the deputy. At least six black-clad soldiers guarded them, and Hopkins stood directly in front of the deputy, speaking into a headset.

"Get them under control. You've got to lock this down." Then he turned to Metzger. "Destiny delayed. Don't worry son, soon you'll be with your friends."

"*These* are my friends," Metzger growled, as the barrel of the gun pushed him into line with the others.

"I meant the ones you traveled in with. The other junkies. We have a place for you, you know?"

"I think I'll pass."

Hopkins shrugged. "Like you ever had a choice."

Deputy Todrunner spat out blood. "So what they told me about you is true."

"They told you I'm a loyal patriot? They told you I'm working for the greater good, getting rid of some of our problems at the same time I'm advancing our space program?" Hopkins held out his arms. "They explained that I was a cultural multitasker, able to help the future while cleansing our past?" Hopkins regarded his prisoners melodramatically. "They shouldn't have. What a nice bunch of troublemakers they turned out to be."

"No. That you're a murderer."

"What words you use." Hopkins's eyes narrowed. "You're a yokel. You've no idea how high this goes, how important this project is."

The deputy was about to answer when they heard a strange sound. It was a song Metzger had heard before, but never quite like he was hearing it now.

The lyrics spoke of lonely streets and heartbreak hotels.

The staccato sounds of automatic gunfire interrupted the accented Elvis dirge as three of the black-clad soldiers turned and fired, but there was nothing to fire at. Instead, they went down as shots came from everywhere, punching crimson-flecked holes in their bodies.

"What the fuck?" Hopkins whirled around, only to witness seven heavily-armed locals leaving their hiding places and fanning towards them in a tightly-disciplined formation.

Leading them was the Romanian ex-Freedom fighter, an AK-47 held in his hands like it was an old friend. He wore a black, bell-bottomed tuxedo with flared sleeves. With him were the Duvall

Brothers, Jimbo Becker, Frank Gillespie, Reginald Johnson and Columbus Williams. Each of them carried a hunting rifle, which they pointed at each of the remaining soldiers.

Metzger took advantage of the confusion and hurriedly grabbed a rifle from one of the dead soldiers; an M249 light machine gun. He'd carried one with him his entire last tour in Iraq.

He locked and loaded, cradling the rifle like a lover. The sound reached Hopkins's ears. He turned and sneered. "You won't be getting very far with that."

Metzger ignored them and waved for Veronica, Natasha, Auntie Lin and Derrick to follow him. He got them to the edge of a nearby trailer before all hell broke loose.

Two more black-clad soldiers had been hiding in the rear of one of the Suburbans. They'd been able to slide around the back of the vehicle unseen and now opened fire on the Romanian Elvis and his rag-tag team of protectors. Metzger had escorted the others away in the nick of time, as a free-for-all broke out between the groups.

It happened so quickly – Metzger saw the light go out of the Romanian Elvis's eyes just as he fired a round into Hopkins's unprotected leg.

Hopkins shrieked in pain, from where he lay on the ground. He held out a pistol in a shaking grip until it was trained on Deputy Todrunner's forehead. Blood bubbles burst from the deputy's mouth, his breathing labored as his chest hitched. He was the worse-off of the two, but he wouldn't need to worry much longer. Hopkins pulled the trigger, his 9mm bullet slamming into the law official's brain and out the other side in a hideous spray of gore.

After that all was quiet, except the sound of wind and rain from TS Hiawatha.

Metzger didn't pause to see who had survived, turning to push the others forward. He was back in Iraq, bad guys lurking around every corner and a squad he'd get home if it killed him. He took the lead and ordered the others to stay close.

No one said a word.

The look in his eyes was grim determination.

Fucking gook zombie *bastard* had got him. He felt the monster badness course through him. He knew that it was only a matter of time before he'd end up like the monster he'd trapped in the trailer – the one that got him. And the worst part about it was that he couldn't work the damn shotgun well enough to blow his own fool head off.

A bottle of 10 year old scotch sat on the table beside his useless 12 gauge, and a glass of the warm brown liquor rested in the hooks of his left hand. He lifted the glass, let the scotch scorch his throat, and in a fit of anger, crushed the glass with the hooks.

He could do almost anything with these damned things except kill himself. He couldn't slit his wrists because he didn't have any to slit. He didn't have any pills around that were useful for that sort of thing, and even if he did, he doubted that he'd decide to end things that way. Somehow, after surviving the way he had and fighting all of these years it seemed like a coward's way out.

No, he wanted to blow his head off, only he couldn't manage to point the weapon at his head and pull the trigger at the same time. A mad, angry part of Gerald believed that it had been a special intention of the prosthetics' makers to create hooks incapable of holding a gun properly for suicide. For a brief scotch-fueled second he entertained killing every hook maker on the planet, if only he could get them in the same room.

He returned to his fugue.

So what was he going to do?

Anger flooded him.

Fucking gook bastards!

His right arm shot across the table, clearing everything from it, smashing the bottle on the floor and spraying what was left of the scotch on the cupboards. Shards of glass ricocheted all the way into the living room.

He remembered the mad hunger in the zombie's eyes as he'd stood before it. Gerald climbed to his feet and stumbled to the bathroom. He'd left the light on. Staring at himself in the mirror, he could see the whites around his blue eyes dissolving and yellow creeping in.

To think that he'd escaped countless of the yellow bastards in Korea only to have them now infiltrate from within. He roared into the mirror. Liking the sound of it, he roared again.

What had they called it, *The Yellow Peril?*

"I got your yellow peril!" he screamed.

Then he paused.

Was he thinking clearly? Were his thoughts right or was he drunk or yellow or monstrous? Then he thought of that girl... what was her name? Her father had gone missing and he'd offered to help her. He giggled. Maybe after he was a zombie, he could go undercover and infiltrate the zombie stronghold.

But then he roared again and the roaring made him feel good.

He glared into the mirror and beheld his yellow eyes. His skin had turned shades of green and he hated green. He hated green almost as much as he hated yellow.

Roar!

He lurched into the hallway.

He felt the last vestiges of his humanity being consumed by something dark and beautiful. He didn't want to be a zombie but he knew he couldn't stop it. He raked the wall with one of his hooks, the metal slicing through the wood like it was butter.

Roar!

Roar!

The hunger ruled him and took him outside in search of something to feed upon.

CHAPTER TWENTY-TWO

The rain had redoubled and now pummeled the town as if to see the place scoured clean. But Bombay Beach couldn't be purged. The town was a great, gargantuan beast brought down before its prime, whose salt-encrusted skeleton had been grown-upon; the houses barnacles, the roads algae, the people mites. And the garbage strewn everywhere was a cancer, sending deep roots into the land. The town was a cosmic road kill, laid low in the desert of a backwater planet by the vicissitudes of a star-crossed providence and a roomful of government hacks, eager to cut corners and touch Heaven the easy way.

Metzger, Veronica and Natasha tore down the street. Derrick pulled Auntie Lin behind him, tottering as quickly as she could on her small legs. When she slipped or slid on the wet road, he held her up and kept her from falling. Everyone knew that they had to keep moving. The wind whipped away their tears as all eyes were upon the neon sign of the Space

Station, the closest place that would provide any modicum of safety.

They passed the Laundromat first. Its windows were lit like bug lights in the night. Two of Carrie's children had their noses pressed wetly against the glass, watching Metzger and the others rush past. Back in the recesses, Carrie stood behind a double row of top-load washers, her arms crossed, frowning at the glass and the storm raging outside.

When they reached the restaurant, Metzger braced against the door and checked behind them as one by one the others filed inside. When they were all in, he took a good long look through the rain and, seeing nothing, backed into the restaurant.

"There you are." Maude was putting food in coolers– sandwiches, hotdogs, cheese and the like. "I'd thought I'd make everyone something before I left."

Derrick stood looking around. If there was ever a moment when he needed his mother, this was one of them. He looked lost, and Maude rushed around the counter and gathered him into her arms. He clutched her tightly.

Maude glanced at the others. "What happened?"

"Hopkins and his goons," Metzger said. "Todrunner tried to save us, but we were ambushed."

"What?" Maude shook her head. "Is this true?"

They all nodded.

"What happened to Will?" Maude asked. She looked to Natasha for an answer.

"He's dead. And so are the others. Elvis, the Duvalls, Frank, Columbus, Jimbo and Reginald."

"All of them?" Maude's hand flew to her mouth. "Are you kidding me?"

Natasha shook her head and cast her eyes to the floor.

Auntie Lin walked up to Derrick, drew him to a table and sat down with him. She put her arms around his shoulders as he lay his head in the cradle of his arms.

"Hopkins snapped," Metzger began. "He had his men take everyone out. The last thing I saw was him blowing the deputy's brains out."

"How did you get away?"

"Metzger took over and saved us," Natasha said. "We came straight here."

"They weren't following you, were they?" Maude ran to the front window and peered out.

"There's no one left to follow us. Hopkins was badly wounded. I think most of his men were dead."

Maude ran back to the counter. "We've got to get out of here."

"How?" Metzger said.

"By boat. Lu Shu has it arranged. He used to be a maintenance worker in the plant when we were running full steam ahead. He always has a boat ready in case we need to escape.

"Lu shu?" Auntie Lin asked.

Maude nodded.

Natasha remembered her Auntie and the small Chinese man rattling off Chinese the other day. She'd asked her what they'd talked about, and Auntie Lin had said something about Lu Shu being from one of the Western Provinces of China. Although she said it with a sneer, there was no denying the twinkle in the woman's eyes at being able to talk to someone from her homeland.

"But the water's dangerous. The zombies come from the water," Veronica said, glancing at the others for agreement.

Maude shook her head. "They can't swim. Whatever else they can do, the zombies *cannot* swim. Get in a boat and you'll be safe."

"Why not just find a car?" Auntie Lin asked.

"Whoever is left will be expecting that. The plan has always been that if they ever lost control, the orders were to keep anyone from leaving at any cost. They'll be watching the roads the most closely."

The door slammed open so hard the glass cracked from the bottom to the top. Wind and rain roared from the rectangular mouth into the restaurant. Metzger scrambled towards the door, slipping and sliding along the floor. He almost had it closed when Hopkins entered the doorway. The wounded man punched Metzger in the gut, then kneed him in his face. Metzger went down, but not before the older man stripped him of his weapon and tossed it aside.

Hopkins's left leg was wrapped with cloth, already soaked red with blood. He yanked the door shut, shoving a barely conscious Metzger out of the way with his foot.

"*You* are a fucking pain in my ass."

Auntie Lin and Derrick remained at the table. Natasha, Veronica and Maude backed against the counter, knocking over a cooler, which clattered to the floor behind them. They ignored it, their eyes on Hopkins.

He smiled cruelly, his eyes twisted by pain and frustration.

Maude, on the other hand, stood tall and mean, with the look of a woman who had taken enough shit. Chin high, chest out, arms crossed.

Hopkins trained his rifle on her midsection. "Maude," he warned, "You better stand down. You don't want a piece of me or what I'm bringing. You want to get out of here, if you can. As far as I'm concerned, your job is over."

Natasha stole a glance at Metzger, but he was still down and didn't look like he was going anywhere. His lips were bleeding where Hopkins' knee had caught him.

"You are a fucker, Samuel. A royal fucker."

Hopkins laughed and nodded. "Tell me something new, why don't you?"

"He said go, Maude." Veronica said. "Get out of here. Save yourself."

Natasha looked startled at the idea.

Seeing this, Veronica added, "Seriously, Natasha. Maude needs to leave. Someone needs to know what happened here."

"He's not going to let us go." Derrick said, trying not to cry.

"Of course you are," Auntie Lin said as if it was a perfectly obvious thing. "You're going to let us go, aren't you, Mr. Hopkins?"

Natasha stared at her Auntie in disbelief. Was the woman trying to change his mind with the singular power of her will, or was this just insane hope?

Natasha caught Hopkins examining Auntie Lin with much

the same expression. Then he shook his head and readdressed Maude. "You've only a short window in which to leave. You need to follow the little criminal's advice and get out while you have the chance and I'm in a good mood."

Maude shook her head. "I'm not going anywhere." She stepped over to Natasha and put her arm around her. "Where would I go, anyway? I've been here most of my life. What friends I have are here."

"Some friends. I left them bleeding in the street a couple of blocks back." Hopkins rubbed his leg with his left hand, holding the rifle with the other. He didn't seem to have the strength to hold it level, so it pointed towards the floor. "You kids have been a pain in the ass, you know?"

Natasha pursed her lips. "You've got more problems than us, Mister. Looks to us like you're losing control. Why are all your zombies escaping?"

Hopkins smiled grimly. "Power surges. Earthquakes. Sunspots. What does it matter to you?"

"So the green flashes are the surges?" Derrick asked. When Hopkins nodded, Derrick looked excitedly from Veronica to Natasha. "Grandpa was right. So was the Mad Scientist."

"Is Andy still making trouble? I suppose I'll have to talk to him next." Hopkins shook his head. "What's this about your grandfather?"

"He had a –"

"Derrick!" Veronica shouted.

"What did he have? What did he leave behind? A video? A book?" Hopkins turned to Maude, making a clucking noise with his tongue. "Shame on you. How did you let him write things down about this?"

"It was in code, asshole. How was I supposed to know what he was doing?"

"So you knew about the book, too?" Natasha looked stunned.

Maude smiled grimly. "I knew about everything, honey."

"It *was* a book," Hopkins said. "Where is it now?"

Veronica grinned. "We mailed it to the FBI with a note telling them to open it if we don't show up on their doorstep within three days."

Hopkins stared at her for a long moment. He aimed the rifle at her belly. "You kids watch way too much television."

"I'm serious."

"I bet you are. Just tell me one thing. I shut off the mail two days ago, so when in between then and now did you manage to get a package out when there was nothing coming in or going out?"

Veronica shook her head and bit her lip. She stared diamond-edged anger at the man, but kept her mouth shut. Finally, "You can't just shut off the mail."

"What? Like I can't just shoot you? Like I didn't kill the deputy?"

"Yeah." Veronica's voice was almost a whisper. "Like that."

"Then why not just kill us all?" Natasha asked. "Who's gonna care about the book then?"

"Call it a loose end. I hate loose ends. So tell me, boy, where is that goddamned book?" Hopkins started to step forward, then stopped when he heard the sound of a vehicle screeching to a stop outside. He stepped back and peered out the door. When he looked back he was smiling like a child. "This is going to surprise the hell out of you. You're going to love this."

Natasha saw that Metzger was coming to, but was being careful about it. He opened his eyes to briefly look around, then snapped them shut.

Hopkins stepped aside to let in two black-clad soldiers and the two zombies they led along behind them. The zombies wore bags over their heads. Iron shackles bound their feet and hands.

"I think it's time we play a little game," Hopkins said happily.

"Oh my God!" Natasha pressed herself against the counter as the creatures approached.

"No, you did *not*," Maude protested. "You aren't supposed to make them that way."

"I'm not supposed to do a lot of things."

Veronica inched away from Natasha and Maude.

"I see you recognize what these are," Hopkins said. "You'll find them hot and fresh out of the oven, so to speak. They haven't had the luxury of testing beneath the water yet. Of course, that also means that their skin is still intact." He look around at everyone in the room, then nodded towards the black-clad soldier. "The water's a good place to hide them from prying eyes, but it does horrible things to flesh, especially dead flesh."

The soldiers reached for the bags on the zombies' heads and removed them, revealing their identities.

"Daddy!" Natasha screamed. Tears ran down her face as she looked at the man who'd put her to bed and told her nighttime stories about fairies and elves and the boogeyman. Now he *was* the boogeyman.

For Patrick Oliver retained only a passing resemblance to the man he'd once been. He still had his father's nose; the curve of his jaw was shadowed in his son; even the eyes were the same shape as they'd been before, worry lines etched into his features. But the unholy yellow light that burned within them told of an entirely different being from the man who'd been father to Natasha and Derrick. The shriveled lips barely concealed gums that had receded so far that his teeth looked like fangs, and when he opened his mouth the sound that came from his throat was like the rustling of pages in a book.

"I believe you've met? Patrick, your daughter. Natasha, your father. Why don't you two shake hands?"

Natasha could almost feel her heart stop beating as she saw what her father had become. He wasn't holed up in one of the trailers, or out finding himself. He was lost to her forever, transformed into a zombie. Not only was Hopkins physically vicious, but fucking cruel with it.

"Well, without any more formalities, I think it's time for dinner. Thurman?"

The soldier nearest him let the chains restraining the zombies fall to the ground.

Suddenly Maude jerked a long-barreled pistol from behind the counter, like something out of a Wild West movie. For all the fear she'd shown when first confronted by the zombies, now she held it straight and true, with not even a quiver. "Get the hell out of here, Hopkins, and take your monkeys with you."

"Don't you think that's too late?"

"It's never too –"

The second zombie suddenly lurched towards Maude. She fired, her bullet hitting the creature dead center in its forehead. It stopped and rocked in place. The yellow of its eyes dimmed slightly, a look of surprise crossing its face. She fired again, this time catching it in the side of the head. The contents of its skull splattered against the black-clad soldier beside Hopkins and the zombie fell to its knees.

Then a third gunshot.

But this time it was Maude who went to her knees. Her arm remained stretched out. Her face slapped against the linoleum tile. Her sightless eyes remained open as blood drained from a hole in her temple.

Natasha recovered just in time to see her dad lunging towards her, his arms outstretched to embrace her in a way a daddy should never embrace his child. She leaped out of the way at the last moment as she screamed.

Thurman stepped back and pulled his pistol, but fell backwards with a clatter. Metzger had crept to the side and had managed to pull a fire extinguisher from the wall, and now swung it full strength at the soldier's knee cap. When the soldier hit the ground, Metzger brought the fire extinguisher down on his face twice.

On the other side of the room, Natasha dodged her father again. Hopkins screamed for everyone to stop moving and only then noticed that Veronica had picked up Maude's gun and was training it on him. She fired, and the round struck the front door, shattering the glass. Hopkins ducked and brought his rifle to bear, but ducked again as Veronica fired once more. This time she missed as well, splintering the wood by the doorjamb. Hopkins dove out the door and was lost from sight. The second soldier followed, leaving them to the mercy of the monster.

That was all Metzger needed. He climbed to his feet, grabbing the pistol from Thurman's unmoving body and his rifle from where Hopkins had dropped it on the floor. He rushed to where Natasha was still trying to hold her father at bay, snatched a chair, and slammed it across the zombie's skull. It went down, but only for a moment.

"Come on. Before it gets up." He grabbed Natasha's hand and jerked her towards the back of the restaurant. Veronica followed, shoving Derrick and Auntie Lin in front of her. Soon they were out the door and into the night. The rain continued unabated, as did the wind.

Metzger looked left and right, then at the water. It flashed a brilliant neon green. "Shit! Where do we go?"

Veronica slammed her shoulder against the restaurant's door, forcing what had been Natasha's father back as it tried to stumble after them.

Natasha found several boards and, with Metzger's help, wedged them beneath the handle. It wouldn't hold forever, but it would buy them some time.

"Does anyone know where to go now?" Metzger asked.

"I do." Derrick straightened his shoulders, pulled a plastic bag from his pocket, and removed the map he'd been working on earlier. He squinted at it, then looked in an easterly direction. "Come on."

CHAPTER TWENTY-THREE

The storm raged around them.

They kept to the shadows as best they could. Occasionally a white Suburban would roar by on a parallel street. Thankfully, they could hear the vehicles even when they were driving with their lights off; when they heard one, they'd stop and hide until it passed.

When Natasha and the others crossed Avenue E, they saw that Lazlo's trailer was lit by the headlights from two vehicles. Shadows moved about inside. But that wasn't their destination.

They turned immediately north and crossed 4th Street one by one, aware that at any moment those in the vehicle could look their way. But they made it safely across, weaving past propane tanks, through yards and out the other side.

Soon they arrived at their destination – Kristov's house. They crashed through the gate, then waded through knee-deep cans. The front door was unlocked. When they were all inside, Metzger closed the door, barricaded it with the kitchen table, then peered out the window to see if anyone had followed them.

Everyone else flopped on the couches and chairs in the living room, defeated and exhausted.

"Why here?" Metzger asked.

"We need to make some plans," Derrick said, his voice a monotone. "They'd be expecting us at some of the other places, like the Mad Scientist's or Maude's trailer. No one would expect us to be here. Here we at least have some time to come up with a plan."

The only light in the room came from an illuminated Elvis clock positioned directly above the couch. Natasha and Auntie Lin sat underneath it, while Veronica and Derrick grabbed chairs on either side. Auntie Lin held Natasha's hand.

"It's like a bad dream," Veronica said.

"It's not a dream. It's real." Natasha's voice was strained.

"How could this happen?" Derrick asked.

"I don't know. It just did." Natasha wiped her eyes dry with the palms of her hands. "People can't leave well enough alone, I guess."

"We need to get out of town," Metzger said. "We can't stay here."

"Maude said to go by boat," Veronica said.

"I don't know if we can trust her."

"She's dead," Derrick said. "Isn't that trustworthy enough?"

Metzger regarded the boy for a moment before he answered. "No." He returned to his vigil at the window. "We need two things. We need a distraction of some sort and we need a vehicle. We either find something drivable and hit the road, or find something floatable and go across the sea. Hopkins be damned."

"Either way we're fucked," Veronica snorted. "I wish I could have shot him when I had the chance."

"On one hand we have Mr. Hopkins to worry about, and on the other we have the zombies," Auntie Lin piped in.

"I don't think we have to worry so much about them," Metzger said. "If we move fast enough, we should make it. Those zombies move slow; if we're in a car or on a speed boat there should be no way they can get at us."

"Don't say '*no way.*'" Derrick frowned. "I bet a week ago you would have said there was no way that zombies existed."

"I bet you're right." Metzger's eyes suddenly widened. He hurried back to the window. "Wait. Shhh."

They heard the unmistakable sound of cans being pushed aside as something waded into the yard.

"Oh, shit, shit, shit," Natasha said. She glanced at Auntie Lin, then tiptoed to where Metzger stood. He put his arm around her waist and hugged her close. "See anything?" she whispered.

He shook his head. "No. Not yet."

An incredible bang made the trailer shudder.

"What the hell was that?" Veronica jumped as the banging came again, from the back of the trailer this time.

Metzger peeked out the door. The yard was empty, as was the street. He moved to the living room window.

The banging continued at regular intervals, moving along the rear of the trailer. Each bang was followed by a shudder as if something immense was ramming into the thirty-foot-long home.

Veronica hefted her pistol and eased towards the back of the trailer. Derrick grabbed a heavy statue of Elvis wearing prison stripes and slashed it through the air a few times experimentally.

Natasha ran to the kitchen and yanked open a drawer. She rifled through it, took out a spatula and tossed it aside. She tried several other drawers and finally found an immense knife. She stared at it open-mouthed for a moment, then tossed it back in the drawer.

All the while the banging continued, the trailer shuddering and shuddering.

"What are you doing?" Derrick asked.

"Looking for a weapon," she said.

"What was wrong with the knife?"

"I just can't... I can't stab someone."

The sound of cans moving grew louder, coming around the front of the house, before stopping at the front door.

Natasha tiptoed to the door, but Metzger, who was peering carefully out the window, put out his hand and shook his head. *No*, he mouthed. *You do not want to see this*.

She stopped, bit her lip, and peeked out the window. There was her father, standing with his head down, his arms at his sides, wearing a military uniform, the front of it stained with blood and gore.

She looked in horror at Derrick.

"It's him, isn't it?" he asked.

Natasha nodded.

"I knew he'd come for us," Derrick said calmly.

Natasha gaped at him, and swallowed hard. She knew what she had to do but she doubted that she had the strength to do it.

Metzger must have seen something in her eyes.

"You aren't going out there."

"I can't leave him like that." She stared at the floor. "He's my daddy."

"But now he's a zombie."

"I know. But he doesn't have to be." She gulped and went over to Derrick. She gave him a hug as she knelt beside him. "We can't let him be like that, can we?"

Derrick shook his head. He wiped his nose with his forearm and stood. Natasha stood with him.

"What are we going to do?" he asked her.

"We're going to kill daddy."

Auntie Lin began to cry.

Metzger looked as though he wanted to say something, but kept his mouth shut. He held the pistol out for her.

She took it. It felt lighter than she'd thought it would.

She put one arm around her brother. "Keep holding me, Derrick. I need you to help me do this."

He did as he was told, his eyes wide with fear.

Natasha held the pistol before her and nodded to Derrick, who yanked open the door. Her father stood at the bottom of the steps to the porch, his head downcast as if he were ashamed at what he'd become. He'd always fought so many demons, never thought himself worthy of what he had, always wanted something more. Now here he was, a monster beyond reckoning.

A small cry escaped from Derrick.

Their father heard it and slowly brought his head up. He stared at them through yellow, alien eyes. Nothing of who he was remained in him.

The zombie began to wheeze and rock back and forth. The cans stirred around its legs.

Natasha brought the pistol to bear and held it pointed at her father's head. Her hand shook, and she couldn't hold the gun steady. Derrick's hand came up and balanced against hers. Natasha counted silently to three, then pulled the trigger. A hole opened in the zombie's forehead. She fired again and again until the gun clicked empty.

The zombie first fell to its knees, then as more shots struck it, fell on its back. For a brief moment, Natasha saw that person who had been her father, and then the rain came down and buried him beneath the sea of beer cans.

CHAPTER TWENTY-FOUR

Metzger took control of Derrick and Natasha. The first thing he did was get them out of harm's way. He knew from experience that being around dead people you once loved could drive a person crazy. He'd seen enough of his friends die and had spent many hours standing next to their bodies, or lying next to them in a roadside ditch, trying to stay absolutely still as enemy fire tore through the air above his head.

Such were the vicissitudes of war.

And this *was* war. Hopkins was the enemy general and the zombies were his troops. Metzger's own ragtag army was made up of frightened kids and their nanny. Pathetic really, but it was all he had. There weren't any Hajji-made roadside bombs, there weren't any skinnys on the rooftops with weapons, and there weren't deliberate ambushes to run into. But there were zombies, and although they weren't trained in military maneuvers these creatures were immune to pain and fear, and every bit as badass as the most hardened soldier.

So they paralleled Avenue G heading north to the Mad Scientist's house, running through the yards, stopping and starting to make sure that zombies weren't lying in wait for them. They crossed Second Street without being seen and sprinted into the Mad Scientist's yard.

They found Andy Gudgel waiting for them at the door. He waved them in, then shut and double-bolted it behind them.

Metzger was immediately struck by the sterility of the place. There was a living room, a kitchen and a hallway, just like every other damned single-wide trailer on the planet, but this one seemed... well, not much lived in. He turned to make a remark to Dr. Gudgel, then saw the man smile thinly and offer him a nod.

"Please, everyone in the kitchen. We'll be safer there."

"What? In the kitchen?" Veronica made a point of looking at where the carpet met the linoleum. "Is there like a force field or something?"

Dr. Gudgel didn't answer, but ushered everyone inside. Once past the demarcation, he grabbed a lever above the sink's water faucet and pulled it up, and the room began to drop on hydraulic motors.

Metzger couldn't help but grin as they were lowered into a secret chamber. They came to a halt in a large room with concrete walls.

Metzger escorted Derrick and Natasha to a sofa and set them down, then turned to appraise his new surroundings.

Here and there sand and dirt trickled from the crumbling mortar. The floor was covered in indoor-outdoor carpeting. It had the feel of a basement: low ceilings, lots of couches, and a big television screen on the far wall, divided into twelve squares. Six of them were lit active. The others were black.

One screen showed the front yard of Dr. Gudgel's house, the angle of the camera capturing the door to the laboratory. Another screen showed the front of the Space Station and part of the Laundromat. The door to the restaurant had been ripped off the hinges. The Laundromat's windows were entirely gone. Suddenly a figure walked into frame and shambled into the Laundromat. It knelt and did something beside the bank of dryers, then lurched to its feet. It turned, and Metzger cursed under his breath. It was his old friend Royland, now a full-fledged, glowing-eyed zombie. They'd met in Norfolk and had both signed up for the program... *There but by the grace of God*, he thought.

Another screen showed the front of the school. Two zombies seemed lost in the intricacies of the playground slide, while one beat his fists on the tire swing, sending the killer bees who called it home into a maniacal swarm, the ensuing cloud virtually hiding the zombie from view.

Yet another showed the view across the seawall, all the way from sump pump #1 to #2. Metzger could see where the wall had been breached, dirt on the road showing where the zombies had climbed over and slid down.

Another view ran south down Isle of Palms Avenue.

The last screen gave them a view of the entrance to the town. A semi-truck had been pulled across it. On either side of the road was an impassable ditch.

"The other cameras have been found, I'm afraid," Dr. Gudgel said, joining Metzger in studying the screens. "Hopkins spied the first one on a telephone pole along the access road to the plant, and he's been looking for them ever since. I used to have this town completely covered. Now..."

"So you were always expecting something like this to happen?"

"It couldn't help but happen. Cut backs. Putting the military in charge rather than scientists." He shrugged and shook his head. "It was bound to happen sooner or later."

"This is how you knew it was us coming." Metzger turned around to look at the rest of the room. Veronica sat on the couch between Natasha and Derrick, speaking quietly, trying to console them.

But for all the attention Veronica was giving her friends, she kept glancing at the screens. She wanted to check on her aunt and uncle, and the kids of the woman who ran the Laundromat. She'd wanted to check on them on the way to Dr. Gudgel's, but Metzger had convinced her to postpone it, stressing that Natasha and Derrick needed her right now.

"Did you see what happened at the Space Station?" Metzger asked Dr. Gudgel.

"I saw them come in, and I saw Hopkins come out wounded, but I didn't see anything else."

Natasha swallowed. "I killed my father."

Metzger strode over to her. "No, you didn't. You killed a zombie. Hopkins killed your father."

"But I saw something in his eyes."

"Nothing more than spastic synapse firing, Ms. Oliver." Dr. Gudgel pointed to his own head. "All the neuron patterns that comprised memory – that which really makes us human – were ruined in the re-making. What you saw wasn't what you saw."

"How bad was Hopkins wounded?" Metzger asked.

"Pretty bad. He had to pull himself into one of those Suburbans in order to return to the plant."

"You know he killed Deputy Todrunner, right?"

"I didn't know. *Damn.*" Gudgel pointed to the screen with the semi blocking the entrance to the town. "Which makes *that* a lot more significant."

"Why?" Derrick asked.

"It means he's going for the 'scorched earth' solution," Dr. Gudgel said. "He's going to kill everyone, then concoct some sort of accident to cover it all up. With no communication or traffic in or out, he can do it without anyone stopping him."

"Except for us." Veronica sat, her elbows draped over her knees. "We have to stop him."

"And how are we going to do that?" Dr. Gudgel said.

"I don't know. That's for the smart people to figure out. But what I do know is that if *we* don't then *he's* going to find a way to stop *us*. So what are we going to do?" Metzger pointed at the boy. "It was his idea to come here. He figured you had a plan."

"I found the crib," Derrick said. "It was *Space Station.*" Derrick spelled out the words.

Dr. Gudgel nodded and chuckled. "It's always something obvious. Did the book go into great detail?"

"It has everything. It has dates and times of the green lights flashing, natural phenomenon, and missing people or mysterious fires in trailers."

"But it doesn't have anything about zombies?" Dr. Gudgel persisted.

"No. But Hopkins found out about it and now he wants the book," Derrick said.

Metzger shook his head. "I think we're past that. The book was a momentary interest. If Hopkins is going to destroy the whole town, then he'll destroy the book along with it."

"Do you still want to see it?" Derrick asked.

Dr. Gudgel waved his hand. "No, I don't need to see it. Mr. Metzger is right. There's nothing stopping Hopkins from destroying everything. Whatever power the book might have held over him vanished when he decided to kill everyone."

"So now what?" Metzger asked.

"I've been dreading this moment for a long time, but like I said, I knew it would come. There's only one thing to do when your back is against the wall."

Natasha looked from one man to the other. "And that would be?"

"Attack," Metzger said.

"Take the fight to them," Dr. Gudgel said.

"I suppose you have a plan for this?" Metzger asked.

"I do." He gestured towards the couch. "Derrick, Veronica, Ms. Lin, could you come give me a hand, please. I need some supplies from the lab."

After they left, Metzger walked to the couch and stood in front of Natasha. Her hair, even tangled and wind-blown, held chestnut curls he'd love to run his hands through. He liked her. He liked her a lot. She'd been through more than anyone should be allowed to go through. He just wanted to make sure she came out the other side as whole as she was when she went in. He sat on the couch beside her. "Hey, are you going to be okay?" he asked softly.

Her eyes were puffy from crying, and her cheeks were red. She stared at her hands.

"You're a terrific girl, you know? What you did out there..."

"My dad told me about this movie once and I never really understood it until now. We were always watching movies, growing up, and my dad said they were nothing like the ones he watched. He talked about the old times when characters were real, before they became space alien monsters and talking animals." She spoke in a monotone.

Metzger kept his mouth shut and listened. She needed to talk.

"I forgot the title of the movie he talked about. I remember that it was about this boy who had a dog. His dad didn't want him to have it, but there's no saying no to a kid when they have a pet and they want it, you know? So the boy, I think his name was Travis, bonds with the dog and they become best friends. Then the dog gets rabies and it begins to attack the family. The father could have taken care of it, so could the mother, but instead he made the kid shoot the dog."

"If he hadn't," Metzger added carefully, "it would have hurt the whole family. People could have died."

"Exactly. I was like, what's the big deal? The family is more important. I thought it would be easy to pull the trigger."

"Pulling the trigger *is* easy."

She shook her head. "No, it isn't. It's the hardest thing in the world."

"Living with the consequences is what's hard," he said. "Especially when it's someone you love."

"Especially." She sighed and laid her head on his shoulder. She grabbed his hand.

"The movie was called *Old Yeller*," Metzer said. "I think it was a Disney movie."

"Those fucking Disney movies."

"I know. They can be really hard."

"Fucking miserable is what they are."

Metzger laughed. "That would be a great marketing campaign for today's youth. Watch Disney movies. They're fucking miserable."

Natasha smiled and closed her eyes. He held her like that until the sound of the lift descending made them stir.

Derrick, Veronica and Dr. Gudgel returned from his laboratory carrying several boxes. They put them on the table, and the doctor had Veronica and Derrick back away.

"Okay. What we have here is Semtex. It's terribly explosive and I'm afraid a little past its expiration date."

"What does that mean?" Natasha asked.

"It means that it's been sweating," Dr. Gudgel explained, "and when it comes to explosives, sweating is definitely not a good thing. The sweat from TNT is called nitroglycerine. One drop can blow your hand off."

Dr. Gudgel fixed everyone with a firm gaze. "Right. We know there's no turning back, so we need to destroy the plant. Are we in agreement?"

Everyone nodded.

"Good. Because I'm going to volunteer to drive the truck that's going to do it."

"What?" Metzger grabbed the older man by the shoulder. "Like a suicide bomber? You can't do that!"

Dr. Gudgel looked at Metzger's hand, then grinned. "What they are doing is wrong. The project has changed from a scientific ideal into an utter nightmare. We never meant to hurt people. It was never meant to be something evil."

"But you don't have to kill yourself," Derrick said.

Dr. Gudgel chuckled and put his hand on Derrick's head. "You're a smart kid. You're going to grow up and do something special. I'm sure of that. But my time," he paused and licked his lips, "My time has passed. My purpose is gone and there's nothing else I want to do with my life."

"But you shouldn't have to die," Derrick said.

"I'm doing what I want to do."

"For the record, I hate suicide bombers," Metzger said.

"I bet you never had one on your side before," Dr. Gudgel countered.

CHAPTER TWENTY-FIVE

Derrick, Metzger, Veronica, Auntie Lin and Natasha sat on the couch glued to the screens. They'd helped the Mad Scientist prepare his pickup truck for the assault. The explosives were attached to the front grill, ready to be detonated by remote control; a video camera installed on the back of the seat provided a view of the road from just over the driver's right shoulder. There was no sound, but the image was clear.

The plan had been argued *ad nauseum* for half an hour until the Mad Scientist let everyone know in no uncertain terms that his mind was set. The plan, such as it was, entailed the Mad Scientist driving his truck through the barrier and ramming into the front of the building. The ensuing explosion should make a decent-sized hole in the plant. Then it was only a matter of time before someone came to investigate, and when they did, Metzger, Derrick, Natasha and Veronica would ascend to ground level to inform the authorities about everything that had happened.

Each of the four sitting on the couch watching the screens now had a 9mm pistol with an extra magazine. Metzger had showed them how to load, chamber and fire the pistol. He'd also shown them where the safety was on the weapon.

Natasha hadn't wanted to touch a weapon, remembering what had happened last time she'd held one. But Metzger had said "*Old Yeller*" as he'd handed it to her, which helped to put the pistol and its use into perspective.

But for now they sat back and watched the silent movie called *The Mad Scientist Blows Up the Zombie Factory.*

The rearview mirror was positioned so that they could see his face in the reflection, which made for an interesting visual experience.

Dr. Gudgel got in the truck and started the engine. The vehicle was one of those big Ford pick-ups with extra large tires.

Gudgel put the vehicle in reverse, backed out of the yard onto Second Street and headed toward the short block to Isle of Palms Avenue. The rain had let up somewhat and the windshield wipers kept the view clear.

"Wait a minute. What's that?" Metzger stood and pointed at the screen showing Isle of Palms Avenue itself. A white Suburban had turned onto it about a hundred meters down, heading north. The vehicle would intercept the Mad Scientist in no time.

They all stared at the feed from the pickup. Gudgel slammed the truck into reverse, backed it near the curb, then turned off the engine. But the windshield wipers were still going. Gudgel hadn't turned the key off all the way. If the driver of the Suburban passed by and saw the wipers flipping back and forth he'd know someone was inside.

"Turn off the wipers!" Veronica shouted at the screen.

Natasha couldn't take the stress. She almost closed her eyes.

Just as the Suburban was about to turn the corner, Gudgel's hand came into the lower part of the picture and turned the key off the rest of the way. Now the wipers had stopped, but the window was clean and dry, rain drops coming too slowly.

The Suburban turned the corner, headlights off, illuminated only by street lights. The tinted windows hid everything but the dim shadow of a man sitting in the driver's seat. Would he see the truck and know it hadn't been there a moment ago? Would he notice the window didn't have a sheen of rainwater like all the other vehicles?

Finally the Suburban rolled past and was lost from view. A minute later, the truck started up again.

Everyone let out a sigh of relief.

Gudgel eased towards the intersection, turned and rolled slowly down Isle of Palms Avenue, doing no more than 15 miles an hour. As he approached Fourth Street, they saw lights blazing from Lot's Church of Redemption.

The front door of the Church slammed open and Kim Johnson ran out into the road. She stood in the middle of the avenue, blocking the truck. She waved her arms, the minister's robe she was wearing fluttering and revealing her nakedness beneath.

The Mad Scientist pulled to within a few feet of her before stopping, providing all of those watching a full-frontal view of Kim Johnson. She came around the front of the truck and began to speak with the Mad Scientist.

Suddenly Metzger stood. "Shit!" he said, pointing at a smear of white behind the church, a Suburban parked in the alley that the Mad Scientist hadn't seen. "Shit! Shit! Shit!" He ran to the platform and leaped onto it.

Natasha shouted, "Where are you going?"

"This is an ambush – I've got to go help him."

As the platform began to rise, Natasha's attention was drawn back to the screen by Veronica's words, "Oh no she doesn't –"

Kim Johnson had pulled a small pistol from the pocket of her robe and pointed it at the Mad Scientist. She said something that was lost to the camera and pulled the trigger. The pistol flashed, the windscreen shattered and red splotches sprayed out over the hood.

Veronica, Derrick and Natasha stared at each other for a stunned, speechless moment, before returning to observe the scene being played out before them.

Metzger was hell bent for leather, running down Avenue G as if he had Saddam Hussein's crocodile mask-wearing Fedayeen Saddam after him, ready to turn him into a red, white and blue target dummy. He held his pistol low against his leg as he ran. His training had kicked in.

He shot past Third Street, only barely registering a zombie trapped beneath a trailer, wedged tight while it had been trying to get at something beneath. He zigzagged between homes and leaped over piles of trash, old engines, and weed-enshrouded pieces of machinery, and soon had the pickup in sight. There was no sign of Kim Johnson. The truck's engine rumbled gently.

Metzger rounded the rear of the vehicle, passing to the driver's side, and aimed his pistol along the side of the truck. He ducked as he spotted the nose of the white Suburban still parked behind the church. He paused to peek into the cab of the truck, just to be sure that Dr. Gudgel was dead. The scientist's eyes stared over Metzger's shoulder, towards the sea and beyond.

Metzger kept moving, veering towards the side of the church that paralleled Isle of Palms Avenue. He sprinted to it and planted his back against it. He held the gun in his left hand, pointing the barrel towards the corner as he crept forward slowly.

When he was halfway there, a weaponless black-clad figure stepped from the alley, completely oblivious to Metzger. Metzger pulled the trigger three times, hitting the man in the face, side and back, as the man spun and fell to the ground.

He went quickly into the alley and was ready to fire at anything that moved. The rear door of the suburban was open and laid flat. A rifle had been field stripped on the carpet of the cargo area, and was ready to be wiped down and re-oiled. The poor sap had picked a poor time for it.

Metzger heard the crunch of gravel from behind him. Without thinking, he rolled forward and caught a glimpse of a second black-clad figure, knife poised to strike. Had Metzger not moved when he had, the knife would have been in his back.

He tried to roll to a sitting position, but over-corrected and fell on his side.

The other man was drawing a pistol from a holster on his thigh. Metzger didn't give him time; he fired five times into the man's chest.

The soldier hit the ground, and Metzger got to his feet. His uniform was covered in mud, and he was soaked to his skin. He looked contemplatively at the man he'd shot. He was about his size...

He approached the fallen figure and reached down.

The soldier came to life and screamed, bringing the knife around and up in a vicious arc. Metzger leaned back, narrowly missing being disemboweled by the wickedly-serrated knife. The man leaped to his feet before Metzger knew what was happening, and delivered a mean left punch to the side of Metzger's chest. Metzger tried to bring the pistol to bear, but the soldier's knife smacked him on the wrist with the flat of the blade, sending the pistol flying.

For a brief moment, Metzger couldn't understand why the man was still alive. Was this a new kind of zombie? Then he saw the tell-tale bulges of the man's body armor, and understood what had happened.

They were now face to face, the man holding a knife, Metzger empty-handed.

"Come on, fucker," he said.

The man slashed, feinted, then slashed again. On the second slash, Metzger grabbed the blade, pinning the weapon between them as they fell to the ground, Metzger on top.

The two men locked gazes; acne dimples marred the soldier's cheeks, and a scar hung beneath his right eye. He twisted his head to the right to get away from Metzger's elbow but Metzger leaned in hard, pressing his forearm against the carotid artery. His assailant's eyes shot wide. His legs bucked as he tried to dislodge him, but Metzger held on, aware that he needed to maintain the superior position.

It took about fifteen seconds, but finally the fight in the man's eyes dimmed as the blood flow to his brain ceased.

But Metzger wasn't done yet. He brought his head back, then slammed it forward as hard as he could, shattering his opponent's nose. Metzger released his hold as he took the knife away from the other's unconscious grip, and then slammed it through an eye socket until he felt the tip scrap against the back of the man's skull.

Metzger climbed to his feet, using the side of the Suburban to help. His muscles flagged as the adrenaline settled. It had been a long time since he'd stared a man in the eyes as he killed him. He felt his own eyes water and pushed the feelings away. He had hoped never to feel this way again.

It seemed as if a full minute had passed since Natasha had last seen Metzger. She'd watched as the black-clad soldier with the knife had snuck behind where Metzger had gone and feared the worst. Now, staring through the red film of blood on the camera, well aware that Dr. Gudgel was very dead, she thought the worst of what could happen.

Metzger could be shot dead in the alley.

Metzger could have been stabbed in the head.

Metzger could have been attacked and killed by a zombie.

Then a figure stepped from the alley.

She gasped. It wore the black-clad uniform of Hopkins's men. She screamed at the screen.

"*No!*"

The man turned back towards the alley, then walked along the wall towards the front door of the church.

"Wait!" Derrick shouted. "That's Metzger. Look!"

He pointed to the screen as the man waved at them, knowing where the camera was.

Natasha sighed with relief.

Metzger entered the church, shut the door behind him, and immediately began coughing. His eyes watered and stung. He tried to open them, but the smoke made them tear even worse.

Fucking incense.

He hated incense.

Long, thin tapers burned in the foyer of the church, replacing the ever-pervasive sea rot with a sweet, noxious odor that threatened to turn his insides out. It was like a barrier to the evil outside. The smell wove its way into him, making him reel as he fought for balance.

Beyond the foyer was a wide open space. Cheap black and white tile covered the floor, and fifty metal chairs faced an altar occupying much of the front of the room. He couldn't see anyone, but that didn't mean someone wasn't there. He stumbled into the main part of the church and away from the noxious odors in the vestibule, pulling his 9mm pistol and surveying the room. On the left wall was a mural of Sodom and Gomorrah. A red velvet curtain covered most of the right wall except for a doorway nearly hidden in the shadows. The altar was made from pressboard, nailed together, painted red, and covered with a white tablecloth. The ceiling was painted to depict the night sky. Here and there glow-in-the-dark stars had been glued to the ceiling to represent specific constellations.

He'd heard that the minister had come from Montana, where she used to preach to a nudist colony. Looking around, the room looked nothing like what he'd expect a church to look like. There were no crosses, no images of Christ, no statues of saints, none of the usual trappings he'd expect in a church.

"You look a little lost."

Metzger whirled and drew down on Kim Johnson. She was completely naked except for a tattoo of a vine weaving up from her ankles and along her legs, past her pubis, around her torso, and stopping at her neck. The vine bore flowers and the occasional red and orange fruit.

"Don't move," he commanded.

She didn't. She only smiled.

He mentally kicked himself for letting her get the jump on him.

"Not feeling as sharp as you're used to," she said.

Her voice had a pleasant, mesmerizing quality.

"Shut up. Is there anyone else here?"

She smiled in response.

"I asked you a question. Is there anyone else here?"

"You told me to shut up."

"Answer this one."

"No." She looked around. "It's just me and you."

He stared at her. She seemed a little fuzzy around the edges. He noticed how she stood with her legs spread slightly apart. He stared at the petals of her womanhood and felt himself stir. He lowered the pistol an inch or two before he realized it.

He shook his head to clear his mind. It was then that he noticed her hands were behind her back.

"Show me your hands," he ordered. He aimed his pistol at her forehead.

She brought her hands slowly around. Both of her fists were closed, but he could tell there was something in them.

"Open them. First the right one."

She obeyed, revealing a glass pipe of the sort made to smoke crack or meth. He'd seen them more often than he cared to. He used to own a dozen of them. Metzger had a sinking feeling. "Now the left hand."

It was filled with a small bag of whitish crystals.

Metzger knew an ounce when he saw it. An echo of the acrid taste of the methamphetamine found a home in his mouth. He began to salivate at the same time his jaw began to work back and forth. His heart beat faster. His body, he knew, wanted him to cut it and snort it, lick it and taste it, bowl it and smoke it.

"Here," she said. "Maybe these will help. Just a little something to keep your edge."

His gaze went from the pipe to her breasts, from the bag to her pubis, from the bag, to her lips, from her eyes to the pipe, then back to the bag again. He wanted all of it. He wanted her. He wanted the drug. He wanted to feel that laser edge once more.

But Metzger knew better. He slapped the stuff out of her palms, shattering the pipe on the hard floor and sending the bag skittering beneath a seat somewhere. He didn't look. Wherever it went, it was away from him now.

"Aw, why'd you do that?" she pouted, slouching and swaying, the motion making it seem as if the vine was tightening around her body.

"I don't want it!"

"Do you really know what you want? Come on. Pick it up. Let's have fun."

His brain felt fuzzy. He wanted to do what she said. "Jesus! What kind of church is this?"

"You mean us?" She laughed huskily. "Not much Jesus in here. Just Lot's Church of Redemption. What does that mean to you?"

"Lot? Wasn't he the one the angels told to leave Sodom and Gomorrah?"

"He was... sort of. So you're a good church-going boy, aren't you?" Kim shifted so her hip thrust to the left, her right leg taking her weight. His eyes were drawn to the tattooed leaves that tickled her privates. "But you have to be very careful with the bible. The old white men who wrote it insist that it's the word of God, but don't you wonder how much of it was influenced by other, more selfish thoughts? For instance, did you know that the destruction had little to do with the quote-sins-end-quote occurring inside Sodom and Gomorrah? Would it surprise you that the whole event was territorial? I doubt it was an angel who told Lot to leave. After all, he'd been taken prisoner."

Metzger tried to follow her words, but his thoughts were having trouble connecting. He shook his head, dazed.

"You see," she continued, "the Cities of the Plain battled the Vale of Siddim, and it was the Vale who had captured Lot. And Lot, the unlucky kid, was Abraham's nephew. No way were the kings of the cities going to let that happen. No way was Abraham going to let one of his blood be captured." Kim winked and nodded. "So they attacked and burned the Vale's twin cities to the ground. Historians said it was God who made it happen. Most rational people think it was Abraham. But there's one thing that can't be argued."

Trying to keep up with the conversation, Metzger asked, "What was that?"

"The Vale of Siddim had another name, a more common one. Locals loved the area around it because it was a bread basket of harvest, much like the Imperial Valley is around here. Can you guess what the common name for the Vale was?"

Metzger shook his head. "The incense. What did you do to it?" His tongue felt thick.

"Don't interrupt, you bad boy. Listen closely. The common name for the Vale of Siddim was the Salton Sea."

Metzger gritted his teeth. His brain was becoming numb. He managed to ask, "What about his wife? Didn't she turn to salt?"

Kim laughed loudly. "There's a funny thing about that. Lot never had a wife. Do you know how we know? It's because she's the only one ever talked about in the Christian bible who doesn't have a name. They never named her, so she didn't exist."

"Then why –"

"Because she was a biblical mnemonic. They wanted the masses to be afraid of salt, as if salt represented everything evil in the world. The twin cities of Sodom and Gomorrah were built on the edge of the Salton Sea."

"You're crazy," he said. But he licked his lips. Her body glistened in the light. Her breasts quivered as she spoke.

"They tried to sell the idea that salt was a bad thing. And here's the rub. We're almost seventy percent water and we have more than six ounces of salt on average in our bodies. We're literally made of salt water, but at the same time we can't metabolize it." Kim smiled and sighed. A blossom grew on her stomach, hatching yellow and pink butterflies. "Yet here we are on the edge of the largest salt sea in America."

Metzger found himself entranced by the way the vines curled around her thighs, fruit growing between her legs. He shook his head. He knew he shouldn't be looking, but he couldn't tear himself away.

"The Vale of Siddim. The Salton Sea. The Sea of Lot. There's an even older name for that place that everyone knows. The Dead Sea. Nothing can live there. It's so polluted by the salt that the shores are like snow drifts. There's an old Arabic saying about it, *An Empire of Salt, ruled by the dead, fit for no man to live or love.* It used to be a place they sent men to die. What do you think of that?"

Metzger shook his head. He was drooling, imagining salt on his French Fries and ketchup on her breasts. "I think salt is bad for you."

She laughed. "That's what the doctor says." Then she ran her hands through her hair and inhaled deeply. He couldn't help but watch the rise and fall of the vine wrapping her body.

"Touch me," she said.

"No." He shook his head. "I can't."

"Touch me."

"I don't want to," he said through gritted teeth.

"Sure you do. Do you really know what you want?" She touched his gun with the tip of her forefinger, then licked her finger. "I said touch me. Touch me. Touch me."

He stared at her body for a long, luscious moment as the words sunk in. Finally he reached out with his pistol to touch it, but she shook her head.

"Not with that. Here, give it to me."

Without thinking, he handed it to her.

"Now," she leaned in close to him, so close he could see what looked like a hummingbird tattoo on her right shoulder. It seemed to be hovering there, its wings blurred from their motion. "Touch me here."

Both her hands went to her thighs. Metzger placed his hand between her legs and found her center. His erection strained at his pants. He gripped her with his free hand and shoved her back towards the altar. When her back hit it, she pushed herself on it into a sitting position. Her breasts were now at eye level and he enveloped them with his mouth, kissing first one, then the other, lathering them with his tongue.

He vaguely wondered what he was doing. But his brain was a hazy muddle as he let his fingers push into her. She moaned, her eyelids fluttering like the hummingbird's wings.

"I can't stop," he murmured.

"No," she panted. "You can't. The incense is made from Frankincense and Myrrh soaked in an orange sunshine microdot solution. Just a little LSD. You have little control over anything you do."

"But..." He wanted to talk, but his mouth was full of her. She was his drug. She was what he needed. He needed to say something, but it didn't seem as important as it had been. Still, he managed to croak, "You killed him."

She paused for a moment and examined him with critical eyes, then melted back into ecstasy. "I've killed more than him."

He pushed her down and climbed on top of her. She began to help him out of his clothes.

"Hopkins," he whispered, pressing his lips against the hummingbird.

"Yes. Sam." She licked his stomach. "We're old friends."

Metzger knew that he shouldn't be doing what he was doing. He also knew that there was some connection between her voice and the incense. She'd said the smoke had been laced with acid. He grinned. He'd loved acid growing up. He and his friend Pete had done microdots for a full summer, never once coming up for air. It had been lost time. He never really knew what had gone on during those three months, but he remembered feeling happy.

"Why'd you kill him?"

"Same reason you're going to die," she said. "You know too much."

Metzger found the idea of dying funny and began to laugh.

She laughed too. Soon, they were both laughing about how funny it was to die.

His mouth was on the hummingbird when his hands found her throat. He squeezed.

"Not so hard," she said, with that voice that made him want to listen. "Softer. Gentler. Lovelier."

He closed his eyes and let his hands relax. He could feel the tips of his boots pressing against the altar. His erection pressed against her pubis.

"Hurry, before someone comes," she urged.

His body jolted as a memory seized him. He'd heard those words before. He was transported from the altar of this church to a ditch outside an abandoned factory south of Mosul, Iraq. He never knew the woman's name. She was a prostitute – at least that's what they'd thought. He was fourth in line and the last from his squad. He lay atop her as she spoke lush Arabic into his ear. She could have been calling him an imperialist pig, she could have been talking about tomatoes, but he remembered pretending that she was talking to him like he was a real man and she was a real woman, and they had something real together.

He'd unzipped his pants but had left his vest and top on. That was the thing that saved him. He was plowing her, using his arms to support his weight and listening to her speak to him, when he heard the first shot. It came from far away. He was so used to hearing them that he ignored it.

Then she said the words in English, "Hurry, before someone comes," and all hell broke loose. Rounds sizzled into his friends from broken windows in the factory. His squad members fired back, but it was too late. A single round hit him in the back. The air left him, but he didn't die. The vest had caught the round. Looking at the whore, he saw the hatred in her eyes and how her gaze flicked to the windows of the factory. That's when his hands had found her neck.

He was hit twice more, but he never let up. Even when she spat on him with her eyes bulging and her tongue seeking escape from her mouth, he continued to squeeze. The hatred faded from her eyes as they turned dull, life fleeing them so quickly that she was there one minute and gone the next.

Metzger opened his eyes and found himself living the scene again, his hands throttling Kim Johnson.

She tried to speak but she could only gasp. She thrashed and kicked beneath him. Her eyes bulged, filling with fear as she realized that this was the end, and that all her planning, her voice – the acid-laced incense – and her gaming with Metzger had somehow turned back upon her.

Kim Johnson died gurgling.

Metzger held himself atop her with his arms outstretched for several moments before rolling off, out of breath. He caught himself before he fell to the floor, staggering, using the edge of the altar to support himself. He found his shirt, holster and vest, and struggled into them.

His mind was beginning to clear, but the fuzziness was being replaced by something else, something dirty and awful that he didn't want to remember. No, now it was *two* awful somethings, each playing in endless loops.

He spied the bag of meth beneath a chair and snatched it. Without even thinking, he poured a quarter of it into the palm of his hand and snorted it. His lethargy disappeared in a rush. His senses expanded. His mind grew sharper.

"Metzger! My God! What are you doing?"

He jerked from his ecstatic moment like a dog caught in the act of chewing something he wasn't supposed to.

Veronica stood just inside the door, one hand gripping the back of a chair, the other holding a pistol. She breathed heavily as though she'd been running. Her gaze went from the naked body atop the altar to Metzger and the bag of drugs in his hand. "What happened?"

He closed the bag and shoved it into his pocket. He found his pistol on the ground, put it back in his holster, snapped it in place and walked towards the exit. He was about to walk past her, when she grabbed him by his arm and spun him around.

"I asked you what happened."

He stared coolly into her eyes as his system raced with meth. "What happened?" he repeated. When she nodded, he replied with one word. "Murder."

Then he shrugged out of her grip and headed out the door.

Metzger was too high to cry. He was too wired to let depression overtake him. His hands gripped the wheel with the same force he'd used to strangle those two women. He sped past the entrance to the quay. He tore down the road towards the plant. He remembered the conversation about suicide bombers he'd had with Dr. Gudgel. It seemed like it had been hours and hours ago. What had the older man said? *"My time has passed. My purpose is gone and there's nothing else I want to do with my life."* Metzger understood those words. He also understood that he didn't want to go on with the images of those women in his head, forever dying, and forever being murdered... by him. No matter how evil they were, he'd stained his soul by killing them.

Metzger took the remote detonator from where it lay in the ashtray. He could make it all go away in a rush of light and heat.

He wouldn't even feel anything. For a moment, he thought he understood the mentality of the suicide bomber.

But then an image filled his mind, which drilled through the chemical high, pried apart his pain and fell into his heart. At the last minute he opened the door and bailed out.

Metzger hit the ground hard enough to rattle his teeth and rolled, tumbling until he was on the shore of the sea, his boots in the water. Somehow he'd kept a grip on the detonator and as the truck plowed through the fence then crashed into the front door of the plant, he flipped the first switch. The explosion shook the world. A moment later he flipped the second switch. This one was double the first.

Pieces of metal and concrete rained down. He covered his head with his arms and concentrated on the good feelings that had returned to him. He had to. Because if he forgot about the good, all the bad would come back to him and he would need the meth which was currently weighing down his pocket.

As soon as pieces of the plant stopped raining down, he dragged himself upright and stared at the sky, wondering if any satellites were looking down.

"Hurry, before someone comes," he said.

When the sea started to flash green, he ran.

CHAPTER TWENTY-SIX

Metzger met the others running towards him.

Derrick's smile was immense. "Holy shit. You blew it all to hell."

Natasha's smile was almost as wide. Metzger remembered the camera mounted in the truck and wondered how much she'd seen. Then he saw Veronica. She smiled as well, but it was more reserved. Auntie Lin followed behind.

Suddenly he realized the enormity of what Veronica had witnessed. Natasha wouldn't understand. She couldn't ever know what had happened in the church or in Iraq. So it was with a heavy heart that Metzger embraced the others as they plowed into him.

"So you got her?" Derrick asked. "Veronica said you got her."

"Yeah. I got her." He shot Veronica a look. "It was close though. She almost had me."

"Did you see the water?" Natasha asked.

Metzger nodded.

"What now?" Veronica asked.

"We gotta get out of here. By the frequency of the flashing lights, every zombie in the zip code could be headed our way." Metzger glanced at Natasha, who'd been gazing at him the whole time. "We need to find somewhere safe."

"Didn't you see?" Derrick asked. "The road is completely blocked. There's no way out."

"We don't have to drive out of here," Natasha said. "We could just run to the road until we meet a passing car or truck."

"We'd never outrun the zombies. We'd tire first." Metzger shook his head. "The only way looks like the sea. Like Maude said."

"We're not leaving without my uncle and aunt," Veronica insisted. "They're the only family I really have."

Metzger stared at Veronica for a moment, then nodded. "Fine. Then go get them."

"She can't go alone. I'm going with her," Derrick said.

Natasha moved to intercept her brother, but he shrugged her away.

"I'm going."

"Meet us at grandpa's trailer," she called.

He waved his hand, then sprinted to catch up with Veronica, who'd already made the turn down Fourth Street. Natasha turned to Metzger. "Are you sure you're okay?"

"Why your grandpa's trailer?" Metzger asked.

"There are some pictures there of my mother and father I don't want to leave." Seeing his expression, she added, "They're all that I have now."

"It's a waste of time to go there."

Natasha narrowed her eyes. "Why would you say that?"

Metzger felt the drug coursing through his system. He fought to control the his twitching jaw.

"You were in there a long time. What happened?" Natasha asked.

Metzger glared at her, hating that he was being asked so many questions. But then his gaze softened as he remembered that the drug could make him mean if he let it. "It was hard.

I had to kill her. I don't want to talk about it if it's okay with you."

She nodded and tried to smile, looking concerned. She took Auntie Lin's hand and hurried forward, avoiding pools of light.

Metzger collected his thoughts. He was embarrassed by what had happened. His body had reacted in a natural way to wholly unnatural circumstances. That it had been a life or death situation didn't matter. Sex and death are close friends; they just never meet in public. No, he wasn't embarrassed by what happened, but that he'd been caught. He had powerful feelings for Natasha, there was no doubt. But the idea of sex on the verge of death, the power of the energy created between him and Kim Johnson where he didn't know how it would turn out, whether he'd live or die or fuck or not, was undeniable.

He realized with a sense of fatalism that if he had to do it again, he'd probably do it the same way, even knowing that Natasha would be crushed if she ever found out.

It was at that moment that Metzger realized that he wasn't the right man for her. She deserved better. She didn't need his sort of damaged goods.

They decided to take a detour.

Well actually, Veronica decided. Derrick followed. Veronica wanted to check on the children first. She'd explained to Derrick how she'd spent a lot of time babysitting Carrie Loughnane's disparate offspring, so much so that she felt like a sort of big sister. There had been several times when Carrie had fallen off the wagon, leaving her kids to be cared for by fate, and Veronica had stepped in and treated the seven little monsters the way she would have wanted to be treated herself.

So she and Derrick ran the length of Fourth Street, then turned down Avenue A. They hadn't seen any zombies yet but the dramatically flashing lights promised that it would only be a matter of time.

Derrick hoped that they were going to make it in time, but when they arrived at the Laundromat, the zombies had been there and gone. It looked as if a herd of rampaging beasts had stampeded through it. Nothing remained of the glass frontage. The chairs had been splintered and twisted into origami puzzles. Washing machines were overturned, posters had been ripped from the walls, the fluorescent lamps that had hung from the drop ceiling were shattered, not a single one intact.

But somehow the children were still there.

And Derrick realized, so was their mother.

Like goldfish in individual tanks, the kids stared out of the glass doors fronting the upper row of front-load dryers, their eyes wide, mouths open and sagging, exhausted from screaming. Blood smeared the outside of the doors. One of the glass fronts had cracked but was still held together by the shatter-proof coating.

Derrick looked at the doors. To open them one had to turn a lever above the coin feed and then pull the handle on the door; too difficult for a zombie for sure.

Then he looked down. On the floor beneath where the children had been saved lay their mother. Carrie Loughnane's eyes remained the sky blue they'd always been. Her face held a knowing smile, as if in the last moments of her life she'd finally understood something important. But the rest of her was mangled. Her arms had been taken, her legs bent at impossible angles, broken and snapped, her ribcage torn open. She'd been emptied out. Nothing remained but a glimpse of vertebrae in the shiny cavity that had once harbored a heart big enough to love everyone she'd ever met.

"Come on," Derrick said, trying not to look at the body again. "We gotta – we gotta go."

"But the children –"

When Veronica put her hand on one of the glass plates, the girl on the other side pressed her cheek against it. "We can't just leave them like this."

"We have to." Derrick looked from one to the other. "Do you really think we can keep them safe? We're barely able to protect ourselves."

"But they're only kids!"

"Look at the front of the dryers. The zombies already tried and gave up. They can't get to them. Let someone else save them in the morning when help arrives."

"*If* help arrives."

"*When* help arrives. I can't believe that a whole factory can explode and an entire town can get eaten and no one will come to investigate?"

Veronica gave him a withering look. "Look around you. This town has never been on anyone's *to do* list."

"No, I guess you're right. Then how about this – *we'll* come back and save them in the morning."

"But what if something happens to us?"

"If something happens to us, then something's going to happen to them if they're with us too. Like I said, they're safer here."

Veronica shook her head, not because she disagreed, but because she couldn't believe this was happening and they had to make these sorts of decisions. Nothing had prepared them for this. There was no *Idiot's Guides to Zombie Chasing*. There were no *how-tos* on how to survive zombie attacks. That they'd survived this long was a miracle. If they made it through the night it would be more than a miracle.

"Let's go." Derrick glanced around once more at the devastation. "The zombies are on their way. I feel it. Anytime now." Derrick climbed over the sill, careful of the broken glass.

Veronica stole a last look at the kids. Their faces pressed against the glass of the driers, terror showing on their faces at the prospect of being left alone. But Derrick was right. They had a greater chance of surviving if left where they were. So she silently wished the children good luck and followed Derrick into the street.

They kept to the edge of the buildings. When they reached the restaurant, they saw hundreds of zombies staggering ashore. The image stunned them for a moment, freezing them in place. By the time they turned and ran up Avenue A, the zombies had seen them and were in full pursuit.

At Fourth Street they zigged east, intending to take Avenue B north to Veronica's trailer. But they saw movement near the intersection and dodged between two trailers. Almost out of breath, they finally got to the back of Veronica's trailer. As they arrived, they heard a scream.

Veronica shot Derrick a wide-eyed look. He waved her to her bedroom window, the screen long since broken. He'd go in the front. A small, chicken part of him wanted to turn that around so that she went in the front, but he squashed it.

A white Suburban was parked in the front yard. The sight of it actually made Derrick smile, not because he wasn't afraid of Hopkins and his cronies, but because he was less afraid of them than he was of the zombies.

Raised voices came from inside. He recognized Hopkins's voice and the deep baritone of Veronica's uncle. At the door, he peeked in, planning to jerk his head back, but the scene captured and held his attention. Veronica's aunt was dead on the couch, her face almost gone. Blood and brain matter were splattered on the wall behind her. Next to her on the couch was Natasha's uncle, his hands out, pleading with his attacker.

Derrick's movement must have caught the uncle's attention, because he looked squarely at Derrick, as did Hopkins.

Derrick brought his crowbar around, but he was too slow and Hopkins backhanded him with his pistol. Pain exploded in Derrick's face; he fell to the ground, wanting to cry and vomit at the same time. He tried to rise, but his breath was stolen away from him as Hopkins kicked him in the stomach. Now he did puke, ribbons of bile sliding down his face. He was jerked to his feet by his hair and spun to face his attacker.

"You motherfucking kids! How *dare* you fuck with me!"

Hopkins brought his fist back and plowed it into Derrick's face. His eyes felt like they'd burst, the pain turning everything red and white. He tried to say something, but could do nothing more than gurgle.

Suddenly he felt Hopkins stiffen. He let go and Derrick fell to the floor.

"You can't punch a kid like that," Veronica snarled. Then she cried, "Oh, Lord – Auntie!"

Derrick didn't see what happened next, but he heard three

pistol shots and the sound of something heavy hitting the floor. It took a moment, but Veronica rolled him over.

"He killed Auntie," she whispered hoarsely.

"And you killed him." Derrick got to one knee. Hopkins lay face down. Derrick got the rest of the way to his feet, then kicked the dead man in the side as hard as he could.

Veronica ran to her uncle, cradling his wife's body.

Derrick rolled Hopkins over. He was happy to see the surprise that would live forever on his dead face. That it was two kids who killed him was all the better. Derrick brought his foot back and kicked the man in the side of the head.

Outside he saw a mass of zombies chasing someone down the street. They could be next.

"Hurry up," Veronica said to her uncle. "We have to go."

Her uncle shook his head. "I'm not going to leave her. I have to bury her."

"But uncle, you have to come or you'll die."

"I let him kill her."

"I don't care about that. I care about you."

"Then take care of yourself. Save yourself. I'm going to die right here."

"But uncle!"

"Veronica, keep your voice down," Derrick hissed. "We have to leave."

She turned to Derrick. "Go without me."

"What? I can't do that!"

She gripped his shirt. "Do it. Just go." She kissed him hard on the lips. "I'll be there, I promise. Now *go*. Before it's too late."

Derrick didn't like the idea of splitting up, but he knew by the look in her eyes that there was nothing to be done about it.

So he did what any hero would do.

He turned and ran.

CHAPTER TWENTY-SEVEN

Derrick's face hurt worse than any other pain he'd ever felt in his life. He'd been hit in the balls with a football and fallen off of his bike going downhill, but he'd never been punched in the face by a fully-grown man. His lips were swelling. One eye was all but closed.

He ran to Fourth Street and was about to turn east for the quickest way back to the trailer when he saw a horde of zombies running down the street. They hadn't seen him yet.

He dove across the road towards a propane tank, hit the ground and tried to roll, but didn't have the athleticism. Instead he skidded to a stop on his hands, gravel and sand biting into them. The crowbar went flying out of sight.

He thought about trying to find it, but the zombies were coming and he didn't have time. He got to his feet and ran, dodging around the end of a trailer and throwing his back against it. On Avenue A an Irish Setter he'd never seen before ran down the street, turning and barking at the dozen zombies who chased it before running again, as if it were leading them away. By the way the dog's tail wagged, it clearly thought it was just a game.

The game would inevitably turn bad. So many people had died that to see an animal die, especially a dog, tore at Derrick's heart.

But he kept going. Now he heard the tell-tale high-pitched wheezing of zombies on the other side of the trailer to his left. He took off running, only to run straight into one of them.

Derrick didn't have time to stop. He went into a baseball slide, like he was going into home plate feet first. The maneuver took him low through the mud and, as he slipped past one of the zombies, he brought his hands across the creature's ankles.

The zombie couldn't take the momentum. Its ankles smacked together; it teetered once, then crashed against the trailer and fell to the ground. Even as it did, it reached for Derrick, but he was too quick. He shot to a standing position and took off again.

He passed a house where a huddle of zombies was chewing at an immense man, lying sprawled in a kiddy pool that was rapidly filling with rainwater and blood. His legs were as big around as Derrick's chest and his arms must have each weighed eighty pounds.

As Derrick sped past the zombies, he realized with horror that he'd been more apalled by the man's waxy, pale skin than by the zombies' feast. He was becoming inured to the sight, and it didn't bother him at all.

For a moment, he had a clear shot to his grandpa's trailer, but a pair of zombies suddenly peeled away from a cat they'd been eating and ran right at him. Derrick ran between the nearest houses, taking him away from his sister.

The zombies' lack of dexterity ran in Derrick's favor. Most of the yards on this block were separated with waist-high chain link fences, and he was able to get over them fairly fast, while the zombies all but fell as they attempted the same.

For a second he was home free. Then the figure of the Klosterman Kid caused Derrick to skid to a stop. He was straining at the end of his chain, howling in frustration as he swung his arms towards an old woman zombie. It would be easy to run around them, but as he listened to the man-boy's howl, he knew he couldn't. Veronica had described the Klosterman Kid as a four year old stuck in a thirty-five year old's body, making him no different than Carrie's kids. They at least had the safety of the dryers; what did the Klosterman Kid have? The door was ripped from the hinges of his doghouse. The Kid really had nothing... and no one, unless you counted Derrick.

Just then the woman leaped atop the Kid's back, moving more like a spider than a person. She was about to sink her jaws into the back of his neck, when he spun, sending her flying into the side of the trailer.

"Hey!" Derrick shouted.

The Kid whirled. When he saw Derrick, he broke into a smile. "Hey!" he shouted back.

Derrick ran to him, intending to unstrap the wide leather collar around the Kid's neck. But the Klosterman Kid wrapped both of his arms around Derrick and hugged him to his huge chest. Derrick struggled for breath.

"Stop... can't... breathe."

The Klosterman Kid let go and Derrick began to work the leather end free of the clasp.

The old woman zombie attacked once more, flinging herself at the Kid, her teeth latching onto his arm. The Kid tried to shake her off, which did nothing to help Derrick.

The zombie came away with a chunk of meat. The Klosterman Kid threw his head back and screamed like a giant baby, kicked out and caught the zombie in the stomach. She bent over double, but was back up in a second.

But that second was enough time for Derrick to finally pull the leather through the metal clasp and free the kid.

But he had no time to celebrate. The zombie was after *him* now and dove on his chest. He was somehow able to grab her by the shoulders and hold her off, but he couldn't hold her for long.

She snapped at his face. Derrick closed his eyes and screamed.

Then she was gone.

Derrick cracked open his eyes and saw her hanging by the leash. The Klosterman Kid had wrapped it several times around her neck and had lifted her from the ground. If she was a human she would have died.

Derrick scrambled to his feet.

Her legs kicked beneath her and her hands tried to pry the chain loose, to no avail. The Klosterman Kid spun her on the end of the chain, twirling her around and around. After four revolutions he let her go. She flew through the air. When she hit the length of the chain, her neck snapped and she fell to the ground.

But it didn't kill her.

She climbed unsteadily to her feet, head lolling on her shoulders.

Derrick searched for something to use as a weapon. He spied a shovel leaning against the trailer, grabbed it and shouted, "Hold her down!"

Doing as he was told, the Klosterman Kid body-tackled the old woman zombie. He lay atop her as she bit him repeatedly in the arm. He screamed, but still held her down.

Derrick swung the shovel trying to take the zombie's head off with the blade, but missed on his first try, the flat of the shovel smacking into her face and shattering her front teeth. He swung again, this time almost hitting the Kid in the back of the head. Derrick realized that it would never work the way he was trying to do it. So he straddled the old woman zombie's head, pressed the blade of the shovel against her neck and then jumped with both feet on it as if he were digging a hole. The blade sliced clean through the neck.

The zombie went instantly still.

He dropped the shovel and reached down to the Kid. "Come on. Follow me."

The Klosterman Kid rolled over. Tears still fell from his eyes as he brought a hand to his bloody wounds.

"Hurts," he said. "Omammie it hurts."

"I know. I know." Derrick put his arm around the Kid's back as he got to his feet. "We'll get that looked at, I promise."

He glanced around. They seemed to be in a zombie free zone. Those who'd been chasing him earlier had given up the chase.

Now in the Klosterman's backyard – with the exception of the dead, decapitated zombie laying in the muddy grass – he could have been anywhere.

Who was he kidding? They had to get out of here.

"Follow me," he said, picking the shovel back up.

He took off at a jog and ran around the end of the trailer, right into a group of zombies.

"Fuck!" Derrick tried to dodge one way, found that way blocked, then spun back towards the other way. All of a sudden he was grabbed from behind, the wheezing so close he couldn't even hear his own breathing. He struggled spastically, flinging his arms and legs wildly about, but couldn't break free. He tried to swing his shovel, but couldn't bring it to bear. A zombie came at him from the front and he kicked out, catching it in the hip and sending it stumbling off balance.

Suddenly teeth bit deeply into his left tricep.

He screamed. His whole body shook as teeth scraped against bone. He struggled again to swing the shovel, but couldn't get it higher than his knee, so he began to rake it across the legs of the zombies nearest him, hoping that they'd at least feel the pain.

But nothing happened. The zombie tore again at the back of his arm.

Derrick screamed again, and was echoed by the Klosterman Kid behind him.

Derrick fell to the ground and saw the Kid swinging a piece of wood torn from the porch in wide sweeping arcs. With each swing a zombie went down. Sometimes it stayed down, but more often it got up.

Derrick found himself no longer the center of the zombies' attention. They surged past him towards the Klosterman Kid.

Derrick climbed to his feet, gripping his bloody arm.

"Homerun!" The Kid broke out into a grin as he stuck his tongue in between his teeth and swung harder. He stared at Derrick and yelled it again, this time breaking it into two words. "Home run!"

Derrick understood and got to his feet, one arm holding the other. For a second Derrick thought he may actually survive the battle, but the wood cracked and splintered, leaving the Kid with little more than a twig to defend himself.

The zombies surged over the Kid, and Derrick turned and ran. His head swam and he was a little unsteady at first, but he found his balance, oriented himself, and took off like a drunken racer down Fourth Street, holding his arm. By the time he'd reached Isle of Palms Avenue, there were a hundred of the creatures hot on his tail. Their combined hissing sounded like a hungry freight train.

Some of the creatures ran at almost regular speed, but many could move no faster than a jog. Some even lurched like the ones in the old black and white movies. Derrick figured maybe it had to do with how old they were, or how much damage the rot had done to muscle and bone. In the zero-gravity environment of space it wouldn't matter, but here on earth, gravity had everyone under its thumb.

Derrick took a corner at full speed, his feet slipping on the wet gravel and mud that had fallen off the seawall where the zombies had broken through. His head had cleared and he was no longer dizzy. He headed south towards the intersection of Isle of Palms and Fifth Street, where the seawalls met in an "L" and the entrance to the plant was – *used* to be, he corrected himself; all that remained was a smoking heap.

He somehow found more speed and bit his swollen lip to keep from crying out. His arm hurt worse than any pain he'd ever felt. Where the beating from Hopkins had been a temporary thing, the horrendous wound on his arm, dripping blood and gore where his muscle had been torn away, affected him as much psychologically as physiologically.

Through the entrance to the quay he observed that the sea was still flashing. It lit the night in green throbs. He wondered how many more zombies there could be waiting beneath the water.

Derrick had been hoping he could circle the block and end up back at his grandpa's trailer. But he was almost to the corner when he glanced through the trailers towards Fifth Street and saw dozens more zombies loping to intercept him. Fear almost stopped him. This was not at all what he'd anticipated.

He couldn't turn around. He couldn't turn the corner. He could go over the seawall, but there were most certainly zombies on the other side, still wading from the sea. He couldn't weave through trailers, because there weren't any this close to the intersection. His only chance was to get to the corner first. As impossible as it seemed, he managed to pour on a little more juice... and he made it a few steps faster than the nearest zombie coming towards him down Fifth Street. Leaping over piles of trash and stacked wood, Derrick ran to sump pump #2. As he grabbed the metal grate, the pump growled at him like a furious chained beast. He remembered when they'd first come to Bombay Beach and the Salton Sea, and how the pump's sound had scared him. That sound was nothing compared to the real horror now in town.

The grate was impossibly heavy. Derrick tugged and heaved until there was a space big enough for him to slip through. He went in feet first and immediately got stuck, but wiggled and shoved with the desperation of someone about to be eaten and finally fell inside. He hit the piping and part of the motor with a painful crash, but he had no time to waste. He stood and pressed his hands against the grill slats, anchored his legs against the concrete wall, and pushed the grate back into place with a clang.

And not a moment too soon.

A zombie crashed against the gate, pushing its fingers through, trying to get to him.

Derrick jerked his hands back and found himself staring into yellow zombie eyes. The creature chewed and gnawed at the grate, breaking teeth on the metal. The zombie snapped like a savage dog on the other side of a fence, unwilling to back down, not knowing that it couldn't chew through the barrier, not caring, driven by a desire it couldn't understand.

Another zombie crashed on top of the first one. It had an eye missing and fungus growing in the empty socket. It hissed and pushed, trying to get to Derrick, fighting the other for position.

Derrick met the dead hungry stares of the zombies as they glared at him, need behind each glowing yellow eyeball. They wanted him. They needed him. They'd do anything to have him.

Then it began to rain harder, as Tropical Storm Hiawatha asserted itself. The sump growled. He peered up at the zombies above him.

A horrible thought struck him. After all this, he might end up drowning down here.

It began to rain harder and Derrick swore that he could see the water level rising even as he prayed for the sump pump to work faster.

CHAPTER TWENTY-EIGHT

Veronica cried wildly into the rain. Zombies had taken her uncle as he'd tried to dig a hole in their backyard. She'd been unable to save him and had barely been able to save herself. Now, staggering down the street, she wasn't sure where to go.

She saw the golf cart swerving down the street and ran towards it. Although the rain was coming down hard, she thought she saw Mr. Duphrene behind the wheel. He'd be able to help. He might even have a way out.

She jumped into the street and began to wave her arms.

"Over here! I'm over here, Mr. Duphrene."

The cart swerved hard to the left, then to the right, and then straightened, as if he was drunk. She lowered her arms. He drew near, but he wasn't slowing, and there was something wrong with the way he looked. Almost too late, she saw what had happened and dove out of the way.

The cart careened past. The zombie that had been Mr. Duphrene turned his head and roared at her, crashed into the side of a trailer and was propelled over the steering wheel and into the side.

Veronica began to back away.

Mr. Duphrene climbed over the ruin of the cart and got to his feet. He stared at Veronica for a moment, raised his hooks into the air and came running at her.

She turned to run, but slid on the wet pavement and fell down hard enough that her knees began to bleed. She staggered to her feet just in time to dodge the flailing arms of the hook-handed zombie.

He skidded to a stop, and fell as he tried to turn around.

She backed towards the wreck of the cart, hoping to use it as a shield between her and the zombie.

It roared and came at her again. She climbed through the cab of the cart as it lunged at her, but wasn't fast enough. One of the hooks snagged the end of her tennis shoe, piercing the leather. Somehow her toes were spared any damage, but the hook was set hard in the leather.

She kicked with her free leg, catching the zombie in the face each time, but seemed unable to hurt it.

The zombie pulled her towards it, and as it did, the other hook came down between her legs. She lurched back at the last moment, barely avoiding being pierced in the abdomen.

She rolled over and tried to pull away, but try as she might, she couldn't get free of the hook. She felt a sharp pain as Mr. Duphrene's teeth sank into her calf and screamed, kicking fiercely with both legs.

The sound of a car engine roaring was followed by a tremendous jerk that dragged her several feet. But she was released, and gathered her feet under her and turned around.

A car had rammed right into the Duphrene zombie, pinning him to the wall of the trailer and hitting him with such force, the straps of the prosthetic had snapped off, leaving the hook still attached to her foot. She freed herself and threw it away.

The driver's side door opened and a man staggered towards her.

Not again!

Then she recognized the driver. It was Frank, the town drunk. She'd thought he'd died during the fight with Hopkins earlier. One of his arms was in a dirty sling. The other held a bottle of whiskey.

"Step right up," he slurred. "The bar is open."

He saluted her with the bottle and staggered down the street and out of sight.

Veronica climbed out of the wreck of the cart, turned and ran. Nothing stopped her until she'd reached the safety of Natasha's grandfather's trailer.

Natasha had seen Derrick scramble into sump pump #2 with what seemed like a hundred zombies clawing at the grate.

Veronica sat on the couch being treated for a bite wound by Auntie Lin beneath the half-roof of the deck.

How were they were going to save her brother? Metzger had planned to set fire to some of the trailers and draw the monsters' attention away, but with the rain coming down, there was no way a fire would stay lit.

The ceiling beneath her feet bumped again and she couldn't help but jump. Zombies had followed Veronica to their trailer and had almost made it up to the roof. If it hadn't been for quick thinking on Metzger's part in breaking loose the boards and knocking down the old wooden stairs, their fate would have been sealed. Now the zombies were in the house, rooting around, doing God knew what. And each bump served to remind her that only sheet metal, wood and fiberglass protected them from the zombies' relentless hunger.

"Have you figured out how to save my brother yet?" she asked.

"We're not going down there, that's for sure."

As if by way of confirmation, the zombies thumped against the ceiling beneath them again. There were others clawing at the metal side of the trailer, searching for purchase. Their fingers sounded like fingernails against chalk boards.

"Then what?"

Metzger peered into the rain and shook his head. "There aren't too many options. We can sit it out and hope that one of them doesn't figure out how to lift the grate or..."

"Or what?"

"Or I can try and make that propane tank explode and see how many of them I can take out."

Natasha turned back to the telescope. The propane tank in question was only twenty feet from the sump and much too close to her brother for comfort. Derrick's chances at surviving were slim. She wanted to tell Metzger that, but they'd run out of options. The cavalry wasn't coming. They had this one chance. The more she thought about it, the worse she felt, but she was certain this was the only way.

Still, she had to ask. "Is that the best you can do?"

He shrugged.

"Isn't it too far?"

"It better not be." He held up the XM8 assault rifle he'd taken from the soldier in the restaurant. "I've never fired one of these 8s before, but they have the same ammo as the M16, so the range is probably similar. It looks to be about a hundred meters. I can hit that."

"In the rain? With zombies milling around?"

Metzger breathed deeply a few times, then fired. But instead of an explosion, he was rewarded with an anticlimactic clang. He tried again with the same result.

"Fuck me. The damned bullets won't penetrate. Must be soft tip."

"What does that mean?" Natasha asked.

"It means they'd tear through the human body, but won't do jack to something made out of metal."

He stared momentarily at the rifle. "Aw, fuck it," he said and aimed again before letting loose a stream of automatic rifle fire. At first it had no effect other than raising a clatter, but then a fireball erupted, followed by a deafening explosion that enveloped the zombies, the sump pump and the piles of trash heaped around it.

Veronica and Auntie Lin ran to the railing. All four watched as the fireball ate itself, leaving a pile of charred zombie parts and a herd of burning, stumbling, creatures, lurching aimlessly back and forth and into each other in various states of dismemberment.

The zombies began to attack each other as the propane-fueled fire ate at their flesh. The sound of the storm resumed, but it was different from before. Now Natasha heard sizzling as the water began putting out the burning wreckage. But the zombies were another matter; no matter how much rain fell upon the flames consuming their bodies, the fire refused to die. All Natasha could think of was the isotope in their blood and wonder if it, too, was flammable.

Metzger stood suddenly and began to open fire at the propane tank next to the house next door. It took fewer rounds this time. The tank exploded like the one before it, lighting every zombie within its proximity on fire. He reloaded from a cargo pouch in his pants and continued firing. Soon explosion after explosion rent the air. All around them were fireballs and burning zombies.

Metzger fired until all four magazines were empty and at least two hundred of the monsters were on fire, some fleeing as fast as they could, fanning the flames even faster. They plowed into other zombies and into trailers, their flaming impetus setting fire to everything they touched.

"Get ready to go." Metzger checked the rifle and his pockets for more ammunition. Finding none, he tossed the weapon over the side, drew a pistol from his shoulder holster, checked to see if it was loaded, and turned to the others. "We're leaving in ten seconds."

Natasha was terrified that her brother had been killed. She wanted Metzger to promise her that he was okay. But he seemed distant, more like a soldier now than he had been. He was a different person. Despite the fact that he was helping them survive, she wasn't sure she liked this version of him.

"Veronica, come and help me." He stood by one of the support posts of the half roof covering the deck. "We need to break this free from the posts. Lean with me."

Veronica got to her feet slowly. Her leg was bandaged tightly, but she seemed to be in another world since her auntie and uncle died. Still, she took one look and seemed to know what to do. They managed to rip the roof free and lower it across the gap between trailers so it could be used as a bridge.

Metzger started to step onto it, when Natasha screamed for him to wait. He stopped and looked back at her.

"Shouldn't we try someone light first? Just to make sure it holds?"

Metzger frowned and shook his head. "It doesn't matter. Either it holds us or we all die. "What are you going to do if it breaks and I fall down there?" he asked, pointing towards the zombies. "What are you going to do if Auntie Lin falls? I'll tell you the answer: nothing. You'll do nothing right until the moment you die. Then that'll be something."

Natasha watched Metzger's back, noticing his hands clenching and unclenching. He was like he'd been when he'd first arrived, acting like an addict. She frowned.

Metzger put down another foot and allowed the wood and metal to take his full weight. Not even a tremble. They crossed quickly.

Natasha stole a glance towards the grate covering the sump pump. It was still there and didn't look like it had been moved. On the other hand, besides a few burning bodies, there were no zombies in the vicinity. If her brother was alive, now would be the time for him to get out of there.

She was about to shout when Metzger came and covered her mouth. His hand smelled like gunpowder. Her eyes narrowed and she tried to pry his hand away.

"Not yet," he hissed. "Wait until we're at the end, then we're going to make a run for that."

Natasha stopped struggling as he pointed at a trailer on the other side of the seawall. The Duvall Brothers used it for salt storage, and the windows were barred to keep out thieves. The distance from the last trailer to the salt storage trailer was about thirty feet; they would have to cross the road and scramble up the muddy seawall. Luckily the explosions had done a number on all the nearest zombies. About half of the creatures along their intended path were on fire.

Metzger removed his hand and Natasha grimaced and wiped her mouth clean of the smell.

Without warning, Metzger opened fire. It took five rounds from his pistol, but the zombies on the other trailer went down, the back of their heads exploding in a shower of bone, brains and yellow ichors.

Together Veronica and Metzger moved the bridge from one side of the trailer to the other. Metzger went first, then the others. He had to shoot a zombie tramping up the stairs at the side of the trailer, but it otherwise worked perfectly.

They repeated the process four more times until they came to the end of the row of trailers and leaned the roof down, making a ramp to the ground.

"Okay, now's the time to call him," Metzger said.

Less than a dozen zombies were within fifty feet of them. Two of those were on fire.

"Derrick!" Natasha screamed. "Come on Derrick!"

All eyes were on the grate, but nothing moved.

"Derrick!" she screamed again. She choked on a sob, suddenly convinced that he'd died down there and she'd never see him again.

"Derrick," Metzger yelled. "Hurry up, bro. We have a plan."

"Yeah! Come on," Veronica yelled, joining in.

Natasha screamed again, "Derrick!"

The grate moved. First a little, the sound of metal grinding against metal a slow, plaintive wail, then a hand came up, followed by an arm. Soon they could see Derrick's head, half of his hair scorched off and his face as black as soot. He pulled himself out of the sump and, as if it was angry to lose a meal, the pump growled as he left.

Natasha let out a laugh, but she had no time to glory in her brother's survival.

Metzger grabbed Veronica's arm. "Now hurry. Down the ramp and up the seawall."

Veronica looked left and right, ran down the ramp, crossed the road, and went up the other side. She made it halfway up the hill before the mud slowed her to a stop. Then it was hand over hand until she reached the top.

Natasha helped Auntie Lin down the metal ramp. The older woman ran like a bowlegged chicken. Natasha ran beside her.

"Run, Derrick!" Metzger roared.

The boy stumbled forward, almost tripping over the blackened corpse of a zombie. Several partially burned zombies jerked around as he passed them. Those that could ran towards him. Those that couldn't clawed and dragged their way in his direction. They all wanted him.

"Take the road around and meet us on the other side!"

Derrick hesitated and looked back at the road that ran to the still burning zombie factory, then began to lope in that direction.

Natasha got Auntie Lin about three feet up the seawall before the old woman came to a complete halt. It was just too slippery.

Suddenly a zombie spotted them and broke ranks, sprinting like an Olympic champion directly at them. Metzger ran down the ramp to intercept, lifted both pistols and fired point blank at its head. It fell, the momentum sending its feet forward, laying it out on its back.

"You *have got* to hurry," he yelled back over his shoulder.

"But she won't move." Natasha pulled and jerked to get Auntie Lin up the hill, but no matter what she did, the older woman wouldn't budge.

"Leave me!" Auntie Lin commanded.

"Never!" Natasha cried.

"Veronica, lay down and give Natasha your hand. Natasha, grab Auntie Lin with your other. Ma'am," he said to the old Chinese woman, "you better hold on." Metzger paused only to shoot another incoming zombie, then turned and, without holstering the pistols, pressed both of his hands against the old woman's butt.

"Veronica, pull!"

With Veronica and Natasha pulling and Metzger pushing, his Army boots digging into the mud, they finally made the top of the seawall beside the storage trailer. Derrick was waiting there as well. Natasha ran to hug him, but he jerked away, holding his arm gingerly. He'd lost a lot of blood. Where his face wasn't covered with grime and soot, it was pale. She examined his wound and knew she'd have to take care of it soon, but now there wasn't enough time.

There were no more zombies in sight yet, which was a blessing. Only the rain and the rotting, white-capped sea kept Natasha and the others from running all the way to Los Angeles.

But there, at the end of a rickety old dock, was one of the boats used by the salt collectors. Flat-bottomed and twenty feet long with an outboard engine, it was plenty big enough to hold them all. If only they could all make it out there in time.

Thunder rumbled from far off. As if in response, the sea flashed green yet again.

They ran towards the boat.

CHAPTER TWENTY-NINE

The dock had seen better days. The wear and tear of the salt and continual use by the Duvalls had turned it into a teetering version of its once sturdy self. As they ran down its worn length, the clomping of their feet made it shudder and sway.

But when they reached the boat, their hearts sank like rusty anchors to the Salton Sea floor. The bottom was a colander of holes that had allowed several inches of water to collect. Had it not been tied so tightly to the dock, the boat would have sunk long ago. As it was, there was no way it could carry all of them.

Abruptly heads began to rise from the surface of the sea as more zombies found the surface.

Metzger howled in frustration. He grabbed Auntie Lin and, carrying her in his arms like she was a toddler, sprinted back toward the trailer. The others were quick to follow. They made it to the trailer as the first zombie made landfall, standing and staring as the rain beat down on its green mottled face.

The door was locked, but two kicks from Metzger's booted foot opened it for them. They piled into the trailer, then hunted for a way to bar the door. The living room was used as temporary storage for the harvested salt. Burlap sacks filled with salt crystals covered most of the floor and were piled to the ceiling. They heaped these in front of the door. The sheer weight of them would keep it closed.

Natasha ran to a barred window and peered out, but jerked her head back as a hand shot through the bars, breaking the glass. The yellow-clawed fingers just missed her face, as she turned to look at the others. "Shit! I should have known better than that."

Metzger ran to the back and made sure that there were no other ways in.

Natasha met him in the hall. "There isn't any food or water."

"What did you expect?" he said.

"Maybe we should have stayed on the roof of my grandpa's trailer. I felt safer there than here."

Metzger scowled. "You want to go back, be my guest."

She went to reply, but kept her mouth shut. He could see the hurt in her eyes, but he hadn't been able to keep the smart-assed remarks from bubbling up.

Finally she asked, "What's wrong with you?"

He gritted his teeth and shrugged. "Dunno. What's wrong with you?"

Her jaw dropped for a moment, then she slapped him hard across the face, turned and stomped back into the living room. No one spoke. No one asked her what happened. They didn't have to. The trailer was so small that they'd all heard.

Metzger wanted to strangle himself. He slid into the bathroom and closed the door, flipped on the light switch and glared at his gaunt face in the mirror. He was a piece of work. When Natasha needed someone she could lean on, someone she could count on, all he could be was an ass. He'd always been a bully when he was high, and nothing had changed. He reached into his pocket and pulled out the bag of meth he'd taken from Kim Johnson. There was enough there for a weekend jaunt. He poured the crystal into his hand. It seemed so harmless. He'd been to enough classes in

Norfolk to understand how it worked. He knew how terrible it was for his system. But damned if it hadn't brought back old memories.

He opened the toilet. A small circle of sludge greeted him in the bottom of the bowl. He held his hand over the water with every intention of flushing it away, but instead of letting go of the crystal, his hand closed protectively around it.

He couldn't help but laugh.

Who was in charge here? Was it him? Or was it the meth?

He tried again with the same result.

Fuck it. The meth made him sharp and helped him think in tough situations. When they got out of here he'd find a way to make it up to Natasha. Until then, she'd have to understand. Yeah. She'd just have to understand.

Metzger poured the crystal onto the cheap Formica counter. Using the butt of his pistol, he crushed it into a fine powder. Without ceremony, he leaned down and snorted the whole shebang. When there was nothing left but residue, he licked his finger, wiped it, then wiped his finger across his gums.

The rush was immediate and all powerful. He was superman. He could not be defeated. He could not lose. He'd save them all. He'd be a hero. He'd get the girl and live happily ever after.

He yanked open the door and stepped into the hall.

Veronica was waiting for him, her eyes glowing yellow. A low growl came from her throat.

"Aw fuck," he said.

Then she attacked and shoved him into the bathroom.

The door slammed shut behind them, and they fell into the bathtub, the shower curtain entangling them. Her teeth tried to find him, but he was somehow able to wrap her face with the curtain. He punched her three times, hard, but it had no effect.

He scrambled over the side of the tub, grabbed the vanity to help him get to his feet, and jerked the door open. He leaped into the hall and closed it behind him. It opened inwards, so he held onto the handle as tightly as he could.

Natasha approached him.

"What are you doing?"

He glanced from her to the door and back. *Wasn't it obvious?*

Veronica began to pound on the door.

"Who is that? Is it Veronica? Let her out!"

Metzger shook his head. "Zombie," he breathed.

Natasha raised her hand to her mouth in shock. Then she glanced down the hall at her brother, who was sitting at the table getting his arm bandaged by Auntie Lin.

"What do we do?" she asked.

"Gotta kill her," he said.

"But..." Although the idea revolted her, he could see the understanding in her eyes. "Oh."

"Grab the door knob."

When she did, he pulled free his pistol, checked the magazine, then stepped to the side and aimed for the door.

"On the count of three, push it open."

Natasha nodded.

"One. Two. Three!"

Veronica stood framed in the doorway. Her hair was wild, her eyes yellow, her skin a sickly green. She growled low in her throat.

Metzger fired three times, catching her in the head and face.

Veronica fell to the ground unmoving.

Natasha backed against the wall, while Metzger pushed the dead girl farther into the bathroom with his booted foot, and closed the door.

Derrick and Auntie Lin met him at the end of the wall in the kitchen.

"What happened" Derrick asked.

"Veronica. Zombie. Killed her." Metzger glared at everyone, challenging them to ask him more, but he'd given enough information.

He went to the front door to see if there was any hope at all. There had to be a way out. There was always a way out. He'd had a sergeant in Iraq who said the only failure of idea was a failure of imagination, and right now Metzger's imagination was a Technicolor dreamcoat of ideas.

The trailer was on the side of the seawall and elevated from the sea, perpendicular to the shoreline. Visualizing the outside, Metzger remembered that the front was supported by iron pylons that had been cranked to level the floor.

He peered out the window. More zombies were coming ashore. Would they never stop? How many were there? How many soldiers suffering from PTSD had Hopkins arranged to be a part of the program? Metzger made a mental promise that when he got out of here, he was going to blow the secret wide open to the national media. Many of those soldiers had been his friends. They'd all been brothers in arms. Regardless of the connection, they were all fellow humans and it just wasn't right. But that would have to wait until they escaped. Right now he had to figure out a way to do just that.

An image flashed through his mind of Noah's Ark, and the beginning of an idea was born.

"What are you doing?" Natasha asked tightly.

"Saving you."

"How can you just go back to this after killing Veronica?"

"I didn't kill Veronica. She was dead the moment she was bit."

"Like my brother."

"I didn't say anything about that."

"Are you going to kill him too?"

He rounded on her. "Do you really want to have this conversation right now? What did you think was going to happen? Did you think we were all going to walk out of this unscathed? This is war and in war people die. That's it. Period. End of fucking story."

She glared at him. "So *are* you?" she persisted.

A thousand responses went through his mind, but he bit every one of them back. Instead he said, "I think I'll leave that up to you."

She glared at him for a long moment, then went to the table where Derrick was being ministered to by Auntie Lin. Metzger stared at her for a moment, then turned away. Like he said, *this was war.* He didn't have time for kid stuff like boyfriend and girlfriend. Someone had to save them, and since he seemed to be the only super-fueled hero around, it looked like that was him.

He searched beneath the cupboards in the kitchen until he found a toolbox and rifled through it until he found what he was looking for – a crow bar in the toolbox, which he used to peel back the cheap carpet. Beneath was old, rotting plywood. He dug at it, stripping away the wood until he'd made a hole big enough to fit his head into.

He shifted position and stuck his head through the hole. Sure enough, the brackets supporting the axels were mounted on concrete bases. He craned his head to see what condition the trailer's wheels were in. They were good all around – relatively new and apparently inflated.

Metzger jerked his head back up and directed everyone to help move all the salt bags from the other rooms towards the front of the trailer. The idea was to put as much weight in the front as possible. It took several minutes, but soon there were so many bags of salt in the living room that the entire floor was covered up to a level of four feet.

"Now what, idea man?" Natasha asked.

"Now we rock it."

The look of confusion on her face was replaced with understanding as he leaped atop the bags, put his hands on the ceiling, and began to throw his weight forward and back like he was standing on a swing and trying to get it to move.

Before long even Auntie Lin was on top of the salt bags, doing the same. It took a minute or to get coordinated so that they rocked in time with each other, but eventually they heard the metal of the trailer begin to creak. They doubled their efforts, slinging their bodies forward and backward in unison.

Metzger felt the support brackets begin to teeter and urged the others on. Then the front end suddenly jerked out and the support brackets lost purchase. The front of the trailer fell with a bone-jarring crash that shook everything, the front door flew open as the trailer frame bent, windows exploded outwards, and Metzger and the others lost their footing and rolled on the floor.

The trailer began to roll on its wheels – slowly at first, then faster and faster.

Zombies ran alongside the trailer as best they could, trying to keep up. Their ravenous faces were fixated on them. Some stumbled, falling to the ground, tripping others as they fell, but there were still enough to make leaping from the door worse than suicide.

Suddenly one reached inside and grabbed Auntie Lin's left leg. She kicked savagely, knocking the zombie away.

"Hold on!" Derrick shouted. "We're going to hit!"

The front end of the trailer plowed into the water in a great plume and everyone was hurled forward into the front wall. Metal scraped and screamed along the ground, then suddenly everything went smooth as the caravan started to float.

Metzger climbed a little unsteadily from where he'd ended up on the floor and jumped over the salt bags to the door. With a hand on each side of the jamb he leaned out. They were about a dozen feet from shore and moving farther out.

"Metzger!" Natasha yelled. "We're sinking."

He glared at the water that was already to his ankles. He directed the survivors to grab their stuff and follow him into the back bedroom where he'd seen the hatch to the roof. It was a moment's work with the pry bar to open the hole large enough for him to get through and then they were on the roof.

The momentum of the trailer had carried them out to sea far enough so that even the most rapacious zombie couldn't reach them.

They'd passed the end of the dock by a dozen feet. Instead of being stranded in town on the roof of an earthbound trailer, they were now on an aluminum island that was inexorably sinking. Bubbles shot free as water ate more of the inside.

The only blessing in the whole damned mess was that the rain had finally stopped. Perhaps Tropical Storm Hiawatha had ended.

Off to the east the sky was beginning to lighten.

Their long night was almost over.

CHAPTER THIRTY

Auntie Lin and Derrick huddled together in the middle of the trailer. She continued to adjust the boy's bandage, concern and fear etched across her face. Metzger stood at one end searching the water for any sign of help. Natasha stood at the other. But no matter where any of them stood or sat, their situation appeared hopeless.

Natasha couldn't believe what had happened to her the last few days. It seemed like just yesterday that they'd been traversing the country in the rolling avocado, looking forward to a life of fun and sun. It was laughable if it wasn't so damn tragic. Fun and sun from an inland salty sea with no access to the real ocean wasn't any fun at all. Rotting fish weren't fun. Dying birds weren't fun. The town filled with lost, miserable people wasn't fun. And the zombies, may they all rot in Hell, had now taken everything she had away from her and they were no fun.

Glancing over her shoulder at Derrick, she knew that soon, very soon, he'd join the ranks of friends and family who'd been turned into zombies and would probably have to be put down. She'd willingly change places with her brother if she thought it would do any good.

It was all just so fucking hopeless.

But then a fishing boat drifted out of the gloom. Its bow was high so she couldn't see who was driving. The sound of the outboard engine rolled over the top of the water.

Soon it was evident that the boat was headed towards them.

"Is that really a boat?" Derrick asked.

"Yes. It is." Natasha squeezed his shoulder reassuringly.

The pitch of the boat's engine dropped, then ground to a baritone hum before it cut off. The boat bobbed in the water, turning so the driver could see them and they could see him. It was Lu Shu, the fisherman. He grinned broadly at them. "I wasn't sure you'd be here," he called. "So I waited out there."

"We weren't sure either," Metzger said. "But we made it... mostly."

The fisherman's expression grew pained, and he rattled off a string of Chinese.

"What was that?" Natasha asked.

"'One day, a thousand autumns,'" said Auntie Lin. "He means so much has happened."

"Is this all you have?" Lu Shu asked.

"We're it. Thanks for coming. I wasn't sure if... well, you know."

Lu Shu nodded. "Those beasts are inventive. No telling what they might think of if you give them the chance, which is why I waited where it's deepest."

"Look!" Derrick pointed. One eye was completely closed. The other was red with blood. "They're going back in the water. They're leaving."

All eyes turned to the shore and witnessed zombie after zombie headed toward the water. The water moved up their bodies, covered their mouths, noses, and eyes, then finally their heads as they disappeared beneath the waves.

Natasha wondered if they were really going back.

"Hold on," Metzger said suddenly. He looked around worriedly. "How deep is it here?"

Lu Shu and shrugged. "About seven or eight feet. It's –"Realizing why Metzger was worried, he reached around and frantically pulled the starter cord on the motor, but it wouldn't catch.

"What's wrong?" Natasha asked. "Where are you going? Don't leave us!"

Metzger jerked out his pistol and aimed towards the water around the trailer. "It's resting on the bottom, isn't it?" He cursed and stomped the length of the trailer. "Fuck! Fuck! Fuck! No wonder we aren't sinking anymore."

Then the truth of it caught up with Natasha. She spun and searched the water. The zombies weren't returning to the depths after all. What had they been thinking? They were coming for them!

Finally the boat's engine coughed and roared to life. It seemed fine for a moment and Lu Shu put his hand on the rudder. But before he could do anything else, the engine gurgled as if it was bogged down by seaweed.

"You aren't leaving us," Metzger commanded. He changed the aim of his pistol to Lu Shu. "If you leave without us, I swear to God I will shoot you dead."

Lu Shu stared at Metzger, trying to get the measure of the man. The boat was spinning around slowly and now faced out to sea, which brought the engine into view of everyone on the trailer. They couldn't see the blades of the outboard, but there was no mistaking the spreading yellow petrol slick on the water.

The engine coughed again, then died.

Lu Shu cursed and struggled to pull the engine out of the water. A decaying hand broke the surface of the water and latched onto the motor, and a zombie hauled itself up the metal contraption. Its scalp had rotted away in places, showing pieces of its skull. Here and there wet wisps of hair lay lank and dirty against its head. Its other arm came up missing a hand, severed by the engine's blades.

Lu Shu didn't panic. He just kept pulling on the starter cord, frowning intently at the engine.

The zombie climbed higher until it straddled the engine, sitting on the axle that held the blades.

Suddenly the engine caught and roared to life.

The zombie shook like it had been struck by lightning as the whirling blades dug into its backside and bore into its midsection.

Lu Shu grabbed an oar and used it to shove the zombie off the motor. The zombie hit the water just as Lu Shu lost his balance and the boat beneath him roared away. The man splashed furiously, kicking and screaming, but was jerked beneath the surface so suddenly it was like he had never been there at all.

Natasha stared at the boat roaring into the distance and all hope she'd managed to resurrect returned to the grave from which it had come. Now they had no chance.

As if to emphasize this, Lu Shu's hand floated to the surface. It bobbed for a moment, everyone's eyes riveted on the appendage, and was snatched back under.

The sound of running feet drew their attention to the shore. Dozens of zombies were charging from the sand to the dock, each running at a dead sprint. When they reached the end of the dock they jumped towards them. Although it was an impossible distance, each leap sent Natasha's heart galloping. The desperation the zombies were showing was horrific. As soon as they hit the water, they sank. And although she couldn't see them, she knew they were there beneath the water.

A rotting hand reached and grabbed the edge of the roof. Auntie Lin leaned over and began to poke it with her umbrella, but it did little good.

Metzger waited beside the old woman, and when the zombie rose out of the water, Salton Sea water pouring from its broken teeth, he shot it in the head. The bullet slammed it back into the water and it rolled on its side and sank.

Derrick pointed. "Look at the boat!"

It was coming around again.

They had only one chance left. Metzger handed Natasha the pistol and removed his vest and his armor, then hurriedly untied his boots and jerked them off.

The boat was closer now, and so were the zombies. She could

see them moving beneath the water as dark shadows. She held the pistol in front of her with both hands and waited for one of the zombies to latch on to the trailer. One did; she fired and missed, three times. Its glowing eyes mocked her before the fourth shot caused the back of its head to explode in a shower of yellow ichor. The zombie fell back into the water and sunk from sight.

She didn't know how many more bullets she had, but they wouldn't last much longer at this rate. She shot a quick glance at her brother and finally understood what he'd told her a few weeks ago, when he'd been playing a computer game and she'd asked him how he was doing. His reply had been to itemize his ammunition.

It was all about the ammo, in both games and reality.

Only in reality there was no restart button.

The boat seemed determined to miss them. Metzger had cleared a path so that he could run the length of the trailer and jump for it. But just like the zombies jumping from the end of the dock to get to the trailer, his jump seemed impossible.

Still, as the driverless boat came back round, Metzger took a running leap, screaming obscenities all the while as if they were fuel for his flight.

He seemed to hang in the air for a long time, long enough for Natasha to be certain he was going to make it... then change her mind and be certain that he wasn't.

He hit the side of the boat at the rear hard, winding herself. He tried to grab the gunwale, but his hands slipped.

Natasha's hands flew to her face. If he wasn't able to grab it, he'd feel the bite of the engine blades, or worse, the bite of the zombies waiting beneath the water. Her heart was caught in her throat as she silently urged him into the boat, and somehow he managed to pull himself in. He rolled from sight as the boat roared away.

Derrick, Natasha and Auntie Lin watched it go, their smiles of hope fading as they saw no sign of Metzger. Finally, he pulled himself to a sitting position, gripped the rudder, and turned the boat around. He throttled down the engine, and the bow slapped gently on the water as it approached. Metzger grinned at them and waved tiredly.

But Metzger's smile vanished as his head suddenly jerked back and crashed against the engine. The engine quit but the boat continued on an intersect course for the trailer. Metzger tried to pull himself up, but his head was jerked back again. A zombie hand dragged across Metzger's forehead, carving deep bloody grooves. The fingers dug into the top of Metzger's scalp, the arm muscles tensed, and the zombie pulled itself out of the water. Even from twenty feet away, Natasha could see the unholy yellow of the monster's eyes as it sunk its teeth into Metzger's face over and over. The one-time soldier, crack addict, possible boyfriend and savior of them all punched at the creature to no avail. He cursed the monster as it chewed. He kicked, he punched, he even shoved two fingers into the creature's left eye. Yellow ichor exploded onto him, but the zombie didn't even slow down. As if sensing the inevitable, Metzger shouted one last curse to the universe – *"motherfuckingcocksucker!"* – pushed with his feet and sent them both over the side, where they disappeared beneath the water.

The empty boat struck the trailer hard, knocking everyone off balance. Auntie Lin toppled into the boat, but Natasha and Derrick fell into the water. They immediately began to kick and scream. Natasha felt hands beneath the water scrabble at her ankles and kicked as hard as she could.

"Kick, Derrick – kick and they won't get you!"

The pistol was doing her absolutely no good so she tucked it away. Suddenly she saw Auntie Lin above the gunwale, holding out an oar. Natasha latched onto it and let herself be pulled towards the boat, all the while kicking as furiously as she could, her feet striking something each time she lashed out, fingers brushing against her ankles like taloned-seaweed. When she was close enough, Natasha hauled herself out of the water.

She ran to the other side of the boat. Auntie Lin had Derrick by the wrists. She pulled as hard as she could, but could not bring the boy from the water. Natasha joined in, but Derrick wouldn't budge.

Then she realized that he wasn't kicking.

He screamed and his body began to shake. "They're eating me! They're eating me!"

Auntie Lin looked once at Natasha, then dove into the water.

Natasha grabbed for the old woman's ankles, barely managing to grab one as Auntie Lin plunged into the depths. Her weight almost jerked Natasha overboard, but she wouldn't let go. She was up to her shoulder in the water, her hand and arm firmly gripping Auntie Lin.

With her other hand, she helped Derrick aboard. He seemed so weak. She roared as she heaved, and he fell into the boat and rolled over. His lower legs were a mess of blood and bite marks, and huge chunks had been torn away. Blood began to fill the bottom of the boat. He moaned for a moment, then his eyes all but rolled up into his head.

Natasha began to pull Auntie Lin, but like Derrick, she wasn't moving. If the zombies had her it was face first. The old Chinese woman began to quiver and shake, and the water began to churn, like a feeding frenzy of piranhas were consuming Auntie Lin. Natasha could barely hang on; her whole body shook as she struggled to maintain her grip on her old nanny. The dun-grey surface of the water suddenly turned crimson as it bubbled and roiled.

Natasha heaved backwards with all that was left in her. She managed to get her own shoulder and arm out of the water. She used her other hand to grip the wrist that held Auntie Lin's ankle, and used her feet to support her and help lever the old woman out.

The water suddenly calmed, and Natasha fell back, her hand still gripping a leg... all that was left of Auntie Lin. Natasha leaned over the gunwale and hurled the limb from her hand. It hit a gory slick, leaving a ripple.

She emptied her stomach, spraying the water with vomit and gripping the gunwale with both hands to keep from falling in. She got to her knees shakily, drool lacing from the corners of her mouth, tears welling from her eyes until they ran dry, until she was empty.

She snapped out of it when knocking began on the bottom of the boat. Natasha lurched to the rear seat, sat down hard and tugged on the starter cord several times before it finally caught. When it did, she turned the handle on the rudder to full and the boat roared away as she turned it out to sea. She glanced at Derrick to make sure was still breathing and not a zombie, before giving one last, hopeless look at Bombay Beach.

CHAPTER THIRTY-ONE

She'd bandaged Derrick's arm as best she could by the time the boat hit the beach on the far shore from Bombay Beach. The paltry supplies in the boat's first aid kit weren't adequate enough for the job. After all, there was no tincture for zombieness. It was only a matter of time.

They climbed out of the boat and began walking towards the highway, visible just beyond the dunes. A blonde woman walking a pair of Great Danes passed them, heading for the water.

"Welcome to Desert Shores," she said with a smile. Then, seeing the state they were in, "Are you kids all right?"

Natasha and Derrick ignored her.

"You need to get that kid to a hospital," she called after them.

Natasha thought about yelling back that there was nothing a hospital could do, but she was so soul-tired that she didn't want to waste a breath. They found a picnic table and sat down. She looked despairingly at her brother and held his hand in hers.

"I'm scared, sis."

"Me too."

"I can feel it inside me. I'm so hungry. I'm so angry." He squeezed her hand. "Promise me that you won't let me bite you."

She shook her head as tears poured down her cheeks.

"Promise me, please." His voice began to change. "You have to shoot me."

She watched as his whole body stilled. He inhaled once, then exhaled, then didn't breathe for a while. She couldn't help herself. She got up and backed away, putting the table between her and her brother, who sat with his eyes closed on the picnic table bench.

Then she heard the sound of a helicopter, coming in low over the water from the direction of Bombay Beach. It was white with no markings. It could have been anyone, but Natasha knew what it was, or at least who it was.

Just then Derrick hissed.

Natasha jumped as she watched her brother come back to life, his eyes glowing yellow, his skin turning green. He glared at her.

She backed away, aware that Metzger's pistol was still in the small of her back. She could grab it and protect herself if she had to. She kept backing away, her eyes never leaving her brother. He of the comic books, and he of the video games, he'd always been so easy to make laugh. He'd been a good kid and a better brother. He didn't deserve this. He didn't deserve to be a zombie. The words *Old Yeller* whispered through her mind and she knew what she had to do.

She glanced at the helicopter. It was getting closer.

But then the image of her brother, shouting *Booya* when he'd figured out the crib filled her vision and she knew that she'd never be able to pull the trigger.

She kept backing away, and found herself on top of a sand dune a hundred feet away.

Derrick raged at the picnic table, howling at the sun, his eyes glowing, his fists clenched, his back arched like an animal.

The helicopter swooped in and landed in a clear space adjacent to the picnic table. The doors slid open. Two soldiers leaped out and took up positions. They each fell to one knee and sighted down their rifles towards the zombie.

Derrick saw them and roared. He took a step towards them.

Natasha found herself hoping that the soldiers would kill him, save him from his horrible existence.

Then she heard dogs barking in the distance. One raced towards her—it was one of the woman's Great Danes, and she was running close behind, waving for Natasha to stop the dog before it got away. The dog ran to her and she snatched a hold of its collar.

Beachcombers from down the shore noticed the helicopter and started towards it. This was no Bombay Beach. People here paid attention. She spied a dune buggy in the distance racing towards the scene. Another couple were getting out of their car and heading her way.

Then three more people stepped down from the aircraft. Two soldiers held a net between them. An officer directed the other two to approach the zombie.

Natasha watched in dread fascination as the net was thrown over her brother, rolled on the ground, and wrapped up. The soldiers picked up either end and bundled him into the helicopter.

The man in charge gave Natasha a cold appraising glare, turned to see the crowd that was beginning to gather – she noticed that although his name tag had been removed, the words "U.S. Air Force" were stitched above his right pocket – then he turned on his heel and entered the helicopter. The two soldiers with rifles filed in next. When the aircraft took off, instead of returning to Bombay Beach, it headed north.

CHAPTER THIRTY-TWO

She made the highway and stood along the edge beside a salt-encrusted mileage marker, thumbs out in the universal sign of need. As she waited, Natasha wiped the sweat from her face with the back of her hand. She tasted salt and angrily spat it out.

A truck roared past, bathing her in hot air and swirls of biting sand. She watched it disappear in the distance, too tired to move, too tired to do anything but stand there. Eventually another truck headed toward her, this one slowing until it stopped a couple dozen yards off. When she stumbled up, the driver opened the door and studied her.

He was a bear of a man with tattoos covering both arms, a head of wild grey hair, and a mountain-man beard. Finally, he asked, "Where you headed?"

"Where are you going?" Natasha countered.

"Phoenix, then up to Denver."

"Are there any Air Force bases in those places?"

The driver looked at her a moment, trying to fathom the reason for the question. He finally nodded his head. "I think so. Phoenix has one for sure."

Natasha had no plan. She had nothing. Right now she just needed a ride, and maybe some peace and quiet.

"Listen, if you want the ride, then get in. I got time to make."

Natasha climbed into the cab and belted herself into the seat.

He put the truck in gear and they were soon rumbling north towards Interstate 10 and beyond.

Natasha stared out the window at the hot, arid desert as it sped past—the yellow brown earth, the green cacti, the scrubby bushes, the rock-strewn sand. Beneath the superheated sun, nothing seemed able to live out there. Not a single living thing could be seen moving on the horizon. But that didn't mean what she was looking for wasn't out there.

THE END

WESTON OCHSE is the Bram Stoker award-winning author of various short stories and novels, including the critically acclaimed *Scarecrow Gods*.

He is much in demand as a speaker at genre conventions and has been chosen as a guest of honour on numerous occasions. As well as writing many novels, Weston has written for comic books, professional writing guides, magazines and anthologies.

Weston lives in Southern Arizona with his wife, the author Yvonne Navarro, and their menagerie of animals.

www.abaddonbooks.com
www.abaddonbooks.blogspot.com
Follow us on twitter @abaddonbooks

TOMES OF THE DEAD

TIDE OF SOULS

SIMON BESTWICK

Now read the first chapter from another
exciting *Tomes of The Dead* novel...

ISBN: 978-1-906735-14-2

£6.99/$7.99

WWW.ABADDONBOOKS.COM

CHAPTER ONE

Katja

The rising of the dead was the best luck I'd had in years. A godsend, even. I was lucky to survive, of course; my owners showed exactly how they valued me when they left me locked in a Cheetham Hill brothel to drown. I was lucky they kept me upstairs; I heard the women on the ground floor. I heard them die. Heard their screams of panic, heard them choked off as they drowned.

At least, at the time I thought they had drowned. Hours later, clinging to a rooftop, holding a gun with one bullet left in it and trying to decide which of us to use it on, I wasn't so sure.

My name is Katja Wencewska. Although my family is Polish, I grew up in Romania. It's a long story, none of it relevant to this. I will tell you what is relevant.

I am twenty-seven years old. My father was a military officer.

Special forces. A good, brave man, always very calm. Tall, as well. A tree of a man. An oak. My mother, in contrast, was like a tiny bird – very bright, excitable. I loved them both dearly. I was their only child. They were proud of me; in school I won prizes in Literature, the Arts and Gymnastics. I have two degrees.

None of that helped when they died. A stupid man, driving drunk, late one night. Their car went off the road, into a ravine. My father died instantly; my mother took several hours. The idiot responsible was cut out of the wreckage with barely a scratch. I wanted to kill him, and could have. Papa had often shown me how. He knew the world is full of predators, and taught me to protect myself against them.

I was studying for a PhD at the time, but of course that had to be abandoned. Bills had to be paid, but there was no work to be found. Then I heard of a job in England. For a fee, strings would be pulled, things arranged. A teaching job.

I spoke good English. I thought I would work hard, make money. Eventually I planned to come home – when things were better there, when I had money saved.

I thought I was so clever. I was well-educated and, I thought, streetwise. I could kill with a blow after all, if I was forced to. But the thought never crossed my mind. I had heard of people trafficking of course, but you never think it will be you. Predators would be so easily dealt with if they came to us as predators.

I was a fool.

You can guess the rest. My passport was taken. There was no teaching job. I was to service men for money. When I refused, I was beaten and raped. Worse than rape. Other things were done to me. I will not talk about those things: they are not relevant, you have no need to know. After this I felt defiled and wretched. I did not refuse again. It was made clear to me – to us all – that if we were too much trouble we would be killed. We were expendable; easily disposed of, easily replaced.

I was kept at a brothel in London at first. After six months they moved me to another, in Manchester. I spent the next eight months there. Being able to kill with a blow means little when there are always more of them, when the doors are always locked, the windows always barred, when you have nowhere to go.

I think that is all I need to say about myself.

I was woken that morning by screams and blaring horns.

I got to the window and squinted through the bars. On Cheetham Hill Road, people were leaping onto the roadway to avoid something pouring over the pavement. At first I thought it was water – dark, filthy water – but when I pushed the net curtains aside I could see it flowed uphill. And over the screams and traffic noise, even the horns, I heard it squealing.

I realised they were swarming rats.

It was raining heavily; water gushed down the pavements and the road into the gutters. There'd been a lot of that lately.

There were rats on the road too – all on one side, the lane for city bound traffic, which was deserted. The road out of Manchester, on the other hand, was jammed solid. I could see the people in the cars – wild, terrified faces, fright and fury mixed, fists pounding windows, dashboards, steering wheels, making their horns blare and blare and blare.

The rain intensified until the road blurred. I stepped back from the window, let the curtains fall back into place. My stomach felt hollow and tight.

We had a television there, but I hadn't seen the news in months. We weren't allowed, and besides, we only wanted to watch things that would take our minds off our lives. I had no idea what had, or was, happening, only that something was very wrong.

Soon, I heard banging on the brothel's front door. I looked outside. It was Ilir, our owner. One of his sons came out of the door; he'd been left in charge. Ilir's black BMW was in the traffic jam, doors open. Ilir dragged his son to it. They slammed the doors; Ilir pounded the horn, but the traffic didn't budge. After a minute, they pulled into the deserted city bound lane. Other cars started following their example, and for a short time the traffic moved forward, but then locked up again. So many people, all trying to leave. Some of the other girls had started screaming, pounding on the doors. They'd abandoned us. They hadn't even turned us loose, just left us here.

People were running along the pavement, clutching their belongings, their children. Their eyes were wild.

An hour or so after Ilir and his son left, the answers started coming. Below Cheetham Hill are the Irwell and the Irk, two of the three rivers that run through Manchester. None are very deep; all have high banks. But water was washing up the street. Lapping up in slow, relentless waves.

Even then, I didn't really get it. It only really sank in when people started abandoning their cars.

It happened very quickly after that. Water washed round the wheels of the cars and rose higher. It lapped round their skirts. It poured over the pavements. Across the street, water flooded under the front door of the kebab house and across the floor. People were wading the torrents, then began climbing on top of the cars.

For a few minutes, I just watched. None of it felt real. It was like watching some bizarre art-house film. But nothing had felt real in that place for a long time. You couldn't let it, if you wanted to stay sane.

The water now started pouring over the crest of Cheetham Hill, and the rising waters now became a surge. A middle-aged Asian man fell over and was swept along, screaming for help. His arms flailed, and a toupee slipped off his head. I heard myself giggle; it was a jagged, ugly sound. I clapped a hand over my mouth. He went under and didn't come up.

Then I heard the girls downstairs begin screaming in earnest, and I realised the waters were entering the brothel.

We were all locked in our rooms overnight. Each one had an en-suite sink and toilet – for convenience, not comfort. The windows were all barred, so there was no escape. Even if the waters didn't flood the upper floors, I could still look forward to starvation.

My father had shown me how to pick a lock. I could've escaped my room easily enough on several occasions. The difficult part had always been what I would do then. There were two front doors, inner and outer, the inner triple-locked. And even if I'd got clear of that, where would I go with no papers, no passport, no way of getting a legitimate job?

But now the rules had changed.

I started searching, trying to find something I could use. The women downstairs were screaming. People on the street were screaming. I blocked it out. It didn't help me to hear it, wouldn't help me do this faster.

I tipped up the wastepaper basket. There were used condoms in it, slimy to the touch.

Ignore them, Papa said.

At last I found a paper clip.

I knelt by the door and set to work. It was a slow job. Trial and error. My fingers got sweaty and slipped on the metal.

Suddenly I realised something.

The girls downstairs had stopped screaming. All but one. Then suddenly, that too was choked off. And there was only silence from the ground floor.

Outside the street was silent. I went to the window. Stopped, and stared.

Most of it was underwater. Brown, dirty water had covered almost all the cars. The roofs of a few vehicles showed. There was a double-decker bus opposite, the top deck still above water. A dozen people were there, slack-skinned faces gazing into mine. Here and there, on the water, I saw reddish stains, dispersing slowly in the current.

There were two other women upstairs in the brothel – Marianna, who was about my age, was praying over and over in the next room. Marta, the youngest of the girls, was sobbing helplessly across the landing. She was only fifteen. A child. Tiny. Dark. Like my mother had been.

I ran back to the door, back to the lock. My fingers shook. I took a deep breath.

Panic is a choice, Papa used to say. You can decide not to be scared, not to panic. You can decide who's in charge.

So I chose to stay calm. I could still hear the rain pelting down outside, but I didn't look to see if the waters were still rising. I couldn't think about that. I had to act as if time was not a factor. I just kept working. Even when the thin carpet I knelt on grew cold and wet.

Marta was sobbing and screaming as well now. From next door, Marianna's prayers had blurred into a rising jumble of sound, fast turning into a wail.

The tumblers clicked.

I got the door open. Water filmed the landing, welling up from the flooded staircase. There was a fire extinguisher on the wall. I could smash the locks on the other girls' doors.

Then there were fresh screams. From outside.

I don't know why, but I went back to the window. I suppose I thought the worst of it was past. The door was open. I had time. Or, perhaps, there was something about the screams that alerted me.

When I look back, I believe going to the window probably saved my life. It forewarned me – just a little, but enough. Even so, as with much else, I wish I hadn't seen what I saw.

It was the double-decker. The waters were still rising, but the top windows and the people inside remained visible. They were scrambling away to the back end of the bus.

Someone was standing up in the water at the front end, near the staircase. At first I thought he was just fat. Then another figure rose up out of the water and I almost screamed. The bus passengers weren't so restrained. I could hear them from where I stood.

The second shape – its flesh resembled well-cooked meat, falling off the bone. I could see the bone of one arm showing through, and when the thing swivelled sideways for a second, showing its back, I saw the flesh coming away from the spine on each side, baring it like a moth's body when its wings are spread. Then it turned my way. God. God almighty. That face. Grinning because so much of the flesh was falling from the skull. And looking at me. The sockets of its eyes were empty. They glared; a greenish-yellow glow, bright. It started forward, the fat shape following – I saw now it wasn't fat, just bloated, from its drowning. And then a third figure rose up into view, climbing up the bus's flooded stairwell, and a fourth... all with those glowing eyes.

The passengers were still. There wasn't really anywhere to go in any case. The rotting thing seized one of them, a woman in her twenties, and bit into her neck. I heard her scream. The bloated figure grabbed her too and they pulled her down; blood sprayed up and splattered the windows.

It was over for them very quickly after that. Sometimes I think they were the lucky ones.

I just wish, before I turned away, I hadn't seen the child, hands and face against the glass, screaming...

But there was nothing I could do.

I grabbed the extinguisher off the wall and smashed the lock on Marta's door. She stumbled out, then shrieked again as she saw the flooded stairwell.

"What are we going to do?" It came out in a wail.

I pointed to the hatch in the ceiling. "Get into the loft, then out onto the roof."

Luckily I didn't have to tell her everything; she clambered onto the landing rail and I caught her legs, boosted her up. She pushed the hatch up, grabbed the edges and started wriggling up into the loft. I ran to Marianna's door and smashed the lock there too.

Marianna was on her knees praying. I dragged her to her feet and out onto the landing. The water there was ankle deep now.

"Climb!" I shouted to Marianna, and started clambering onto the banister. Marta reached down to grip my hands. Then her gaze drifted past me and her eyes widened.

I looked.

Wished I hadn't.

Down in the dark water, in the flooded stairwell, I could see movement. And lights. Pairs of yellow-green lights, rising towards the surface. And then I could see their faces.

**Continued in Simon Bestwick's Tide of Souls,
from Abaddon.**

TOMES *of the* DEAD

TIDE OF SOULS

SIMON BESTWICK

Visit www.abaddonbooks.com for information on our titles,
interviews, news and exclusive content.

 ISBN: 978-1-906735-14-2
UK £.6.99   US $7.99

 Abaddon Books

Follow us on twitter: www.twitter.com/abaddonbooks